THE WOLVES OF WODEN

Alison Baird is the author of *The Hidden World*, *The Dragon's Egg* (nominated for the Ontario Library Association Silver Birch Award and designated a regional winner by the participating children) and *White as the Waves*, which was shortlisted for the IODE Violet Downey Book Award.

THE WOLVES
OF WODEN

ALISON BAIRD

Puffin Books

PUFFIN BOOKS

Published by the Penguin Group

Penguin Books Canada Ltd, 10 Alcorn Avenue, Toronto, Ontario, Canada M4V 3B2

Penguin Books Ltd, 80 Strand, London WC2R 0RL, England

Penguin Putnam Inc., 375 Hudson Street, New York, New York 10014, U.S.A.

Penguin Books Australia Ltd, 250 Camberwell Road, Camberwell, Victoria 3124, Australia

Penguin Books (NZ) Ltd, cnr Rosedale and Airborne Roads, Albany, Auckland 1310, New Zealand

Penguin Books Ltd, Registered Offices: Harmondsworth, Middlesex, England

First published in Penguin Books by Penguin Books Canada Limited, 2001

Published in Puffin Books, 2002

1 3 5 7 9 10 8 6 4 2

Manufactured in Canada.

"We'll Meet Again" by Hugh Charles & Ross Parker © 1945
(Renewed) Campbell, Connelly & Co. Ltd.
All Rights Administered By Gordon V. Thompson, Ltd.
All Rights Reserved   Used by Permission
Warner Bros. Publications U.S. Inc., Miami, FL 33014

"A Nightingale Sang In Berkeley Square" Lyric by Eric Maschwitz
Music by Manning Sherwin
Copyright © 1940 The Peter Maurice Music Co., Ltd., London, England
Copyright Renewed and Assigned to Shapiro, Bernstein & Co., Inc.,
New York for U.S.A. and Canada
International Copyright Secured   All Rights Reserved   Used by Permission

NATIONAL LIBRARY OF CANADA CATALOGUING IN PUBLICATION DATA

Baird, Alison, 1963–
The wolves of Woden / Alison Baird.

Prequel to the author's The hidden world.
ISBN 0-14-131180-0

I. Title.

PS8553.A367W67 2002   jC813'.54   C2002-901222-8
PZ7.B617WO 2002

Visit Penguin Canada's website at **www.penguin.ca**

In memory of my great-grandfather
Thomas Moyst
An officer with SS *Caribou*
lost at sea, October 14, 1942

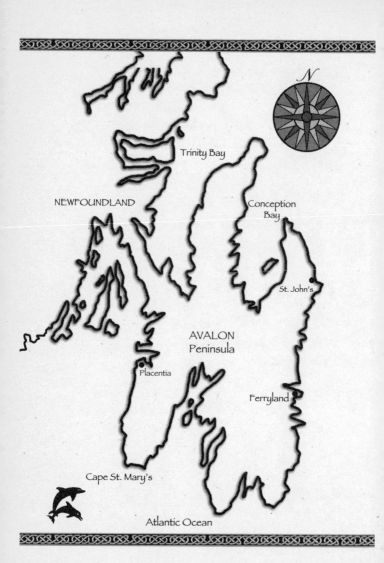

N

Trinity Bay

NEWFOUNDLAND

Conception
Bay

St. John's

AVALON
Peninsula

Placentia

Ferryland

Cape St. Mary's

Atlantic Ocean

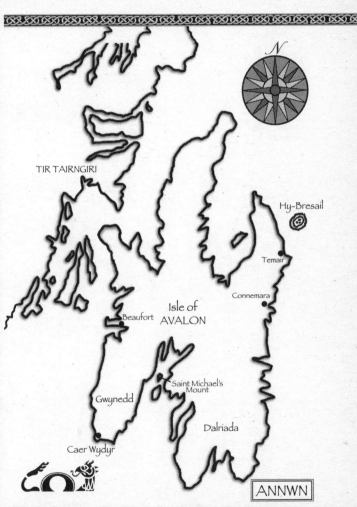

TIR TAIRNGIRI

Hy-Bresail

Temair

Connemara

Isle of
AVALON

Beaufort

Saint Michael's
Mount

Gwynedd

Dalriada

Caer Wydyr

ANNWN

Thou wast not born for death, immortal Bird!
    No hungry generations tread thee down;
The voice I hear this passing night was heard
    In ancient days by emperor and clown:
Perhaps the self-same song that found a path
    Through the sad heart of Ruth, when, sick for home,
    She stood in tears amid the alien corn;
        The same that oft-times hath
Charm'd magic casements, opening on the foam
    Of perilous seas, in faery lands forlorn.

from *Ode to a Nightingale*
John Keats

I may be right, I may be wrong
But I'm perfectly willing to swear
That when you turn'd and smiled at me
A nightingale sang in Berk'ley Square

from *A Nightingale Sang in Berkeley Square*
Lyric by Eric Maschwitz

Pronunciation Guide

IRISH WORDS

(Author's note: the language I call "Gaelic" in this book is really known as Old Irish. There are some differences between Old and Modern Irish pronunciations, as shown below.)

Put the stress on the syllable written in capital letters. Letters in brackets should be pronounced very softly.

* *ch* at the end of a syllable is a guttural sound (made in the back of your throat) such as the "ch" in the name "Bach"; "gh" at the end of a syllable is a softer guttural sound as in "lough" (i.e., Lough Ness).

** *ch* at the start of a word is a guttural sound such as the "ch" in "chutzpah."

ard-righ	ard-REE
Cailleach Bheur	KY-yuck VAIR (rhymes with "fair")
Ciaran	KEER-awn
Cromm Cruach	KROM KROO-ach*
curragh	KUR-agh
Dairmait	D(y)EER-mud
Dana	DON-a
Daoine Sidhe	DIN-a shee
Dubthach	DUV-thach*
dún	DOON
Éire	AYR-a ("ay" as in "hay")
Emain Ablach	EV-in OV-lach*
fidchell	FID(th)-(c)hill** (Old Irish)
	FI-(c)hill** (Modern Irish)
Fomori	FOE-m(w)ir-i ("i" as in "riddle")
Fragarach	FRA-gar-ach*

xi

Pronunciation Guide

Grainne	GRON-ya
Hy-Bresail	EE BRESH-il
Lia Fail	LEE-a FAW-il ("faw" rhymes with "paw")
Lochlannach	LOCH*-lon-ach*
Lugh	LOO(gh*) (Old Irish)
	LOO (rhymes with "blue") (Modern Irish)
Medb	MAYV
Morrigan, the	MO-ree(gh*)-an
Nuada	NEW-ed(th)-a
péist	PAYSHT
Temair	T(y)OW-ir
Tir Tairngiri	T(y)EER T(y)AR-in-gri ("gri" as in grizzle)
tuath	TOO-ath (Old Irish)
	TOO-a (Modern Irish)
Tuatha de Danaan	TOO-ath-a DAY DON-in

WELSH WORDS

Please note: In the Welsh language the consonants C and G are always hard (as in *car*, *goose*). The "dd" sounds like the "th" in "the" (not "thorn"). The "ch" is pronounced as in the name "Bach." The "ll" sound is made by placing the tip of the tongue against the roof of the mouth, just behind the front teeth, and breathing out: a "hissing" sound.

In modern Welsh the stress is normally placed on the penultimate (second to last) syllable.

Annwn	an-oon
Arawn	are-own (as in "ounce")
Arianrhod	air-ee-an-hrod
Caer Wydyr	k-eye-r we-dr

Pronunciation Guide

Craig yr Aderyn	kr-eye-g uhr add-air-in
Cymru	kum-ree
Gwragedd Annwn	goo-rah-geth an-oon ("th" as in "the")
gwyddbwyll	goi-th boi-ll (hissing "ll")
Gwydion	goo-uh-dee-on
Gwyn ap Nudd	goo-in ahp neeth ("th" as in "the")
Gwynedd	gwen-ith ("th" as in "the")
Merioneth	mayr-ee-on-ith ("th" as in "thorn")
Myrddin	mur-thin ("th" as in "the")
Tylwyth Teg	tul-oith tayg
Ynys Afallon	uhn-is avallon
Ynys Witrin	uhn-is wit-rin

ACKNOWLEDGEMENTS

I would like to express my appreciation to the Canada Council for its generous assistance. I would also like to thank my editor Barbara Berson, Cynthia Good, and Meg Masters who first suggested a prequel; Mary Adachi; Judy Diehl and David Plumb; Celtic language experts Anne Connon and John Otley; Carlie Clough; Helen Fogwill Porter; and Brian Deines, for his lovely cover art.

Many thanks also to all those members of my family, both here in Ontario and in St. John's, Newfoundland, who shared with me their expertise on World War II and their memories of the war years in Newfoundland. I could not have done this without their help.

Chapter One

THE VISION CAME TO JEAN IN THE early hours of the morning, when the sky outside her window was still night-blue, and the birds in the trees around the house had begun to chirp intermittently, but not yet to sing. Jean saw the sky and she heard the birds, for the visions always came when she was awake, not in sleep as dreams did. One after the other the images came, in quick succession like a montage in a film; and then it was over, and she was shivering as she lay in her bed, though the summer morning was not cold.

She sat up in bed and looked around her room, reassuring herself with its soothing familiarity. The floral design of the wallpaper was still only a mass of dim grey blotches, but there was enough light for her to make out its pattern. It had hung on the walls for more than ten of her fifteen years. And there on her bedside table was the reading lamp with its white china base—she had had it even longer than the wallpaper—and beyond it were the shelves with her books, and her desk with its plain rung-backed chair. The desk faced the

1

window: when she sat there she could look out on the harbour of St. John's and the Southside hills. She got out of bed, very quietly so as not to wake the rest of her family, and went to sit in the chair.

Dawn was near. As she sat there, gazing out towards the harbour mouth, the sky beyond the Narrows lightened to grey and then turned a rich butter yellow, and Cabot Tower changed from a faint shadow to a sharp, black silhouette. On the Southside, where night still lingered, the big oil tanks and the houses clustering atop the Brow were only pale blurred shapes. When she was very small, Jean had believed those houses really were as tiny as they looked: fairy houses that would come up only to your knees if you went among them, houses inhabited by little people. She could still recall the bitter disappointment she had felt on learning that the houses of the Brow were really as large as anyone else's, with perfectly ordinary people living in them.

Somewhere down the street a car engine coughed as it started, and then there was a rumble of wheels and hooves as a delivery cart went by. The city was awake. Before long there came a clatter of pans and cutlery from the kitchen downstairs as Annie, the maid, began to prepare breakfast. The birds were now singing with full-throated abandon. It was the morning of a fine summer day—the sort of day everyone in Newfoundland dreamed about during the long damp cold of winter. And before long it would be September again, and Jean would have to throw on her school uniform and gather her schoolbooks and rush down to breakfast every morning, instead of taking her ease like this. Besides, today was the day her family was going to visit the

O'Connors in Mary's Bay. A day like this one was a gift, not to be wasted on fretting over silly pictures in your head. And what had she seen, after all? A high cliff overlooking the sea, with white seabirds whirling around it; the face of an old man with grey eyes and white hair and a long white beard; a standing stone, tall and grey and columnar, rising from a misty mound; a solitary tree on a bleak moor, with lights glowing among its leaves—almost like the lights on a Christmas tree, only these were a ghostly greenish white in colour. And that was all. None of the images meant anything to Jean; they were odd rather than frightening. It was not like that night in the outport, years ago, when she had looked out Mary O'Connor's bedroom window and seen the soldiers.

"How did you know they were soldiers?" Andy had demanded.

"I—I'm not sure." Jean felt her certainty waver in the face of her older brother's skepticism. "I think they were wearing some sort of uniform, but it was more than that. I just—*knew*." There had been four of them, and a fifth lying on a sort of stretcher which two of them carried—a still, shrouded form. Along the field at the back of the house they had walked with their solemn burden, on into the woods beyond. Everyone told her she must have dreamed it, and she had let herself be convinced. She was, after all, only eight years old at the time; and to be honest, she preferred not to believe that she had really seen the phantom figures. But four years later when the trees were cleared and a foundation for a house dug on the spot, the bones of a man had been found. Old bones, long buried and forgotten. With them a rusted piece of metal had been unearthed: a protective breastplate from an eighteenth-century soldier's uniform.

The visions had always been there, an accepted part of Jean's being: like dreams, or like the vague muffled voices she sometimes thought she heard when she lay at the edge of sleep. Sometimes, as now, the images were just inside her head; sometimes they blended with the real world, like the soldiers, and seemed for an instant to be part of it. "It's the second sight," Grandma MacDougall used to say, nodding her neat white head. Absolutely nothing ever ruffled Grandma. "It goes with the Highland blood, or so I've heard." Jean did not want to have the second sight, whatever it might be. It made her flesh creep to think of it, and so she tried hard not to think of it at all.

She shrugged its spell off now as she tossed her night-gown to the floor, and began to dress.

Downstairs Mum was helping Annie cook the breakfast, and at the dining-room table Dad and Andy were discussing last night's newspaper. Her little sister, Fiona, was leaning over their shoulders and chattering, but Jean automatically went to the kitchen to lend a hand. She glanced a little enviously at her siblings as she passed the table: Andy's thick thatch of hair was glossy as a chestnut in the morning sun, and Fiona's mop of curls shone strawberry blonde. How could her brother and sister be so striking when Jean herself was so plain? Her own straight, shoulder-length hair was the flat colour of sand; and though her brother and sister had inherited Dad's dark blue eyes, Jean's were green like her mother's.

4

Andy and Fiona were the pride and joy of the family, she thought. Andy of course was the pride, being the eldest and the only son, while little, laughing Fiona was the joy. And Jean . . . *I'm just—here*, she thought. Like the grandfather clock whose constant deep ticking they no longer heard, or the paintings on the walls which no one really looked at any more, Jean was ever present but at the same time unobtrusive. And yet there was so much more to her than that. Everyone was two people, she thought, an inner self and an outer. Jean's outer self, whom everyone knew, was the quiet, dutiful, probably rather dull daughter of Pat and Allister MacDougall. The secret inner self was the one who revelled in tales of adventure and wonder, of King Arthur and his knights and the Holy Grail; the one who saw strange things no one else did; who was, even now, deeply in love . . . A little secretive smile curved her lips as she tipped the sausages from the frying pan onto a plate.

How *that* would surprise them all!

Part of the problem was her name, she reflected. It was such a dull one. Jean Anne MacDougall: the given names common as bread, and then that silly-sounding surname—like a car tooting its horn, she thought. It was not her fate to be beautiful, she had accepted that. But if only she could have had a beautiful name, like the names of the ladies in the King Arthur stories: Guinevere, Vivien, Linet. Or one of the romantic old names from the Celtic sagas—Deirdre perhaps, or Maeve. *Maeve MacDougall* would have sounded so much nicer. It even made the surname sound dignified instead of funny.

Dad was talking to Fiona as Jean brought the sausages to the table. "There's nothing to worry about," her father was saying as he brushed crumbs from his neat, clipped moustache. "I've told you before, the Nazis won't come here."

"But the sirens—" Fiona began.

They went off once a week now: the high wailing air-raid sirens that raised the hair on the back of your neck and made your heart beat faster, even though you knew it was only a test. Every Thursday at ten in the morning they were sounded, regular as clockwork. "If Hitler has any brains," Andy remarked flippantly, "he'll bomb us at ten a.m. on a Thursday. Who'd pay any attention?"

"They won't bomb us. The drills are just a precaution." Dad speared a sausage with his fork and waved it about in a dismissive gesture. "It's hardly likely they'd send the Luftwaffe all the way over here. The Atlantic's too wide, the planes wouldn't be able to stop and refuel."

"They might build aircraft carriers," Andy argued, turning serious again. "Why else are we putting up anti-aircraft guns? And what about their submarines? I hear they're coming over to our side of the ocean now."

"They can't come in our harbour." This was true. A giant underwater net had been strung across the Narrows, to bar the entrance of any U-boat. "Believe me, there's no danger to us."

It was hard not to think of the war. Every time you thought you had forgotten it, it intruded once more. Whenever she looked across the ocean, Jean imagined she could *see* it looming on that far horizon like the dark rack of an approaching storm. Signs of it were everywhere you looked. Huge rectangular water tanks stood in the streets like wooden sheds, in case a bombing attack cut off the water supply. Here and there a house had the letters "SP" posted on the front, to show there was an emergency stirrup pump inside. And there was the sugar ration; and the blackout regulations, strictly enforced by the air-raid patrol; and the metal hoods that had to be fixed to the headlamps of all cars, to reduce the light they cast.

It had all begun as a distant rumour, reports of events occurring beyond the sea: events which had no bearing on life here and now. Even the bulletins on the radio had had no power to alarm, describing as they did far-off places one had never visited, never would visit. The newsreels that ran before the movies in the theatres seemed as dramatic and unbelievable as the movies themselves. Austria was taken, then Czechoslovakia, without any strong reaction. Only when Poland's turn came did Britain declare war on Germany; and still nothing happened. The drama played out far away, on its unseen stage. To be sure, the re-broadcasts of Hitler's speeches on the radio *were* rather frightening. Though Jean did not understand the alien words, the harshness and fury of them seemed to spill into the room as she and the rest of the family sat listening. The pictures of Adolf Hitler were not alarming: with his lank hair and little moustache he even looked a bit comical, like Charlie Chaplin. It was hard to believe he was the owner of the terrifying voice.

Then this spring Denmark and Norway had fallen, with shocking suddenness; then the Netherlands, and Belgium and France. *France!* It didn't seem possible. Paris, the city of wine and fashions and the Eiffel Tower which Jean had so often seen in pictures—occupied by the Nazis? For the first time Mum and Dad looked grave as they listened to the radio, no doubt thinking of the Great War that had been fought in Europe long before Jean and her brother and sister were born. *Another* Great War? It couldn't happen—not again. That had been the war to end all wars. So, at least, Jean told herself, over and over again.

But as she went back upstairs after breakfast she over-heard Andy say to her father: "It's those oil tanks on the Southside that bother me. And all those wooden row houses downtown. If the tanks are bombed and the burning oil spreads across the harbour, the whole city will go up like matchwood. All the water tanks and stirrup pumps in the world won't be much use then. This city's burned to the ground before, Dad, and it can happen again."

At a quarter to ten they all piled into the car, the three younger ones in the back seat. Fiona sat by one window, bouncing with excitement as if she were five years old instead of ten, while Andy sat at the other looking rather sullen—he had been hoping to drive the car this time, but Dad said it was too risky on the rough country roads. A smashed car could not be replaced in wartime.

Jean, as usual, was stuck in the middle without a window, but she made no complaint. She had put on the nicest dress she had, apart from her Sunday best: a green plaid with white collar and cuffs. Not all colours looked good on Jean, but green brought her to life, drawing out the green of her eyes and harmonizing with her skin tone and her sandy hair. Perhaps Jim O'Connor would even notice . . .

Dad backed the car carefully down the short drive and swung it out into the street. The engine thrummed with a deep note of power and the navy blue hood with its chrome fittings shone importantly in the sun as they drove on, out of St. John's and into the countryside beyond. The farther they drove, the more the car seemed to grow in magnificence: when the paved streets gave way to the narrow dirt roads of the country, people gathered at the doors of their houses to stare and wave, and little boys ran shouting in the dusty wake. Outside the city automobiles were seldom used or seen. No one in the small fishing villages they passed had ever owned one, let alone a fine '38 Chrysler like Mr. Mac-Dougall's. The gawking and pointing people made Jean feel rather like visiting royalty. But Andy only grumbled.

"Why do we still drive on the left in Newfoundland?" he complained, watching his father carefully navigate a bumpy stretch of road. "It's stupid. We buy American cars with left-hand steering, but we drive on the left like the British!"

"Better this way." Dad was succinct as always. "The driver can see the ditch, and not fall into it."

Andy opened his mouth again and Jean spoke up quickly to avert a quarrel. Her brother seemed so restless and angry these days. "Look, aren't the wildflowers pretty?" she exclaimed, pointing.

The flowers in the ditches *were* beautiful, with the deep vivid colours that made you think of autumn. Loveliest of all was the fireweed, spreading in great pools of purple through the empty fields and meadows they passed. Jean felt a little ache at the thought of summer's end. There would not be many trips to Mary's Bay once the weather turned cold. And then there would be no Jim for months and months at a time, and Jean would have to hold fast to her memories of him. She had only one photograph of him, and it was merely a group shot of the two families, with Jim a faint blurred figure in the back row. She had asked Dad for it, blushing and fearing absurdly that her reason for wanting it was too obvious. It was now hidden away in her closet, together with her diary and the stories she had written at the back of her old school notebooks. She had written "Jean & Jim" over and over again in the margins of these notebooks, and once, greatly daring, "Jean O'Connor": it had given her a secret thrill but she had later blacked it out, afraid that Fiona's prying eyes might come across it.

But today she would see Jim in person. This was a day to savour, before it became merely another cherished memory. Nothing must spoil today: not the war, nor anything else.

The road wound on, familiar at every turn. They had been driving out to see the O'Connors for many years now. When she and Andy and Fiona were younger, they had even begun to catch the contagious outport accent, saying "I does" instead of "I do" and "I wants" instead of "I want." Mum hadn't liked it and had told them to stop.

"You sound like a lot of baymen," she scolded.

"But you talk like that yourself sometimes," Andy had countered. Andy was never intimidated by Mum.

"That's different," Mum answered readily. "I was born and raised on the Southern Shore, can't help slipping into it sometimes—but you, you've got no excuse. You'll never get anywhere, talking like that."

It had been another of Jean's childhood disappointments to learn that her mother came, not from Fairyland as she had first supposed, but from an outport called Ferryland. This was the original Avalon, the site of Lord Baltimore's old settlement. Mum often spoke of the wondrous buried objects the outport people found when they dug in their gardens: cannonballs, fragments of ancient glass, bits of pottery. "Such lovely pottery," she would say softly, "with beautiful colours and designs, made a long time ago and very far away."

Jean looked at her mother sitting quietly in the front seat, trying to imagine her as Patricia Reilly, the vivacious strong-willed girl who had disgraced herself by falling in love with a young commission merchant—a Protestant. Setting faith and family aside for love: could there be anything more romantic than that? But she was just Mum now, slight and small-boned with a strong-featured face under short, dark, tightly waved hair. Jean turned her attention back to the road.

They arrived at Mary's Bay before noon. Suddenly there were the rows of small wooden houses before them, and the rolling hilly headlands they knew so well, and the great blue dazzling sweep of the bay. On through the outport they drove, past O'Connor's general store, past strolling people and wide-eyed wondering children. Fishermen painting the bottoms of upturned dories, women hanging up the laundry on lines, old men sitting on the doorsteps of houses—all looked up as though they had never seen a car before. *Looking at us*, thought Jean with a glow of pleasure. *They must think we're rich!*

And yet, oddly enough, it was the O'Connors whom she envied. They were not wealthy, despite owning a store. They could not afford to live in town as the MacDougalls did, on a fashionable street like LeMarchant Road. Their own house was not smart: it was an old traditional saltbox house that had belonged to their family for generations, and its white paint was flaking in places and the roof needed repairs. There were four children sharing the two small bedrooms at the front of the house: the youngest child had to sleep in her parents' room. But Jean loved the house, with its view of the sea from the front windows and of the wild green woods from the back; loved the torrent of activity that seemed to stream constantly through its doors and eddy throughout its rooms. The O'Connor home was always full: of children, of cats and dogs, of visiting neighbours—*of life*, she thought. It was a house in which no one could ever brood or feel cut off. And best of all, the house contained Jim. How lucky Jim's family was, to live with him, to see him every day!

He was there in the front yard as they drove up, standing by the road with his father. He was taller than Mr. O'Connor now, lean and long-limbed, but his glossy black hair and warm brown eyes were the same. Those eyes always reminded her of a dog's, not so much for their colour as for the fact that they held the same open friendliness and good humour and loyalty. He came running to meet them, a welcoming smile on his face. It did not matter that he only said "Hello, Jean," before moving on past her to greet Andy and admire the car. He and Andy were the same age—seventeen—and shared many of the same interests: it was only natural that Jim should spend more time with him. She stood watching him talk to her brother, and was content.

"That engine's some smooth—did you put some new rings in her?" Jim asked.

"That's right," Andy replied. His sullen mood had lifted

and he was now eager to show off the Chrysler. "Have a look inside."

"You should have been here yesterday," Mr. O'Connor was saying to her father. "What a commotion! They're going to use the bay as winter anchorage for merchant ships, since your harbour up in St. John's is getting so crowded. There'll be a marine railway and repair site, barracks, everything. The Canadian Minister of Defence passed through here to have a look around, and he brought some Canadian troops along with him."

"Quite an invasion," grunted Mr. MacDougall.

"Not at all! They were welcome—everyone here enjoyed meeting them. The minister was held up here by fog—couldn't catch his flight out—so he spent the day going around to people's homes, introducing himself. Did you know his background's Irish, too? His name's Power. And the Canadian soldiers were nice young men. It got some of us thinking about whether we could be one people some day—one country."

"Confederation with Canada?" Jean's father snorted derisively. "Now, Matthew, you know what that would mean. You'd lose your living. All those big chain stores of theirs would start moving in, and that'd be the end of O'Connor's General Goods. What we really need is to get rid of this Commission Government, and start running our own affairs again—"

Mr. MacDougall and Mr. O'Connor seldom agreed on anything, but they seemed to enjoy arguing, even though neither ever convinced the other. Jean and Fiona and their mother left the two men to their genial debate and headed for the house—though Jean cast a longing backward glance at Jim, who was now examining the Chrysler's engine while Andy stood proudly by. As the women approached the house more O'Connors came running around its side, yelling greetings: fourteen-year-old Rick promptly joined the two older boys by the car, while his younger sisters ran up to the MacDougall girls.

"Come on!" Mary, the elder, invited them breathlessly. She caught hold of Fiona's hand. "Duchess has had her kittens. They're some cute! We're giving most of them away, though. Come and see them—"

"And then let's go to Dougherty's. It's a new place just down the road, they sell ice cream—" explained her sister Colleen.

"No, the barrens first! The blueberries are ripe, Mummy says we can go pick some—"

Jean followed the younger girls—first to the woodshed at the back of the property, where the calico cat presided over her mewling litter, then into the back door of the house. No one ever used the front door, with its little flight of stone steps. The back door was the main entrance, opening and slamming all day as young O'Connors rushed in and out. Here, in the part called the lean-to, was a long narrow room with a sink and a place to put boots in wintertime. A tiny room to the left of the door had once been the birthing-room: these days it was used for a sick-room or spare bedroom. Directly ahead was the kitchen. It too had a door but this was never closed. Indeed Jean could not remember ever having seen it shut in all her visits here. She knew this place as well as her own home, from the ground-floor rooms right up to the tiny attic, where the girls liked to put on hats and dresses from the battered boxes and pretend to be ladies. Some of the dresses were very old, with tiny wasp waists and great dusty skirts. The women who had worn them must have been very small, for they fitted the children perfectly.

As Jean entered she saw her mother sitting with Mrs. O'Connor and an older grey-haired woman, one of the neighbours. The youngest O'Connor child, four-year-old Lizzie, was playing at their feet with a doll: it was battered and had only one eye, no doubt a hand-me-down from her older sisters. "Mummy!" shouted Colleen. The O'Connor children always shouted, indoors and out. "Can we go to the barrens and pick berries? Can we go *now*?"

"In a moment," said Mrs. O'Connor, smiling. She was plump and round-faced and affable, like her husband.

"I want to go too!" Lizzie cried, springing up from the floor.

"Jean, you're not dressed for berry-picking," said her mother. "Why ever did you put on such a good dress? It'll get stained."

Jean's heart sank at her mother's tone. Now she would have to stay indoors with the women, and listen to them talking about births and deaths and marriages in the outport while everyone else was out enjoying the sun and fresh air.

"If Lizzie goes, she'll need someone older to keep an eye on her," said Mrs. O'Connor. "Will you look after her, Jeanie?"

"Of course," Jean replied gratefully. If she couldn't be with Jim, at least she needn't be cooped up in here.

"Shouldn't go out in that dress," said the grey-haired woman sitting beside Mrs. O'Connor. It was Mrs. Doyle, a widow who lived alone in a house several doors up from the O'Connors.

"Oh, she can have one of my old aprons, Maggie," Mrs. O'Connor replied easily. "That'll cover some of it up anyway."

"Not what I meant," Mrs. Doyle said. She shook her grey head. "It's green, that dress. Unlucky. They won't like it."

"Who won't?" Jean asked, bewildered.

"The good people. It's their own colour, that. They won't hold with others wearing it."

"Here are some buckets and sieves to put the berries in," interrupted Mrs. O'Connor. "And here's an apron. Lizzie, take Jeanie's hand. That's right. Off you go, and be back in time for lunch."

"What did Mrs. Doyle mean?" asked Jean once they were out of the house. "Why won't the people here let anyone wear green?"

"She meant the fairies," said Mary carelessly. "That's what they calls them round here—the Good People, the Good Neighbours. It's bad luck to speak ill of the fairies, they says. But Daddy says it's just a superstition."

"I like fairies," said Fiona. "They're so pretty, with those little wings. I collect pictures of them for my scrapbook." She began to skip about, pretending to fly.

"Fairies here are different," Colleen told her. "They're bigger and fiercer, and they hates people. They carries you off, like the Bogey-man."

Lizzie squealed. "That's enough," said Jean quickly.

"Maybe they'll get *you*," Colleen teased Fiona. "You

should cross yourself, like this." With one finger she sketched the shape of a cross on the front of her blouse. "And say a Hail Mary."

"I'm *Presbyterian*," reproved Fiona.

Religion, the children had been told many times by their parents, was a topic that must never be raised among them. The O'Connors were Roman Catholic and the MacDougalls Protestant, and this was a matter of some delicacy. Though Mrs. O'Connor had once been Protestant, she had avoided any difficulties by converting to her husband's faith, unlike Mum who had never changed her religion. It was all very complicated. But the children, despite the warnings, had had many frank discussions when out of their elders' hearing.

"You don't really believe that piece of communion bread is God," a twelve-year-old Andy had once challenged Mary.

"Yes I does. The priest turns it into God," the little girl had replied.

"Well, can the priest do anything then? Is he magic? Could he turn you into a frog?"

"Sure he could, if he wanted to," Mary had responded stoutly. Jean had not really believed this, but for some time afterwards she was unfailingly polite to black-cassocked Father O'Neill whenever she passed him on the road—just in case.

"Come on," she said now, as they passed the last few houses of the outport and headed over the fields towards the barrens, "let's talk about something else."

"Look at the fog!" exclaimed Fiona, pointing.

A long white bank was advancing across the flat stretch of the barrens, one of the dense sea fogs so common to the

Avalon Peninsula. Overhead was clear blue sky, and the hot sun burning down at them; ahead, the thick cottony mass like a low-lying cloud. Fiona gave a whoop and ran to meet it, waving her bucket. She was joined by Colleen, brown pigtails flying.

"Don't get too far ahead!" called Jean. The mist was so very thick: Fiona's figure already seemed only a grey shadow in its whiteness. "I don't want you to get lost." Their laughter floated back to her out of the fog. Jean reached for Lizzie's hand, but the little girl made a whimpering sound and clung to her sister Mary instead.

Jean sighed. "All right, just don't let her run off on her own, will you, Mary?"

"Come on, Liz, let's get some berries!" said Mary. "We'll get more than anyone else!"

The fog had reached them now: its cold damp blankness was all around them, and overhead the sun had turned to a bleached, heatless circle. They could see no more than a few yards in any direction. But they could see the ground clearly, and all around them a rich crop of blueberries waited for the picking. The younger girls fell silent, absorbed in their harvest now that it had become a race. Jean also stooped to pluck the little blue-black berries from their low-growing stalks, though she moved at a more leisurely pace. Occasionally a red partridgeberry showed itself, gleaming like a ruby, and she picked these too. It took only minutes to fill the bottom of her sieve.

After a while she straightened to ease the strain in her shoulders, and looked around her. The mist was starting to thin slightly. A few feet ahead of her a dark grey shape loomed, and she frowned. It was a tree: a tall one, with wide-spreading boughs and a thick canopy of leaves. That was odd. She had never noticed a tree growing out on the barrens, all by itself. She went up to it, touched the rough mist-damp bark of its trunk. A maple tree, it looked like. And there was another, just a few yards away: a tall branching shape in the mist.

Jean realized that she must have wandered all the way to the edge of the barrens. She'd lost track of time: it hadn't felt as though she was walking that far. She turned and looked about her for the other girls.

"Mary! Lizzie!" She could not see them anywhere in the grey void. They hadn't been all that far behind her, had they? She called again: "Mary, Lizzie, where are you?"

Silence. She could hear only the distant sea, a breathing sound in the stillness.

Jean began to backtrack, her heart beating uncomfortably fast. Why didn't they answer? Surely something couldn't have happened to both of them at once? But they ought to be able to hear her at this distance. She called again, raising her voice to a shout: "*Mary!* Where are you? Fiona! Colleen! I told you not to go too far!"

Still there was no reply. Perhaps they were playing a joke on her. It would be just like them: lie low in the fog and make worry-wart Jean run around yelling like an idiot. They'd be snickering as they listened to her . . .

Jean abruptly came to a halt. There in the mist before her was another tree, and the dim outlines of two more behind it. She'd thought she was retracing her footsteps, but she must really have been going around in circles. As she stood there the sun brightened: the mist turned pale gold and began to lift. Jean looked around her in bewilderment.

She was standing alone in a forest of huge, ancient trees which stretched around her for as far as she could see in every direction. There was no one else in sight.

Chapter Two

JEAN STOOD ABSOLUTELY STILL, staring around her. Long aisles of tree trunks spread before her, fading into green distances. This was not the forest of scrubby pines and firs that surrounded Mary's Bay. These trees were much taller, and many were deciduous: maples and oaks and elms whose branches supported a thick ceiling of leaves. Overhead the fog lingered, hanging like heavy white smoke among the branches. She could still hear the sea, and birds were singing far off, somewhere in the wood. But there was no other sound. She almost thought she heard, as well as felt, her own heartbeats.

How long she stood there Jean could never afterwards say for certain. There was nowhere to go, no direction which did not lead to more forest. There were no roads or paths. *How could I have come so far into this wood without knowing it?* she wondered. The fog hadn't been that thick, surely? But it must have been, she told herself firmly, or she would not be here.

After a few more minutes' standing and staring about her, she decided that she must at least try to find a way out. *I can't stay here 'til I take root!* She chose the direction from which she had originally come—at least she thought it was the right direction. She had turned around so many times as she scrutinized her surroundings that she was no longer sure. The forest floor was rough and uneven beneath her shoes, full of little dints and mossy hollows and criss-crossed with networks of tree roots. More than once she tripped and had to grab a projecting branch to steady herself. Occasionally she called out to Fiona and the others, but was unsurprised to receive no answer. They would be out on the barrens still, wondering where she had got to, no doubt. It would be embarrassing to admit she had gotten lost in the fog—*she*, the eldest, to whom the others were supposed to look for guidance. How they would laugh! But the adults wouldn't be amused.

I didn't know there were woods like these anywhere near, and the fog was so thick . . . Already she could hear her own excuses.

The forest continued, vast and uninterrupted. Dense mist still trailed through its upper branches in cold white waves, and the sky was only a lightness overhead. The grey veil of suspended moisture gave a flatness to the further reaches of the forest: they seemed to have no more depth than a painted backdrop. She was beginning to feel unnerved when she heard a sharp cry from somewhere above her, and looked up to see a small shape circling in that pale blankness. It was only a grey outline in the mist: the flying form of a bird. But somehow it was a relief to see another living thing in this trackless forest. She stood for a moment watching as it darted to and fro above the trees, wondering why it didn't settle. Her presence must have disturbed it. She walked on, but the bird followed her, still uttering its shrill cries. "Chaw—chaw!" They sounded almost like the caw of a crow, but higher in pitch, less harsh, more musical. The bird brought a voice into the silence, motion to the unnatural stillness of the wood, and a momentary easing of her fears.

Why was I so nervous, anyway? It's only a wood, an ordinary wood! I'll soon find my way out, get back onto the barrens. I'll find the girls and we'll all have a laugh. Jean's told to watch the young ones, and she's *the one who ends up getting lost!* Lost . . . How she wished she had not thought of that word: the forest seemed to fling it back at her, as though she had shouted it. *Of course I'm not lost! I wandered a bit off track, that's all. I'll be clear of this place soon, it can't go on forever!*

Forever . . . Again her own word loomed before her. She felt the tightness below her ribcage that was the first symptom of panic.

"Chaw!" She looked up, saw a mist-grey shape perching now in the boughs of a tree. The bird again. But no—it wouldn't be the same bird. There were probably dozens like it in this forest, hundreds. There was no reason at all for a wild bird to be following her . . .

She started to walk a little faster, jumping over thick protruding tree roots. There was a rustle overhead, a soft sound of feathers fanning the air, as the bird swooped above her. It kept pace with her, alighting on branches when she slowed or halted, launching itself into flight again as soon as she moved on. Jean was becoming thoroughly unnerved. The bird, whose presence had been a reassurance at first, was now suddenly a part of the strangeness that surrounded her—a strangeness she was only beginning to admit to herself. There was no comfort anywhere now, not even in the distant sound of the sea—for no matter how long and far she walked, it still did not come into sight. Shouldn't she have reached the barrens by now? Was she walking in the wrong direction entirely?

She stopped dead. There was a large, thick-boled tree directly ahead of her, with a humpbacked root arching up from the moss at its foot. She knew it: she'd seen it before, a few minutes ago. She was going around in circles.

Suddenly the bird flew down to a low branch, then to the forest floor. Now that it was no longer half-hidden by mist she saw that its plumage was dark in colour, a shiny blue-black with faint glosses of green along its wings and tail. Its beak and legs were red. It perched there for a moment, its bright eye cocked up at her, showing no fear of her at all. Then it opened its wings again and flew a few yards away, settling on a branch.

"Chaw," it said. "Chaw, chaw."

Jean could not explain even to herself why she followed it. She was, perhaps, tired of following her own instincts, which so far had only led her astray. The direction in which the bird had flown seemed as likely as any to lead her out of the woods. The ground was less smooth here: there was more undergrowth, short prickly bushes that scratched at her stockinged legs, and clumps of taller saplings covered in clusters of orange-red berries. Dogberry trees. She pushed past them, and began to feel more optimistic. At least this part of the forest looked different: it had lost that disturbing sameness.

The bird flew on before her. Before long the undergrowth cleared again and she found herself on a path—a real path, not paved but still clearly the work of many feet wearing a flat track through earth and moss. Human feet. Her spirits lifted. So she wasn't all that far from the outport then.

And now she heard voices coming from ahead of her. The bird flew high up into a tree.

Several figures were approaching through the forest, mounted on horseback. Through the low-hanging screens of leaves and rows of trunks she could catch only partial glimpses: a flash of bright blue or scarlet here, the mottled flank of a horse there. Voices murmured, muffled by distance and the soft thud of hooves. At last! People—comforting human presences, locals from whom she would get directions and reassurance. She ran towards them, tearing her way through the impeding undergrowth so that fragments of twigs caught in her hair and burrs clung to her skirts. Scratched and panting, she ran onto the path just as the riders came around a bend.

The leader was a man on a big bay horse, much larger than any outport pony. It snorted softly through flared nostrils as Jean burst onto the path in front of it, but did not rear or startle, as though it had been trained to remain calm in such situations. It was the rider who reacted, shouting something and reining in his mount—so suddenly that the horses of the riders behind him all collided with one another like dominoes.

Jean could only stand and stare, wide-eyed. The men at the front of the group were wearing what looked like steel battle armour.

The man in the lead crossed himself, as Colleen had done, and spoke in an urgent tone. "It is one of them—the Tylwyth Teg!" He was staring at Jean, who gazed back in bewilderment.

"It cannot be," said another voice behind him.

"But see how she is clad! No mortal would dare wear green, not here." The big armoured man reached out and snapped off a red-berried twig with his gauntleted hand. "A sword is of no use against them. But the fairy people fear the rowan!" He dismounted and advanced upon Jean, grim-faced, brandishing the dogberry twig. "Back, you cursed creature!" he bellowed. "You'll work no spells on us."

Jean could not stir a limb, or give voice to her own amazement. She could see, now, that there were about seven armoured men in all, and with them some women dressed in long bright-coloured gowns. It had happened again: the thin veil between times had lifted for her, opening a window on some bygone age. But never before had the phantoms of the past come so close, nor had they ever seen or spoken to her. They had always passed on unheeding, as the soldiers had done, through their own mysterious, parallel reality. She stood and stared at the armoured man, paralyzed not by fear but by utter astonishment.

He halted a pace or two away from her, clearly perturbed and puzzled that she had not fled from him. "Back, I say!" he roared again, waving the dogberries almost in her face.

Jean's voice came at last to her rescue. "Stop that!" she ordered automatically, just as she might have rebuked a misbehaving Fiona or Colleen. The man recoiled, a look of comical surprise and dismay on his face.

A woman's merry peal of laughter rang out from the back of the group, followed by her teasing voice. "Well, Sir Owen, this is a strange sort of fairy you have found! She does not seem to know what is expected of her." Jean could not see which of the veiled and mantled figures had spoken, but the voice sounded young. Then there was a chuckle, and another man rode forward from the back of the line.

He was clad in what looked like a robe of some home-spun fabric, ashen grey in colour: but it was his face that Jean's eyes fastened on. It was an aged face, much lined about the mouth and eyes, with long furrows across the high brow. His hair and beard were wool-white and extremely long, the former falling to his shoulders and the latter sweeping his chest. His eyes were deep-set, grey as his robe, his nose thin and high-bridged.

"You . . . I've seen you before," Jean blurted out. Who was he? One of the outport people? Then it was all right after all: they were just folks from Mary's Bay, putting on some sort of history pageant . . .

The grey eyes dwelt on her thoughtfully, and a bony hand in a wide sleeve came up to stroke the falling fleece of his beard. "Indeed?" he mused. His voice was not thin and reedy like an old man's, but deep and resonant. "Now that is most curious. For if I mistake not, you are not a dweller in these parts." He too dismounted, and walked towards her.

She continued to stare at him—the one familiar element in this strangeness; and then with a kind of despair she recognized him. It was the old man whose face had appeared in her early-morning vision. So he was not anyone she knew

27

after all: he belonged to the strangeness, to this unknown time and place.

The young woman called out again. "Is she truly one of the Good People then, Druid?"

"No, indeed: something more curious still."

And as Jean stood there, the woman rode forward on a horse white as snow. She was, Jean saw, little more than a girl, perhaps eighteen or nineteen years of age. Her hair was bound in long corn gold braids under a veil of blue cloth, and her gown was blue also and so long that it covered all her horse's left flank—for she rode side-saddle, like a woman of olden times. Her clear blue eyes gazed at Jean directly and without a trace of fear.

"Is she one of the wild people then—the Forest Folk who live in the deep woods?" she asked.

The big armoured man shook his head. "They wear only garments of deerskin; and they also paint their faces, or so I am told." The blonde girl rode her horse closer, and he spoke to her nervously. "Your Highness, please! Not so near. It is not safe."

And now Jean saw the band of gold that circled the young girl's brow, its lustre lost in the gold of her hair. She was royal. That explained the elegant gown, the regal and stately bearing. Before Jean's eyes there flashed the memory of last year's royal visit: the procession along LeMarchant Road, King George VI and his smiling dark-haired queen waving at the crowds from their car. Jean remembered standing with her family on the front steps of their house, cheering and waving the Union Jack—for a thrilling instant she was convinced that the eyes of Queen Elizabeth had rested on *her*. Could this young girl be a queen? But then the man would have said "Your Majesty," wouldn't he? A princess, then. In the confused welter of her thoughts this one idea shone through. Perhaps it was all only a dream—perhaps she had never really awakened, never driven with her family to Mary's Bay, never picked berries on the barrens. She might well be still in her bed back home. But even as she thought this her knees were already bending in the clumsy curtsey she and Fiona had learned for the royal visit.

"There!" the white-bearded man said. He sounded amused. "Would one of the Tylwyth Teg make obeisance to a mortal? Green gown or no, this is a human child, Your Highness."

"A pity!" the girl on the white horse said, and her voice too held a hint of laughter. "I should have liked to see a real fairy. Well, let us ride on, then!"

The terror of being left alone in the wood again seized Jean, and she cried out: "Please—!"

The smiling blue eyes—so like those of Queen Elizabeth as she rode past in the royal car—looked down at Jean with a kindly expression. "What do you wish?"

"Please—couldn't I come with you?" implored Jean. "Your Highness," she stammered as an afterthought. She turned to the white-bearded man, who still seemed to her the central figure, the half-familiar key to the mystery into which she had been plunged. "Couldn't I come? I'm lost, I have no place to go."

He considered a moment before speaking. Under their white brows his eyes were cool and remote, like wintry lakes beneath banks of snow; but there was no wariness in them such as she had seen in the other men's eyes. "Druid," the princess had called him: but that was a title, wasn't it, not a name? In school she had learned of the Druids, pagan holy men of ancient Britain. They were all gone now, had vanished thousands of years ago. And she had never heard that they lived in Newfoundland.

"I think she must come with us," the old man said to the princess. "There is no harm in her, of that I am certain. And if she cannot return to her own place she will need a roof for her head."

"We go to the Abbey of Saint Michael," the princess told Jean. "It lies not far off, by the Bay of Connemara. From there it is but a few hours' journey to Temair. But we shall stay the night, as the abbess is a dear friend of mine. You shall have shelter and food there too, for they make all travellers welcome."

The place names meant nothing to Jean, but she did not expect them to. She let the man called Sir Owen help her up into the saddle behind one of his comrades. It was almost a relief to feel the strong grip of those powerful hands, and the sun-warmed metal backplate of the man sitting in front of her. She could touch these people, and be touched by them; she was part of their world; and though this thought was frightening, it was better to be in the company of flesh-and-blood beings than ghostly shades. She had companions now, and protectors. Whatever bygone age they belonged to, they were human as herself and they had offered her help. For the moment she felt only small, immediate fears—of tumbling off this man's mount, for instance. Its back seemed very high off the ground to a girl who had ridden little outport ponies many a time, but never a full-sized horse. She put her arms timidly around the man's armoured waist.

The big man named Owen swung himself back up into his own saddle and spurred his steed forward, and the Druid remounted his own horse. As they rode on through the forest Jean cast one glance behind her, in time to see the little black bird wing away through the wood.

They saw the abbey's spire long before the trees thinned, glimpsing the green copper pinnacle through gaps in the forest's leafy canopy. Then slowly the track widened, the woods gave way on either side and they were out in a sunny clearing with a broad bay to one side.

Mary's Bay.

Jean knew it at once: the headlands with their rolling hills, the crescent of shingle beach and the rust-coloured rocks of Sunker Point. But in this unknown other-time there was no outport: no houses, no roads, no wharves lay before them. Instead there was a sort of fortress with low stone walls on the summit of Dutton's Hill, over on the north side of the bay; and here on the nearer side the Abbey of Saint Michael stood. It was a great church quarried of grey granite, entirely surrounded by a stockade of rough-hewn tree trunks. Before the gates of the stockade was a cluster of little hovels, built it seemed from interwoven sticks daubed with mud; there were little vegetable patches lying between them, and farmers' fields beyond, and an apple orchard. Men and women in plain homespun garments were busily harvesting the crops, but at the approach of the riders they set their tasks aside. Several children came running up to the knights, who reached down grinning and hauled some of them up onto the pommels of their saddles. Others clambered up behind the men, squealing with delight.

"The holy brothers and sisters have many more tenants," observed the golden-haired princess, smiling and waving back to the people. "It really is almost like a proper village, with all these families."

"There will be quite a large village here," commented the Druid, "one day." He said it not as though he were speculating, but as though he were pronouncing a certainty.

Jean found her voice, which had once more deserted her at the first sight of the transformed bay. "Why is there such a large fence?" she asked, staring up at the stockade.

"To keep out the enemy," replied the man she rode with. He spoke without turning and his voice was grim, and some of the men and women in the party crossed themselves. Jean did not like to ask anything else. She could feel the fear in their abrupt silence, and it reminded her too much of the cold dread she herself had felt during the past year. She looked up instead at the stone walls of the abbey as the riders passed through the wooden gates and into an unpaved forecourt. The tower was as tall as that of the great Kirk in St. John's, but rounded in shape, not four-sided; it looked to her more like a tower from a medieval castle, and she could see arrow slits set into its walls. A secondary defence, then, should the stockade be breached? Whoever their enemies might be, these people plainly lived in daily terror of them, and had left nothing to chance.

The mounted party rode right up to the heavy arched entrance of the building. At the door a middle-aged woman stood, wearing a plain white veil and robe, and behind her stood several other women similarly clad. Nuns, they must be, and she would be their abbess. The woman came forward, her arms outstretched in welcome as the visitors drew up before her door. The golden-haired girl swung herself lightly down from her horse, and went to meet her. Jean was surprised to see that the princess was quite small, her head not even as high as the older woman's. On horseback she had naturally seemed much taller, and her regal bearing had added to the illusion. But her air of calm confidence more than compensated for her lack of inches. She glided gracefully across the yard, indifferent to the churned-up mud and dirt through which the lovely blue train of her gown trailed, and smiled as she took the nun's hands in her own. The veiled woman curtseyed.

"Princess Gwenlian—"

"Dear Abbess Brigid—"

The women embraced warmly, cheek to cheek.

"Ah, Princess, it is so good to see you! And such a happy occasion, too," the abbess said. Her face was rose-cheeked and sun-browned, like the face of a woman who spends much of her time out of doors. "We have all hoped for this betrothal ever since you and Prince Diarmait were little children, fostering together at Temair. If ever a marriage was meant to be, it is this one."

"He was a terrible boy," recalled Princess Gwenlian. "Always teasing and pulling my hair." But there was no complaint in her tone as she said it. If duty demanded that she marry a terrible boy, this young woman clearly meant to do it without any fuss.

"But come in, come in," invited Abbess Brigid, gesturing to all the party. "It is almost time for Sext, and afterwards we will all dine together. Be welcome in our house!"

White-robed men came forward to take the horses' bridles; everyone dismounted and headed for the stone entrance. In the tower high above a bell had begun to peal. The man Owen helped Jean down off the horse, and she turned anxiously to the old Druid. "What is it? What are we going to do now?" she whispered.

"We will attend church with them. This is the hour of Sext, their midday service," he whispered back. "Eight services are held each day in the abbey: Lauds, Prime, Terce, Sext, None, Vespers, Compline, Matins. The holy brothers and sisters observe them all, and while we are under their roof we must attend some of them at least." She started to ask another question, but he smiled slightly and shook his head at her, as if to say *Not now*. There was nothing else to do but follow him and the princess and her retinue into the dark entrance of the abbey.

Chapter Three

JEAN HAD NEVER SEEN ANYTHING LIKE THE INTERIOR of that church. Its ceiling was not, perhaps, as high as it seemed at first sight; but the arching stone vaults conveyed to her the impression of an exalted, airy space. The windows were rather small, but they contained fine stained glass in rich and vivid colours: ruby, amber, violet. Their transmuted light fell here and there on the figures of kneeling peasants, casting here a rose-red halo on a bent head, there a wash of blue on a pair of clasped work-worn hands. A fine embroidered cloth covered the altar. Behind it there spread a screen of intricately carved and gilded wood, showing a nativity scene, and topped by a wooden statue of a spread-winged angel.

Those in the abbey's religious order sat at the front, in special pews that faced one another across the central aisle. In addition to the white-clad nuns, Jean saw, there were a great many men wearing white robes: monks, they must be, though it seemed odd that they should share the same living quarters as the women. Weren't nuns and monks always kept apart, in separate communities? And the men did not wear a tonsure at the crown of the head, like monks in all the pictures she had seen: instead, they had shaved a swath through their hair from ear to ear. It was rather like looking at a drawing in which certain details had been made deliberately wrong. *Was* this place real—had she crossed some unseen threshold, bodily entered some past era in which the Island she knew had belonged to these people? Had things somehow been reversed, so that this time it was she who was the intruder, the otherworldly phantom moving through an age in which she did not belong? But this culture was medieval. Surely Newfoundland had not yet been settled in the Middle Ages. And this *was* Newfoundland, of that one thing she was certain. The bay was there, unchanged, perfectly recognizable, even if these people called it by another name.

She cast her eyes up at the ceiling as the monks and nuns commenced a plainsong chant. How could such a large building, with its thick walls of granite blocks, have vanished utterly by her day? In Europe there were many ruins of old abbeys and churches. But she had never seen any trace of such a ruin in Mary's Bay, not so much as an outline of a foundation. Mr. O'Connor had told her all about the outport's past, from the arrival of the first Europeans who had come there only to fish, to the colonists who had come later, in many waves spanning the centuries. The crumbling remains of a medieval abbey in an empty wilderness would surely have aroused wonder and curiosity among the early settlers. Even if the last weathered stones had been taken away, there would have been *some* mention of it in the local histories.

Her eyes drifted downwards again and came to rest on the wooden angel atop the carved screen. Its wings and halo were plated with gleaming gold leaf, as was the knightly armour in which it was clad and the sword it held aloft in one hand. Beneath its golden feet a hideous demon sprawled, with a scaly half-human face turned up in a fanged howl. The archangel Michael, it must be: God's champion against the Devil. She had seen pictures of him in books, though the Kirk where her family went every Sunday held no image of him. "Idol worship!" Grandma would have said of this golden figure; it was what she always said when she passed a Catholic church with its statues of saints on pedestals. "As bad as the heathens!" A much younger Jean had worried that this might mean God was angry with the O'Connors. "Grandma told me it's wrong, all these statues of saints and things. The Commandments say so. It's adultery," she had informed Jim anxiously.

"You mean idolatry," Jim corrected her. "And it isn't, either. We don't worship the saints, we pray to them."

This had sounded like hairsplitting to Jean, but even then she had been too fond of Jim to argue with him for long. Now she sat looking timidly about her, feeling the foreignness of this great stone temple, its forbidden and alien sanctity. She was in a *Catholic* church—a place she had no business to be: she had never even ventured inside the O'Connors' church in Mary's Bay, though once or twice she had peered in its front door at the plaster images and banks of glowing votive candles. It was not at all like the Kirk, that big, solemn, austere building with its plain interior and the tall clump of organ pipes at the front . . .

But she must *not* think of home, not now: that only heightened her fear.

She stole a sidelong glance at the white-bearded Druid sitting beside her in the pew. Why was *he* here? He was another discordant element: for the Druids had worshipped pagan gods, hadn't they? Yet he sat there gravely and quietly, his crag-like face impassive as he listened to the hymns and chants of the Christian service. He seemed very wise; somehow she felt certain that he knew or suspected more about her presence here than he had admitted. If she could just talk to him alone . . .

The final hymn ended; the robed men and women began to file out of their pews, heading for a low-lintelled door to the right side of the sanctuary. The peasants left by the main entrance, but the princess and her retainers followed the monks and nuns. Jean walked slowly behind them.

The little door led into a narrow, low-ceilinged passageway. To either side were tiny cells of rooms, their wooden doors open to show their Spartan interiors: each held a wooden bed and hanging crucifix and little else. There were also a couple of guest-rooms, larger than the cells though no less plain, with several beds each. The largest room of all they called a "refectory": it was a sort of dining-hall with a number of long wooden tables running down its length. Here the visitors were invited to sit while a meal was served to them.

The meal like everything else was very plain, consisting for the most part of fresh fish, boiled eggs, a few vegetables, bread, cheese, some of the golden yellow apples from the orchard and wild berries of various kinds. Looking at these, Jean remembered suddenly her sieve full of blueberries and partridgeberries: she could not recall where and when she had lost it. The people around her helped themselves to the food, eating it off flat trenchers that were themselves made of hard, brown bread. Earthenware pitchers of rich, creamy milk were passed around to fill the wooden cups. There was no meat to be seen. Neither was there any conversation. Instead, Abbess Brigid and an older monk took turns reading aloud from a small vellum-backed book: the readings all seemed to be prayers or religious poetry. Unable to ask her hosts any questions, Jean simply took the food offered her and ate it. There could be no doubt that the food was real: the crusty brown bread still hot from the oven, the apples whose burnished peel snapped as she bit it, the berries that burst into sweetness on her tongue, all drove away the dreamy strangeness. *You are here*, they seemed to say to her. *It is all true.*

But where was "here"? Or rather, *when*?

A bell chimed softly, and the abbess set down her book. The monks and nuns rose, and began to file out of the refectory. A few remained behind to remove the empty trenchers and wipe the tables clean: the others all walked out into the sunny enclosure. Jean was surprised to see most of the holy men and women go out the main gate, and start to work alongside the peasant folk in the fields. The rest, a small group of a half-dozen or so, headed for some wooden benches set along the abbey's outer wall.

"Now, Princess, perhaps you will tell us all your news," invited the abbess. "And introduce this young handmaiden to me, for I see that she is newly come into your service." She beamed kindly at Jean.

"She is not of my company, Reverend Mother," the princess replied, and proceeded to tell the abbess and her subordinates how Jean had been found in the forest.

"Indeed!" said the abbess, looking interested. "Well, Mistress Jean, how did you come to be wandering all alone in the wild woods? Were you with a group of travellers, perhaps, and did you become separated from them?"

"I was with my sister and some friends," said Jean slowly. The image of Fiona and the O'Connor girls running through the mist came to her, but it seemed vague and indistinct, like a memory from much longer ago than that morning. "We were on the barrens, in a fog . . . and I lost sight of the others, and when I called they didn't answer . . . and then I was in a forest. Just like that."

"The barrens?" repeated the elderly monk.

"Where your forest—used to be," said Jean unhappily.

They all looked at her in bewilderment; all but the Druid, who sat thoughtfully combing his beard with his fingers. "*Used* to be?" said the old monk, echoing her words again.

"In—my time." Jean knew she was explaining it badly, but what did it matter? They would never believe her in any case; she could scarcely believe it herself.

"But this *is* your own time. You are here, are you not?" said Abbess Brigid, smiling.

"No. At least, I am here but I don't belong here." She took a deep breath. "I'm from—from the year nineteen forty."

She waited breathlessly for their reaction, but there was no amazement on their faces, only a mild puzzlement. "But so are we, also," the abbess said.

Jean stared. Now she had confused them: they plainly didn't understand what she meant. "No, you're not," she corrected, "you belong to the Middle Ages—to the past, my past. You're all from a long time ago—"

"Ah! You think that we are ghosts!" the abbess exclaimed. "Poor child, you cannot truly believe that. Have you not joined us at our table, and shared our food? We are flesh and blood, like yourself."

"Perhaps she believes we are fairies, and are deceiving her senses with magic," suggested a young nun. "She was wandering in the woods, you say; and her garment is green, which puts her in their power. She may think that she has been fairy-led, and that all this"—she waved her hand to indicate the abbey, its enclosure and the fields and orchard beyond—"is only a fairy *glamour*."

"Ah, I see!" Princess Gwenlian held a slim beringed hand out to Jean. "Truly, we are mortal as you are, Jean: I swear it."

"No—" Things were becoming more confusing by the minute: Jean's head was starting to swim. She stood, clutching the back of the bench for support. "I *don't* think you're fairies, or ghosts, or anything like that. I only meant that we're living in different times. I don't belong here, I came here by—by some sort of accident and I want to go home. Can't you please help me go back home?" She was close to tears now and could no longer keep a quiver out of her voice. They looked at her—all these people who in her own time were long dead, vanished without trace—then as one they looked to the Druid. He rose to his feet.

"Perhaps you do not understand as well as you think, young Jean." His face was serious, even stern, and at the

41

sight of it her next words died on her tongue. "But explanations can come later. For now, I must tell you that no one here has the power to return you to your own place—no, not even I. Indeed, I feel certain that you have been sent here for some purpose, and until that purpose has been fulfilled you cannot return."

Jean sank back onto the bench, overcome with helplessness. There were a few sympathetic glances, but the people around her soon turned back to ordinary conversation. Jean might feel herself to be the centre of a drama, but these people had other concerns to occupy their attention and they obviously meant to get on with them. She subsided into silence, only half-listening to their talk, which all seemed to be of the abbey's doings, this year's crops of fruit and vegetables, the births of foals and kids, and births and deaths and weddings in the small human community outside the stockade. But presently Jean's ears pricked up again.

"And has the enemy been sighted?" Gwenlian asked.

The abbess's face grew grave. "No, I am glad to say: but the Lochlannach are wild in their ways and their attacks are quite random. One never knows when a longship might appear."

"There have been attacks on other villages along this coast, I hear," said the princess.

"Yes: but usually only animals are taken by them, for food—*strand-hogg* as they call it. They seem to feel they have a right to take whatever they please."

"They sometimes take prisoners too, Abbess Brigid—for slaves, most likely. And always they are attracted to monasteries because of the jewels and gold leaf on the reliquaries and missals. I fear my family did you no favour by giving you your golden Michael."

Jean felt that cold shiver again. "Who are the Lochlannach?" she asked.

At last she had the reaction she had been seeking: there was a speechless pause following her query. "I would that I might go to your homeland, Jean," exclaimed the young nun, "if the Lochlannach are unknown there! It must be a lovely place."

"It isn't. We're at war," Jean told her, "with the Germans." The old cramping sensation in her midriff came back: the feel of a fear, briefly set aside, returning. What things she could tell these people of, if only she could make them understand: air raids, U-boats, convoys, rationing. What were a few roaming pirates compared to terrors like these?

"I know of no such race," the abbess said. "And your own people—what is your land called, Jean?"

"Newfoundland. We're part of the British Empire."

"And are you a Christian?"

"I'm Presbyterian," came the automatic answer. The blank bewildered look that by now was so familiar crossed every face present, and she sighed. "Yes, I'm Christian."

"Perhaps we should pronounce a blessing on her all the same," said the old monk, "or sprinkle her with holy water. She may not be what she claims, and none of the fairy folk can endure contact with anything holy."

"Now why is that, good prior?" asked Gwenlian. There was a twinkle in her eye. "They were angels in Heaven once, were they not?"

The prior nodded, his thin face serious. "Yes, Your Highness—just as the devils were, before they turned against their Creator. When Satan and his followers rebelled, Michael's angels made war upon them; but some of the heavenly host stood aside and took no part in the battle. These too were cast out, being fit neither for Heaven nor Hell: they fell down, to the earth and the seas and the lower air, and they became the fairies."

"Yes, that's so," the young nun said eagerly. "I know a story about it. There was once a priest, I have been told, who lived in a parish that was troubled by the fairies. One day he stood on the threshold of his church, and commanded the fairies to show themselves. He saw nothing, but a voice spoke out of the air and said to him, 'Tell us when our salvation shall be!' And he answered, 'Unclean spirits! Sooner shall my walking stick give forth shoot and bloom than you have forgiveness for your treason. Now be gone!' And there was a great sound of wailing, and then silence, and that parish was never troubled by fairy mischief again."

There was a long pause, and then the Druid spoke. "I know that tale, sub-prioress," he said. "I heard it many years ago. It is older than you think, for it comes from the old country across the sea. But there is more to it than you have told."

"There is? Then will you give us the rest, Lailoken?" the sub-prioress asked.

"In the version that I heard," said the Druid, "the priest went back to his house afterward, satisfied with his good work. And when he went in, behold!" Lailoken raised his arm, as though pointing at some marvel. "The dead wood of his walking stick had split asunder: and from it there came forth green shoots, and buds of fragrant blossom."

That afternoon passed for Jean with agonizing slowness. Abbess Brigid, Princess Gwenlian and the Druid Lailoken went apart to talk—about her, Jean suspected. The holy brothers and sisters and the princess's handmaidens looked as though they wanted to question her further, but Jean was not in a mood for talking. She went apart and sat on a bench by herself, staring listlessly out the open gate of the stockade, with its view of the little wattle huts and the fields and the orchard's fruit-laden trees. Peasants went to and fro, picking the golden apples, bringing baskets of fresh fish from the bay, feeding their goats and hens. Gwenlian's ladies worked quietly at pieces of embroidery, while the knights sat in the sun polishing their armour and sharpening their weapons. Everyone was busily involved in some activity or other, leaving her isolated in her idleness.

In mid-afternoon came the ringing of the chapel bell for None. Jean did not attend with the others. When she saw them all filing into the church she ran—out of the fenced enclosure, out to the bay beyond, where she stood, her chest heaving, staring at the great sweep of land where the outport should have been. It was disturbing to see the familiar hilly headlands and the stony beach, but no houses or fishing boats or piers. A few small primitive-looking coracles were drawn up on the shingle. Several yards away reared the large lopsided boulder which the O'Connor children called "the Whale," and which she could remember climbing and playing on when she was small. On its flat grey back some filleted codfish had been spread out to dry. She went up close to the huge rock, searching for the place where Andy had chipped his initials years ago. They were not there. But of course they would not be, she told herself: for back in this day and age Andy had not been born. An appalling loneliness fell on her, bringing with it a sharp surge of panic.

She began to run along the beach, heading for the grassy slope on the north shore where the O'Connor house had been. *No: would be.* It was not to be built for centuries yet. She dropped to her knees in the empty meadow, trying to conjure up the white saltbox house out of the air. What if it *wasn't* there in the future? What if everything had changed and the O'Connors would not ever exist, after all? Time seemed to shift and waver all about her, distorted and changed, like a broken reflection in a pool. But the mild wind off the sea blew into her face, setting all the feathery headed grasses rustling around her; and the sunlight warmed her head and shoulders. Even without the house this place had a gentleness, a kindliness about it—as if something of the O'Connors came through it to touch her. Folding her hands in the faded red-checked apron that still hung at her waist, she reached out across the gulf of unknown centuries that separated her from them. *Oh, where are you?* she silently cried. *Jim, Andy, Dad, Mum: hear me, help me find the way that leads back to you.*

She returned to the abbey in late afternoon. There was another meatless meal, which she ate without relish and without meeting anyone's eyes. When it was over she went straight to one of the guest-rooms, tore off the apron and flung herself down on a bed. After weeping quietly for a while she fell asleep, despite the thin straw pallet and the hardness of the bed beneath. Her dreams were dark and confused, woven throughout with a sense of fear and loss. When she woke it was with bleary eyes and aching head, to stare blankly at a golden splash of late-evening light on the stone wall opposite her bed. Then memory brought back a rush of misery.

She walked out of the building, across the enclosure and out of the gate—not, this time, heading for the bay and the empty place where the O'Connors should have been, but back along the rutted path which led to the forest. The sun was setting, but there was still enough of an afterglow for her to find her way.

She had not been walking long when she heard her name called from behind. She turned, and there were the blue-gowned princess and the Druid following her. She slowed to let them catch up, but did not stop walking.

"Jean, it is no use," said Lailoken, coming up to walk at her side. "You may have come to us from the forest, but that does not mean it can take you home again. The door by which you enter is not always that by which you leave. And you *cannot* leave—not until the fates that brought you here permit it."

Jean's legs trembled, and she sank down wearily onto a fallen tree trunk beside the path. They sat with her, one on each side. After a moment the princess laid her soft pale hand on Jean's.

"Lailoken and I have talked long about your arrival and what it may mean," said Gwenlian gently. "And he thinks that you are mistaken: that you come not from another time, as you suppose, but from another world altogether. He did not want to tell you this before, as he did not want to frighten you. But we cannot let you wander away and get lost again."

"If I am right," the Druid said, "it is no great rift of distance or time that separates you from the world you know, but only the thinnest of veils. So take comfort: you may be nearer your home than you think."

Another world? What did they mean? There was only one world—unless one thought of the past as a different world, in its own right. She had often thought that herself, after seeing the shadowy soldiers of Mary's Bay and those other dim figures—great-skirted and bonneted women, stiff-collared men—whom she had sometimes thought she glimpsed in the streets of St. John's when she was very young. Perhaps, she had thought, time was in layers: like an onion, or like those pictures of the Earth's crust with all the different strata of soil and stone lying one atop the other. If the physical world had all these different layers, what others might it have? All of its bygone ages and epochs might lie piled invisibly atop one another, with the boundary separating each becoming thinner in certain places so that a person could look *through*. Hadn't she seen with her own eyes things thought long gone and vanished?

There was a little sharp cry and a bird flew overhead to settle on a branch high above them. It was now dusk, but Jean recognized its shape.

"There it is again!" she said, pointing. "That little black bird that led me to you—but I suppose it can't be the *same* one, can it?"

"It must be, if you saw one like it before," said the Druid, gazing up at it. "There could be no other bird of that kind here."

"What is it, Lailoken?" the princess asked.

"It is called a chough."

He pronounced it in the old way, *chow*. Jean turned to him. "You mean, a chough?" she asked, giving it the modern pronunciation of *chuff*. "Like a Cornish chough? But they're European birds, aren't they? They don't live on this side of the ocean."

"No," the Druid agreed.

"It's wandered a long way from home then."

"Yes," he repeated, "a long way from home." In his voice her phrase had a deep sadness, the haunting quality of an echo flung back from cliffs of stone. Lailoken stood and held his hand out to the bird. It cocked its head and half-opened its wings, and for a moment Jean thought it would fly down to the Druid. But it only fluttered up to a higher branch, and his hand fell back to his side. For no reason she could understand, tears came suddenly to Jean's eyes. Perhaps it was simply because the little bird was so lost and alone, cut off from its own country and kind. *Like me* . . . Or like Lailoken, perhaps? If he could recognize a bird from the old world he must have been there himself—perhaps had even lived there.

"You have always had such a love of birds, Lailoken," remarked Gwenlian, smiling. "I have seen him charm them into alighting on his hands, Jean: it is part of his magic."

"I have a close kinship," said the Druid, sitting down again, "with the things of the air."

"And no wonder," the princess said softly. "But of course Jean knows nothing of that."

"Of what?" Jean asked dully.

"An old story I heard once. It's said that some evil demons of the air once plotted to enslave all mankind by fathering a half-mortal child. Because he would possess their magic powers but live as a man among men, he would become a great tyrant—or so the demons hoped. But the poor innocent maiden whom they chose for the babe's mother ran to her priest for help, and he watched over her until her son was born, and baptized him, and schooled him in the ways of righteousness. And so he became a great power for good, and not evil, and the demons' plans were thwarted."

Lailoken smiled. "That is so."

"*You* . . . ?" exclaimed Jean.

"It is one version of the tale of my birth," the Druid said.

"But you don't—*believe* it?"

"The versions differ slightly in their details, but in the main the tale is true. I have no mortal father."

While Jean was trying to absorb this the sound of footsteps came along the forest path, from the direction of the abbey. They all turned and saw Abbess Brigid coming towards them, her white robes gleaming in the twilight under the trees. "Ah, there you are, my friends!" she called. "The abbey's gate will be closing soon for the night. Will you be much longer?"

"We will come now, I think, Reverend Mother." Lailoken rose, casting an inquiring look back at Jean. She knew she had no choice but to comply—she could not spend the night alone in the woods—but she still felt a rebellious surge of irritation.

"I don't understand this!" she burst out petulantly. "Nothing here makes any sense. You're a Druid, she's a nun. How can you two be friends? Don't you worship different gods?"

"There!" said Lailoken, gesturing to the abbess and Gwenlian. "What further proof do we require? She speaks exactly as a child of the Shadow-world would."

"But of course!" Brigid exclaimed. "In that case she would belong to the church of Rome. And so did our ancestors here in Annwn, child, once upon a time when the paths that ran between our worlds were open. We were in communion then with the Holy City of Rome and its Pope. But they did not approve of our joined monasteries, nor of our friendship with the Druids. Had the paths not been closed, I have no doubt that our church would now be under Rome's rule. And I, as a woman, would not be allowed to lead a community with men in it; nor would any of our monasteries enjoy any importance—for Rome's chief regard was always for the priests and bishops. But here it is abbots and abbesses who lead the church. I took my vows in the grove that lies on the northern side of the bay, where a spring that is sacred to the Druids wells up out of the earth. For all places are holy to me, and there is no grove or hill or vale where God is not."

There was a pause. "I don't belong to the Roman church either," said Jean. "I'm Presbyterian. Our church broke with Rome ages ago. There are lots of churches now, the Roman Catholic Church is just one of them."

"I see. How sad, though, that your people should be so divided. At least here in Avalon the church is one, and we look on the Druids as our brethren, fellow-travellers on the sacred ways."

The bird suddenly flew up from its bough with a startled cry and winged away over the trees. Lailoken swung around.

There were shouts in the distance, and the sound of running feet coming down the path.

"What is it?" said Gwenlian, springing up from the log. "Something is wrong, Abbess!"

"Reverend Mother—Reverend Mother!" A monk and a nun were speeding towards them through the dusk, robes drawn up to their knees in their haste.

"My children! What is the matter?" The abbess strode calmly forward to meet their headlong rush. The young nun fell at Brigid's feet, sobbing and clutching at the older woman's robes. Her brother monk stood doubled over, panting so hard he could barely speak.

"Lochlannach—the Lochlannach!" he managed to gasp.

"Sea raiders—here?" Brigid exclaimed. Princess Gwenlian and Lailoken stepped forward, but Jean's heart seemed to stumble at the terrible words and she could not move.

"Where are they now?" asked Gwenlian urgently.

"They came ashore." The monk was getting his breath back. He straightened. "The guards in the hill fort sent us a messenger. They said they had seen a longship in the bay. We could not find you anywhere, Reverend Mother, and so the prior and sub-prioress commanded everyone to come within the stockade. We two went to find you—"

"We could not bear to think of you out here, in danger," said the nun, "and the princess too—"

"Where are my men-at-arms?" interjected Gwenlian.

"Searching for you, Highness."

"They should have stayed to help defend the abbey." Gwenlian was moving with swift determined strides along the path, and the others made haste to follow her. There was a reddish glow through the trees ahead of them, and an acrid odour of burning. When they arrived at the forest margin, they halted in dismay.

The stockade was on fire. A column of flame as tall as the abbey's tower rose from the seaward side of its fortifications, throwing up red fountains of embers and streams of smoke. All around the wooden wall ran figures, black against the blaze, shouting and thrusting burning brands at the logs.

Hooves came thudding from their right, and a mounted knight drew up next to them. "Highness! Thank Heaven you are safe. You must come away with me now—"

"No! We must help them!" As Gwenlian spoke, the shape of another rider raced across the fire-glow between them and the abbey. "Where are the other knights?"

The second mounted man turned and rode towards them. A sudden terror seized Jean. "Look out!" she screamed, pointing to the rider.

Gwenlian looked, glanced away again. "It is only one of my knights."

"He isn't, he isn't! He's one of *them*!" How she knew this Jean could not say. As he drew nearer, the black fire-limned figure of the armoured man on the horse filled her with a dread unlike anything she had ever experienced.

The others all stared as the rider continued to gallop towards them. He wore knightly armour and rode a war-horse, but there was something about him . . . Then when he was almost upon them Jean saw the long bristling beard, the long tangled locks that flowed under the helmet.

With a startled oath the princess's knight spurred his own mount forward to block the disguised attacker's path. The two horses neighed shrilly as they collided, and the bearded man raised a huge battle-axe, and swung it at the knight. The latter parried the blow with his sword.

Jean screamed again. She saw, somewhere in the red-lit night, the abbess with her mouth wide open—calling out something Jean could not hear; and Lailoken with his robed arms raised and his eyes shut as if in prayer. Then out of the red glow a shadow came running towards them—a shadow that, as it came, resolved itself into a man.

It was a Viking. He could not be anything else, this wild-eyed barbarian: tall and broad and bearded, swathed in bristling furs and mail with a conical helmet that glowed in the firelight. Behind him many armed warriors were fighting blade to blade, while others came rushing towards her—friend or foe? Jean did not stay to see.

She ran—blindly, in panic; ran until the fire-glow was replaced by a thick blackness, and still she could not stop. There was nothing but darkness and fear and her own frantic flight. And then suddenly a woman's voice cried, ahead of her: "Oh, Jeanie, thank God!" And out of the darkness came hands that clutched and held her.

It was her father and Mrs. O'Connor. Turning wildly in their grasp, Jean stared behind her. There was no forest, no abbey, no twisting tower of flame. The barrens stretched around her in all directions, dark and empty and still.

Chapter Four

JEAN SAT AT THE O'Connors' kitchen table. Surrounded now by friends and family, by warmth and safety and familiar things, she had stopped trembling, although she still felt dazed and confused. Mrs. O'Connor had given her some hot tea to drink. Holding the cup in unsteady hands, she sipped at its steaming contents while everyone bombarded her with questions, reassurances and recriminations.

"But where *were* you?" Mum demanded for the fifth time, and for the fifth time Jean answered, "I told you—I got lost in a wood."

"You mean the woods on the south side of the bay?" Mr. O'Connor asked.

"No—I don't know—there were lots of big trees. I walked on and on but I couldn't find a path, and then . . ." Her voice trailed away. How to explain what had happened then?

"But how could you be lost in the woods *all day*?" her mother persisted. "It's just turning dark now. What were you doing in all that time?"

Jean struggled to answer. "I—I think—I must have dozed off."

"Dozed off—in the woods? Why in the world would you go to sleep there in the first place? And why were you running when your father found you?" Jean had run so hard that both her shoes had fallen off; they had been found lying on the ground some distance apart, though there was no trace of Mrs. O'Connor's checked apron.

"I had—a bad dream." She saw, again, the strange medieval figures, the abbey, the fearsome attackers. A nightmare: that was what it must have been. And yet—

Mrs. Doyle chuckled unexpectedly from her corner of the kitchen. "Ah, some do think they only fell asleep and dreamt it. Others say they can't remember a thing, not even if they've been gone for days."

"What do you mean?" Mr. MacDougall demanded, turning to her sharply.

"There was one woman down by Trepassey went missing all night long, in the pouring rain—but when she was found her clothes was dry. She said all she could remember was being in a lovely great house, with music and dancing. That's how it is when you're taken."

"Taken—?"

"By the Good People, into their world."

Jean's father glared at the older woman, and Mrs. O'Connor quickly intervened. "There now, never mind what happened. We've got her back again. Nothing *bad* happened, that's the main thing."

"She lost your apron, Sarah," said Mum.

"I'm sorry," apologized Jean.

"Goodness, that old rag! It doesn't matter in the least," retorted Mrs. O'Connor. "Now, I'm going to go tell all the neighbours she's been found."

The adults began to stream out of the kitchen—to talk about her some more, Jean suspected, outside her hearing. Now that her fright over the dream had lessened she was close to tears with humiliation and disappointment. The whole day, lost and ruined: the precious Mary's Bay excursion she had been looking forward to for days. She had seen hardly anything of Jim, and now she was going to be taken home—in disgrace. Andy and Fiona were looking askance at her, with a touch of malicious glee behind their disapproving scowls. They were usually the ones who caused all the rows: coming home after their curfews, going off to visit friends without telling Mum or Dad first. Jean, on the other hand, had always been reliable and punctilious. For *her* to get into trouble was an unheard-of thing.

"You spoiled *everything*," Fiona began as soon as their parents were out of the room. "We had to spend the whole day looking for you, instead of having fun. We found your sieve lying on the barrens, all full of berries, but we couldn't find *you*. Mum was so upset she had to go and lie down, she thought you'd been kidnapped or attacked by a bear or something. And Mary was *crying*."

"I'm sorry," said Jean again. She was consumed with guilt. Jean, the worry-wart, could not bear the thought of someone else's mental anguish.

"Boy, are you in trouble," gloated Rick, grinning all over his round freckled face. "I bet you'll be punished when you get home, all right. I bet—"

"Shut up, Ricky," interrupted Jim.

The deliberate use of his hated childhood nickname had a dampening effect on Rick: he flung a shocked, hurt look at his older brother, then turned away and said no more. "Leave her alone," Jim went on, speaking to all of them. "It isn't as though you were perfect yourselves. How many times have *you* all gotten in trouble, and caused worry for your families? And did Jean ever nag you about it—ever?" Silence. Even Andy and Fiona said nothing. "She's said she's sorry, more than once. How many times does she have to say it before you're satisfied?" Jim got up and headed for the door, pausing briefly to lay a hand on Jean's shoulder. "Don't you mind them, Jeanie," he said. "You're back safe: that's all that matters." With that, he left the room. After a moment all the others slunk out, too.

Jean was left alone, with the comfort of those words, and the feel of Jim's hand still on her shoulder: the memory of its pressure, and its lingering warmth.

Jean did not forget the odd occurrence on the barrens, but it was soon overlaid and obscured by other things, the busy clutter of life. Summer ended and time no longer flowed free, like some wide slow-moving river. With the beginning of the new school year the days were once more regimented and partitioned and filled with activities. They seemed to move more swiftly than before, and soon they were literally shorter.

Jean was now in her second year at Prince of Wales College. It was only a few doors down from her home on the opposite side of LeMarchant Road, and a year's familiarity had given it a comfortable feel. But she felt a little lonely this fall. Last year Andy had still been at PWC, and though he had, of course, spent all his time over on the boys' side of the school, she had often glimpsed him at a distance and had waved to him cheerfully. Now Andy was in his first year at Memorial University College, several streets away. The year before last, Jean had still been at Holloway School with Fiona. She remembered walking down the street to Holloway on crisp autumn days, remembered the sun on her little sister's curly head, the book bag clutched awkwardly in the small hand, the feet in their little black shoes trying to keep up with her, the timid upward glances at the big sister who would be there and explain everything. Fiona had hung back when she first saw the playground, swarming and noisy under the Kirk's massive red-brick tower. Jean recalled the warm, protective love she had felt for her sister then, and she sighed. Fiona now had lots of friends her own age, with whom she went happily to school each morning. She no longer needed Jean to comfort her.

Jean had friends as well: not a great crowd like Fiona's, but there were two girls whom she had known since her Holloway days, Penny Ross and Laura Macrae. They had spent many after-school hours together as children, dropping by one another's homes to talk and play and cut interesting pictures out of magazines to paste in scrapbooks. They had pored, together, over newspaper accounts of the royal family's doings, and their favourite was Princess Elizabeth since she was nearest them in age: sometimes in their games they would pretend to be princesses too. As they grew older, however, Jean became aware of a gap widening between herself and her friends.

Penny was in many ways the same as ever, plain and clever with a tongue that was often sharp, while blonde Laura was as pretty and easy-natured. But there was a change, and it was not only in their budding figures and lengthening limbs. They talked of different things now, and try as she might, Jean could not feel any interest in how much Jenny Fifield's new fur-top gaiters cost or what Penny had bought on her trip to Corner Brook or whether Steve Morrison in Grade Ten was better looking than Gary Butler in Grade Eleven. For Jean there was only one boy, Jim O'Connor, and talk of others bored her. The little giggles and squeals that punctuated the boy-talk grew especially tiresome. Penny and Laura had declared their intention to study Latin and chemistry next year: not because they had any interest in those subjects, but because they were the only courses at PWC that were coeducational.

Perhaps that was why Jean was not paying much attention to her friends' talk that grey September morning as they clattered up the staircase after assembly. It was only when they and the rest of their navy-uniformed classmates were settled behind their desks that Jean realized what Penny and Laura were discussing.

"They're just putting a good face on it, my dad says," Penny remarked. "The newspapers always do, in wartime. But even they had to admit Buckingham Palace was hit, and there was lots of damage."

Jean felt again the sick, reeling sensation that had struck her at the sight of the newspaper headline two weeks ago. The *palace* bombed! It had been on a Friday—the thirteenth, she thought with a little shiver—and she had agonized about it all the following weekend. "But the king and queen weren't hurt," she reminded Penny, forcing a cheerful tone.

"So the papers *say*," replied Penny darkly. "But it must have been a near thing. My dad says we may never know just how close they came to being killed. Would *we* be told?"

Laura's pale blue eyes were very wide. "Imagine if the Nazis had killed our king!"

"It would have been his own fault if they had," sniffed Penny disdainfully. "They were told to leave the palace, he and the queen, but they wouldn't listen. They think they're invulnerable."

"That's not true!" Jean protested. "They just don't want to run away and leave their subjects to suffer through the bombing. They won't even send the princesses out of the country for safety. They won't *let* themselves be safe, when so many other people are in danger every day." Jean saw again in her mind's eye the royal procession on LeMarchant Road, the cheering crowds, the king and his smiling queen. "And they go around visiting places that have been bombed, talking to the survivors and trying to comfort them. I think that's very brave and—and noble of them."

She looked up at the map of the world hanging at the front of the classroom, with all the nations and colonies of the Empire shown in pink. Newfoundland looked terribly small and alone on the map, a little pink island surrounded by blue sea: how vulnerable it was, and also how desirable to the enemy. A safe haven for British cargo ships and military vessels; a base from which Nazi warplanes could launch air attacks on North America. How many U-boats were prowling beneath that blue sea? Was Newfoundland already surrounded? At least no Nazi bombers had come to the Island yet. But they came many a night in her dreams: again and again she had started awake with her heart pounding in her chest, convinced that she had heard the drone of engines high in the sky.

Miss Manley, the history teacher, swept into the room and called for their attention. The buzz of voices obediently ceased. Impulsively Jean put up her hand.

"Yes, Jean?"

She swallowed, lowering her hand again. There was still time to change her question, or to say that she had forgotten what she meant to ask; but she had been burning to ask it for weeks now, and she suddenly found herself blurting: "Miss Manley, was there anyone in Newfoundland long ago? Very long ago, I mean—in the Middle Ages?"

A disconcerting hush had fallen: everyone was staring at her, including the teacher. "In the Middle Ages?" Miss Manley repeated. "Well, there were the native people, of course—Indians and Eskimos and so on."

Jean persisted. "No one else? No one at all?"

"There weren't any Europeans, if that's what you mean. John Cabot didn't arrive until 1497, and there were no permanent settlers until a long time after that."

Jean saw, again, the terrifying fire-lit figure with its bristling beard and armour of steel. "What about—Vikings?"

"Vikings?" Miss Manley seemed taken aback by the question. She glanced around at the map. "I couldn't say . . . There *are* some old Norse sagas that tell of Vikings voyaging to countries beyond the western sea. Leif Eriksson, the son of Erik the Red, was supposed to have set up a home base—*Leifsbudir*—in some unknown western land. And others were said to have made the same journey after him. But if it was Newfoundland they sailed to we've yet to find any trace of their presence here."

Jean had not expected this. "Still—they *could* have come here," she said slowly.

"Well, yes, in theory. The Vikings were master mariners, they'd already colonized Iceland and Greenland. And Greenland isn't so very far away from here."

"Are there any Norse people left in Greenland now?" another student asked.

"No, no, they all vanished centuries ago. We don't know what became of them. They may have died out from some disease, or interbred with the natives." Miss Manley picked up the pointer and ran its tip across the map. "Old-time Greenlanders could have made landfall here at Baffin Island, or lower down in Labrador, and then sailed south to the northern tip of Newfoundland. And the sagas do mention natives, who might have been our Indians. But there's so much in these old tales that can't possibly be true. The land the Norse wrote about was called Vineland, or Vinland, because it was supposed to have grapevines growing in it: but of course grapes only grow in warm climates. And there's some nonsense about a prophetess, and ghosts, and a tribe of one-legged men. The whole thing may just be pure fantasy. Jean, this is all very interesting but it's got nothing to do with today's lesson. If you want to know more I can recommend some books for you to read."

"Yes, Miss Manley," said Jean meekly. Inwardly, she felt a great rush of relief. It couldn't possibly have been real, then.

What had happened to her on the barrens had been only a dream, not a true vision of, or journey into, the past. She could see Laura and Penny giving her odd looks and knew they would interrogate her later, but she didn't mind. *None of it was real.*

"Now will you all open your textbooks to page fifteen," Miss Manley began. But she got no farther than that.

From outside the window there came a noise, high, keening, piercing: a noise they all knew well. A murmur of consternation went up from the girls, and even Miss Manley turned slightly pale. She snapped her book shut. "The air-raid sirens," she said unnecessarily. "You all know what to do. Stand up." The girls sprang to their feet and stood beside their desks. "Now walk out of the door, single file, and go straight down the stairs and out of the building. And no running!"

Jean's heart skipped a beat. "But it's not Thursday," she exclaimed, staring up at the classroom clock. Half-past nine. *It's not a drill, it's not the right day, the right time—*

"Single *file*!" shouted Miss Manley as some of the girls jostled one another in the doorway. They slowed down, streaming down the staircase to join the navy blue torrent of students headed for the girls' entrance. Once they were outside they could see the boys pouring out of their own door in a mass of navy and grey flannel. The girls crowded together, some whispering, others tittering nervously or casting anxious glances up at the overcast sky. They could still hear the wavering wails of the sirens coming from every quarter of the city, and Jean knew every ear in the place was straining, like hers, for another sound: the thunderous rumble of the bombers, flying high and invisible above the clouds . . .

"Is it—real, do you think?" asked Laura in a low voice.

"It's Woden's day," said Jean, shivering. A chill ran through her. "Something terrible is going to happen, I know it!"

Laura and Penny stared. "*What* did you say?" Laura asked.

"I said it's Wednesday. So it can't be a drill, something must be wrong—"

"You didn't say Wednesday, you said something else."

"Woden's day." Penny's sharp ears never missed a thing. "That's what you said. Woden's day."

For some reason Jean felt a little jab of fear. "I did not!" she protested.

"Jean, what is the matter with you?"

Jean was wondering the same thing. *Why did I snap at her? And did I really say that?* Her head was spinning; she took a staggering step to one side as her vision clouded over and was replaced by a seething grey void. Through it she could still hear the sirens, but they sounded different to her: almost like the voices of dozens of women, raised in an ululating lament . . .

"She's fainting!" somebody—was it Laura?—cried, far away in the greyness. Jean felt an arm slip under her own, supporting her suddenly sagging weight. Her knees buckled: she could feel herself gently sliding downward.

There were more voices. "Stand back, girls! Don't all cluster around. Give her some air!"

There was a brief silence, then the all-clear sounded in the distance. Jean realized she was crouching on the pavement with her head on her knees while Miss Hanson, the

English teacher, knelt beside her. The other students were walking back into the girls' and boys' entrances, some throwing curious stares in her direction.

"Oh—what happened?" Jean gasped, looking up. "Did I faint?"

"Not completely, I think." Miss Manley was standing over her. "You were very close to it, though. Are you feeling better now?"

Jean struggled to her feet with Miss Hanson's help. "I feel a little bit dizzy, but I can see again. I've never done that before."

"Are you sure you're all right?" the English teacher asked, still holding on to Jean's arm.

"You say this has never happened before?" Miss Manley pursued. "Didn't something rather odd happen to you this summer, Jean? I seem to recall hearing your friends talk about it. It was when you were visiting an outport with your family, they said. A bout of amnesia, wasn't it, or something like that?"

Jean looked away. "It was nothing," she mumbled.

"I think perhaps you should go home and rest," suggested Miss Manley. "You live right on this street, don't you? We could send someone with you, if you're afraid of fainting on the way—"

"No, I feel better," said Jean. It was not entirely true, but she was beginning to feel embarrassed and a bit unnerved by the history teacher's penetrating gaze. And if she went home it would only worry her mother needlessly. "Really I do. I just want to go back to class now."

There was a little pause. The two teachers looked at one

another. "All right then," Miss Manley said at last. "Off you go." Relieved, Jean headed for the girls' door. But she could almost feel their eyes on her as she walked away from them.

The sirens wailed again that night in her dreams.

It seemed to Jean that she heard the eerie keening as she lay in her bed—and then, more terrible still, the other sound she had feared to hear that morning: the reverberating drone of the enemy's planes high in the sky. As always in her nightmares, she dreamed that she sat up in bed, with her heart hammering in her chest; then she leaped up, and stumbled over to the window to stare out into the night. She saw the dark winged shapes shadowed against the sky and cried out, but no one came to her: everyone else in the house seemed locked in slumber. She could only watch in horror as the planes dived—by the moon's light she could clearly see the white-edged swastikas painted on their tails—and then with a shrill whistling sound the bombs fell, and the oil tanks on the Southside hills erupted into rolling billows of flame. She tried to scream but could not, her mouth rounded in a soundless No. Down the steep slopes poured the yellow flood of fire, engulfing all in its path; reaching the harbour, it did not stop but spread like burning lava over the surface of the water. It moved with amazing speed: in mere moments she saw the high tongues of flame and roiling smoke-clouds that told her the wharfs were alight.

"Dad!" she shrieked. "Mum, Andy—"

She fled her room and ran through the house, only to find each bedroom empty. They had all gone, they had run away and left her . . . The sky was red with fire-glow: all the downtown core must be in flames now. Staring out Andy's bedroom window, she saw a great shower of blazing embers spread like a net to drop over the houses of LeMarchant Road. As she flung up the sash Jean felt the furnace-blast on her face, heard the crackling roar of the approaching conflagration.

Terrified, she tore downstairs and out of the house. If it caught fire she would be trapped inside. She ran out onto the street, feeling its pavement ice-cold under her bare feet, looking wildly up and down its length for another human figure. There was no one to be seen. Houses were burning wherever she looked, red-lit smoke belching from their eaves: doors and windows were caverns of fire. Flying sparks and cinders spun around her. In a moment she too would be burned. Panic-stricken, she fled down the street, screaming for her family.

Above her the winged shadows swept back over the city, flying low over the flaming roofs: in the fierce glow she saw them distinctly. But now they had changed. They were women, ghastly winged women in black tattered garments, white-faced, white-haired; they shrieked in triumph as they flew like carrion fowls above the city, fanning the flames with their wings. And with them was a shrouded form on a grey gaunt steed, a wraith spun out of smoke and cloud. And she heard a noise like the howl of hounds, up there in the sky; and she cowered back as the aerial hunters circled, again and again, coming lower, closer . . .

Then she woke, to darkness and silence, with the sound of her own voice echoing in her ears.

It's Woden's day. Something terrible is going to happen.

Chapter Five

"I THINK IT'S AN ANTIMACASSAR," said Mrs. MacDougall. But she sounded a bit uncertain.

"A what?" asked Andy.

It was Christmas day. The MacDougalls were sitting together around the tree in a rustling mass of brightly coloured gift wrap, along with Grandma and Grandpa MacDougall, who had come over from their home in Mount Pearl. It was Mum's turn to pick a present, and she had chosen the one sent by Grannie-from-Ireland, the only one of her Ferryland relatives with whom she remained close. Grannie-from-Ireland was really a great-grandmother, Mum's grandmother who came over from the old country long ago, and every year she sent Mum a gift of handmade lace or crochet. Some of these gifts were quite beautiful, some unexpectedly entertaining—like the stiff round cushion that Andy had discovered could be thrown like a discus—and some merely puzzling, like the object Mum was holding up now. It was about a foot and a half long, made of ivory-white crochet, and had an odd hour-glass shape.

"It's a covering to go over the head of a chair," Mum explained.

"No, I think that's meant to go on a side-table, Patricia," declared Grandma, leaning forward to look at it through her lorgnette.

"I know! I know what it is!" Grandpa took the object from Mum, and with a grin he spread it sideways across his chest.

"Frederick! That's not funny," reproved Grandma as Fiona rolled howling on the floor.

"But I always *wanted* one of these!" piped Grandpa in a falsetto voice, and Grandma's next reprimand was lost in laughter.

Jean tried hard to smile too. That morning she had kept her own personal Christmas tradition of rising early to watch dawn break: she had sat in her chair gazing out on roofs covered in snow, thick as the icing on the Christmas cakes, and at the Southside hills all blanketed in white, and the grey harbour below clotted with slob ice. She had heard Fiona's small bare feet go padding downstairs at about six a.m.—Fiona was the only one who still had a Christmas stocking—and then come up again, followed by little soft rustlings from her bedroom as she removed her treasures from their casing of lisle. Oranges, sweets, small toys: how well Jean remembered them tumbling out of the stocking, and the sharp tang of the oranges as the peel came off. She had felt a sudden fierce love for her little sister as she listened to the sounds—for all the children in all the houses outside. At least the holiday could still be happy for them.

But would it ever really be the same? More memories filled Jean's head: of going out in the evenings to neighbours' Christmas parties, of the front windows of all the houses along LeMarchant Road filled with happy holiday scenes—glowing and glittering trees, smiling faces, cozy vignettes of other people's celebrations. Tonight the black-out curtains would be drawn, the festive lights and the merrymakers inside all hidden from view. Try as she might, Jean could not find the joy that this season had once brought her.

Of her family, only Andy seemed to share her mood, and she could not talk to him about it: she no longer felt as close to her brother as she once had. Andy's increasing restlessness and dissatisfaction seemed to be pulling him apart from her and everyone else, out of the circle of the family, drawing him away—where? Sometimes she felt that Andy himself did not know.

Grandma raised an imperious hand. "Hush, everyone: here's the king's message coming on. Fred, stop your fooling and let's listen." Grandpa, who was dancing a little jig with the piece of crochet draped over his head like a bonnet, obediently subsided, and they all listened as King George's voice came over the radio.

"In days of peace the feast of Christmas is a time when we all gather in our homes, young and old, to enjoy the happy festivity and goodwill which Christmas messages bring . . ." The familiar voice sounded thin and far away, but there was still a note of determination in it. ". . . War brings among other things the sadness of separation. There are many men in the forces away from their homes today because they must stand ready and alert to resist the invader should he dare to come . . ."

Jean stared at the grill on the front of the big floor-model radio, with its Gothic arches like a church window, and listened along with the others. *It doesn't seem real, everything here is so normal,* she thought. There was the tree, as always, glimmering in the corner of the living room with its tinsel and candy-coloured lights and the pink angel on top. The air of the house was already warm and savoury with the smell of roasting turkey; at midday they would eat Christmas dinner together as always, followed by Mum's wonderful Christmas cake, dark and dense and jewelled with fruit under its almond icing. Every detail of the holiday was exactly as it had always been, down to the holly on the mantelpiece and the evergreen wreath on the front door with its big red bow. Between now and New Year's Eve they would visit with friends and neighbours, and have their traditional holiday trip to see the O'Connors in Mary's Bay. And her parents had given her a new party dress of holly green velvet, and a silver locket to go with it: she had already decided to cut out the little faint image of Jim from her hidden photograph, and put it in the locket opposite her own. Some day she would find a better photograph of him to place there.

She *should* be happy, she told herself, looking forward to days of parties and visits and fun. But she only felt worried and miserable, and the king's brave, pathetic broadcast did not help. Looking at the tree, she could only think how each shining strand would have to be taken off for recycling: in wartime no metal must be wasted, not even a bit of decorative tinsel.

"To be good comrades and good neighbours in trouble is one of the finest opportunities of the civilian population. By facing hardship and discomfort cheerfully and resolutely they not only do their own duty but they play their part in helping the fighting services to win the war. . . ."

What hardship and discomfort were the MacDougalls enduring? The English had suffered bombing raid after bombing raid: it was a wonder, some people said, that there was anything left of London. And in last night's paper a whole page had been dedicated to the mothers of young Newfoundland servicemen killed overseas. *To You Who Have Lost*, it said in big black letters. How many of those snow-clad roofs outside hid a tragedy? In how many was a father, a brother, a son missing?

". . . We do not underrate the dangers and difficulties which still confront us. But we take courage and comfort from the successes of our fighting men and their allies who have won at heavy odds by land, on the sea and in the air. The future will be hard. But our feet are planted on the path of victory, and with the help of God we shall make our way to justice and to peace. . . ."

But does he really believe that? she wondered as the broadcast concluded. *Or is he just trying to boost morale?*

The next day they went to Mary's Bay.

Here at least there were no troubling signs of war: Christmas in the outport was like Christmas a hundred years ago. As the early winter dusk settled there came a jingling of bells across the snowy fields, from the little pony-drawn sleighs that the outport people used. The O'Connors' Christmas tree was not decked out in coloured electric lights like the MacDougalls', but decorated with real candles attached to the boughs by special holders. It stood in the parlour, glittering and magnificent, its living flames casting their flickering glow upon the walls.

The two families were standing around it together, laughing and talking, when there came a heavy knock at the front door—so heavy that it must have been made with a stick or cane rather than a hand. At the sound Jean's heart leaped, and the younger children began to chatter excitedly. Mrs. O'Connor went to answer the door, and they all heard the shuffling of many feet, felt the ice-cold draft and heard a curious high-pitched voice say: "Is janneys allowed in, Ma'am?"

"Yes!" cried a chorus of young O'Connor voices before their mother could get a word out, and they all ran into the passage.

Mr. O'Connor went to join his wife at the door. "Right, in you comes then—straight on into the kitchen, now."

The janneys, or mummers, came around every year, but not always when the MacDougalls happened to be visiting: Jean had not seen them since she was ten years old. This was a rare treat. Anytime between Christmas and Twelfth Night they might come, whenever the fancy took them. She watched in delight as they trooped into the front hall, a big group of strange, faceless, scarecrow figures, in costumes cobbled together out of odds and ends from their attics. All were masked: some wore old pillowcases or flour sacks over their heads, with holes cut for their eyes and mouths; some had more elaborate masks of painted cardboard. Some wore wool caps or ladies' broad-brimmed hats; one had a pair of caribou antlers strapped to the top of his head. A tall thin figure with a flour-sack mask was attired in a wedding dress, complete with flowing white veil. But beneath its lace hem clumped a pair of great black fisherman's boots.

They came in singing, all in peculiar piping or croaking voices to further conceal their identity. One carried an accordion, another a fiddle, and as they stood there they began to sing *Jingle Bells*. It was a weird noise. The younger O'Connors and Fiona promptly joined in. When it was over they began *Squid-Jigging Ground*; and when that had concluded Mary cried: "Let's have a dance, like last year! Please, Mummy?"

Chairs and tables were pushed back against the walls. "Mind the stove now," cautioned Mrs. O'Connor. The masked man—or could it be a woman?—with the accordion began to play again.

And the mummers danced. With a pounding of booted feet on the floorboards, and a swishing of skirts and scarves and hanging bed sheets, the swathed figures spun around the room. Mary and Colleen joined in, then Rick and Fiona; finally the older ones let themselves be swept up into the dance.

"I know you, I know you!" Mrs. O'Connor panted, laughing. She pointed to a heavily padded figure with a man's felt hat and a pipe protruding from its masked mouth. "It's Sally Maloney—isn't it? That's your Jerry's old hat!"

Masks began to come off, one by one, as identities were guessed: flushed and smiling faces emerged. Jean found herself laughing out loud, for the first time in many days. The wild, exuberant dancing had helped; also Jim had told her that she "looked like Christmas" in the holly green dress.

"Great fun, isn't it?" Mr. O'Connor laughed to Mr. Mac-Dougall. "Takes me back to my boyhood, mummering. My mum said it was just the same in her day, only they called it 'going out in the fools.' They always invited the fools in for a drink and a bite—but they didn't sing and dance like this. They used to put on a play: some silly nonsense about Father Christmas, and Saint George fighting with a knight."

"Goes back a long way, I imagine," said Jean's father. He had held aloof from the mad dance, looking on indulgently.

"As long as anyone here remembers. Goes back to the Middle Ages, I allow: it came over from the old country."

Jean's mother was sitting in the corner with Mrs. O'Connor and Lizzie and plump, red-cheeked Mrs. Maloney. "Sure I feel like I'm home again," Mum was saying with a smile. "Haven't danced with the janneys in years, we don't get them in town."

Jim and Andy were standing apart from the rest. Presently Jim asked, raising his voice above the hubbub: "Is the Horse out tonight?"

Heads nodded. "We seen 'im. Chased us all along the Bayshore Road."

Jean felt a curious sensation at the mention of the Horse, a shivering thrill that was not quite fear. She'd seen him too, on that evening five years ago: he'd come and looked in at the kitchen window, and Fiona, who was only a little girl then, had screamed and run from the room. The Hobby Horse was a part of the mumming festivities, and yet also independent from them. The man who dressed up as the Horse might join with the mummers, even dance alongside them; but more often he roved about the streets on his own and pretended to attack people, mummers included. Sometimes he did not pretend, but attacked in earnest, even charging at women and children. People had been hurt by the Horse.

"Where did he go after that? Did you see?" Heads shook.

"We'll go find him then," said Andy.

The mummers were still talking and sipping their wine, masked or unmasked. The two boys threw on coats and scarves and headed for the door. Jean, watching them, felt a sudden, inexplicable dread: a kind of horror at the thought of the two of them leaving the light and warmth, being swallowed up by the cold darkness outside. Her own joy fled; the hot air of the kitchen seemed to stifle her. As the boys headed out the door she too edged towards it, looking for her navy coat and her beret. Even as she put them on, she wondered at herself. *What am I doing?* she thought as she eased the door open. Her place was with the others, with the other women and the children, in the safety and light and warmth of the house. If Jim and Andy chose to go out into the night and face the Horse, that was their right. Young men did these wild and daring things. They could look after themselves . . . But again she felt that twinge of sourceless fear, and beneath it something else: something almost like the first faint stirring of rebellion.

When she stepped out the door her first breath of wintry air seemed to cut like a knife through the stuffy air in her lungs. There were ice crystals in it, and the salt tang of the sea, and as she rounded the corner of the house she felt the wind's strength. Andy and Jim were striding down Bayshore Road with their hands in their pockets, talking and laughing together, strong and confident. She followed them at a distance, not wanting to tag along and annoy them, but still somehow unwilling to let them out of her sight. The sky was heavily overcast and it was very dark, darker than night ever was in the city. She could not see anything of the houses farther down the street but their lighted windows, and the sea was only a roar in the blackness beyond.

Some other mummers were making the rounds: as she walked along the road she saw them moving in groups between the houses. Jim and Andy walked up to a small clump of them, and the wind blew their words towards her. "Where's he gone now? Can anyone tell us where the Horse is to?" Jim was asking.

The mummers all spoke at once, and she could not distinguish their intertwining answers, but she distinctly saw some of them wave their arms and point back down the street.

The two boys turned, moving towards her: in a moment they would see her, and Jean, seized with a sudden shyness, ran up a little side path that led between two houses. Behind lay a dark wall of evergreen trees, the margin of the forest: she could hear voices coming from its depths, and a faint chiming of far-off sleigh bells. She stood there, feeling a little foolish, as her brother and Jim walked back along the road. They might be irritated, thinking she was trying to join them uninvited, or—even worse—Jim might guess she had a crush on him and be embarrassed, which would embarrass her even more. If she told them she was worried about their safety, they would laugh her to scorn. She would wait until they had moved out of sight behind the row of houses before she started back towards the road.

But as soon as they passed from her sight and she began to move, the shouts from the forest grew louder, and nearer. There was a rustling and the soft sound of footfalls half-muffled in snow, and when she whirled around in alarm the Hobby Horse was there.

He was standing under the trees, half-hidden in shadow so that it took her a moment to make him out: a figure from a dark dream, nine feet tall and swaying from side to side like the windblown trees. He had no body: the figure of the man who carried him was swathed and shrouded in a bed sheet and she could see nothing of him, not even his boots. Above the pale cocoon of cloth jutted the pole that was the Horse's neck, and on it perched his head. It was not like a horse's head, not like any animal to which one could put a name. It was huge, made from a log split in half to form a pair of great snapping jaws lined with nails for teeth. The eyes were circles of glittering glass, the bottoms of bottles; the head was covered in the thick black pelt of a bear. She froze where she stood, too fascinated to run. The Hobby Horse was more than a costume: it had about it an aura of ancientness. The man inside it was no longer a man. He was a part of the Horse now, part of the winter night's wildness, and there was no knowing what he might do.

There were more loud, excited shouts from the darkness under the trees, and a group of young men came bursting out of it and rushed at the Horse, taunting and teasing him. "Lop Chops! Here, old Lop Chops!" one called. "I'm over here!" Some threw snowballs. But none of them dared go too near, and as the big black head bobbed towards them they yelled and scattered like children.

In a moment Andy and Jim would hear the noise and come to join them.

At that thought Jean started to run—not away from the Hobby Horse, but towards him. She plunged right into the whirling circle of bodies, directly in front of him. The head swung at her, eyes flashing like frost in the scant light, and as she ducked she heard the *snock* of the jaws as they snapped shut, nail-teeth clashing on air. Jean sprang back a step, but she did not flee. She was afraid, but it was a better kind of fear than the lurking, gnawing anxiety that had held her captive all these months: it brought her a sense of release. As the Horse turned towards the road—towards Andy and Jim—she rushed in again, making him lunge after her. Around and around she went in the dangerous dance, darting in and out again, running and dodging.

And then Andy and Jim were there, shouting, grabbing her arms and pulling her back, away from the whooping and howling men as they and the Hobby Horse charged back into the trees and disappeared.

"What were you doing?" cried Andy in amazement. She could not find her voice, and he looked exasperated. "I don't know what's come over you lately, Jean. You've been acting so strange."

Her beret had fallen off; Jim retrieved it for her, brushing the snow from it as he handed it to her. He said nothing, but she sensed his puzzlement, saw him looking at her as he might look at a total stranger. It disturbed her, and she dropped her own eyes as she put the hat on again.

Andy was still scolding as they walked back towards the

road. "Maybe you really *were* switched by the fairies, back there on the barrens."

The door to a cottage on the opposite side of the road had opened, spilling yellow light out onto the snow: the figure of a woman stood there, watching them, her wiry grey hair waving stiffly in the breeze. Mrs. Doyle. She chuckled as the three young people walked past. "Oh, it's Jeanie Mac-Dougall. I should have known. She *isn't* the same," she said to Andy, "they never does come back the same once they've been to that place. Makes changes, it does. Some comes back simple, or scarred—"

"Ignore her," said Jim, taking Jean's arm.

"Peggy O'Brien now," rambled Mrs. Doyle, following them along the other side of her little picket fence. "She were the loveliest girl in the outport, back in my mother's day: had lots of boys pinin' for her. But she *would* go berry picking alone on the barrens. 'I don't believe in no fairies!' she'd say, tossin' her pretty head. Well, the day came when she went missing—almost a week she were gone—and when they found her they couldn't hardly recognize her. All withered and wizened she was, like an old old woman, and her wits so addled she couldn't say where she'd been or even who she was."

"How'd they know it was Peggy then?" Andy shot back over his shoulder.

"Oh, she'd a birthmark on her cheek, like a little red heart; her beauty spot, she always called it. And of course her clothes was the same ones she wore when she vanished. She died not long after, poor thing. The Good People punished her, you see, for her unbelief. But even when they doesn't change your outside, they makes changes inside of you. No, you never comes back the same." She had come to the end of the fence now, and was calling after them as they walked away.

"Never mind old Maggie Doyle," Jim said. "She's touched in the head. Remember how we used to call her Mad Maggie behind her back?"

"What's wrong with her, Jim?" Jean asked in a low voice.

"I don't know. People say she lost her husband back in the Great War, and she never recovered from it. She used to say she'd had a vision of him standing by her bed, the same night that he died. But that's probably just more of her craziness."

"After tonight everyone will think it's Jean that's crazy," grumbled Andy. "Maggie Doyle will tell everyone in the outport about it, you bet. What made you act like that?" he demanded of his sister again.

"I don't know," Jeanie answered slowly. "I just saw the men and the Hobby Horse dancing around, and I wanted to join in. It looked like—fun." Even as she said this, she knew it was not the whole truth. But how to explain to him something she couldn't quite understand herself?

"Fun!" snorted her brother. "You could have been hurt, do you know that? The Horse is dangerous."

"*You* went out looking for him!" returned Jean, with such force that both boys looked taken aback. "Was it all right for *you* to get hurt then?" Her words fell into a little silence.

"Never mind," said Jim, before Andy could find his tongue, "it's over, and there's no harm done. Let's all go back."

Later that night, Jean sat with her family by the fireplace in her own home, staring into the fire's red heart, seeing before her eyes the towering, swaying form of the Hobby Horse. *What* has *come over me?* she wondered as she watched the charred logs crumble. *I never used to be like this—I'm a stranger even to myself. Everything I did made sense, once. People always knew what to expect of me. Perhaps it's all this worry over the war: it just has to come out somehow. . . .*

Fiona, who was sitting on the hearth, gave a wide yawn and was promptly sent to bed, protesting all the way up the staircase that she wasn't sleepy; Mum followed her, and the sound of their voices went up to the second floor and faded. Normally Jean would have gone up with them, but not tonight: she was not tired, and the odd, contrary mood was still on her. She remained in her chair as Dad and Andy talked quietly, then they too left. "Turn the lights out when you go, Jean," Dad said, pausing in the door, "and the tree."

"Yes, Dad."

She sat alone for a few minutes, then rose and turned off each of the lamps. Now the only light came from the fire's dying embers and from the tree: the latter seemed to come into its own with all the other electric lights extinguished. It glowed softly, seemed to float in the darkened room: its tiers of tinsel changed their glitter for a subtler gleam, the glass birds on the boughs looked more real, poised as if for flight. She noticed how the light bulbs created little patches of colour, tinting the needles red or blue or golden, and how they were reflected, like tiny bright-coloured stars, in the shining glass balls. Above them the smiling pink-robed angel on the top of the tree spread her feathery wings. She was a little worn and tattered from her long years of service, but the children could not bear to replace her: she went back to their earliest Christmas memories. Jean felt comforted by the little winged figure. Gazing up at it, she suddenly recalled another angel, with armour of gold and bright-bladed sword, and wings outspread for battle.

A voice spoke in her memory. *When Satan and his followers rebelled, Michael's angels made war upon them* . . . Oh, for an army of shining angels to come and drive *this* enemy away, to free sky and sea and let the lights shine at night again!

She went and sat by the tree, breathing in its heavy balsam scent, sheltering under its branches. Closing her eyes for a moment, she almost imagined that she could feel something flowing from it into her. *Life*, she thought: not the finite life of the tree itself, but some greater, deeper power of which it was the symbol—of which every living thing was a branch, and that power the root and stem. Far away in the night she could hear voices and laughter, and the sound of many feet trampling the snow. A group of Christmas revellers, it must be, returning home late from a party. They would be heading for their warm beds; and so should she.

With a sigh she rose and switched off the tree lights, plunging the room into near-darkness: the fire was almost out. The tree was only a shape of shadow now, the darkened electric bulbs clustered on its boughs like strange, exotic fruit. The house was utterly still. She might almost have been alone in it. She could still hear the laughing voices outside, and snatches of song. A sudden craving for other human company filled her. If only she could join those people, whoever they might be: join in their jokes and their comradeship, instead of going upstairs to lie in her bed, staring up at the dark and yearning for sleep to claim her. As she passed by the bay window she peered out through a gap in the blackout curtains, looking for the revellers. If she could at least look at them, it would almost be like sharing in their gaiety, their guiltless enjoyment of the holiday season.

Through the narrow space she glimpsed some people straggling by. To her surprise they were all dressed in outlandish costumes: masks of painted cloth, and long cloaks with hoods and fur trim. One carried a torch—not an electric one but an actual torch, its flames flowing back in the wind like long yellow streamers. Mummers! They were the first she had ever seen in the city. They had a Hobby Horse with them, too, but theirs was different from the one in Mary's Bay. Its head was not made of wood, but of the skin of a real horse's head, stuffed and mounted on a pole. The head had glass eyes to replace the real ones, but its teeth were actual horse's teeth, their yellowed bone flashing in the torch light as the man holding the pole pulled on a rope, making the dead jaws open and shut.

Jean pulled the gap wider to get a better look, then gave a little gasp.

LeMarchant Road was gone. Where its rows of houses should have been there was nothing: a vacant field covered in deep snow, stretching for as far as she could see. Jean recoiled, letting go of the heavy black curtain.

Impossible. She must be imagining it. With a racing heart she went to the window again and lifted the curtain. The mummers were no longer there, but she saw their trampled tracks in the snow. And still there was nothing where the houses should be. They were all gone.

She ran to the kitchen and peered out the window over the sink, lifting its curtain with trepidation. There were the Southside hills, whitened with snow. But even as a relieved sigh was forming in her throat, Jean realized there was something strange in the once familiar scene. She could see no houses on the Brow: not the remotest trace of a roof or wall. There, far below, was the ice-filled harbour—and the Narrows beyond—and as she craned her neck she saw the rounded mass of Signal Hill, looming against the dark blue sky. But there was no Cabot Tower on the hill's summit. Instead she saw many towers, tall and topped by battlements, and joined together halfway down by high walls of stone. A castle.

She ran back to the front of the house. At the door she hesitated, then opened it just a crack. Of course there would be nothing there: only the quiet darkened street, the neighbours' familiar houses across the road. But the door opened onto the same scene of snowy fields. The mummers were walking a few yards away, wading through the thick snow, and in the distance she saw some small buildings, too humble to be called cottages. But no houses anywhere. Jean swallowed: she was trembling, though not with fear. She drew back, but left the door open, afraid that if she closed it the otherworldly scene would vanish. Going quietly to the coat cupboard, she took out her winter coat and a pair of sturdy boots. Her hands shook as she put them on. *Stay there, don't go away; I'm coming—please, please don't go away.*

She went back to the door, and all was as she had seen it a moment ago: the white fields, the parading mummers, the snow-roofed huts. She looked eastward, and again she saw the castle on the hill: a fairy-tale keep, cast in evening shades of blue and silver. "*Camelot*," she whispered. Jean stood on the threshold, half-exhilarated and half-afraid, like a swimmer poised to plunge into the swell of a heaving sea.

Then she stepped out into the snow, and left her world behind.

Chapter Six

THE SNOW WAS DEEPER HERE: it must have been falling for much longer in this place. As she struggled through it, the thick white drifts sometimes reached almost to her knees. There was a road—it showed through here and there, where the snow had been trampled thin by the mummers—but it was earthen, not paved. Once or twice she stumbled in a frozen wheel-rut.

She was not surprised, on looking back, to see that her house had gone. It did not belong here; and somehow she knew that it and its sleeping occupants had not vanished, but were still safe in their own place, on LeMarchant Road. The thought comforted her, and she turned her gaze forward again, focusing on the castle and the mummers who were now walking about twenty yards ahead of her. Either they had not seen her, or they did not consider her to be of any importance: they strode on through the drifts in the patch of light cast by their fluttering torch, their voices carrying back to her in the still, clear air. She could hear snatches of song, and loud bursts of laughter. The Hobby Horse's clacking jaws made a sort of accompaniment to their mirth, like the click of castanets.

As she walked, the little snow-roofed huts gave way to larger clumps and clusters of cottage-sized dwellings, and some bigger structures which she took to be stables and granaries. Passing a gate in a high stone wall, she glimpsed a small orchard, its trees laden with snow thick and white as the blossoms they must bear in spring. Under the moon everything was as bright as day. Then, farther down towards the harbour, there were rows and rows of stone houses, enclosed within a wall: a city, much smaller than St. John's but built upon the same sheltering slope. The mummers turned aside from its torch-lit gate, though, and headed on across the snow-covered barrens, on up the hill to the castle.

It really did look a great deal like the pictures of Camelot in her King Arthur books. Only when she was halfway up the slope did she think to ask herself whether its occupants were friendly. This was not her own familiar world, and she knew very little about it and its potential dangers. But she had no doubt that it was the same place where she had encountered Lailoken and the princess—*and they were friendly and kind*, she thought. Besides, the mummers were heading for its gate as though happily confident of a welcome.

As she climbed the steep path she saw, a little distance away on the hillside, a pattern of raised wrinkles and folds too regular to be natural: earthworks of some kind, they must be. In the midst of them was a low tumulus from which rose a grey upright shape, topped by a cap of snow. It was the very same standing stone from her vision, although the view of it was different. Human hands must have set it atop the mound long ago, but it looked to Jean as though it had always stood here: as if erosion had merely exposed it, like the great rugged rocks of the hillside. Somehow she knew it was much older than the castle.

She struggled on through the thick snow, and about twenty minutes later arrived at the chill summit, and the castle's entrance.

The mighty gates were open, the portcullis drawn up: light flooded out onto the trodden snow beneath, shadowing the many dints and hollows made by hooves and booted feet. Lamplight glowed in the tower windows high above, and smoke from dozens of chimneys mounted the cold clear air, leaning landwards in the wind off the sea. The great stone blocks of the walls were rimed at the seams, glittering as if they had been mortared with crushed diamonds.

Through the gates the mummers went, into the outer ward and towards the massive inner keep, while Jean crept along in their wake. At the entrance to the keep armed guards stood, with tall halberds in their hands. After a moment's discussion they admitted the mummers, but at the approach of Jean they lowered their halberds.

"You—girl. Why do you follow the players?" one barked.

"I don't know—that is—" Jean swallowed. "Whose castle is this, please?"

Their eyes went narrow with suspicion under their steel helmets. "Who are you, that you do not know the *dún* of King Ciaran?" one demanded.

"I'm not from here. My—my name's Jean MacDougall."

Now the eyes under the helmets went wide. "The Shadow-child? Can it be?" said one to the other, almost whispering the words. "She wears the fairy colour—look!" He aimed the point of his halberd at Jean. She glanced down, saw a fold of holly green velvet protruding from the front of her navy coat.

"I'm not a fairy, really I'm not!" she cried.

"We must take her to Princess Gwenlian," the other guard said, after a pause. "She will know if it is the same maiden she met with in the wood."

"Princess Gwenlian? She's here?" Jean felt a sudden lift of the heart. "She escaped, then—the Vikings didn't hurt her?"

"Come," the guard ordered, and leaving the other man at the door he led her inside, through long stone corridors lit yellow by wall torches and hazed with their smoke. Great rooms and chambers opened to either side. One was a banquet hall, its rows of long wooden tables still holding tankards and crusts and other remains of a feast, while a fire burned low in a huge fireplace like a red-lit cave.

Jean and her guide came at last to a great hall from which the sound of laughter and music swelled. Here were roaring fireplaces, and bright banners hanging from the rafters and wreaths and boughs of evergreen on the walls, and men and women in bright jewel-coloured clothes dancing across the floor in long rows. On a carved wooden throne below a vast tapestry of a stag hunt sat Princess Gwenlian, in an ermine-trimmed gown as red as a rose. To her left sat a middle-aged woman and a grey-bearded man in thrones much like hers, but with taller and more ornamented backs; in a matching throne to her right sat a young man of about nineteen or twenty. All four wore crowns—not tall, top-heavy crowns like those of King George and Queen Elizabeth, but simple medieval-style circlets that seemed to sit lightly on their heads.

Jean started eagerly forward, forgetting the armed guard in her excitement. Then a hand came down on her shoulder and spun her around. She found herself looking up into a lined, smiling, grey-eyed face surrounded by snow-white hair and beard.

"Welcome, welcome!" said Lailoken. He was wearing a plum-coloured robe, also trimmed with white, and looked like Father Christmas—not jolly red-suited Santa, but more like the older and more dignified figures from Victorian Christmas cards. "You have returned to Annwn!"

"Annwn?" she repeated.

"The name of this world. You stand in the great *dún* of Temair, in the Isle of Avalon."

She looked at the dancing couples, the evergreen wreaths that were mounted on the stone walls. "This really *is* a different world, isn't it—not just another time? It's Christmas for you, too."

"It is. And in a few days' time we celebrate the new year, Anno Domini nineteen hundred and forty-one."

"So do we." She looked back at him and was glad: glad that he and the rose-gowned princess and everyone in the hall was alive in this moment as she was, and not mere phantoms of some bygone era. "So—there are *two* worlds, right alongside one another?"

"There are three," the Druid told her as he led her up the hall, moving alongside the dancers. "See the shadows there on the wall, of the people dancing to and fro. For a shadow to exist, one must have two things: an object to cast it, and a light to shine upon the object. Think of your world as a shadow of ours, like it and unlike—as those shadows on the wall are like but not like the people who cast them. Above both worlds, on a higher plane, is a realm of divine Light. That higher world burns with the power and beauty of its divinity; this lower world of Annwn shines in its reflected glory; and the third, the Shadow-world, is like a dim copy of Annwn."

"Can you come into my world?" she asked him.

"Alas, no. Those of us who were born in this world, who have lived all our lives eating its food and breathing its air, can never leave it for yours. You can return there because you were born there and belong to it, but if you were to marry here and have children, they would belong to Annwn. Our spirits, you see, are drawn always to the Light: it pulls us ever onward and upward, towards itself. For you to move *upward*, to our plane, is therefore quite natural, since you are moving closer to the Light; but for us to go *downward*, into your Shadow-world, would be counter to the inclinations of our spirits." He beamed down at her. "I am glad to see you: I did not know whether you would return to us, once your deed had been performed."

"Deed?"

"It seems that the fates decreed you should save the princess's life when the Lochlannach warrior attacked. Had you not alerted us to his disguise, he might have taken Gwenlian by surprise and held her hostage before her knight could come to her aid. My attention was otherwise engaged, at that instant: it was fortunate that you were there. You must have the second sight, to have seen past his ruse."

"I'm glad you're all safe," said Jean shyly. "Is—is that Prince Diarmait?" she asked, gesturing towards the young man at Gwenlian's side. He did not look "terrible" to her. He was quite handsome—tall and lean and dark-haired like Jim, though his hair was curly rather than straight. He was smiling at the dancing courtiers, a good-humoured and pleasant smile. As Jean watched, the princess leaned over to murmur something in his ear. He laughed, throwing back his dark head, and Gwenlian looked at him with eyes that sparkled like a sunlit sea.

"It is," the Druid said. "They are husband and wife now."

"But—she loves him!" exclaimed Jean in surprise. There could be no mistaking the look in Gwenlian's eyes.

"She has always loved him," the Druid said. "Ever since she fostered here with him when they were children. Sometimes a friend is the best choice for a life companion."

Jean thought of Jim, of all their childhood games and shared memories. "So she was only joking when she said he was a terrible boy?"

"Oh, no doubt he was quite terrible at times." Lailoken chuckled, then turned serious again. "Diarmait is the son of King Ciaran of Temair—the older man on the throne to Gwenlian's left. And beside him is his queen and Diarmait's mother, Rhiannon of Gwynedd. Avalon, you see, was once two separate kingdoms. This eastern land of Temair was settled by people from the isle of Éire, who sailed across the ocean seeking the lands of the west; and Gwynedd, the realm that lies to the south and west of this one, was founded in later times by Prince Madoc of Cymru. Gwynedd's reigning king, Arawn, was made High King over all Avalon's monarchs twenty years ago."

"*All* the monarchs? Are there more than two then?"

"There is . . . one other." He looked grave. "A queen named Morgana rules a small *tuath*, a people of her own, not far inland from this city of Temair. But she is a sorceress, and has an evil name at Ciaran's court."

He broke off at that point, because Gwenlian had caught sight of Jean, and had risen from her carved throne to greet her with outstretched arms. Jean ran to meet the princess, dropping a curtsey, only to find herself warmly embraced. The king and queen and the young prince too came forward, and welcomed and made much of her. She was relieved of her coat and her heavy wet boots, and a chair with a soft cushion was brought for her, and warm slippers, and a hot spicy-smelling drink like mulled wine was thrust into her hand.

"What happened at the abbey, Your Highness?" she asked, feeling a little giddy from all their loving attentions. "How did you escape the Vik—I mean, the Lochlannach?"

"A great storm blew up at that instant," replied Gwenlian, "so the enemy could not flee in their longboat, and the rains quenched the fire they set on the stockade. A most fortunate chance."

"Fortunate indeed," said Lailoken with something like a twinkle in his eye, "if chance it was."

"The enemy fled overland, thinking it was sorcery. But the princess's men captured some of them," Prince Diarmait told her. His face was even more attractive when seen close up, with fine strong bones and clear blue eyes like his father's. "They are being kept in a cell below the keep."

"But enough of those dreadful pirates," said Queen Rhiannon. She was a short, plump, rather round-faced woman, with a motherly expression on her features. "Let us have our entertainment, now that the dancing is done and we have a distinguished guest here with us!" She beamed at Jean, who smiled shyly back.

Minstrels began to play again, in a gallery which Jean had not noticed when she first entered. There were some familiar Christmas carols, like *Here We Come A-Wassailing*, and others that she did not know. One was about a boar's head being carried into a feast, a merry rollicking song in which everyone joined; another, called *Adam Lay Y-Bounden*, had a tune so sweet and haunting that it brought tears to Jean's eyes. Before she could stop herself they were streaming freely down her cheeks.

Lailoken saw, and moved to stand next to her chair. "What is wrong?" he asked her in a low voice.

Jean fumbled in her pocket for a handkerchief. "I just feel badly, celebrating Christmas when there's a war on at home."

"All the more reason to enjoy yourself. No, it is not heartless. Mirth and revelry are the weapons that we wield against our enemies. We in Annwn also hold our winter feast, to keep our spirits high. For if the enemy drives out joy from our minds and lives, then he has truly won."

At that moment there came a loud knock at the door of the hall; the music ceased and everyone looked to see one of the mummers standing in the doorway. He wore a red coat trimmed with rabbit fur, and a cloth mask to which a quantity of wool had been attached to form a lengthy beard. On his head was a crown of bright-berried holly. Stepping forward, he gave a deep bow and began to recite:

> I stand at your door; pray let me in,
> I beg your welcome I may win.
> When once I stand within your hall,
> My best I'll do to please you all.
> What wonders I shall show you here!
> What knights, what battles shall appear:
> Activity of youth, activity of age—
> Now come, Saint George, and take the stage!

A second actor entered. This one wore a large white surcoat with a red cross stitched to the front, and a wooden sword at his side. He recited in his turn:

> Saint George am I, my exploits you all know;
> I fought a fiery dragon—ran him through!
> I've battled lions, giants, Saracens,
> Foes of all kinds, and every one I slew!

"Hail King George!" cried the audience.

Lailoken bent and whispered in Jean's ear. "This is an old solstice play: its theme goes back to ancient times, before Saint George and the coming of Christianity. It may seem like an amusing little comedy to you, but it is about light battling darkness, hope triumphing over despair. After the solstice the days lengthen, and winter will eventually end.

You see the evergreen wreaths hanging there, upon the walls?" She nodded. "The wreath too is a very old custom, and goes back to the earliest days of the Druids. It has the sun's round shape, and the boughs that do not lose their green in winter signify immortality. It reminds us that every dark time will end, that we must never lose hope. The hero of the solstice play is also a symbol of the sun, of light and life. Saint George slays the dragon as the sun defeats the darkness—as spring conquers winter."

"Our king's name is George," Jean whispered back. "Well, his first name's Albert actually: George is one of his middle names, but he's used it since his coronation. What a funny coincidence."

"Coincidence? I think not. That was a most auspicious choice of name for a king in time of war."

"Oh, but he didn't know there'd be a war then," explained Jean. "This was years back."

"All the same, it cannot be mere chance that he chose the name of the warrior-saint. That is a portent, I am sure."

"*I'd* like to choose another name." Even as she said this Jean was surprised at herself: she hadn't meant to say anything so personal. But something about the kindly old man drew the admission out of her.

Gwenlian overheard. "You do not like your name?" she asked, leaning towards Jean.

"I hate it!" exclaimed Jean. "It's plain and ordinary and dull." *Like me*, she thought glumly.

"It is a very good name," said Lailoken. "It comes of the same root as *Jane, Joanna, John*: a Hebrew name that means, roughly translated, 'Gracious gift of God.'"

"It's so *common*, though," Jean sighed. "There are four other girls at my school named Jean."

Gwenlian looked thoughtful. "Perhaps it could be altered a little to suit you. There are the French forms of the name, Jeanne and Jeannette: they are pretty, are they not? Or . . ." She looked thoughtful. "I remember now, there is an even older form of the name, *Jehane*. I saw it once in an old ballad."

Jean was charmed. "How beautiful! I've never heard that one."

"Shall I call you Jehane instead? It is still your own name, and has the same meaning."

"I'd love that, Your Highness." Jean felt warmed and comforted. The hot spicy drink and the blazing heat from the nearby fireplace had driven the chills from her body, and the kindly words also had their effect. She snuggled contentedly into her cushioned chair, watching the boisterous antics of Saint George. The actor was a natural comedian, revelling in his role: he threw out his chest as he bragged about his deeds, struck comic poses that made everyone in the hall laugh. Presently another actor entered the hall. He wore a black surcoat, and wielded a wooden sword like Saint George's.

> In I come, the fearsome Turkish Knight,
> To seek King George, and challenge him to fight!

There were loud hisses and catcalls, then more laughter as the dark knight glared and brandished his wooden sword at the courtiers. He and Saint George traded haughty insults for a few minutes, then the latter approached the royal dais.

"Will a good lady of this house give me her favour, that I may stand as her champion?" he implored.

Princess Gwenlian whisked one of the red ribbons from the evergreen garlands and tied it, with a straight face, around his arm. He bowed low over her hand, then promptly turned and charged at the Turkish Knight. "Have at thee!" he roared.

A spirited sword-fight followed, the two knights tearing up and down the hall as the crowd cheered and booed. Then the Turkish Knight thrust his wooden blade at Saint George's broad emblazoned chest, and the latter dropped his own weapon and fell to the floor with a loud exaggerated groan. After a few twitching convulsions, he lay still.

"He *dies*?" cried Jean in disbelief. How could the play end like this? "But I thought you said he was the champion! I thought—"

Lailoken laid a reassuring hand on her shoulder. "Like the sun," the Druid whispered in her ear, "he dies but to rise again. Watch."

The dark knight had thrown down his own sword, and was now wailing and clutching at his head. "Oh woe is me, what evil have I done?" he cried. "I've slain this hero, like the setting sun!" Pretending to weep with remorse, he ran from one to the other of the courtiers, pleading with them to fetch a doctor. They waved him away, laughing.

Another knock came at the door, and a stooped figure in a black robe and big, floppy hat entered the hall. The Turkish Knight ran to him, asking him if he was a physician, and if he could restore the dead to life.

"Why, certainly. I've pills for palsy, unguents for gout," the doctor replied querulously. "There's no disease on earth I can't drive out!" He shuffled over to the corpse, pretended to examine it, mimed popping a pill into its mouth and stepped back. The revived saint sat up, stretched, sprang to his feet and began to dance about the hall, along with his former foe, the doctor and the Father Christmas actor. Everyone clapped and cheered, Jean included.

Then the man with the Hobby Horse stepped forward. Pointing to the stuffed head, he announced: "Here's another who has died, yet lives again. He may look like a lifeless head stuck on a pole, but my Horse can answer any question he's asked."

"Who is the boy who steals the sweets?" called a female courtier.

The man with the Hobby Horse circled the room, then made the bony jaws snap at a little page boy, who grinned back.

"Show us the maiden who dreams all night of her sweetheart!" a man shouted next. The Hobby Horse picked out a plump, fair-haired girl who burst into giggles and blushes.

The questions seemed to be part of a ritual. Lailoken leaned over and explained to Jean that the Hobby Horse, too, dated back to pagan days. "He is a symbol of the oracular beast, the sacred horse or bull who foretells with his actions—or the state of his entrails, when he is sacrificed—what the future holds."

A young man standing nearby overheard. "Tell us what the future holds, Horse!" he demanded loudly, in the slurred voice of one who has drunk a little too much. This time there was an uneasy muttering in the room, as though he had broken with tradition, asked the wrong question. Defiant, he repeated it.

The Horse's jaws opened wide. In the same instant there came a terrible sound—not from those jaws, as everyone for a wild instant imagined, but from outside—beyond the castle walls. The voice of a woman raised in a piercing keen.

There were gasps and murmurs from the courtiers and the mummers alike, and one girl gave a faint scream. In the winter night outside another woman's cry joined the first, then a second, a third, a fourth. The wailing voices rose and fell, rose and fell, ululating like another sound Jean remembered all too well. *The sirens!* This was wrong, evil. That sound should not come here—not intrude upon her safe haven.

Then as suddenly as the unearthly cries had begun, they ceased. And the room erupted into movement and a din of frightened voices.

"Could the Lochlannach have done this?" asked Gwenlian above the confusion of the court.

"Not they," said Lailoken. "They have not the power. It was the Banshee, no doubt of that." Gwenlian paled slightly and sank back in her seat; Diarmait laid a hand on her arm.

"Banshee?" echoed Jean faintly; but for once they paid her no heed.

"All the same, I would speak with these Lochlannach." Prince Diarmait rose grim-faced from his seat. "If there is aught evil afoot, I have no doubt they are a part of it. Father, will you come with me to their cell?"

"Gladly." The king's face was stony too.

Gwenlian and Lailoken joined them, but the queen would not. "I cannot bear the sight of those terrible men!" she declared with a visible shudder. "Jean, you may stay here with me if you prefer it."

But Jean felt a sudden terror at the thought of being separated from Lailoken. He was a pillar of strength, an island of calm amid the tumult. Stammering her apologies to the little queen, she hastened after the Druid and his companions.

The cellars of the castle were reached by a winding stair, rough-hewn from the living rock of the hill on which it stood. Jean and her hosts descended the steps in single file—it was too narrow for them to walk abreast—until it opened into a low-roofed, dim-lit passage far below the keep. The granite walls were damp and breathed out a piercing chill, driving the last lingering warmth of the throne room from their bodies. Jean thought she could hear the muffled thud of the surf, far away, and another sound much nearer: a sound as of many loud, deep voices raised in anger.

Prince Diarmait led them along the passage, to a place where it turned a sharp corner: here a single wall torch burned and two guards stood. They snapped to attention at the sight of the king. The sound of yelling voices was louder.

"How are your charges, Cathal?" Ciaran asked one of them.

The man bowed. "Lively, Your Highness. We gave them some ale with their meat and bread, and it has made them merry. Listen to them sing!" The noise coming from around the corner did not sound much like singing to Jean: it was loud and raucous and dissonant. Presently, however, one deep voice came to dominate the rest.

"He is telling the tale of Thorfinn Karlsefni's quest," said Lailoken. "They have their heroes and legends too. I will translate."

"You know their language?" said Jean, surprised.

"Lailoken knows all the tongues of men," said Gwenlian. "For the son of an angel, even a fallen one, there is no Babel-curse."

Lailoken began to speak softly, almost chanting:

> Helluland, the stone-slab-country,
> First before their prow appeared:
> Barren, and with great stones scattered.
> Thorfinn did not linger there,
> But sailed onward, boldly seeking
> Vinland fair, and Leifsbudir.

Jean pictured in her mind a Viking longship, plunging like a bucking horse through icy waves, flinging back spray like a flying mane from its dragon-headed prow.

> Markland next the Northmen sighted,
> Dark with forests, haunt of bears.
> Shores of sand there stretched unending,
> Far as mortal eye could see!
> Furdustrandir, Wonder-beaches,
> Was the name they gave its coast.

The big powerful voice grew louder, and Lailoken had to raise his own to be heard above it.

> Then at last they came to Vinland,
> Green and rich with grapes and grain.
> Natives dwelt there, coward Skraelings:

Many did the Northmen slay.
But long after, battle-wearied,
They took ship and sought the sea.
Up a river sailed Karlsefni,
With his men he disembarked.
And they saw a wonder there—
A Uniped, most strange to see:
Man-like, yet with but one leg!
Hopping like a hare it came,
Holding in its hands a bow.
With an arrow it slew Thorvald
Ere he could lay hand to sword.
Angrily they chased the monster,
But it leaped into the river,
Disappearing from their sight.
Sailing north again, they saw
The homeland of the Unipeds—

"Enough, Lailoken," interrupted King Ciaran. "Let us speak with them."

They followed him around the corner. And there in a cave-like space, behind a barrier of iron bars, were the prisoners. They were huge and brawny with bare, well-muscled arms, their long matted hair and beards mingling with the furs they wore. They seemed to Jean more like large and dangerous animals than human beings. They fell silent, glaring, as Princess Gwenlian and Diarmait and the king approached. Captive animals, straining at the bars of their cage.

"*Berserkers*," said Lailoken to Jean. "Warriors capable of

berserk rages. By wearing the skins of animals they feel they are imbued with animal strength."

"What do your leaders want with us?" demanded Diarmait of the Lochlannach. "I demand an answer! There have been too many attacks of late for mere random pillage. What are your designs on our land?"

"Vinland was our desire," said one man. "Not your little island." He had a narrow triangular face framed with heavy black hair and beard, and his eyes were colder and calmer than his comrades'. They were grey: not dark and deep like those of Lailoken, but a hard pale grey like steel or stone.

"He speaks English?" exclaimed Jean.

"This is Jarl Ulf," the princess told her. "'Jarl' means Earl, he says: he is a nobleman among his people. And his name is the Lochlannach word for *wolf*. But he is not pure Lochlannach. He says that his mother was a Gael, captured by the Northmen long ago when an Avalonian ship ran aground on one of their northern isles. He was born to her and a Lochlannach lord, and learned our tongue at her knee."

"And from her I learned of this island," said Jarl Ulf. "The Northmen knew it as Hvitmannaland, or Irland Mikla—Greater Ireland. The old sagas spoke of it, but we knew not where it lay. Nor did we care, while Vinland the Good was our goal. But Karlsefni abandoned that country, because of the Unipeds and the assaults of the savage Skraelings."

"The Weaklings," Lailoken translated.

"For weaklings, they seem to have done very well at driving out your brave warriors," observed Diarmait.

Grim-faced, Ulf translated the prince's words for his fellows. One big brown-bearded man bellowed and rushed the bars with such force that for an instant they thought the iron would give. Foam flecked his open mouth, and his bloodshot eyes rolled in their sockets. "*Nithing!*" he howled.

Ulf smiled thinly. "He says you are without honour."

"Without honour!" Diarmait snapped. "Did we not spare all your lives?"

The smile shifted to a sneer. Jean realized the Lochlannach felt only contempt for people who refrained from killing. These were men to whom mercy was a weakness, and not a cause for gratitude.

"Why did you attack the abbey?" demanded Diarmait. "What harm had the monks and nuns ever done you?"

"We had heard that the princess would be there," said Jarl Ulf. "It was my intention to capture her and present her to my king as a slave." Gwenlian's expression remained cool, but Diarmait flushed angrily.

"We shall have this island for our own," continued the jarl. "The northern lands are too bleak and barren and Vinland the Good is barred to us. We have need for living-space."

Diarmait glared. "And you think you can take what you please!"

"Think it? I know it for truth. At the approach of the wolf the fox leaves his meat; the hawk cedes his prey to the eagle. To the greatest and strongest go the spoils, always. That is the way of the world."

"You, at any rate, have not proven strongest in this contest, Lord Wolf," Gwenlian pointed out coldly.

"I come but as the thrall of a greater one, who will grant me power in return for my services. I and my men are his hounds, sent ahead in the hunt; the huntsman himself you have not seen."

"You speak of your king?" said Diarmait.

Again the flinty eyes flashed contempt. "Nay, not King Einar. He is old now, and grows more feeble by the day. I speak of another, far greater than he—greater than you can imagine."

There was an uneasy pause. Then King Ciaran touched his son's shoulder. "Come, Diarmait. There is nothing to be gained from talking to these barbarians, and Lailoken has said they are not responsible for . . . what we heard. Let us go back to our hearths and our revels, and leave them to their wild tales. Lady—" to Jean—"you will stay the night with us, will you not? I will see that you are provided with a bed-chamber, and all that you may need."

How she longed to accept his kind invitation. But as they walked back along the passage she said regretfully, "I should try to find my way home. I really shouldn't have left. If I go missing again my family will be so worried."

"I will take you back to the place where you entered," offered Lailoken. "It may be that door will not open again, unless the fates wish it. But we can at least seek it out."

Jean and the Druid left the castle and walked down the hill-side together. The moon was setting, but the snowy slopes were still bathed in its light. It was easy to retrace her foot-steps and the mummers'. Lailoken said that they would try to find the place where her prints joined the larger group's, and track them backwards.

They talked on as they made the descent together, about

her world and his, of the comings and goings between them
and their separate histories. She told him of the Vikings, and
the Greenlanders, and how she was certain that these must
be the ancestors of the Lochlannach. He agreed with her
that it must be so.

"And Avalon—what did they call it?" she asked.

"Irland Mikla."

"It's the Avalon Peninsula, in my world. Isn't it odd that
they have the same name?"

"Perhaps not. Those who gave that name to your peninsula had no doubt heard tales of the lands of the west—
lands that are not real in your world, but are in ours."

"But our Avalon is only a little part of Newfoundland.
Where is the rest of the island here?"

"There is a larger island near our small isle of Avalon: Tir
Tairngiri, it is called. It is a lovely land, rich in gems and
flowering trees and vines."

"Vines? Then that's their Vinland! But Unipeds—*that*
part can't be true, even here. One-legged people—"

"Perhaps they are not *people*. There are beings called the
Fomori who dwell in the deeps of the sea, and have the
power to alter their forms at will. They may appear with one
leg or arm—or one eye, like their King Balor who ruled the
isle of Éire in ancient times. Or they may wear the heads of
beasts. I suspect that these Fomori are in fact allied with the
Norsemen now. Nor am I alone in that suspicion. The Gaels
name them the 'Lochlannach' after the Fomori city of
Lochlan that lies on the sea's floor."

They were halfway down the hill now. The standing stone
reared up from its mound, large and imposing but at the

same time incomplete, like an empty plinth waiting for its statue.

"The Lia Fail," he told her, seeing her look at it as they passed by. "The Singing Stone. When a true king or queen sets foot upon it the stone gives a great cry, to signify its approval of that monarch's reign."

"It's very old, isn't it?" she said.

"Old beyond all reckoning. It was brought here from another place, a land now vanished beneath the sea."

She was silent for the rest of the walk down the slope, and he did not interrupt her thoughts. When the path led them onto the level fields she finally spoke again.

"That person Jarl Ulf mentioned—the one he said was more powerful than a king. You know who that is, don't you? I saw the look on your face."

"Yes, I know. He spoke of Woden," said Lailoken.

Jean gasped aloud. "Woden?" *It's Woden's day . . .*

"You know the name?"

"I—I didn't know it was a name."

"Woden is our name for Odin, chief god of the Northmen. To them he is the wise All-Father, ruler of the gods, who hanged himself on the World-tree and gave one of his eyes to obtain the secret of the mystic runes. The Northmen revere and serve him: that is why some refer to the Lochlannach as the Sons of Death, or Odin's Wolves. But to us he is Woden, the Gallows Lord, bringer of war and death. He leads the Wild Hunt through the sky, seeking whom he can destroy. With him fly his war-maidens, the Valkyries: the Choosers of the Slain."

"But—he's not *real*? He's just a myth, isn't he?" The Druid made no reply. "Isn't he?" she persisted fearfully.

Lailoken looked out over the moonlit fields. "I told you that your world was like a shadow of ours," he said presently. "But they are not the same. What is untrue in your world may be true in ours."

She stood for a moment aghast, sharing his silence. "Things like that are real here," she said at last. "That's what you're telling me, isn't it? Gods, and fairies, and magic: in this world they really do exist."

"With your own ears you heard the Banshee, the fairy women. A Banshee laments when a mortal is soon to die—and when many of them mourn, as we heard tonight, that person will be a great lord or ruler. It is an evil omen."

Jean shuddered and looked down at her booted feet. "I know it's selfish, but I was hoping everything would be all right in your Annwn. So I could always come back here when I needed—when I needed—"

"To run away?" he asked gently.

She nodded mutely.

"Our two worlds are more closely linked than that. If your world suffers, then so will ours. It fits with a certain old prophecy." He gazed out over the bleak fields of snow. "The time that is to come shall be a dark one for both our worlds: a wind age, a wolf age, that shall bring with it evil and strife. But that means we are fellow-warriors, if the thought brings you any comfort. Your struggle shall be ours as well."

His last sentence sounded faint to her ears, as though he had suddenly moved very far away. She looked up, and started: there was no sign of Lailoken anywhere. The moon, the castle, the empty fields were gone. She was standing alone in the middle of LeMarchant Road, and only one set of footprints—her own—marked the snow. Before her was her own house, looking peaceful with its darkened windows, and the Christmas wreath on its front door—the green circle of the undying sun.

Chapter Seven

WINTER WORE ON, cold and bitter. There was no change in the situation overseas: London endured some of its heaviest bombing raids yet, and St. Paul's was damaged, and whole neighbourhoods were destroyed in a rain of incendiary bombs. Despite this, the newspapers remained obstinately optimistic. Casualties could have been worse, they declared, the Allies were holding firm, and Britain's coast had not yet been invaded. But both sides intensified their air war as the winter waned, and the U-boats were now sinking cargo ships on both sides of the Atlantic.

For some time following Christmas Jean had felt a glow of comfort. *It was real,* she would think. *I was really there. I drank that spiced wine, and I heard those carols, and I felt the warmth of the fire on my face. And the people were real, as real as the ones around me now.* She wished she could tell her family about them. *But who would believe me? They still don't really believe in my ghostly soldiers, not even with those bones that were found. Coincidence, Andy always says*. Sometimes she wondered and worried what had become of Gwenlian and the others, in that world where magic existed. At such times she tried hard not to think of her nightmare about the winged women, and the grey wraith that rode the sky. But in time her memory of the Otherworld faded. By early spring the night of revels in the fairy-tale castle seemed very faint and far away, like a memory from a distant time, or like a dream. She would read in her little blue-backed journal the words: "*I entered the Otherworld again today. Or perhaps I should say tonight, because it was late in the evening, after we got back from Mary's Bay . . .*" And it would seem to her like something that she had made up, one of the fanciful stories she sometimes wrote for her own amusement.

Annwn still intruded into her life on occasion. She was talking to Andy one evening in his room when her eyes strayed to the big map of the world which he had hung on his wall. There were white and black pins stuck into it in places, showing where the Allied and enemy troops were positioned—for Andy followed the radio and newspaper reports attentively. Suddenly she found herself gazing at Greenland, following an imaginary path from it to Baffin Island—that desolate, treeless, stony country—then down past Labrador's long coast to northern Newfoundland. *Helluland, the stone-slab-country . . . Furdustrandir, Wonder-beaches, was the name they gave its coast . . . Vinland green and rich . . .* Her eyes moved on down, to the Avalon Peninsula that was almost like a little island in its own right. Irland Mikla?

Andy broke off in the middle of a sentence. "What are you staring at?" he asked.

"Oh . . . nothing."

She had looked up the name *Woden* in her father's big dictionary which listed names as well as words, and found that it really was another name for Odin or Wotan, the chief god of the Norse. The name meant madness or fury; it came from the German *wut*, meaning "rage." She also looked up *Ulf* to see if it meant "wolf," but could not find it. She was on the point of closing the book's heavy cover when a thought occurred to her. Of course, she reasoned as she turned to the A section, that was likely just a coincidence. Just because they sounded a bit similar, that didn't mean the names were actually—

As she read the definition on the page before her, she had an odd reeling sensation, as though the floor had shifted beneath her feet.

Adolf (ad'olf, ä'dolf) [Old Ger. ATHAL + WOLFA] German masculine name; literally, "Noble Wolf."

"So what are you wearing to the dance?" Penny asked.

She and Jean and Laura were walking along the south side of Water Street, peering in the windows of Bowring's and Ayre's and the other big grand stores. It was a grey, windy day in early May, not the sort of weather for lingering at storefronts, but the girls could not take their eyes off the evening gowns on display. The haughty-faced mannequins were swathed in satin or shining metallic lamé, in gowns frosted with sequins, in strapless shoulder-baring ball gowns with huge skirts, in tight seductive dresses that showed the curve of the hips.

A streetcar clattered past, its side bearing the sprawling slogan BUY WAR SAVINGS CERTIFICATES; Jean raised her voice to be heard above the noise. "I've got a new dress, from my parents. It's floor-length crepe."

The dance was a school fundraiser for the war effort. It was going to be quite grand, with live music and a singer, and every girl in PWC was desperate to go. Jean and her friends had no dates, but as Laura had one older brother and a cousin in town, and Jean had her brother, Andy, they had begged the boys to accompany them and Penny. "It's for the War Effort!" they had pleaded until the boys gave in. Andy would take Laura, her brother, Neil, would accompany Penny and Laura's cousin Dan had agreed to go with Jean.

If only it were Jim! she thought wistfully. But at least she was going to the dance.

The three girls walked on along Water Street. Presently they saw a group of young men in navy blue uniforms walking towards them.

"They're Canadian sailors," declared Penny. "I can tell by the uniform."

"They're awfully handsome," said Laura.

"I think the uniforms are ugly, though."

"What does it matter? It's what's *in* the uniforms that's important!" Laura batted her eyelashes and showed her dimples to the young sailors, who laughed and stopped to talk to her.

"Who's this beauty? Did you step down off a movie screen?"

"Oh, you servicemen—!" Laura laughed and tossed her blonde curls as they teased and flirted with her. Penny and

Jean they paid no attention to. Jean did not mind—the opinions of boys who were not Jim O'Connor meant nothing at all to her—but Penny's thin cheeks held a flush of anger when the sailors moved on. Once they were out of earshot she rounded on Laura. "What did you go and do that for? Making us *all* look cheap!"

"Cheap?"

"Chatting up sailors like a—a hussy!"

Jean could see Laura debating whether to retort in kind or cry to arouse guilt. In the end she did both. "Penny Ross, you're so mean these days I just don't want to be near you any more!" she accused through quick-welling tears.

The two girls threw sidelong glances towards Jean as they argued, expecting her to step in and play the peacemaker as she always did. But Jean was annoyed with them both, and kept on walking. She took a side street down to the harbour and walked along the docks, past the outthrust piers. These were very old and the wood of which they were made was rotting in places, grass and weeds sprouting between the planks, and some of the pilings beneath them leaned tipsily. But as always there were lots of ships moored alongside them. There was a troop ship resting there at anchor—a large converted passenger liner, rows of extra life rafts hanging along its sides—and a convoy of several large freighters was just coming into the harbour, shepherded by the warship that had evidently been guarding it across the Atlantic. All the ships looked the worse for wear: how relieved the sailors would be when the submarine net was winched up behind them and they knew they had found safe haven at last!

A small dory rowed past the piers and alongside the troop ship: she could hear the three men in it talking excitedly as they looked up at the vast steel hull. There were other people standing about on the wharf, staring at the moored ships and watching the convoy come in. Suddenly she noticed two boys standing together on one of the piers. One she recognized instantly as Andy, with his thick thatch of chestnut hair. But the other, lean and tall and dark-haired—it couldn't be. It *couldn't* be—

"Jim?" she whispered, incredulous. And then, running towards them, she called out loud: "*Jim O'Connor!*"

They both turned at her cry and she saw the dark-haired boy's face clearly. She hastened towards him, smiling in undisguised delight.

"Jim! I didn't know you were in town!" she exclaimed. "It's so good to see you!"

He grinned back at her. "I just came up spur of the moment, on the bus. Your brother's always after me to come to town, and Dad doesn't need me at the store this weekend."

"Then you're here through Sunday?" she asked. This was too good to be true, she thought dazedly as he nodded. She must be dreaming. Jim here, in St. John's—staying at her *home*. And on the weekend of the dance!

"Yes, I thought I'd look in on that dance of yours," he said when she mentioned it, hardly daring to hope. "And help to keep an eye on you," he added, teasing.

Andy turned Jim's attention back towards the convoy. "That one took a hit, look."

They all stared at the freighter as it limped up to one of

the piers. There was a great, gaping, jagged hole in its starboard bow, extending well below the waterline.

"What did that? A mine?" asked Jean, shaken.

"Torpedo, more likely," said Andy.

As they watched, the dory with the three men rowed right through the hole and into the huge metal cavity beyond. The men's voices echoed hollowly inside.

"They're really at the mercy of the sea wolves, out there," said Jim, shaking his head.

Jean swung around. "The what?"

"That's what the sailors call the U-boats," Andy explained, "because they attack like wolves."

"Are you cold, Jeanie?" asked Jim.

"N-no."

"Thought I saw you shiver."

"I'm all right. Is that a destroyer?" Jean asked, pointing to the warship, and feeling a little ashamed that she didn't know. It was a sleek, streamlined vessel, smaller than the cargo ships, with a single funnel and a deck gun mounted at the front.

"Canadian corvette," corrected her brother. "Destroyers are bigger, but they cost a lot of money to build and there aren't enough of them to go around."

"If only the Americans would enter the war!" sighed Jean. "They've got the money to build anything. *Why* won't they help us fight the Nazis?"

"They can't," replied Andy. "Not with their neutrality laws, and the America First people putting pressure on the government to stay out of it. A lot of Americans don't want to get into another European war."

"Can't blame them really," Jim commented. "They lost a lot of men in the last one."

"So did everyone else!" protested Jean.

"Well, it's no use talking about it," said Andy. "They've decided to be neutral this time, and that's it. It's up to us to do the fighting now."

Jean shivered again, huddling into her coat.

"You're so lucky!" moped Fiona, sitting on the edge of Jean's bed. "I wish *I* was going."

"You'll get to lots of parties when you're my age," Jean comforted her. "I think you're going to be really pretty when you grow up, Fiona."

Jean turned back and forth in front of her mirror. She wished she had a full-length one, so she could see her whole figure. Her new dress was ashes-of-roses crepe, with little rosettes on the bodice, and its frilly hem swept the floor. There was even a little matching rosette for her hair. She had changed her usual pageboy hairstyle for a rippling mass of waves: it had taken sixty pincurls to get this effect, but it was well worth the effort. After putting the gown on she had hidden in her bedroom, waiting for Jim and Andy to leave. Jim must not see her yet, not until they met later at the dance: he *must* look at her tonight as though he had never seen her before.

"Growing up takes forever," her sister complained.

"Not as long as you think." *And what will the world be like when you're grown?* she added silently. *Will anyone be holding dances then?* She quickly suppressed the thought. Tonight, she told herself firmly, was going to be perfect.

"Jeanie! The Macrae boys are here!" Mum called up the stairs.

"Coming, Mum." Jean gave a last glance at her reflection and hastened downstairs. Neil and Dan Macrae were there, dressed in their best suits, and looking as much alike as brothers with their straight fair hair and blue eyes. Dan had turned nineteen this year, and he looked especially grand with his recruit band on his arm. RN, it said, for Royal Navy. Like all the new recruits, he had not been given his uniform yet. This very weekend he would be heading out on the same troop ship she had seen in the harbour, off to Halifax and then to Britain for his naval training. Penny was there too, also looking quite splendid in a long velvet evening cloak. Jean smothered a sigh; why hadn't she asked for a fancy wrap, too? She only had an old cloak of her mother's. But she forgot everything when she saw the corsage Dan was holding out to her. "For you, Jeanie," he said shyly.

A pink rose corsage—Jean loved roses. She held the moist buds to her nose and breathed in their sweet fragrance before pinning the corsage to the front of her dress.

They walked over to the dance together, laughing and talking of the old times when they had played at one another's houses after school. The dance was not being held at PWC itself, since Methodist rules outlawed anything but square dancing on the premises: instead, the organizers had reserved the dance hall at the Guards Club over on the corner of LeMarchant and Barter's Hill. But it was better than dancing in a gymnasium, Jean thought: more grown-up. They arrived to find the party already in full swing, with the band playing loudly at the far end of the room and dozens of little tables set out, each one with a twinkling candle. Dozens of young couples dotted the dance floor, and there were several Royal Navy arm bands to be seen on the older boys. *It's nice that they can get to a party like this,* Jean thought. *One last little celebration, before going into service overseas.* Dan took the girls' wraps for them, and they settled at a table to sip glasses of punch and gaze rather timidly around the room. As they sat there Laura came in with Andy, her date for the evening, on one arm and on the other, Jim, looking somewhat sheepish.

"Isn't he a looker!" said Penny, putting down her punch glass and sitting bolt upright. "Who's that with your brother, Jean?"

"Just an old friend." Jean, seeing Jim in a proper suit for the very first time, realized with a little pang just how handsome he really was. He seemed taller and slimmer than ever, and his dark hair was neatly slicked back from his forehead. Laura looked unexpectedly glamorous: her scarlet satin dress had a plunging neckline and only the thinnest of shoulder straps: it showed off her full figure and her soft, plump shoulders. Penny's dark blue gown was expensive-looking too, its neckline just as daring, but she hadn't the right curves to carry it off: it just seemed to hang on her thin frame, and the sulky look on her face suggested that she knew this only too well. Jean secretly wished she had been a little bolder as well. Her own dress, with its demure rosettes and sweetheart neckline and shy, self-effacing colour, seemed almost designed to fade into the background.

Laura, Andy and Jim came and joined them at their table. The band finished its song and started playing a popular new one, which had many of the older students singing along.

> We'll meet again
> Don't know where
> Don't know when
> But I know we'll meet again some sunny day
> Keep smilin' thro' just like you always do
> Till the blue skies drive the dark clouds far away . . .

The three girls took to the floor with their designated partners, all casting longing backward looks at Jim, who was sitting alone at the table, looking acutely uncomfortable. When the song ended Penny struck up a conversation with Andy, hoping no doubt to get to know Jim through him. But it worked against her, because Andy promptly asked her to dance, leaving Jim to Laura as the only possible partner aside from her brother and cousin. As Jean circled the dance floor with Neil she could not take her eyes off the couple. Of course Jim must be terribly impressed by Laura's beauty. He would never have seen anyone remotely like her in the outport. *She's like a flower at full bloom,* Jean thought. *Not a rose though: something more exotic, a tropical flower. She'll never be lovelier than she is just now. And I'll never be lovely at all.*

For perhaps the first time in her life, this fact truly hurt her, and she turned her eyes away.

Jim asked Penny to dance next, then sat out the next one with Laura. Jean, who was trying hard to listen to Dan talk of his upcoming naval training and hopes for a career at sea, could not help hearing little snippets of their conversation. Laura was doing most of the talking, as usual, but Jim was looking at her very intently as he listened. Was he fascinated by this showy city girl, or merely being courteous?

"Ooh, I love this song!" Laura exclaimed as the band began a new piece, and Jim promptly asked her to dance. Of course it was only the proper thing to do. Of course—

". . . as good a way as any to see the world, my dad says. War isn't all danger, you know: it's travel and adventure," Dan was saying earnestly.

Jean realized guiltily that she had been listening to her date with only half an ear, and quickly turned her attention back to him.

It was only towards the end of the evening that Jim came and asked her to dance; he spent most of the rest of the time talking to Andy and Dan. "Let's try this one," he said casually as he led her to the dance floor. "If you can put up with my two left feet, that is." There was no difference in his voice or in the way he looked at her, she thought unhappily; he might have been inviting her to go for a walk around the outport with him. *It's no use,* she thought despairingly, *he's used to me, I'm like a sister to him. And I'll never be anything else.*

A girl not much older than Jean herself, dressed in a floor-length gown of shimmering silver lamé, came to the microphone, and began to sing in a pure, clear voice.

> That certain night, the night we met
> There was magic abroad in the air

There were angels dining at the Ritz
And a nightingale sang in Berk'ley Square

Of course he had only asked her to dance out of polite-
ness, Jean thought miserably as they circled the dance floor
together. But it was better to dance with him as a friend than
not at all. She had never imagined that this would actually
happen—that she would feel his hand holding hers, lean her
face so close to his. And it was a beautiful song . . .

The streets of town were paved with stars
It was such a romantic affair
And as we kissed and said goodnight
A nightingale sang in Berk'ley Square

The song ended, and with it the perfect moment. They
walked back to the table and rejoined the others.

"Isn't she a wonderful singer?" exclaimed Laura, address-
ing them all but eyeing Jim flirtatiously as she spoke. "As
good as Vera Lynn!"

Jim stood by the table, but made no move to sit down.
"It's stifling in here," he said to Jean in his offhanded way.
"Want to go outside for a moment, Jeanie, and get some
fresh air in our lungs?" She agreed—not, she hoped, too
eagerly—and he went to fetch her cloak. Together they
walked outside into the cool evening air. He didn't stop, but
led her across the street, then on a little way until they had a
partial view of the harbour. It was dark as always—how nice
it would be if there were just a few lights shining romanti-
cally on its surface! Then she could pretend that they were

having a romance. At least there was a full moon throwing its wide glittering track on the water. *There's one* bright light the war can't put out, Jean thought.

"Nice to get out of there," said Jim. "That hall's hot as blazes. And I never was much of a dancer—but I guess you noticed that! Made a complete fool of myself in there."

"No—no, you were fine," Jean fibbed loyally.

"Liar." He laughed, then turned serious once more, gazing out across the water. "Jean, have you ever thought about what'll happen when the war is over?"

"No," she answered, moving to stand beside him. "I've tried to imagine it ending, and everything going back to normal, but I can't seem to picture it in my head. Right now it doesn't feel as though it will ever end, does it?"

"It will end, though, one way or the other," he said. "The fighting men will come home, and marry the girls they left behind, and life will carry on somehow."

"They may have to wait a long time. Years, if it's anything like the last war."

"People waited then." Jim looked at her; his face was more solemn than she had ever seen it. "But things are going to change here in the city, in the meantime. There'll be lots of soldiers and sailors coming in—lots of men. More dances and parties will be put on for them. You're young now, Jean—"

"I'll be sixteen this summer," she said quickly.

"That's what I mean. These years are going to fly by. You'll be a grown woman before you know it, going to grown-up parties."

"I hope you'll get out to a few, Jim. It was . . . nice, having you here."

His dark eyes were unreadable; when he spoke again he looked away from her. "I don't want to work in Dad's store forever, and he's got Rick: it isn't as though I was the only son. I want to go to the College like Andy, get an education. But for now I can't afford it, so I won't be able to come here very often, and . . . I guess what I'm asking is, would you wait for me? To go out with me one day, if I can come here to live?"

Jean gave a little start. He was saying it, actually saying it: what she had dreamed and hoped and imagined he would say to her, one day. And she was speechless. All the charming, clever and kind words she had rehearsed over the years—just in case—completely deserted her. She could only stare at him, and stammer: "Oh, ahh . . . of course!"

"You mean it? Only if you want to, Jean—"

She wanted to kick herself; she wanted to laugh and cry. "Yes, yes, yes, I mean it!"

Then he put his hands on her shoulders and drew her close, and she realized that words were of no importance, after all.

The real excitement came later, when she was alone again in her bedroom.

Too restless and excited to sleep, she paced about the floor for a while, then flung open the window and leaned out to gaze over the roofs and the moon-reflecting harbour. *He loves me*, she thought, and briefly considered announcing it out loud to the sleeping neighbourhood, only stopping herself in time. It was just like one of those romantic movies—*no, better,* she corrected herself happily. *It's real.* Though if a nightingale *were* to start singing right now, like in the song, it could hardly seem more miraculous. Especially since there were no nightingales in Newfoundland . . . Her thoughts darted to and fro, as restless and unwilling to settle as her body. There was something at the back of her mind, about birds that didn't belong on this side of the ocean, some half-faded memory. *"It's wandered a long way from home, then."* No, she couldn't recall it. And what did it matter? Nothing in the world mattered, except that Jim loved her and the moon on the water was beautiful and life was like the movies. He would come here, to Memorial University College, live close by. They would go on dates; they would walk together to the soda fountain after school or to the cinema, strolling arm in arm while other girls turned and watched . . . She and Jim. It was too much, too wonderful to be true; but it was.

Jim O'Connor loved her.

When at last Jean fell asleep from sheer exhaustion, she dreamed that she was back in the dance hall again. The music was playing and Jim was there. But though she could see him through the mass of whirling couples, she could never quite seem to reach him. It grew hot, and very dark, and suddenly the Hobby Horse was there—now bear-furred and nail-toothed, now bone-jawed with dead dry skin. Every time she tried to push her way through the crowd she found herself face to face with him. And then she could not find Jim anywhere, and the hall grew darker and darker, and she was alone . . .

Jean woke with a gasp. The sun was already high, shining in at the window: she'd slept in very late. She kicked off her rumpled bedclothes and sat up, blinking. There was a steady drone of deep voices coming from downstairs: Jim and Andy, it sounded like, talking with Dad. She sprang hurriedly out of bed. The view outside was very different from the moon-washed scene of the previous night. How drab everything looked in the harsh light of day! But Jean's heart was light as she dressed in a clean white blouse and her best skirt, and she found herself humming the song from last night, the one that they had danced to. *Our song*, she was calling it already in her mind. A few minutes later, washed and dressed, she went down the staircase—skipping on the treads as she had done when she was a little girl.

The voices were still coming from the sitting room: arriving at the foot of the stairs, she saw everyone gathered there, her parents and the two boys and Fiona. Why were they all sitting together in the same room? she wondered, puzzled and a little disquieted. What were they talking about?

"—too young," Mum was saying. "You're too young, both of you." Her voice was tense, strained.

"I'm eighteen this fall," replied Andy. "And Jim's birthday's in August. Come on now, that's just an excuse—"

Jean still stood on the last step, clutching the newel post with one hand as she stared into the room. Fiona's eyes were red, as though she'd been crying. Andy stood by Mum's chair, Jim at his side. Then she saw the arm bands the boys were wearing, with the letters RN. Her eyes swam, and she gripped the newel post hard. RN. Royal Navy. Jim and Andy had joined the navy.

Andy glanced deliberately up at the framed MacDougall clan badge over the mantel, with its crusader knight's arm holding a cross and the Gaelic motto, *Buaidh no bas*: To conquer or die. "Don't you want to be proud of me, Mum? Don't you want to know I'm doing my part?" he persisted. Mum's face was deathly white.

"Don't press her, Andrew," Dad said. "She needs to get used to the idea. Just give her a little time!"

"It was you, James O'Connor!" Mum accused suddenly, rounding on him. "*You* came here and gave him the idea—"

"That's not true, Mum." Andy's voice was still stern. Jim stepped forward, between the two of them, and spoke to Mum gently and respectfully.

"I'm sorry, Mrs. MacDougall, but we have to leave now. Our troop ship goes at one o'clock, and we should be gathering now at the Armoury with the others. We'll all be coming down Long's Hill, later, if you want to see us off."

She said nothing, and the two boys headed for the door.

"Andrew!" cried Mum. "Stop him, Allister, he doesn't understand—"

"Stop him?" Dad replied. "He's a man, Patricia, and he's made a decision. He'd just tell me I'd have done the same thing at his age, and what could I say to that?" Fiona was sniffling again. None of them noticed Jean at all, except for Jim.

He saw her on the stair and stopped, gazing at her. "Jeanie—I'm so sorry. I wanted to tell you last night, to explain, but you were looking so happy I couldn't get it out. I didn't want to spoil everything for you. You don't really have to wait around for me to come back."

She couldn't speak. Her throat was closed tight and her heart seemed to be pounding inside her head. She held the newel post with both hands now, afraid that she might fall if she let go.

"I have to leave now," Jim said. He seemed almost to be pleading with her. "You do see that, don't you? I have to do my bit, and so does Andy."

Now: she must cry, beg him not to leave, scream at him even, fill him with guilt. But she could only look at him wretchedly. Jean always said the right thing—always. "I know," she heard her own voice say, though it sounded as if it came from a long way off.

"Oh, Jeanie!" Jim leaned forward and kissed her cheek. "I knew *you'd* understand." Then he turned to follow Andy.

Jean stood motionless as the door closed on them, her hands still clutching the wooden post.

"There they go," called Fiona.

They were standing together on the sidewalk of Long's Hill, watching as a great stream of men and boys came flowing down the steep street—an orderly march, like a military parade, though none of them had a uniform yet. Andy and Jim must be there somewhere, and Dan Macrae, but though she craned her neck Jean could not see any of them. They had already been swept up into the stream of bodies, blended in with it; had already disappeared. Crowds lined both sides of the street, all the way down to its foot, cheering, waving, a few pressing handkerchiefs to their faces. The recruits were heading down to the harbour, where the long dark-hulled troop ship waited to take them—where? Did they even know? Jean turned away from her family and began to run downhill, keeping pace with the procession. When it poured itself through the downtown core and onto the docks, she changed direction, heading eastward, running out towards the Battery.

If only Signal Hill were not fortified and off limits to the public! She could have gone up there, up to the very top as she used to do in the old days; from there she could have seen the ship put out to sea, watching and watching until the earth's curve took it from her sight. But she would get as close to the Narrows as she possibly could. As long as there was a ship to look at, a speck of a shape on the far horizon that contained Andy and Jim, she would continue to gaze after it.

But as she sped towards the shabby wooden houses of the Battery there came a great blast of sound, a tremor that shook the air around her. Jean reeled back as it struck her and roared through her—a massive reverberating sound she heard not only with her ears but with her bones, nerves, sinuses, every vessel and fibre of her body. Then it faded away again; but with its passing all did not return to normal. Everything had changed in that fleeting instant. Her whole world had gone.

The harbour was there, but the troop ship and the crowds and the huge sprawling city had vanished. There was another city there, in its place: its houses were of stone, and so were those of the Battery. Far away, silhouetted on the barren hillside—a hill no longer guarded by sentries—the ring-shaped earthworks rose, and there was the high central mound with its dark grey monolith. Hundreds of people had gathered there, around the stone: on its top two figures stood, outlined against the sky.

She walked slowly uphill in a sort of trance, heading for the crowd. As she drew nearer she saw that the two figures on top of the stone were mantled with purple and ermine:

one had flowing fair hair, the other was tall and dark, and both were crowned with gold.

Gwenlian and Diarmait.

"Yes—they are crowned king and queen today." She turned sharply, to see Lailoken walking towards her, his face grave. "King Arawn is dead: it was he whose death the Banshee foretold, back at Yuletide. I wish I had a happier welcome for you, Jean MacDougall, but we must go now to the *dún* and hold an urgent council. Will you come with us?"

As when she had stood confronting Jim in the hallway, she found she could not speak. He drew closer, asked: "What is the matter, Jean?"

She looked up into his worried, kind face. "Andy and Jim have gone to war," she said, simply.

And the tears that would not come before streamed freely down her face.

Chapter Eight

THE NEW KING AND QUEEN processed back to the *dún* with their courtiers and attendants, all in a solemn silence. No trumpets rang out, no minstrels played: the stone song of the Lia Fail had been the only music to accompany their crowning. King Ciaran and his queen followed their son and his wife, their greying heads bent against the sea wind; with them walked Abbess Brigid in flowing white and gold robes, leaning on a tall carved crozier as though it were a walking stick. A score of nobles and some courtiers walked in a huddled mass behind; the watching crowds had dispersed, heading back to the city. No one spoke. It was so quiet that the flapping of the banners on the castle towers high above seemed loud.

Jean and Lailoken walked at the rear of the group. In a low voice she told him everything, fighting to keep her tears back; and though he could only make sympathetic murmurs, even talking about it was a vast relief to her. Up the winding hill-path they went, up to where it joined the paved road leading to the castle. As they went in through the gate-house Jean glanced up at the keep. She saw, standing atop its nearest tower, something dark and erect. A human figure, she thought, garbed in something black—a robe or cloak; she had the fleeting impression of a face, half-hidden by a shawl or hood—a mere gleam of white at this distance, like the moon when she hides half her face in shadow. These things registered on her brain in a fraction of a second. And then the figure, horribly, was toppling from the battlements, was falling through the air. Jean tried to scream, but only a little choking sound came from the back of her throat. In the next instant she saw that the black, tumbling shape was not a human body, but only a large dark-plumed bird. It circled the tower on black wings, uttering harsh cries, then flapped back up to the sill of a high window and vanished into the darkness within.

It's just my nerves, thought Jean. The tower rooms were likely old and abandoned, and ravens were nesting in them. With her sense of perspective distorted by distance, she had imagined the bird's figure to be much larger than it really was, and her imagination had provided the rest. But her heart still beat so hard it hurt her.

Once they were inside the main keep, Lailoken took Jean gently by the arm and led her apart from the others. "Where are we going?" she asked. "Aren't we going to this council you were telling me about?"

"Not just yet," he replied. "First you must have some rest and food, I think. You are very pale, as though you might swoon at any moment."

Jean realized that she had forgotten to eat any breakfast

that morning. "But I want to know what's happening," she protested, looking back over her shoulder.

"It will take some time for the council to begin. There are a few formalities that must take place first. I will send for you when it is time, I promise. Aoife, Sinead—" He beckoned to a couple of Queen Rhiannon's handmaidens.

Jean followed the two young women up a steep stone stair and along seemingly endless corridors with large rooms opening out of them. People were hastening to and fro, mostly young pageboys and servants. A castle, she realized, was not so much a large house as it was a small, compact city. There were hundreds of residents, hundreds of rooms and passages and stables and storage places. The chamber she was finally brought to was simply furnished with a few large chests, fur rugs on the floor, a sort of low couch covered in embroidered cushions, and a bed with tall bedposts of dark carved wood. Its one window was set deep into the thick stone wall and had a cushioned wooden seat. The small leaded panes were of thick, ripply glass, but she could tell that they looked onto the outer ward and curtain walls. Here Jean was made to sit and rest while food was brought to her: bread and cheese and some kind of smoked fish on a wooden platter, and a metal cup filled with white wine. The wine made Jean's head swim a bit, but also took the shivers out of her and loosened her tongue. Soon she and the court ladies were talking and commiserating and even crying together, like old friends. They cast some odd looks at her clothes, however, and it occurred to Jean how peculiar these must look: the short-sleeved tailored blouse; the heavy sensible shoes; the skirt falling to just below the knee, in order to conserve fabric for the war effort. She let herself be persuaded into donning a gown from one of the oak chests: a lovely thing of soft sky blue material, with a floor-length hem and long dangling sleeves. The sort of gown she had once dreamed of wearing, straight from the days of Camelot . . . As she was walking to and fro, getting the feel of it, she saw Sinead and Aoife both turn towards the door and curtsey deeply, and she turned, too, to see Queen Rhiannon standing there. Jean quickly made an awkward, lopsided curtsey: she was hampered by the long skirts, and still feeling slightly tipsy.

"You poor child," the queen said, going to Jean and taking her hands, "Lailoken has told me all. I am so sorry to hear of your troubles."

"Thank you," said Jean, then quickly added, "Your Majesty." It was so hard to think of this plump, smiling, unaffected little woman as a queen. "And I'm so sorry to hear about Princess—I mean, Queen Gwenlian's father."

"Ah, yes. Poor Arawn." The queen shook her head sadly. "It was not unexpected. He was in poor health, and he had never ceased to mourn for his wife, Queen Angharad, though she died many years ago. It was not love from the first moment for them, as it was for Diarmait and Gwenlian, but they grew fond of one another over time. I like to think they are together again, in a place where no trouble can touch them."

"It's lucky that Gwenlian and Diarmait love each other so much, isn't it?" Jean remarked. "Because I guess they *had* to marry."

"Had to? No, indeed." The queen smiled. "They pleaded hard to be allowed to wed, and it was only with reluctance that their fathers consented. For each is sole heir of a great royal house of Avalon, and should any ill befall them or their heirs, then both those lines will perish.

"As Lailoken may have told you, my people and Gwenlian's are descended from Prince Madoc of Cymru, who came here with his followers long ago. Their children's children clashed with Ciaran's people, the Gaels, in ancient times, but they made their peace afterwards. It was then that this isle—*Emain Ablach* to the Gaels, *Ynys Afallon* to us Cymri—was made one realm, to be ruled by a High King or Queen chosen by the nobles from one of the royal lines. Dalriada, to the south of here, was also once a kingdom in its own right, but that royal line has died out."

"What about Queen Morgana?" asked Jean, remembering what the Druid had told her.

Rhiannon frowned. "That sorceress! She is no queen, though she may call herself that. She was never crowned at the Lia Fail, and she is no king's daughter. Her father was a Druid who claimed descent from King Arthur's half-sister Morgan le Fay, but there is no proof of that. Still she has come to our royal council, as though she has a right!"

"She's here?"

There was a knock at the door and a pageboy looked in. "Please, Your Majesty, Lailoken the Druid says that the council is set to begin."

"We are coming," Rhiannon replied. "Do you still wish to join us, Jean? Would you not prefer to rest?"

"No, thank you, Your Majesty," Jean answered. "If something awful is happening here I'd rather know about it." It would be better to be with lots of other people, than stay here and be all alone with her thoughts. At home she could only bear listening to the war reports on the radio if the rest of her family were there with her. Fear could be borne in company.

She followed the queen and handmaidens back along the stone corridors and down the great staircase. As they passed the open doors of a chapel Jean saw a woman in white nun's veil and robe coming out. It was the abbess. Jean saw that the glow of healthy colour had gone from the soft rounded face, and there seemed to be more lines about the woman's mouth and eyes than she remembered. "Abbess Brigid?" she called.

The abbess turned and smiled, the brightness coming back into her blue eyes. "Why—it is Jean MacDougall! You have come back to us again. I heard that you paid another visit—here, was it not, at the feast of Christmas?"

Jean nodded, and motioned to the queen and her ladies to go on without her. "Are your monks and nuns all safe, Reverend Mother—and the people who lived by the abbey?" she asked.

"All safe," the abbess replied. "But we had to flee our homes, and seek refuge here in Temair. Our abbey was too close to the sea, and the Lochlannach might come again. We must live on charity now, until we can build a new abbey for our community."

"I'm sorry."

"Ah, well," the older woman waved her hand in a gesture of resignation, "these are difficult times. Perhaps another community can use the buildings that we left, in years to come. And many of our tenants have vowed to return to their village one day. But I would gladly know how it is with you, and your world. Will you be attending the council?"

Jean nodded again, and looked into the chapel's interior as she passed its door. She paused. A large brightly coloured fresco on its plaster walls and ceiling showed a scene of armed angels fighting hideous, demonic creatures. Over the plain stone altar and cross swooped one large painted figure, clad in a gold Roman-style breastplate and tunic and carrying a sword.

"There's Saint Michael again," said Jean. Abbess Brigid nodded.

"Yes—this, too, is one of his holy shrines. Saint Michael, the defender of Heaven, is the patron saint of high places, of hills and mountains. Long ago, before our abbey was built, there was a little shrine to him on the hilltop where the fortification is now. He is also the patron of the healing arts, and of reconciliation." She gestured to the mural covering the ceiling and walls. "Here you see the War of Heaven: Michael and his angels repulsing the assault of the army of Satan."

"That's when the fairies are supposed to have been sent to earth, isn't it?"

"Yes—and so Michael is patron saint of the fairies as well. But the great War is not over. It has never really ended, but continues to this day, the struggle between dark and light, evil and good. Our little human wars are but minor skirmishes by comparison—part of an older and greater conflict. 'For we wrestle not against flesh and blood,'" she quoted, "'but against principalities, against powers, against the rulers of the darkness of this world, against spiritual wickedness in high places.' These great powers are often involved in the strife of earthly nations. The scriptures tell us that Michael intervened with the angel-prince of Babylon, when his kingdom enslaved the Israelites."

"The Israelites?" said Jean. "Do you know, there are terrible things happening to the Jews in Europe—in my world. They're being murdered, persecuted, by the Nazis. Thousands and thousands of them—"

The abbess's face turned an ashen colour, and for a moment Jean feared she was going to faint. "It is worse than I thought, then," she murmured, bowing her head. "He always takes their part. When those the Archangel loves are made to suffer, it is a sign that he is losing ground."

"But—he can't lose!" Jean wondered, even as she spoke, whether her words were to comfort Brigid or herself. She pointed to the winged figure, with its golden armour and sword. "He's an *angel*. A—a great power, you said."

"So are those who fight against him. And their human servants are many, and strong—particularly in your world, I think." She straightened up, with a visible effort, and held out her hand. "But we shall be late for the council. Let us go."

Together they walked on, and came to the vast throne room where the Christmas revels had been held. It was filled now with chairs, three rows on each side facing each other, and Gwenlian and Diarmait were seated on the dais with the older king and queen. But now it was the two young people who had the largest thrones. With the death of Gwenlian's father they were now High King and Queen of all Avalon. Lailoken, who was seated close to the dais, motioned to Jean and Abbess Brigid to join him.

"Let the prisoner enter, and the priestesses also," commanded Ciaran.

Everyone turned to look at the entrance. A pair of armoured guards entered, leading Jarl Ulf in chains. They brought him up the aisle between the chairs, and forced him to stand before the dais. He looked a strange, uncouth figure in contrast to this elegant company, with his chain mail and rank furs, his matted hair tumbling about his shoulders. But he held his head high, meeting the eyes of the seated kings and queens with a stare as bold as a beast's.

Jean was so intent on the Lochlannach leader that she did not hear or see the next group of people enter. When she glanced towards the doorway again she gave a violent start. A row of silent and motionless figures stood in front of it: they must have walked in very swiftly and quietly, but to Jean it was as if they had appeared out of nowhere. There were nine of them altogether. All were clad in long black robes, with veils of some heavy black material that covered the upper halves of their faces. They appeared to be women, all smooth-featured and beardless, though the one who stood in the centre of the row was as tall as any man.

Other people had seen the still black forms now, and an uneasy whispering went through the assembly; but the kings and queens upon the dais said nothing, and gave no sign of having noticed them.

"Lochlannach," said Ciaran sternly, bending forward to fix the warrior with a steady gaze, "I want you to tell everyone here what you told me in your cell, two days ago."

"As you wish," replied Ulf in English. His tone was deliberately insolent, and his chest swelled out haughtily as he half-turned and spoke to the assembly. "My forefathers came from the island of Greenland, many ages ago—"

"I know of no island by that name," interrupted one of the nobles.

"It does not lie in the world that you know," Lailoken told him. "It is a land of the Shadow-realm." A murmur went up from the court.

"Continue, Ulf," ordered Ciaran.

"As the Northmen sailed, their longship passed through an unseen gate and entered into this world. They landed in Vinland, that you call Tir Tairngiri: but the Skraelings and Unipeds who dwelt there repulsed all the Northmen's efforts to settle the land. They returned again through the gate, never knowing that they had journeyed to another world, and went back to Greenland with their story. No one who heard the saga wished to make the westward voyage again.

"But many years later sickness came to Greenland, and at that time certain of my ancestors turned from the Christian god and prayed to their forefathers' ancient gods. The greatest of these, the All-father, allowed their ships to come again to the world of Annwn, and this time the Northmen struck a cunning bargain with the Unipeds. They would not attempt to settle in Vinland, but would take instead this smaller island of Irland Mikla, that you name Avalon. And the Unipeds in return promised to make no move against our people."

There was a brief silence after he had concluded. "So these Lochlannach are not of our world at all, but belong to the Shadow," said another of the seated nobles at last.

"All our ancestors came from thence in the beginning," said Lailoken. "Gael, Cymri, Lochlannach, and all who followed after. Annwn is the fairy world: we mortals have strayed into it over the ages, drawn to the higher plane of which it is a part."

"It is said that there is a young maiden here who has come to us from the Shadow," the first noble remarked.

"Aye, there is: this maiden, Jean MacDougall," Ciaran said.

To Jean's horror everyone turned towards her, and she had to stand up and be stared at and asked countless questions. They made her tell them all about her own world, and the war that was being waged there.

"Can this be true? Men warring in the sky like angels, and sending down fire upon the earth?" one man exclaimed. "Ships that move unseen beneath the waves?"

"All true," the Druid said. "But in many ways her world is very like our own, with only small differences. Our Avalon and Tir Tairngiri are to her one island, New Found Land. Her Éire is Ireland; her Cymru, Wales; Kernow she calls Cornwall, and Logres, England. The Shadow-lands are similar to the countries that we know. The chief difference is that there is no sorcery there, and the beings we call fairies are unknown to them save in legend. The Shadow bars all but the weakest magics from its realm. That is why the rebel angels who became the devils were cast down into that place: it puts limits on their power."

"Devils or no, it must be a blessed realm if its people are free of sorcery and fairy magic," said Queen Rhiannon.

"But there are other terrors in that place, as Jean has told you," said Gwenlian. "Mortal foes who are far worse than the Lochlannach. The dark angels may not be able to work strong magic in the Shadow, but all the same I think they have not been idle."

"But Lailoken tells us it is not only the sea raiders who threaten Annwn," the first noble said.

All eyes turned to the Druid, who looked grave. "That is so. The Lochlannach are but the vanguard of a greater and older power. Somehow, they have awakened that power, and are now controlled by it and are a part of its designs."

"What is this 'power' of which you speak?" an old thane asked.

"I speak of Woden, god of the Northmen," Lailoken answered. "The one-eyed warrior, leader of the Wild Hunt, whom you call the Gallows Lord."

There was a silence, followed by another uneasy murmur. "But Woden is only a tale to frighten children with," said the grizzled old thane.

"If only it were so."

The old man stood and pointed with a gnarled hand. "The abbess, there, will correct you. Druids may believe in such things, but she is a good Christian, and will tell you that there are no gods but the One."

The abbess rose. "That is true, my lord; but I also believe there are many unseen beings that share this world with us. Fairies, neutral angels, and those whom the pagan folk call gods: the names we mortals give them are legion, but their nature is the same. I have studied the treatises of many learned theologians on the subject of the *cacodemones* who dwell in the sublunary realm, below Heaven but above the abyss of Hell. They are immortal spirits, older and mightier than we, and many of them wish us ill. Lailoken knows this. He is the offspring of one such spirit, an incubus who sought through him to rule all mankind."

Lailoken concurred. "It is as the abbess says. These beings are all around us, but work their will chiefly through human servants. The ancestors of the Lochlannach called on the spirit we know as Woden, and woke his power."

"So I said," Jarl Ulf broke in. "They called on the great god, Odin All-father, to deliver them. It was he who opened the world-gate, and it is he who will deliver your island into our hands. For we desire living space, and we shall have it."

"But Woden is not a god of loving kindness. What is his price for delivering our island to you, and do you believe he can be trusted to keep any bargain? Your own bards call him the Trickster, the Shifty-Eyed One."

"He has promised," said Ulf, "that those of us who fall in the battle for Irland Mikla shall become *Einherjar*."

The face of the Druid grew very still; then slowly he nodded, as if at the confirmation of a suspicion long held. "Of course," he said softly. "The Glorious Dead."

"What do you mean, Lailoken?" asked Queen Rhiannon, looking at him worriedly.

"The Einherjar are the shades of dead warriors, Majesty, who go to serve Woden in Valhalla, the Hall of the Slain," he told her. But his face looked pale and drawn, and Jean had an uneasy feeling that he had not told the worst of what he knew. He turned back to Jarl Ulf. "Do you covet that fate, Wolf?"

"Not all of us will die," said the jarl with an ugly smile.

Lailoken nodded again. "And for those who do not, there will be Irland Mikla."

"Barbarian! You shall not have our island," cried Gwenlian hotly.

"*Your* island! Fools!" called a voice at the back of the room before Jarl Ulf could respond.

Everyone in the room turned sharply. One of the black-robed women had spoken. As they stared, she tore the thick veil away from her head to expose her face. She was a mere girl, perhaps a little older than Jean, with unkempt and lustreless hair the colour of straw. Her face was thin and her nose and chin sharp: there was a sharpness, too, in her grey eyes as she confronted the assembly. "Avalon belongs to none of your peoples!" the girl declared. "By rights it is we, the priestesses of Dana, who should rule here. My queen is the heiress of Morgan le Fay, who reigned here with her fellow-priestesses long before your sailor-monks and Cymri princes ever reached its shores. Magic ran strong in this land when Morgan ruled it, but you have turned from the old gods, and this is the consequence—"

"Peace, Grainne," said a clear strong voice behind her.

The robed girl fell sullenly silent as the tallest of the black-clad figures drew back its veil. Jean gasped. This woman was beautiful—a more perfect symmetry of feature she had never seen; but her skin was very pale, so pale that it was hard to believe any blood ran beneath it. It made an eerie contrast with the woman's long, coal black hair. And the dark-lashed eyes she turned upon the assembly were green—not like Jean's own eyes, but as vividly green as a cat's. *Who is she?* Jean wondered in awe. This was clearly no ordinary woman.

"I am Morgana," the woman said, as if answering Jean's unspoken question. "And Grainne speaks true. Had you not turned from the old ways, you would know that you have in this place two of Avalon's oldest and most powerful treasures: the Lia Fail and the Sword of Nuada."

"But we do know it, Priestess," returned Diarmait. "Only today we made use of the Stone for our crowning, and heard it speak to us. And the Sword my father keeps in a safe place in the *dún*."

"Aye—both in the same city," said Morgana coldly, "so that if it is taken by the enemy, both are lost. And the other two treasures, the Spear of Lugh and the Graal—"

"Graal?" Jean exclaimed. "You don't mean the Grail? The *Holy* Grail?" A picture from her King Arthur book floated before her eyes: a jewelled chalice on an altar, kneeling knights, angels hovering like doves . . .

Morgana ignored her outburst. "You do not seek after them—even though the Spear has the power to grant victory in battle to its wielder."

Lailoken spoke in his deep calm voice. "The Spear is a perilous weapon. It is true that it can magically turn the tide of any battle in favour of its wielder. But only, mark you, of its wielder. Once you have cast a spear forth in battle you are its wielder no longer, and any foe who takes it up can use it against you."

"But ought we not to seek after it, if it is so powerful?" Diarmait asked. He looked at his father, but Ciaran shook his grey head.

"Son, you are now *ard-righ*, High King of Avalon. It is for you to say what shall be done, not I."

Diarmait swallowed and gripped the armrests of his throne. To Jean he looked very young in that moment. "But I would still be glad of your guidance, my father."

"And I, too," said Queen Gwenlian.

"I think there is much in what the Priestess of Dana says," Ciaran said reluctantly. "To have two such powerful talismans in one place is tempting to our enemies. It would be better if they lay farther apart, thus forcing the enemy to divide his strength in the attack, and leave us some hope should one be taken. The Stone cannot be moved—at least, not without great difficulty—"

"Let the Sword go south then," said Gwenlian, "to my castle of Caer Wydyr in Gwynedd. It is a strong and defensible place."

"Its defences may work against men," Morgana said. "But your worst foe cannot be held back by mere walls. The Gallows Lord rides the sky at the head of the Wild Hunt, and battlements are naught to him. You will need potent magic to aid you. This Druid—as he calls himself—can use his arts to protect one fortress. But what of the other? Give me the Sword of Nuada, that I may keep it safe; or else send Lailoken south with it, and I will watch over the Lia Fail and cast spells of protection on it."

There was a long pause following this speech, followed by much whispering among the nobles. It was very evident that none of them liked or trusted the dark-clad priestess. Gwenlian and Diarmait conferred together quietly, then Diarmait rose from his throne.

"The queen and I go south to Caer Wydyr," he announced in a clear, carrying voice, "with the Sword. Lailoken shall remain here to guard the Lia Fail. If the Priestess of Dana wishes to accompany us, she may do so. But we shall not delay: we leave tomorrow morning."

Jean saw a look of fierce anger pass swiftly over the high priestess's white face. Then an icy calm replaced it, and Morgana turned without ceremony and strode from the room. The eight black-robed women filed silently after her.

Chapter Nine

JEAN SPENT A MISERABLE NIGHT, tossing and turning restlessly as sleep eluded her. Her bed was stiff and hard, the chamber cool despite the banked fire glowing on its stone hearth, and her mind was in turmoil. What must her poor parents be thinking at this second, even more alarming disappearance? They were already worried enough over Andy. Perhaps they would think she had run away. They had certainly enlisted the help of the police by now. If only she could send a message to them somehow, reassure them! But she could not, any more than she could leave Annwn just by wishing to do so. The mysterious power that governed her exits and entrances had chosen not to release her yet.

Opening her purse at bedtime to look for a handkerchief, she had discovered her little navy-covered journal. She had taken it with her the last time she went out shopping, she now remembered, not wanting Fiona to find it and read some very private things written in it; she had later forgotten to put it back in its hiding place in her room. Opening it to the last entry, she had sat staring dully at the scribbled words. "Jim's going to be at the dance!!! I can't believe my luck. He's going to be there & see me in my new dress. Will he like it? Will he dance with me?! I can't wait to see the words that will fill the blank pages after this one!! What will they say?"

Another girl had written that, ages and ages ago. Jean no longer felt any connection with her.

She managed to sleep a little towards dawn, dozing off from sheer exhaustion. A little after daybreak she was awakened by a page, who knocked at her door and told her that the morning meal was ready. She dressed, putting on her own clothes for their safe and comforting feel, then went to the window. The leaded panes opened outward, she found, and she gazed down on a scene of almost frenzied activity. The whole outer ward of the castle was full of people, rushing to and fro: little pageboys, servants, courtiers, and—this gave her a thrill despite her worn and ragged nerves—knights in full armour, with knee-length surcoats over coats of glinting chain mail. The surcoats were white, emblazoned with a red cross like Saint George's. A little farther away two large brown horses were being hitched up to a primitive-looking coach bearing the painted crest of Gwenlian's house, a red Welsh dragon on a white shield. More horses were being led out from the stables beyond. All was bustle and haste, and raised voices shouting for this or that.

When she came down to the banquet hall, she found it full of men and women queuing up for food. King Diarmait was there, talking with his father.

"I only hope I have made the right decision," she heard the young man say as she entered.

"Sometimes there *is* no 'right' decision, my son, merely a decision that must be made," his father replied. "Kings learn that very early in their reigns."

Diarmait still looked troubled. "I know that my wife and I should not risk our lives together. But Gwenlian wishes to be with her people, in Avalon's capital. They will want her to be there, now that Arawn is no more and she is High Queen. And I cannot live apart from her, Father."

The older man shook his grizzled head. "You two are the hope of Avalon—you, and your heirs. There are many dangers on the way to Caer Wydyr, of which the Lochlannach are merely one. There will be wild beasts, highwaymen, even fairies may be encountered on the roads you will be taking."

"I know, Father—but if Gwenlian and I are not with one another, how then can there be any heirs?" Diarmait grinned.

Ciaran returned his son's smile, and clapped him on the shoulder. "Go safely, then! Heaven knows you *should* be safe enough—with my soldiers to guard you, and the Knights of Saint George as well. I am a doting old dotard, and in matters concerning my son and heir I worry overmuch. But I would that this priestess, this witch-queen, were not going with you."

"I too, Father—but what would you? I dare not leave Morgana here in command of the Lia Fail—the crowning stone of the monarchs. What if she were to cast some spell upon it that would allow no one else to come near it, ever again? The Sword she will not dare to seize from us. It was given to our house by the Daoine Sidhe themselves, and to steal it would likely bring ill luck upon her. And even if she *were* to snatch it from me, well—it is but a weapon, after all. But you have told me many a time that the Singing Stone is the heart and soul of our realm."

"That is true, my son. But this Lochlannach scoundrel, now: need you take *him* as well?"

"We may need Jarl Ulf to act as interpreter, should any of his people be captured in Gwynedd. No one at Caer Wydyr will be able to understand their tongue, as Lailoken can."

"And you think Ulf would be a truthful translator? Diarmait, be cautious! I have learned over time to take a man's measure very quickly. That one is full of cunning and deceit."

"I will be careful, Father. You have my word."

Both men turned as a large oaken chest, richly carved and almost as long as a man is tall, was brought into the hall by four servants. There was a silence as King Ciaran opened it, and its contents were revealed. There on a scarlet cushion lay a long, slender-bladed sword of polished blue-grey steel, its hilt adorned with fine traceries of silver.

"*Fragarach*, the Answerer," said Ciaran, removing the weapon from the chest. "The Sword of Nuada. From generation to generation it has been passed down, ever since the fairies first placed it in the hands of the first king of Temair." He hefted it. "My great-grandsire adorned the hilt with silver and gems after winning a battle. But though I dreamed of taking it up against some foe when I was a youth, I have never had occasion to wield it. Take it, Diarmait, and guard it well."

Once Diarmait, with a solemn face, had received the Sword from his father, Jean stepped forward. "Please," she began.

Ciaran turned. "What is it, child?"

Jean licked her lips, which had gone dry. "If you don't mind—I'd like to go with King Diarmait and Queen Gwenlian. Through those places where the fairies are."

He looked surprised. "Go on the journey? But why? Have you not said that your home is in the city that mirrors Temair in the Shadow-realm? You would be going very far from your own place."

"I know, Your Majesty, but I'm very worried. I still haven't been sent home, and my family must be afraid something awful has happened to me. I want to ask the fairies to use their magic and send me back. After all, if they'd give your family an enchanted sword they must be helpful and good. Perhaps they might even help to save my world."

"It is doubtful that they will. The Daoine Sidhe confer favours when they see fit, not for our asking. But if Diarmait and Gwenlian give their consent, then you may go with them."

"Have you spoken with the Druid on this matter, Jean?" Diarmait asked.

"Not yet, Your Majesty. I just thought of it now, when I heard you both talking about the fairies."

"Lailoken is in the throne room if you would speak with him," Diarmait told her.

Jean obediently headed down the passageway to the larger hall. But at the sound of a voice coming from behind its closed doors she halted. It was the woman Morgana, and she sounded angry.

"Why will you not help me? You and I were born to be the rulers of this world. We are not as common mortals, but are descended from the Sidhe themselves! A great spirit was your sire, a prince of the power of the air. And yet you bow and scrape before those who are not worthy to kiss your sandal! Why do you not sit on that royal throne yourself? It is yours for the taking, Druid."

Jean stood transfixed, her heart in her mouth.

"I have no wish to rule this world," Lailoken's patient voice answered, "or any other."

"Because that old priest who raised you made you into a weakling like himself, and filled your head with his folly." Morgana's voice was scornful.

"Not so," said Lailoken mildly. "I was, on the contrary, the most heedless and rebellious of youths. My guardian's kind words and lessons were wasted on me. He was more than half a Druid, as so many priests of Cymru and Éire were in those days, and unlike a Druid he wrote down all his knowledge in books. Many times did he seek to teach me the wisdom of weather and healing herbs, of stars and spirits and portents. But I would have none of it. I was impatient to go out into the world and leave his quiet woodland cell behind.

"In those days a war raged in Cymru, a petty quarrel between two tribal chieftains, and I was fired with the desire to see battle. I offered my services to one of the warring kings—not out of sympathy for his cause, but rather from youthful passion for adventure. I was given sword and shield and a little training, and when the day of battle came I joined willingly in the fray." There was a long pause. Jean dared not move. If her footsteps were heard by Morgana, the priestess would know that her treacherous words had been overheard.

"Of that battle I will say nothing," said Lailoken at last, "save that it was like all battles since the world began; and when it was over, and blood pooled like rain where men and horses lay slaughtered, and gore crows gathered on them thick as flies, I was left wounded and dazed. I wandered into the woods, vowing that if all men were like this I would live among them no more. Tales are still told in Cymru of the madman who lived as a beast in the wilderness, and rode on stags and had wolves for friends. Those tales are true, by the way: for wolves are not so fierce as men believe. It is a great flattery to the Lochlannach to compare them to such wise and gentle beasts."

"If there is a point to this tale, I would gladly hear it." Morgana sounded impatient and irritable.

"It is this: that with my horror and hatred of what I had seen, I might then have used my powers to enslave mankind and bend it to my will. But one day I chanced to hear a lone minstrel playing on a harp in a woodland glade, and it soothed me, and I came to my senses. If men could make such wondrous sounds, I reasoned, work such beauty with their hands and minds, then they were not wholly evil after all. It was then that I returned to my old guardian's cell, and read his books of knowledge."

"Then you were a fool," said the priestess disdainfully. Jean backed away quickly as the doors opened and Morgana came striding out. The girl need not have worried: the priestess paid her no more heed than if she had been an ant, but swept past her without a single glance. Relieved, Jean went into the throne room. Lailoken was standing there alone, looking tired and old: the lines on his face seemed more deeply graven than before.

"Lailoken!" she exclaimed, running up to him. "I overheard

what that woman was saying to you. Shouldn't the kings and queens be warned about her?"

"I will tell them, certainly," he answered, and there was a hint of weariness in his voice. "But I will be telling them nothing that they do not already know. Morgana is a powerful enchantress, and would long ago have used her sorcery to drive all the Gaels and Cymri out of Avalon had I not opposed her. It is true that her ancestress, Morgan le Fay, came to this island long before they did, and she views it as hers by right. She despises the Avalonians as weaklings and traitors, who turned from their old religions to follow the New Faith. Naturally it would solve her predicament to forge an alliance with me. But she must be desperate indeed to make the attempt."

Jean recalled the white angry face of the priestess. "She frightens me, Lailoken."

"She is dangerous, yes. But she is to be pitied too. Her mother was a lady of the Sidhe—a fairy—who loved Morgana's mortal father and then abandoned him and their child. Morgana grew to womanhood knowing that she was different, that her inborn fairy powers set her apart from all other mortals—even her own father. For years, they say, she searched Avalon for her mother, without success. She must yearn constantly for the company of others like herself, and there are none to be found in all the land."

"Except for you."

He nodded. "Except for me—and I am the sworn protector of the rulers she hates."

They were both silent for a while. Then Jean told him of her plan. "I suppose you'll say what the others have," she said. "That the fairies won't help me return home."

He shook his white head. "I do not say that they will not—merely that it is not their way."

"I know they're not like the fairies in nursery tales, little winged people who grant wishes. But there *must* be some fairies who are good to mortals. What about the ones who gave King Diarmait's ancestors the Sword? And those fairy women who mourned for King Arawn?"

"They may have had reasons of their own for those actions, reasons we know nothing of. They have not intervened in any of our battles so far. There are fairies dwelling on the island of Hy-Bresail, so it is said. You may have seen it: the larger and more distant of the two isles off Temair's coast." She nodded. She had noticed them on her walk up the hill: two small islands that did not exist in her world. "The fairies of Hy-Bresail have done nothing to halt the attacks of the Lochlannach, though it would be well within their power. They stand aloof, observing but taking no part."

"But who is it who lets me come into your world?" Jean persisted. "Isn't it the fairies?"

"That I do not know. There are other powers in Annwn, higher powers of which we know very little. It may be fairies who open the doors between worlds for you—or something else. Some being, or beings, for reasons unknown to us."

"You think it's no use for me to go with the king and queen, then?" she asked, her hopes dwindling.

"Even I cannot foresee that, child. You must do as your heart tells you."

She looked up into his face. "Well, right now it's telling me that I want to try and find the fairies."

"This is not only for yourself, is it?" he asked softly. "You are thinking of the boy Jim, and your brother."

She glanced down at her feet again. "They went away to fight in the war," she said. "I'm a girl, so I can do nothing but stay home and help Mum."

"That is not nothing," he chided gently.

"I know, I know: 'keep the home fires burning'! King George said something about that at Christmas. But I worry and worry and worry," she said wildly, "all the time, and now that Jim and Andy are out there on the sea it'll be worse than ever. I can't stand it, I have to *do* something—anything! And there's nothing I can do at home, in my world. If I could just talk to the fairies—ask them if they're the ones who keep letting me into Annwn, and why. There may be something they want me to do here. And if so, I might be able to ask for a favour in return. I know they can't work their magic in the Shadow, but if they're immortal they must be incredibly wise. There might be something they could tell me that would help us win the war in my world." *And bring Jim and Andy home safe*, she added silently.

The Druid gazed down at her thoughtfully. "Go then," he said simply. "And may you find what you seek."

Those who were making the journey to Caer Wydyr had gathered in the outer ward of the fortress, in front of the gates of the *dún*. There was a company of twenty soldiers from the castle, and a dozen knights, two of the latter guarding Jarl Ulf, who sat astride a horse, his hands bound in front of him. Jean, now wearing a warm fur wrap over her light spring coat, walked towards the royal carriage. She wanted to be as close as possible to Gwenlian and Diarmait, wishing their courage could somehow rub off onto her. The young king and queen were bidding a cheerful farewell to a very worried-looking Queen Rhiannon, laughing and patting her hands reassuringly. If those two were ever afraid of anything, Jean thought, they would never show it.

"They're so brave," she sighed to Lailoken, who had followed her from the keep and was standing by her side.

"A little braver than they are wise, perhaps," said Lailoken with a sigh of his own. "They are both very young."

"They're older than I am."

"But yours is an old soul." He looked at her affectionately. "Older and wiser than your years. Since I cannot go with them, it lightens my heart to know that you will be there, Jean of the all-seeing eye."

"Then I'm doing the right thing by going?" she asked him anxiously.

He looked thoughtful. "Do you mean, is it the right thing for *you* to do? That you alone can say. It was your decision to make."

She felt suddenly reluctant to leave him. It was not merely his knowledge and the hint of power about him that made her feel safe, but his personality, the blend of strength and kindness she had always sensed in him. She said, "King Ciaran says sometimes there's no right decision—just a *decision*."

"He is wise too, in his way. Those words are true."

Several large, long-haired men rode past, singing loudly. They wore only the simplest armour, breastplates of stiff leather, and they reminded her of the Lochlannach with their shaggy beards and braided hair and rough voices.

"The *Fianna*," Lailoken told her, pronouncing it *Fee-na*. "They are warriors who follow the ways of the ancient fighting men of Éire. They rode here with Morgana and her priestesses, and some of them will be coming with you on the journey."

They must be an escort for the high priestess, Jean thought. But as the company mounted their horses and prepared to set out there was still no sign of Morgana.

"Is the priestess not coming after all?" Jean asked hopefully. One of the Fianna overheard her.

"The Queen and Priestess of Dana, travel with *us*?" The man laughed, and gave her a lofty look. "She is a great enchantress, and has no need to make long journeys over land like a common mortal. She takes the paths of the air, travelling unseen."

"Oh . . . but *you're* riding with us. Aren't you her guards?"

Again he laughed derisively, as though she had said something absurd. "We, guard Queen Morgana? She has no need of our protection or anyone else's. No, we merely help to guard the Sword of Nuada."

"That will not be necessary," said one of the knights, riding past on his big bay charger. His mail and gauntlets gleamed and his surcoat was dazzling white, as though it were newly washed. Jean recognized him as Sir Owen, the knight who had led Gwenlian's company through the forest. "The Knights of Saint George will see to its safety," he declared. "We have never failed in our duties."

The Fianna warrior only smiled contemptuously.

Abbess Brigid, who was standing calmly in the midst of the hasty activity, raised her wooden crozier and called a blessing on the departing company. "A safe journey to you all, and may God go with you!"

"Come, Jean." The young king and queen beckoned to her from the door of their carriage.

She turned to Lailoken. "I have to go now. I hope I'll see you again, some day." There was a lump in her throat as she spoke, and she held out her hand to him.

He took it in both of his, warming her cold fingers. "We will meet again."

As always, he made it sound like a certainty, and Jean was comforted.

When they were about halfway down the winding road a dense fog rolled towards them, billowing past them up the slope to surround the castle. Only the tops of its tallest towers were visible when Jean glanced back through the little window in the carriage door. A figure was standing atop the nearest of the outer towers: a tall robed form, recognizable even at this distance. Lailoken. Was it true that he commanded the elements? Was it he who had called up this unearthly mist?

When she suggested this to Queen Gwenlian she nodded, as though there were nothing extraordinary about it. "He is a great Druid," she said simply. "And he has sworn to protect the *dún* and the Stone." The mound with its tall monolith was already beginning to fade in the thick white fog. Jean felt a flickering instant of déjà vu; then she suddenly recognized this as the scene from her vision last summer. *Then—I must be doing what I'm meant to do!* she thought, reassured.

Once they had come to the bottom of the hill and left both it and the city behind, the fog ended like a wall; before them the road was bathed in sun and the sky was clear and blue. A black bird flew high overhead in the same direction in which they were heading: a large crow, or perhaps a raven, Jean wasn't sure which. For a while she thought it was keeping pace with them; but then it suddenly swung away across the sky and vanished to the west.

That first leg of the journey was quite pleasant. The carriage jolted and bounced over the uneven pavements, leading Diarmait and Gwenlian to discuss elaborate plans for the repaving of all the kingdom's main roads; and the air was rather cool. But the sun was bright, and they were greeted with joy and enthusiasm by the inhabitants of all the little crofts and villages along the way. Jean was reminded of riding to Mary's Bay in the Chrysler. But this was even more impressive, for Gwenlian and Diarmait were royalty, and in this medieval-style society kings and queens had an aura of grandeur that even her own world's monarchs no longer commanded. It must be a great relief to these people to know that Avalon had two new rulers, and life would carry on as before.

At noon Diarmait, who had been growing restless in the carriage, decided to ride along with the escort, and a spare horse was saddled for him, leaving Gwenlian and Jean alone together. The two girls whiled away the long hours of the journey with talk, each telling the other of her world, its history and customs and stories. Jean was fascinated that the old myths of King Arthur and Merlin the wizard (Myrddin, as Gwenlian called him) and the knights of the Round Table were known here as well. But of course, Lailoken had said there were many comings and goings between Annwn and the Shadow. It would be wonderful to see the other two treasures, especially the Holy Grail. Could it really *be* the same magic cup that had featured in the King Arthur stories?

She also told the queen about Jim, of her feelings for him and all that had happened. Gwenlian sympathized. "Ah, how hard it must be to be separated from your beloved! Diarmait and I could not bear to be parted. I hope that we are never, ever forced apart! And if we must die, I pray we die together."

Jean shivered a little. "Don't say that, Your Majesty! I'm sure it won't come to that."

"Please, Jehane, we are friends! Will you not call me by my name?"

"But—but you're royal," stammered Jean.

"What of it? I have royal blood in me; but truth to tell, Madoc my ancestor was not the legitimate son of King Owain Gwynedd. For that matter, your Jim may have a more kingly lineage than I. O'Connor is an ancient name among the Gaels. Those who bear it are said to be descended from the great kings of Connacht in the isle of Éire."

But Jean didn't care what sort of blood he had. Jim was Jim: that alone was reason to love him. She unburdened herself further to the young queen as the carriage rattled on. "I'm afraid it was all an adventure to Jim, going off to war—like a play or a movie, and that having a girl to say goodbye to was just part of it. Something he needed. And so he doesn't really love me, deep down."

"Is that your fear?" asked Gwenlian. "Oh, Jehane, I am sure it is not so. You say that your father and his are friends. Tell me, would a man make such a promise to the daughter of his father's dear friend, knowing that he might not keep it?"

"No," said Jean, a rush of happiness returning to her. "To another girl, he might, on an impulse—but not to a friend."

"You have his love then, and nothing can take that from you—not even death. It is true forever. Do not doubt him!"

"Oh, it's not really Jim I doubt. It's myself. You're lovely, Gwenlian, and you have a beautiful name. Boys just don't fall in love with girls like me." She grinned wryly.

"Ah, Jehane, why are you so hard on yourself?" sighed the queen.

They journeyed on, pausing only in mid-afternoon so that the horses could rest. Diarmait dismounted and joined the queen in a short walk to stretch their legs, while Jean sat down on a flat stone to write in her journal. When she looked up she found herself completely surrounded by handmaidens and knights, who were all staring in amazement at her fountain pen. One knight declared that it must be magical, since it never needed to be dipped in an inkwell. Her explanation about ink reservoirs only fascinated them further. They were filled with the greatest curiosity about her world, and she answered as many of their eager queries as she could. Her spirits lifted a little as she spoke. She even sang for them a marching song from the last war which her father had taught her. She could only remember one verse, but the men did not mind. *It's a Long Way to Tipperary* proved a great hit with them, and as the royal procession moved on they sang the one verse over and over again, seeming never to tire of it, though Jean was beginning to by the time they all halted for the night.

They made their camp on a barren, rocky plain with no sign of civilization apart from a few tiny hovels on the horizon. A large tent was taken from one of the supply carts and set up for the king and queen and handmaidens to sleep in: its sides were embroidered with the dragon emblem of Gwynedd, and rugs and cushions in rich warm colours gave its interior a luxurious look. Two guards were to sleep within it, before the door; the rest rolled themselves up in cloaks and blankets and slept on the bare ground.

"You must join us in the tent, Jehane," invited Gwenlian, to Jean's relief.

The men lit large bonfires to help keep themselves warm, and over these a supper was cooked in big pots like witches' cauldrons. When the meal was over the men sat around their fires singing—ballads and war songs, mostly, with the occasional snatch of *Tipperary*—and the king and queen and her handmaidens joined them for a little while. The Fianna kept to themselves, sitting by their own fire some distance away. When Jean and the others retired, Morgana's warriors were still sitting up, talking and singing together in the old Gaelic tongue.

That night Jean dreamed that a horde of hideous, black-clad women rode across the rocky barrens, mounted on the backs of giant wolves. One of the women gave a piercing cry as she rode past the tent, echoed by the howl of her terrifying mount. Jean woke with a start, feeling cramped and stiff and disoriented. *Had* there been an actual sound to wake her, or had it all been just a dream? All the others were sleeping peacefully under their furs. She threw off her own fur rug and peered out through the tent flap.

She saw only the prone bodies of sleeping men, knights

and soldiers, and two sentries keeping watch by a bonfire. The other fires had burned down to a bed of embers. Jean relaxed: had there been any actual sound they would have heard it, but they did not appear to be alarmed. But she still did not feel sleepy. The fresh air was welcome after the stuffy interior of the tent. As she walked towards the fire the two sentries turned sharply, then smiled when they saw her. She saw Jarl Ulf a few feet away, his legs and arms bound fast by cords. He was awake and sitting bolt upright, seeming to strain against his bonds as he stared out across the dark barrens. What was he doing—watching, listening for something? Suddenly she felt uneasy again.

She went up to the sentries. "Is everything all right?" she asked in a low voice.

"Naught is amiss, so far as we can see," one of them told her.

"You didn't—hear anything, just now?" They shook their heads. "Oh, well, it was only a bad dream then," said Jean uncertainly.

"Small wonder that you dream. This place creeps my flesh," complained the other sentry. He looked quite young, not much more than a boy. "These rocks, all around—I swear they seem to move at times."

"It is just the firelight playing upon them," the older man said.

Jarl Ulf turned his narrow black-maned face towards them, his eyes glittering with reflected flame. His bearded lips stretched into a sneer. "So, the king's bold warriors take fright at shadows? You had best return to your safe keep if your courage falters so easily! There is far worse that awaits you on this journey."

"I am no coward, Lochlannach scum!" retorted the young sentry. "Hold your foul tongue!"

"What is all this noise?" A few feet away Sir Owen sat up, and flung off the cloak he was using for a blanket. "All of you hold your tongues, and let a man get some rest!"

"Your pardon, Sir Knight," began the older sentry. "We meant no—"

"Hold!" cried the other, his body turning rigid. "I am *certain* I saw something that time. Look, over there—"

Sir Owen stared in the direction the boy was pointing, then he sprang to his feet. "Arms! To arms!" he roared. "We are surrounded!"

The men woke, grumbling or calling out in alarm. There was a frantic scramble for weapons and armour, but even as they mobilized themselves there came a chorus of yells from out of the night beyond. Out on the rocky barrens dark figures suddenly leaped into view, springing up from behind huge boulders and from hollows in the ground. Wild, savage figures, clad in rough furs and mail.

The next few moments—hours as they seemed to the terrified Jean—were a nightmarish confusion of shouts, screams, plunging shapes, fire-lit steel, blades clashing together. She ran for the royal carriage and leaped inside, slamming the wooden door after her. Through the tiny window she watched, biting her lip, as fighting men plunged in and out of the circle of firelight, grappling fiercely like partners in a wild and grotesque dance. One huge axe-wielding Lochlannach made for the royal tent, tearing his way through its cloth side with the heavy blade.

"No—no," Jean whispered through chattering teeth.

Then Diarmait came running out of the ruined tent, closely followed by Gwenlian. The queen was clutching a long dagger, and in the young king's hands was a sword. It was Fragarach. As he raised it a blaze of blue light sprang from its blade, bright as a thunderbolt.

Howling like frightened animals, the Northmen recoiled, shielding their eyes. Diarmait himself seemed stupefied. All along the blade of his weapon a blue fire ran, flowing and flickering, as though he clutched a burning brand: the young king's face, gaping in wonder, was lit up by its unearthly glow. Everywhere Jean looked there were blue-lit faces with expressions of amazement, bewilderment and awe.

Then there were loud howls of fear, as one after the other their attackers fled into the night. Any physical danger they could face, but not this unknown power in the young king's hands. When they were all gone, the sword's blue fire dwindled and died, leaving only the bonfire's embers to light the scene.

Diarmait, relieved, lowered the quiescent blade. "Is all well?" he called out hoarsely in the darkness. "Is anyone hurt, or slain?"

Voices answered him from all sides. There were some injuries, apparently, but everyone seemed to be accounted for.

"Jehane!" cried Gwenlian, a note of panic in her voice. "I cannot find her anywhere. Has anyone seen Jean MacDougall?"

"I'm here!" Jean called back, throwing the carriage door open. "I'm all right!"

"Ah, thank the Lord! I thought they had taken you," exclaimed the queen in relief, casting down her dagger and running to embrace Jean.

Then there was another cry in the night. "The prisoner!" yelled one of the soldiers.

They all turned, and saw in the firelight the torn ropes lying loose upon the ground. Jarl Ulf was nowhere to be seen.

Chapter Ten

"WELL, WE HAVE HAD A NEAR ESCAPE," observed Diarmait.

A wan grey day had broken over the barrens, and they could now more clearly see the aftermath of the battle. The torn tent still stood, listing to one side, and the ashes of the fire were strewn everywhere. Sir Owen was limping about the campsite, groaning. His left leg bore a great gash from knee to ankle, and he could not bear weight on it. Another knight had tried to bind it up. Furs and cloaks were scattered for a long distance beyond the campsite, and one rock was splashed with blood. If any of the enemy had fallen, the bodies had been taken away along with Jarl Ulf.

"No matter: we lost no one, and the Lochlannach did not capture us or the Sword," Gwenlian reminded him.

"Majesty, there is someone coming," warned a soldier, drawing his sword.

Across the grey barrens a tall dark figure could be seen, striding towards their camp with a swift confident gait. At first Jean thought it was a man; then as the figure drew nearer she recognized the pale face and billowing black hair. It was Morgana. The priestess wore a long black gown under a cloak completely covered in black feathers: neither garment bore any stains of travel, and there was no horse or carriage to be seen anywhere upon the plain. The Fianna all bowed deeply; the others simply gaped at her as she came up to them.

"Where did *you* come from, witch-queen?" snarled Sir Owen, turning on her a face twisted with pain, fear and fury.

"I have been riding the winds of the upper air," she answered calmly, "far ahead of you. I wondered why you took so long to set out this morning. I did not know that you had been waylaid."

"A pity. You might have helped us in the battle, with your black arts. Or was it you who set those vermin on us?" He sat down with a grunt on a boulder.

She ignored this, eyeing his bound leg. "I can heal that wound with those arts you despise," she declared, stooping to examine the bloodstained bandage.

"Get back!" He recoiled, casting a look of appeal at his young king. "Majesty, do not let this witch touch me!"

Morgana's face turned cold, and she straightened again. "As you please."

"Don't make her angry," Jean implored the king. "She'll turn against us!"

Diarmait nodded and spoke to Owen. "Let her help you. No protests, man: that is my command as your king." He turned back to Jean as Morgana undid Owen's dressing. "I hear that we have you to thank for our escape."

"All I did was hide in the carriage," replied Jean, embarrassed.

"But had you not awakened and alerted the others, we might all have been taken unawares. Most of us would still have been asleep when the Lochlannach came."

"And how did the enemy come so near?" Morgana demanded, taking some leaves from a small pouch and packing them into a new dressing.

The two sentries dropped their eyes. "We never saw them. Perhaps there was some witchery there," the youngest said.

"It could not have been carelessness on the part of the watchers, of course," said Morgana dryly, rising to her feet again. The boy's face flushed.

"It is fortunate that there were not many," the king said. "No more than a dozen, I would say. But they were confident of catching us sleeping."

"They will attack again, Sire," Sir Owen warned. "Depend upon it. Be careful, you son of a dog!" Jean jumped slightly before realizing that his words were directed at the soldier who was rebinding his wound. Hissing through his teeth with pain, he turned once more to the king. "And they will likely come in greater numbers next time."

Jean's heart sank. Another attack? Would they be assaulted every night on this lengthy journey? They would none of them be able to sleep a wink for fear, and sooner or later there would be lives lost.

"What are we to do, Sir Owen?" the young queen asked.

"There is naught that we can do," the rugged knight answered, standing on his injured leg and wincing. "We do not know how many of those devil's spawn are out there in the countryside. We must double our watch by night, and hope for the best. Unless Your Majesties wish to return to the safety of your *dún*?"

"We have already said why we cannot," replied Gwenlian. "The Sword and the Stone must be kept apart."

"Excuse me," said Jean. They all turned to her. "I think I know what the problem is," she began, stammering a little. "You see, we're travelling in such a big procession, like a parade almost. There are all these knights and soldiers, and a royal carriage and a royal tent. And everyone for miles around knows about it. We're awfully conspicuous, aren't we? The enemy can see us from a long way off, and hear about us from the villagers and learn where we're going."

"But we cannot travel any other way," Gwenlian said, frowning. "And we must have guards."

"The more guards there are, the more obvious it is that there's something important to guard," Jean explained. "What if you were to send most of these people back to the castle, with the royal carriage, so it'd look as though you'd given up? Then the rest of us could disguise ourselves with some old clothes, and stick the Sword in a hay wagon or something, and pass for peasants."

"There is something to what the maiden says," Sir Owen remarked.

"Could we get to Caer Wydyr by foot?" asked Diarmait.

"It need not be all the way to Caer Wydyr," said Owen. "Once we come to the western coast, it is but two days' march to the castle of Beaufort where my order is based. The Grand Master will give you shelter, Majesties, and a hundred knights to escort you the few remaining leagues to Caer Wydyr."

"Very well then," said Gwenlian. "Let us do as Jehane suggests."

Diarmait sent a soldier to the distant crofts with a handful of coins, and he returned an hour or so later with a rickety two-wheeled cart full of musty straw, a sturdy pony very like the ones Jean had often seen in the outports, and a heap of clothing, old and torn and stained. "Perhaps we should have bought a goat too," mused Gwenlian, "to walk behind the cart on a rope. It would have added to the look of the thing!" Her eyes shone as she spoke. She and Diarmait had recovered from their anger and shock at the enemy attack, and seemed to be looking on their new plan as a sort of adventure. They had quickly disappeared into their tent with some of the old rags, and returned a little while later dressed up in them. Diarmait wore a coarse brown tunic that was too large in the waist, belted with a length of rope, while the queen had donned a shapeless brown sack of a dress and had tied an old stained cloth over her hair. Both had shabby cloaks that further concealed their figures, and the weapons they were carrying. But there was still something wrong in their appearance, Jean thought as she watched Gwenlian walk towards them with her head held high and a pleased smile on her lips.

"You're still walking like a queen," Jean told her. At once Gwenlian let her shoulders slump and adopted a slow shambling gait. Diarmait followed her example. Sir Owen declared that their faces were perhaps too recognizable still, and they proceeded to smear their faces with dirt, laughing when they saw one another. Jean felt they were possibly enjoying themselves too much, and hoped they wouldn't overplay their roles.

Must I always play Mother? she wondered ruefully.

Jean threw on a long hooded cloak that covered her from head to foot. The knights and fighting men tried dressing up too, but with their great shoulders and bulging arm muscles they still looked too much like warriors. In the end the king and queen decided that only two men-at-arms would accompany them, one knight and one Fianna warrior. Sir Owen now vehemently insisted that his wound was only minor, and proved it by vigorously striding about the camp. He was chosen, and Morgana selected a Fianna named Dubthach. He was one of the quieter men among the warriors, a big dour-faced man with a crooked nose and masses of dark brown hair. Once Morgana had chosen him, she left the camp and proceeded to walk away across the barrens, heading towards the south-west. When Jean glanced after her a moment later, she had vanished.

The Sword was bundled up in some old rags, and the king slipped it under the straw in the cart.

"We really should put something else in there," remarked Jean. "People don't just cart straw around, do they?"

This proved to be something of a problem. It was too early in the season to be transporting vegetables or hay. "Firewood, perhaps?" suggested the queen.

Diarmait gestured to the stony barrens. "There is scarcely a stick to be seen."

"A sick person then," suggested Jean. "Sir Owen is hurt. We could say he was in an accident and we're taking him to the doctor."

They all looked at her as though she had committed a *faux pas*. "No knight will ride in a cart," Diarmait explained to her. "It would dishonour him utterly. Knights only travel on horseback."

"I will be the injured one, then," Gwenlian offered.

"What if Your Majesty was recognized? It is possible: we are not far from Gwynedd. I will ride in the cart," Owen said. But he wore the air of a martyr as he spoke.

Oh, for goodness' sake! thought Jean. "*I'll* do it!" she said. "I promise you, no one will look at me."

One of the queen's handmaidens now went into the tent and donned the queen's blue travelling dress and veil, while a young soldier put on the king's royal attire. Then the tent was folded up again and placed on a wagon, and the royal doubles got into the carriage. The little party that remained watched as the procession headed back down the road towards Temair, Jean feeling some serious misgivings now that her plan had been adopted. Then they set out in the opposite direction with the pony-cart. It had been decided that whenever they passed anyone on the road—even if it was only a humble farmer—Jean would lie down in the cart and do her best to look wan and weary. As the day wore on she found this less and less difficult to do.

"This sword is awfully hard and bumpy to lie on," she remarked, squirming around, "and I hope it doesn't decide to go all fiery again. All this straw would go up in an instant." It didn't smell very pleasant, and from the number of feathers scattered through it she suspected that chickens had been nesting there. As soon as the road was clear again she was actually glad to get out and walk.

But Diarmait and Gwenlian were quite untroubled by the hardships of a journey by foot. No doubt they had both led such sheltered lives that they were eager to escape into the outside world. Certainly Diarmait must have been raised on tales of daring deeds and heroes of ages past. It would be an important part of the training of any young prince. Their discomforts seemed a positive joy to them: the rougher the road, the plainer the fare, the happier they seemed. Indeed Jean felt obliged to remind them that real peasants would not look so cheerful. As the day wore on they grew a little quieter, but they still did not complain.

At noon they bought a frugal meal of warm beer, hard bread and rank-smelling goat's cheese from a lone farmer for a few coppers. As they were eating it by the side of the road some rough-looking men approached, their lean and tired horses bearing marks of ill use. Jean quickly hopped into the cart and lay flat. Sir Owen rose, his hand clenching and unclenching in the eagerness to get at his concealed sword.

"Highwaymen, I'll be bound," he hissed. The big Fianna warrior stood too.

The ruffians dismounted and looked them over, leering at the queen in her soiled rag coif. One grabbed her by the arm, grinning into her face; another started to rummage in the straw of the cart, looking for valuables.

"So what ails you, missy?" he sneered at Jean.

Jean thought frantically, trying to remember what illnesses were common in medieval societies. "The plague!" she burst out.

"Plague?" He stared, drew his hand back. The man

gripping Gwenlian's arm released his hold with an oath and took a step back.

Inspired, Jean sat up. "Oh, no: I shouldn't have said that! Don't tell anyone, will you? You see, it's very catching. No one will give any of us food, or let us near, if they know I've got the—"

But the men had already fled back to their horses. In a few minutes all that could be seen of them was a faint cloud of dust.

"Now by all that's holy," said Diarmait angrily, "we should have fought them!"

"Nay, Majesty," said Owen, though he too looked wistful. "There were too many of them for our three swords—and how if Fragarach had shown its fire, and the tale of it had spread? Your Majesties' safety must come first."

"All the same," vowed Gwenlian, rubbing her arm and gazing after the men with a hard look in her eyes, "we must see that their kind are dealt with in the future. I did not know that our people were subjected to such villainy while using the royal roads."

"Well done, Jean!" said the king, turning to the girl. "Once again we owe our escape to you. We shall see that all who come after us remember the courage and cunning of Jean MacDougall."

"You mean," said Gwenlian with a smile, "*Jehane* Mac-Dougall."

By day's end they had come to a settlement surrounded by a tall wooden stockade, like that of the Abbey of Saint Michael at Connemara Bay. There were armed men at the gate, heavy-set men with bows and full quivers who watched all the approaching traffic warily.

"I know this town," Owen declared. "It is called Merioneth: a small outpost, and a safe enough place to spend the night, I think."

"Merioneth is a Cymri name," commented Diarmait. "We are in the old kingdom of Gwynedd then?"

"On its border, Majesty. In a day or two we shall reach the west coast, and the fortress of the knights."

"Perhaps we should tell these men who we are," said Gwenlian as they drew closer to the armed guards. "Else they may not permit us to enter."

"And will you stop their tongues from wagging, my queen?" asked Sir Owen. "I am sorry, Your Majesties, but your lives may be in danger even here. We must be very cautious until we are come safely to Beaufort."

They went up to the gate. The king and queen, Sir Owen and Jean (who was once more reposing in the cart) went unchallenged by the guards, but the Fianna warrior Dubthach was told to halt. The larger of the two guards eyed him narrowly. "You—speak to me in English or in Cymraeg," he ordered.

The Fianna raised a bushy brow. "What would you have me say?" he retorted. "Well: that is English. The Cymri tongue I know not. Would you hear me speak in Gaelic?" He added several words Jean could not understand.

The man grunted. "These tongues you may have learned long before you came to our island, if you are a spy."

"You think I am one of the Lochlannach?"

"You have the look of the sea raiders about you," the other

replied, eyeing Dubthach's long curly hair and beard, his broken nose and the swordsman's muscles on his bare arms.

Dubthach raised his shaggy head proudly and looked the other man in the eye. "I am no spy. I am Dubthach son of Seanchan, of the Fianna."

"You are very far from home, Dubthach of the Fianna. And dressed as a pauper, and consorting with vagabonds." The guard gestured disparagingly at the king and queen, who had to look down to suppress their smiles. "That is odd behaviour for an honest warrior. And the Fianna have a bad name."

"Please, sir—he has been our friend," Gwenlian appealed to the guard, looking up at him in beguiling fashion from under her coif. "We have been twice waylaid upon the road, and each time he came to our aid unasked. Please let us all come into your town: we truly mean no harm."

Her sincerity and the beauty that even ground-in dirt could not hide appeared to sway the guard. "Enter, then—but not with your sword." He pointed to the scabbard that could be seen hanging below Dubthach's short cloak. "That you must leave outside. You may pick it up again when you leave."

Reluctantly the big man complied, though he looked as though he would rather engage the two guards at once with the weapon than lay it down at their feet. "And you"—the big guard added to Jean—"what is your ailment? Nothing of the sort that can be spread to others, I trust? If so—"

"Oh, no," said Jean quickly. "I've been sickly since—since I was a child, and I couldn't make the long journey on foot. That's all."

"You'll be heading to Saint Michael's Mount, then," said the guard.

Jean turned to the others, only to see them all looking as puzzled as she felt. But apparently it was just a comment, not a question; the guard waved them through impatiently, and turned to the next group of travellers.

Once through the gate they found themselves in a good-sized village, with rough dirt roads running between small wooden houses roofed with thatch. There was a little stone church, not much bigger than the largest of the houses, and a crude market full of flimsy stalls selling cheap goods, and one inn. The latter was dark and fusty inside, its common room smelling strongly of smoke and stale beer and un-washed bodies. A fire burned in the large smoke-blackened fireplace in the west wall, and the little narrow windows let in a few rays of fading sunlight. While Sir Owen and Dubthach attended to the stabling of the pony (and watched over the hidden Sword) the rest of them ordered a meal. The fare was coarse and plain, as might be expected: the menu consisted of a rather soggy version of fish-and-brewis and some roasted rabbits, or "coneys" as they called them here. Everyone here spoke English, to Jean's surprise: apparently it was a sort of lingua franca for Avalon, used by all its people so that neither Gaelic nor Cymraeg would be seen as being favoured. As she ate she listened with interest to the con-versations of the locals.

"They do say the sea raiders are striking farther inland now."

"Why don't the king and queen put a stop to it?"

"Them! What do they care, sitting all day in their safe castle?"

For a moment Jean was afraid Gwenlian or Diarmait

might say something in response to this last remark, but though both their faces reddened they went on silently picking at their food.

The innkeeper's wife was especially kind to Jean. She was a big, stout, red-cheeked woman with a mass of bushy red hair, and as she passed their table repeatedly while waiting on others she kept bringing tidbits and cups of goat's milk to Jean.

"I can spare a cup or two of milk, heaven knows!" she said in her big hearty voice when Jean thanked her. "Poor lamb, so you're not too strong, are you? I hear you were brought in lying on a cart. Pale as milk yourself, you are, and not much on your bones neither. Never mind, love, you'll likely bury us all. Though with the world in such a state, sometimes I think those that live on are the unlucky ones."

Some men a few tables over began waving their cups and tankards and bellowing, "Gwen—Gwennie!" She glared.

"Oh, be quiet, the lot of you! I'll be there in a moment!" she shouted, and turned back to Jean. "Never thought I'd live to see the day—sea raiders stealing and burning, aye, and killing too! Dozens of folk used to come through Merioneth on their way to Mount's Bay, but no more: they're all coming t'other way now. And there's some says they've heard the Wild Hunt galloping through the sky of nights, with all the hell-hounds baying and the devil himself leading the souls of the damned. But 'tis likely only wild geese flying north for the summer: make a fearful noise, they do. There, drink up your milk, love. I hope you're well again soon."

"I'm sure I will be." Jean felt rather guilty about lying to this good-hearted woman, and tried to assuage her conscience by eating and drinking everything she was given, though it all tasted quite vile to her. The innkeeper's wife went off to deal with the rowdy customers, and after some shouting and slamming down of ale tankards she returned, looking hot and somewhat flustered. "What was I saying?" she asked, pushing her tangled hair out of her eyes with a broad forearm. "Oh, yes, the good times. No, there aren't so many as goes to Saint Michael's Mount now."

"What *is* Saint Michael's Mount?" asked Jean, curious.

"You don't know? I thought for certain you'd be heading that way yourself, seeing as you're such a sickly thing," Gwen said, with more kindness than tact. "Well, don't you bother about it, then. It's better not to go any place too close by the sea these days. 'Tis an island in the bay just south of here, linked to the shore by a causeway you can take at low tide. There's an old monastery there, the Llanfihangel Monastery, set up by some good monks long ago. There's many says that those who are desperately ill may find a miracle cure there. I've never been there myself, but we've had many a pilgrim come through here, hoping to be healed of this or that. They've got a holy relic there, it seems, brought from the lands across the ocean. Some say it's a spear, but I don't see how that could be. No spear ever healed nobody, quite the opposite, you'd think—"

"A spear, did you say?" Diarmait looked up sharply from his plate of overdone rabbit.

"Ah, bless you, I've no time to tell of that now. Talk to old Evan there by the fireplace, he'll give you the whole story." And the woman Gwen bustled off, waving her plump arm in the direction of the fire. The three of them stared. An elderly man was sitting on a stool close to the fire, his gnarled hands folded on the head of an equally gnarled walking stick.

"What do you make of that?" Diarmait whispered to his wife, leaning across the table. "Could it be the Spear of Lugh, do you suppose? Have you ever heard of such a place?"

"There are so many shrines to Saint Michael in Avalon," said Gwenlian, shaking her head. "He is much loved by Gaels and Cymri both. I cannot remember them all. I think I have been told there was one on an island, but I recall no more than that."

"Then let us talk to the ancient storyteller, there, and see what he has to say," the king suggested.

The elderly man glanced up as Jean, Diarmait and Gwenlian approached. "Good sir," said Gwenlian, "we've been told that you know a tale of Saint Michael's Mount. A tale concerning a magical spear."

"May I fill up your cup, friend?" added her husband.

"Ah, that'd be kind of you, young man," the old man wheezed. The faded eyes in their deep sockets brightened as he held his tin cup out. They rested longest on Gwenlian. "So it's the old story of the monks and the madman you're wanting, is it? Thank you kindly—" as his refilled cup was pressed into his hand. Some of the other patrons sitting near the hearth grew quieter to listen: no doubt they had heard the tale many a time, but had no objection to hearing it again. This was probably the only form of entertainment available in lonely little outposts like Marioneth. As she watched them, Jean was reminded of her own family listening to a radio play.

"The story begins nigh on a thousand years ago," declared old Evan, indicating the great span of years with a sweep of his rheumatic hand. "That's when the first monks came here to Avalon, from the land of Logres across the sea. They were looking for a place to start a new monastery, they said, to house a holy relic they had brought with them; and they looked high and low for the right spot. Weren't so many people on the isle back then, I reckon. Hardly anyone in Gwynedd. Well, the monks asked the few fisher-folk and farmers that lived hereabouts, and they all said there was a lone hermit living on an island in the southern bay—a hermit who had the power to restore people to health. That must be a holy place if ever there was. So off they went, carrying with them their sacred relic, and they got a boat and rowed out to the island. And there they found the old healer-hermit, sitting alone in his cave. He told them they might build their monastery there, so long as they took a vow always to shelter and succour the sick. They promised, and suddenly his face changed: it grew younger and beardless, like a lad's, and it shone like the sun so they couldn't look at it and turned away, dazzled. When they dared to look at him again, the man had vanished. But it was no man. It was the Archangel Michael himself! And so they named the island after him, and at the Llanfihangel Monastery they treat the ill and the lame to this very day."

"And what was this holy relic of theirs?" Diarmait asked.

"Ah, well may you ask! A most wonderful magical spear it was, with the power to heal anyone who touches it. It was first seen in the land of Logres two thousand years ago, they say, when it belonged to a wandering madman named Longinus.

He claimed to be a centurion of old Rome, a man escaped from the Shadow-realm. Wherever he went he took the spear with him, and he ranted about it to anyone who would listen, speaking of it now as a thing accursed, now as the holiest of relics. Finally he became a hermit, and kept the spear with him in his cell, and there he ended his days. Later some monks found the weapon and took it to their monastery, and there it stayed for hundreds of years—until one abbot had a vision in his sleep, telling him to take the spear west, to the sacred isle of Avalon. For they do say that the spear is the same, the very same . . ." Here he paused for effect.

"Yes?" three voices said breathlessly. The locals leaned closer.

"The very same spear," declared Evan, raising one quivering finger, "that the centurion Longinus used two thousand years ago, to pierce our Lord's side when He hung upon the Cross!"

There was a deep satisfied sigh from all the listening locals, but the hearts of the three visitors sank in disappointment.

"So it is not what we thought," said Diarmait sadly as they stood in the stable-yard afterwards, waiting for Owen and Dubthach to have their meal. "Not the Spear of Lugh, after all."

Gwenlian stroked the pony's brown muzzle, looking thoughtful. "And why, my love, should it not be?"

"You heard him say it was the spear from the holy scriptures. True or false, that is the reason for its fame."

"Perhaps. But why can it not be both? It is told that the Spear of Lugh passed out of all reckoning ages ago: could it not have been taken right out of the world we know, and into the Shadow-realm? And then brought back again to Annwn by this man Longinus? Diarmait, we must go and look at that spear!"

Jean jumped down off the cart, where she was perching. "But won't that delay us terribly, Your Majesty?" she asked, worried.

"But if it *is* the enchanted spear . . ." Diarmait too looked eager, "it would have the power to destroy our enemies!"

"Lailoken said it could be used by our enemies too," Jean reminded him.

He turned to her, a look almost of appeal in his blue eyes. "Jean, you heard those poor people in the inn. Every day they go in fear of the Lochlannach. How can I not help them if there is even a slight chance? How could I ever live with myself, knowing that I might have found the weapon that could have saved all Avalon, but put my own safety first? You and Gwenlian can journey on to Beaufort; I will remain behind, and seek the spear."

"Nay, Diarmait!" cried the queen. "You promised that we should not be separated. I will go with you."

Jean groaned softly to herself, but she knew that it was no use. The king and queen could not be dissuaded, and when Owen and Dubthach came back from their meal and were told of the magic spear, they agreed to depart from their chosen route and visit the monastery. They called for the innkeeper, and inquired the way to go. From the maps he drew for them in the earth of the stable-yard, Jean managed to get a fair idea of where they were. The island of Avalon had the same general shape as the Avalon Peninsula:

two large capes jutting north into the ocean and two extending southwards, with large bays between them—like a butterfly's two sets of wings. The castle of Caer Wydyr, she gathered, was on the south-western cape: on the tip of the butterfly's lower left-hand wing, as it were. The bay between it and the south-eastern cape—called St. Mary's Bay in her world—was here known as Mount's Bay. She wondered if there were an island like Saint Michael's Mount in St. Mary's Bay, or if, like the island of Hy-Bresail off the coast of Temair, it was a feature unique to Annwn.

To minimize the delay they chose to set out immediately, even though it was growing dark, seeking the road the innkeeper had told them led to the bay and its famed island. At the town gate they were greeted unexpectedly by Morgana, standing tall and imposing in the torchlight. She was holding Dubthach's sword. "This is yours, is it not?" she said dryly, and his hairy cheeks flushed as he took it from her. When they explained the change in plan to her, she looked annoyed, but chose to walk with them all the same. "These roads at night are no place for fools," she said. "You may well have need of my arts." Jean, who was feeling tired and anxious and irritable, wanted to ask her where her arts had been when the Lochlannach and the highwaymen threatened them, but she knew better than to say any such thing to the dark priestess.

The road they took through the woods to the south was not paved, but looked rather as though it had been formed by the tramping of innumerable feet over time. Their hand torches gave only a fitful flickering glow, so that it was hard at times to find their footing on the uneven surface. Hour followed hour until Jean began to feel that she was walking in her sleep, no longer aware of her surroundings apart from the dark shapes of fir trees and the fire-lit road leading on and on into blackness, with no end ever in sight.

They were all weary enough to collapse by the time the bay finally came in sight, well after midnight. There before them they saw the glittering expanse of moonlit water, and rising from it the black shape of a small island topped by the high walls of an abbey. A tall, conical steeple rose from the summit to pierce the sky like a silver lance. The tide was at the full, hiding the causeway of which the innkeeper's wife had spoken. They would have to wait for it to ebb.

"I will watch over the camp this night," Morgana announced as they all sat down wearily on the rough grass and rolled their cloaks about them. "We of the fairy blood do not need to sleep as often as other mortals. If any Lochlannach come near, they will repent of their boldness."

Jean lay down and shut her eyes, but a few minutes later she sat up again in alarm. Into the night rose a chorus of eerie but strangely melodic cries, hollow and haunting, seeming neither human nor animal. "What is *that*?" gasped Jean. The others were already sleeping soundly, and had not heard the cries.

"Have no fear, Jean Mac Dhughaill," the sorceress said in her cool superior voice. "They will not harm you. They are only singing to the moon."

"They?" Jean, looking out to sea, thought she could see figures swimming across its moonlit surface: dark round heads were bobbing among the waves.

"They are the sea people, the Selkies."

Jean clearly saw a long dark shape slip through the water not twenty feet from shore, its form outlined by the gleaming moon-path. A tail of paired flippers lifted briefly, and splashed down out of sight again. "Oh—*seals*!" she said with a laugh, lying down again.

But the wailing cries followed her into her sleep, and her dreams were dark and strange.

Chapter Eleven

WHEN JEAN WOKE, shivering with the cold and damp, she saw that Morgana had gone. Dawn had come, shedding a wan, diffused light through an eastern sky the colour of watery milk. The sea was calm and silver-white, and when she rose and went to the edge of the low sandy bluffs that overlooked the beach she saw, with a little stirring of excitement, that Saint Michael's Mount was a lone island no longer. It was now connected to the shore by a long road of wet, gleaming stone that had appeared as if by magic. *The causeway*, she thought in delight. *The tide's low again at last. I must wake the others!*

Boulders and stony beaches girded the island's base, and its grassy sides, patched here and there with grey groves of still-leafless trees, sloped gently up to a rocky summit. From this granite base rose the monastery: square and sheer-walled as a little fortress, with the grey spire lancing skyward to terminate in a tiny copper cross. She was reminded of pictures she had seen of Mont St. Michel in France—though this island was nowhere near as large, nor was it surrounded by tidal flats. Jean started to turn away from the view; and then suddenly she saw Morgana.

The sorceress was standing some distance away at the far end of the beach, among the weed-green boulders and the pools and sea wrack left by the retreating tide. She was not alone. Grouped around her in a half-circle were about a dozen long, grey, mottled shapes that Jean might almost have taken for more rocks had she not seen one or two of them move slightly. Then she saw the smooth rounded heads with their deep, dark eyes, and she realized that they were seals. They were not afraid of Morgana, who seemed to be talking to them, gesturing with her long white arms. And as Jean gazed at the largest—a big, long-whiskered bull— she had a fleeting mental image of an old man, grey-haired, long-bearded, seated on a throne in some dim-lit hall.

As she stood there one seal looked at her and barked, and they all began to move away towards the sea, their long bodies undulating like waves. Morgana turned sharply, and saw her.

Jean wondered for a moment if she had seen something she should not, and angered the sorceress. But Morgana's features were perfectly composed as she walked back towards the bluffs.

"You have been favoured with a sight few mortals have known," she remarked as she came within earshot. "The high court of the Selkies, and their king."

"King?" What did she mean? Could animals have kings? She saw again the picture of the bearded old man on his throne.

"What did you see just now, girl? Only seals?"

Could Morgana possibly know about Jean's vision? There was a shrewd look in the sorceress's green eyes. "I saw a—a sort of picture in my head. A man sitting on a throne."

"Ah. It is true, then: naught is hidden from you."

The woman gazed at her in a cool, speculative way that made Jean feel uneasy. Did Morgana approve of Jean's ability, or did she feel threatened by it?

"Wake the others," said Morgana abruptly. "It is time we went to the island. The tide will be at the full in a few hours."

Gwenlian, Diarmait and the others were stiff and tired from lying on the cold ground, but it was decided that they must not waste time preparing a hot meal. Diarmait took the Sword and put it in a scabbard at his waist, and they left the cart behind, tethering the pony to a stunted tree. Then they all set out across the causeway. It began a few yards from where the land-road ended, a broad lane of stone covered like the surrounding rocks with mats of flaccid seaweed, purple and brown and olive green. The stone was wet and slippery with algae in places, and down the centre a long shallow depression had been worn by generations of pilgrims' feet. Farther out Jean noticed the rocks gave way to fallen trunks of long-dead trees, bleached with age and exposure to the elements; they could not be mere driftwood, for there were stumps too, with long rambling roots disappearing into the mud. The sea level must have risen a long time ago, drowning a forest that had stood here in ancient times.

It was going to be fine, unlike the preceding day: the rising sun shone in a sky of vivid blue, and there were only a few delicate high-altitude clouds. The wind blowing across the causeway was brisk but not bitter, its sudden gusts and buffets almost playful. Great swarms of seagulls circled overhead, flapping and gliding on motionless wings. Their yelping cries filled the air, utterly wild and piercing. In the clear air the travellers could see every detail of the island: its green slopes, leafless groves and the tall, grey-tiled spire of the monastery. There was a belfry, and as they drew nearer they could see the dark shapes of the great bells hanging motionless within. It all looked more ordinary in the strong daylight, prosaic and stripped of mystery. The place was certainly nowhere near as impressive as Mont St. Michel, with its steep streets and tiers of houses leading up to the mighty fortress at the top. Michael's *Mount* seemed a rather grandiose name for this islet, Jean thought. It was hardly a mountain, and humble even for a hill. She wondered where the hermit's cave was—if there really had ever been a hermit. Perhaps none of that fanciful tale was true. And if not, then what of the Spear? The whole thing was beginning to feel more and more like a wild goose chase, she reflected glumly.

They saw no one on the island as they approached it and came ashore. A winding dirt path led up to the monastery, with wayside crosses at each turn. They followed it up to the building's mighty oaken doors, which stood ajar as if in invitation, and peered in. There was still no one to be seen, and no sound of any human activity: only the distant crying of the gulls broke the silence. Entering the great front hall, they found themselves confronted by a huge statue of white marble, more than life-size: a figure of the Archangel

Michael, with carved breastplate and outstretched wings, treading upon the coils of a hideous dragon-like monster. His hands were raised, as if in rebuke, but the marble face with its curling stone locks and halo was utterly calm and serene. Dubthach went down on one knee.

"You Fianna honour Christian saints?" said Owen, raising an eyebrow.

"Michael we pay homage to," said Dubthach, standing again. "Because he is a warrior, like the god Lugh, and fights to protect his people."

"Where is everybody?" asked Jean, unnerved. "Someone must have heard us by now."

From room to room they went. Vast chambers with oak-beamed ceilings stood silent and empty, with open doors: a sanatorium full of unmade beds, a common room, a refectory. In the latter the remains of an unfinished meal still lay on the tables, while flies buzzed above it. The chapel, a grand high-vaulted space with elaborate carving on its arches and pillars, had clearly been ransacked. Missals and reliquaries were scattered about the stone floor, broken and torn.

"The Lochlannach," said Owen bleakly. "I know their ways. The Lochlannach have been here."

"But how could they have broken in? This abbey is like a fortress!" exclaimed Diarmait.

"They could have used guile to enter," replied Owen, looking grim as he picked up a slashed altar-hanging. "If I have learned one thing about these Northmen, it is that they have no true sense of honour. They will sail up to a village in their longships, pretending that they come only to make peace and barter goods. Then when the villagers lay down their weapons, armed warriors leap up out of their hiding places in the bottoms of the boats, and kill everyone within reach. They spare no one—not even women and babes."

"They are not still here in the building, I hope!" said Gwenlian, whirling nervously around.

"We would have been challenged by now, Majesty, had that been the case."

Diarmait fingered Fragarach's hilt. "Perhaps they saw us coming, and are lying in wait."

There was an uncomfortable pause, then: "There is no one here," Morgana told them. "I feel no life in this place."

"I suppose the Lochlannach have taken the holy relic," said Gwenlian, her face bleak. "There is no spear in the chapel, and that is surely where it would have been kept. We can only pray that it was not the Spear of Lugh after all."

"I knew the weapon was not here," Morgana declared. "I would have felt its power being used."

"Why did you not say so?" demanded Diarmait irritably.

"Would you have believed me?" Another uneasy pause fell as four of them reflected on their reasons for distrusting her. "You had to see for yourselves."

They walked in silence back to the main hall, and stood for a while gazing sadly at the statue of the Archangel. It stood in such a curious pose, Jean thought. One clenched hand raised, the other held low: no weapon in either, though he was supposed to be fighting a dragon. She walked up to peer more closely at the marble hands. There was some crumbly substance, like old plaster, sticking to the curved palms; and the dragon had a round hole bored right through his upturned neck. It lined up perfectly with the holes formed by the Archangel's clenched stone fingers. "Look," she said, dully. "The Spear was *there*—in the angel's hands. You see the holes? They tore it out, and took it away with them."

There was nothing more to be said, or done. The travellers replenished their provisions from the monks' abandoned larders, then left the building to walk slowly and dejectedly back to the hill path. At Gwenlian's suggestion they sat down on the grass to eat some bread and cheese, as they were all quite famished by now. Only Morgana declined, and walked away on her own.

"Bother these flies," said Jean, brushing one away. "You wouldn't think there would be so many, would you, out here with a strong wind blowing?"

"Let us have one more look about the place," said Diarmait. "The trees in that grove are quite thick. Someone might have hidden in there." He finished his bread and strode back uphill, to a grove of tall deciduous trees growing just below the rocky summit. Jean, following him, spied some shapes dangling from the lower boughs of trees, further in where the light was dimmer. Laundry drying, perhaps? Or scarecrows, to drive birds away from newly planted seeds? Or . . .

Diarmait had stopped, his back rigid as he stood staring at the things in the grove. Jean too froze where she was. There was a loud buzzing in her ears as of countless swarms of flies, and the air blackened around her, and she realized she was fainting. And then she was lying on the grassy ground, though she could not remember falling.

"There, there, Jehane!" It was Gwenlian, helping her up. "Here is some water—drink, and you will feel better. Can you stand?" Jean struggled to her feet as her vision cleared.

"Come with me, this way—no, do not look back! Ah, those poor people!"

She led Jean to a little knoll overlooking the sea, and they both sat there for a while. Jean swallowed, trying hard not to be sick. "What happened to them?"

Gwenlian hesitated. "They were sacrificed to the Gallows Lord."

"Sacrificed . . . ?"

"I am afraid so. Lailoken warned me that such things might happen when the Lochlannach come in force and try to claim our island. Worshippers of Woden perform human sacrifice: they kill people and hang them from trees, just as Woden hung on the World-tree in their old tale. It is done to honour him. They will want to convert all Saint Michael's holy places to the worship of their god, Lailoken said. For Woden is a god of hills and high places, and in Avalon all of these are consecrated to the Archangel."

Jean scrambled up again. "Please, Gwenlian, can't we leave this horrible place now?" she begged.

"Soon, soon, I promise you," Gwenlian soothed. "But first we must give those poor monks a Christian burial."

"That will delay us," said Dubthach, coming up behind them. "The tide will rise and cover the causeway."

He was right. There was always a six-hour gap between low and high tides: how many hours had they already spent here? The sun was high in the sky, and they could see waves breaking over the stone road that was their only connection with the mainland.

"Then we shall wait for the next low tide," the queen said sharply.

Suddenly they heard a shout from the direction of the grove. Diarmait and Owen had emerged from the trees, propping up between them an aged, white-haired monk.

"This man survived by hiding in a cave," the king said.

The old man sobbed and trembled uncontrollably as they lowered him gently to the ground. At the sight of the long-haired Fianna warrior he flinched, and Gwenlian quickly knelt at his side. "There, we will not harm you, I promise," she said, taking his hand in hers. He relaxed at the sound of her soft voice, and looked up into her pretty, kindly face. "We are friends. Tell us what happened here, Brother."

"Portents," the old man mumbled. "There were portents. We were warned. Had we only understood . . . Some of the brothers had terrible dreams. Brother Edgar told me he saw a black-clad woman, a giantess taller than an oak, walk across the island carrying a sword that dripped blood. Others dreamed of wolves and ravens—"

"The Lochlannach came here, did they not?" said Diarmait.

"The sea raiders—yes," he quavered. "Two days ago they came. Some they killed, others they took away for thralls. I fled to the hermit's cave . . . I have not dared to move in all this time." He clutched his head, moaning. "*Gungnir*, they kept saying, where is *Gungnir*? We did not know what they meant. Then they said, Where is the magic spear *Gungnir*? But we could not tell them where the Spear is. It is gone."

"Gone?" echoed Diarmait.

The old man was gasping now, struggling to catch his breath. "The Spear of Longinus . . . it has been gone for more than . . . a month. Three women came, lovely maidens . . . they appeared from out of thin air. They removed the

Spear from the statue as we watched . . . and then they vanished. Angels . . . they were angels. They took the Spear back with them, to Heaven . . ."

"Fairy women, more likely," murmured Gwenlian to the others. "Ah, well: at least the Lochlannach have not got it. For I think it must have been the Spear of Lugh. Why else would the Good People take it?"

The man suddenly gave a rattling sigh, and his eyes rolled up and closed. His head fell back heavily against Diarmait's arm.

"He is dead!" exclaimed Owen, touching the monk's throat. "There is no pulse."

"But there is no wound on him," the king said in dismay, lowering the still form to the ground.

"I think his heart must have been weak," the knight answered, shaking his head.

"Then he too must be buried." Diarmait stood, pale but resolute. "Gwenlian, you and Jean must go back to the mainland before the causeway is submerged. Take Sir Owen with you for protection. I will join you when I am able."

"No, Diarmait, we should not divide our party. And you will need Sir Owen to help you build the cairns." Dubthach stood apart, showing no inclination to assist the king in his melancholy task.

Jean was of two minds: like Gwenlian she hated the thought of their party being split up for hours while they waited for another low tide to reunite them. But she badly wanted to leave this island, with its terrifying aura of violence and death. In the end she agreed to remain with the others, despite her misgivings. She knew she could not expect the king and queen to leave the Lochlannach's victims without a proper burial. It was not only that Gwenlian and Diarmait belonged to a chivalrous society, and had been trained from the cradle to behave honourably; they would do the decent thing because they themselves were decent to the core, kind and caring and devoted to what they believed was right.

As the two men set about their grim business Jean wandered back up to the monastery, still feeling sick. *Control yourself*, she thought. *There are boys not much older than you who have seen even worse things, over in Europe on the battlefields.* But still her eyes swam as she sat and watched the sea rise and reclaim the causeway. How strange to think that the day should be so beautiful, the sun shining strongly out of a cloudless sky, the sea blue and dancing with sun-pennies. Far out in the bay she saw some sailboats—fishermen, perhaps . . .

Then her heart began to pound as they drew nearer and she saw the high carved prows, the sails that hung broad and square on the masts.

She leaped up and pelted down the hill path, to the beach where her companions were busy raising seven cairns. Dubthach had lent a hand after all, though Morgana was nowhere to be seen. Gwenlian had found some wild violets somewhere, and was strewing them over the makeshift graves.

"The Lochlannach!" Jean yelled. "They're coming this way—in ships," she added as they all turned, like startled deer, to look at the submerged causeway.

Owen swore an oath. "The very same raiders as came here before, I will be bound. They must have been lying up in coves along the shore. They are going to try again to find the Spear."

Diarmait blanched. "This is my doing. I have doomed you all by keeping you here on the island."

"No," Jean said, "you told me and Gwenlian to go ashore, and we wouldn't."

"You told me back at the inn that we should not make this journey. Why did I not listen to you?"

He was distraught, and she pitied him even in the midst of her fear. "Never mind all that now," she said rapidly. "Quick! Is there *anywhere* on this island where we can hide?"

They could all see the three longships approaching, their striped sails swollen with the strong wind, bucking and plunging on the big waves.

"Did they see us, do you think?" Jean asked as they all turned and raced back up the hill.

"It matters little if they did or not," Owen retorted. "They will have no trouble finding us. We are trapped here, just as the holy brothers were."

They sped on up the path, past the dark groves where the sacrificial victims had hung—*The Lochlannach will know someone's been here*, Jean thought in panic. *They'll see the cairns, then the empty trees, and they will know . . .*

"What about . . . the cave where . . . the old monk hid?" she panted.

"It is small, a mere alcove in the rock. It could not hold us all," Owen replied.

"Could we go into the monastery, and bar the doors?" suggested Gwenlian.

"We can try—but they will soon find a way to break them open."

Near the top of the path Morgana met them, striding

along with no sign of fear on her face. "You have seen the raiders? Come with me," she said curtly, turning and heading for the southern slope of the island. "Their weapons are of cold iron, I can feel it from here. I cannot ensorcel them. And they are too many for us to fight. I shall take the paths of the air, but the rest of you must escape another way. Follow me, and I will show you."

On the island's seaward side the grass and trees gave way to a sheer precipice of black basalt, plunging into a rock-strewn swirl of seething waves. Morgana led them right up to the cliff's edge and stood there, her long black-feathered cloak blowing back in the wind like a pair of giant wings. The others came and stood beside her, gazing down at the churning white surf below.

"Escape?" said Owen. "How—by growing wings?"

"You must leap into the sea," she replied.

Jean gasped. It was not, perhaps, as far down as it looked. One could probably survive it. But that frothing maelstrom would surely suck them under, and the bitter cold of the water would be deadly after only a few minutes. And where would they swim to, even if they could swim? The mainland was much too far away, even for a strong and experienced swimmer, which Jean certainly was not.

"Madness!" said Diarmait. "We would drown."

"I have friends who will bear you up and see that you come to no harm," the sorceress replied. "Look, they await you below."

And now Jean saw that a number of sleek, round, grey shapes she had taken for small rocks were in fact heads bobbing like buoys in the foam. "The seals?" she cried.

"Even so. Will you all trust me, now that you have no other choice? See, the first longship has landed on the beach."

As they all turned to look, Morgana went up to the very edge of the cliff. She stood there for an instant, poised on the tips of her toes, then she flung herself over.

Jean screamed as the dark figure plummeted swiftly towards the sea, dwindling to a tiny blot as it fell . . . She blinked. No—it was actually *shrinking* in size. That black fluttering shape halfway down the cliff's face could not be more than two feet across. It was no longer Morgana. As Jean and the others watched, a wind off the waves took the black thing, and tossed it into the air again. A harsh, croaking cry echoed back from the basalt cliff and a night black bird, a raven, rode the wind upwards.

"God in Heaven!" Diarmait said hoarsely.

Owen too looked shaken. "I have heard of such things, but I never truly believed . . ."

Only Dubthach showed no surprise. Stepping up to the cliff, he too jumped fearlessly off its edge. He did not change his form, however, but plunged feet-first into the swell. The other four watched the roiling foam in horror, but he did not rise to the surface again.

Shouts came from the beach on the island's eastern side, and the thud of pounding feet. The Lochlannach had seen them, outlined against the sky on the clifftop. Owen turned, sword drawn, like a cornered and desperate animal.

"So this is what it comes to," the young king whispered. "Death by swords—or drowning."

Swords hurt more, thought Jean. And she remembered,

with a flash of terror, the macabre scene in the grove. Anything was better than that . . .

"Take my hand, Jehane," said Gwenlian, "and you, Diarmait, the other. We will close our eyes and leap together. Are you ready?" The shouts and the drumming feet were closer. "Now!" the queen cried.

They closed their eyes, and jumped.

Chapter Twelve

FALLING, plunging, wind shrieking past her ears; her friends' hands pulling away, her eyelids fluttering open to show her the seething cauldron of surf below, a voice screaming—hers, she realized, in the blurred instant before impact. Then a shock of cold, a bone-jarring crash, dull green light—and darkness.

Am I dead? she wondered a short time later. *Did I die there, in the sea? I must have, but—where am I now? Am I anywhere? Am I still Jean?*

She was adrift in darkness; not standing on or touching anything, but hanging weightless in a void. She no longer felt cold, and there was an impression of light coming from above—was it the sun, beating through her closed eyelids? She opened her eyes, looked blearily about her. She was surrounded by a muted green light. Directly ahead of her a mass of shining, silver shapes were swirling and darting, like shards of light. They drew closer, and her eyes focused. Fish: a great school of small herring-like fish, swimming in close formation. As they swept past her in a thick silver cloud she tried to move towards them. Her body was perfectly at ease in the water now. *Am I dead? Is this what death is like? But why do I still feel my body? Perhaps I'm still drowning, and it doesn't hurt . . .* Several large grey shapes swung by, scattering the fish in all directions: watching the graceful movements of these larger creatures, she suddenly understood. She was one of them.

She was a seal.

But it was good: better to be a seal than Jean MacDougall, that unfortunate girl who had plunged into the sea and drowned. This new seal-self was alive and free of fear, and the water was not her enemy. The other seals swam past her again. Watching the sleek grey shapes, she felt that "swim" was hardly the right word for their effortless motion: like birds they swooped, glided, soared through the emerald element that was their home. Clumsily she tried to follow them. Raising what once had been a hand, she saw a stout grey-furred limb ending in a webbed claw. She beat at the water with her new forelimbs, and felt herself propelled forward. The strong supple column of her seal's spine undulated, a wave-like rhythm: the sea's own motion. She knew she must not be left behind: she could not bear to be alone, now, in this strange new life and body. As the other seals rose towards the surface immediately above her, she saw their shapes black against its transparency, silhouetted against sky and clouds as though they were truly flying. She realized that they were rising in order to breathe. She felt that same need in herself now. Her new form was swift and agile and very wonderful, but every cell of it was crying out for air.

Hastily she rose to join them. Her head broke through the luminous surface and she gasped, dragging the fresh cold air greedily down into starved lungs. Several seal heads floated among the waves a few feet away. Their great liquescent eyes looked full into hers for a moment, and she saw the intelligence in them. Then they all dived again, glossy backs and flanks rolling in the sun. She drew a last deep breath, and submerged once more. They were leaving her, sinking into the green deep. She could not call out to them to wait. Panic filled her: she plunged after them with urgent strokes of her seal limbs, and in a few minutes began to close the distance.

Through the depths they led her, down and down, until they came to a great undersea cliff or barrier of rough granite. Perched at its top she saw the shapes of needling towers. A castle—*under* the sea? But she could waste no time on wonderment. The seals swam on, and once more she had to work to keep up with them. Further down they went, to where a cave opened like a black mouth in the cliff's face. She did not like the look of this, but her fear of being left alone was greater than her fear of what lay within its gaping darkness. Into it she went, in and down—and then up—up into a vast echoing space, a natural cavern filled with air. A platform of grey basalt sloped gradually upwards, like an uneven floor or the heeling deck of a ship, to meet a rock wall. Its surface was covered in the forms of reclining seals, and the walls of the rock chamber echoed with their mournful cries.

She turned and saw other seals coming up out of the water. Two of them, a pair of dark grey bulls, tilted their heads sharply upwards—and then, in the flicker of an eye, they were gone. Grey seal hide fell in loose folds to the rock, and two men rose to their feet: tall and broad-shouldered men with dark eyes, clad in plain grey tunics. One of them leaned down to touch the head of another bull that sprawled nearby. Its hide also loosened and fell away, like a split husk, and from the falling folds emerged the hunched figure of Sir Owen. He looked dazed, like a man half out of his wits. Jean tried to speak to him, but only a seal's barking cry came from her mouth.

And now she saw, in a dim corner of the cave, Gwenlian and Diarmait huddled together on seal hides spread out on the rock. The pale grey-green light was coming from another cave-like opening farther along the wall. There were steps in it, rough-hewn from the living rock.

She heaved herself up onto the rock floor, as she had seen the other seals do. The men immediately approached her, and one reached down to touch her head—and then she was kneeling, wet and shivering with cold, with an empty seal's skin lying crumpled beside her.

She and Owen got somewhat unsteadily to their feet and went to join the king and queen. The two men—if men they were—went to the small cave-like opening and disappeared up the steps. "Who are these people?" Jean whispered. "Are they fairies?"

"I do not know," answered Gwenlian in a low voice. "Many tales are told of the Selkie-folk. Some say they are seals that can speak and take human form, others that their true shape is human and they use seal forms to travel from their castles in the sea to dry land. Some say they are fairies, others that they are mortal and only distant kin to the Good People."

"Fallen angels," Owen rasped. "That is what they are. Spirits condemned to dwell in the deeps, far from the glory of Heaven—"

Another seal came heaving and splashing up the stone beach. It was a great, silver-white animal, spotted with black, and its huge dark eyes looked on them haughtily for a moment. There it flung up its head and cast off its skin. In its place crouched Morgana. She was not wearing her feathered cloak, and her long black hair flowed over her bare white arms and trailed upon the rock. Both hair and gown were perfectly dry.

She stood, sweeping them all with her green gaze. "So you did not drown after all?" she commented, raising one black brow. "Well and good. Where is Dubthach?"

"We have not seen him," replied Diarmait, "or the Sword of Nuada either."

"Why do you not ask your *friends* where he is?" said Owen.

Morgana turned, no doubt to make some acerbic remark, but at that moment there came a sound of feet descending the rocky stair. Two tunic-clad men—not the same two Jean had seen before—entered, holding spears. Behind them came Dubthach.

"Majesty," he said to Morgana with a bow, "we are summoned into the presence of the Selkie king."

They were led up the granite stair and into an upper passage—this one floored with flags, and walled with blocks of quarried stone; and there were windows high up on those walls, tall narrow casements from whose panes a dim green light fell. Jean remembered the castle she had seen atop the submarine cliff—strange and dream-like it had seemed to her then, but here were its solemn halls stretching before her, lit with the cool undersea light. They were damp and chill, water trickling in long rivulets down their walls and beading on the stones like sweat. In some places shallow puddles had formed on the floors, smelling strongly of the sea; out of one of these a large crab crawled as they walked past, sidling away with pincers raised. The place echoed with the sound of falling droplets, like a cave.

At length they came to a large hall with more and larger windows, and here they saw a great gathering of people, like a royal court. All were arrayed in fine clothing of sombre hues—or so they seemed in that sombre light—and throned on a dais at the end of the hall was an old man, silver-haired with a hoary beard and deep, dark eyes. Jean recalled the old silver-muzzled seal she had seen on the beach, and knew even before he spoke that this must be the Selkie king. He was holding the sword Fragarach in his hands, poring over its blade and hilt design, but glanced up as they entered with their guards.

"Well, Morgana, you are welcome here," said the king of the Selkies. "But who are your companions?"

"They are my allies against the Lochlannach, King Fingal," Morgana replied. "We are at war on the land."

"Please," Jean exclaimed, forgetting in her anxiety that one should never speak to royalty uninvited, "you're magic, aren't you, King Fingal? Could you help us?"

"Help you?" King Fingal frowned—not in anger, but merely as though he were puzzled. "But this is not our struggle. Why then should we help you?"

Jean thought of the angel statue in the monastery's empty hall, and of what Abbess Brigid had told her. Michael was the patron saint of the fairies, she had said. "For—for Saint Michael's sake," she heard herself say.

Fingal gave a dry laugh. "Ah! This is a cunning companion you have here, Morgana. She knows well we can refuse nothing asked in that name. We are close kin to those who forsook Heaven"—Owen let out a hissing breath—"and owe a debt to the one who took their part, long ago."

Jean opened her mouth to protest that she hadn't known they could not refuse her plea. But she realized that anything she said now would sound insincere and unconvincing, so she remained unhappily silent.

"You say you are fairies?" Diarmait asked, as Fingal handed Fragarach back to him.

"Nay. We are living flesh and spirit, even as you are: but our ancestors were of the fairy blood, like Queen Morgana. In the fairies' mortal offspring the spirit is so strong that we may live for many centuries. Nigh on a thousand years have I lived, but my strength is waning now. My eldest son will reign soon in my place."

"King Fingal," Gwenlian said, stepping forward—a graceful, gracious queen still, despite her sopping rags—"was it your people who took the sacred spear from the monastery of Saint Michael? Is it in your keeping now?"

"Nay, my folk have naught to do with the monks, nor with any people of the land," answered Fingal. "I have heard of the Spear that Wounds and Heals, but I did not know it had been taken."

"Some fairy maidens appeared before the monks, and

took the Spear and vanished some time ago," Gwenlian told him. "We had hoped to find it, for it is a very holy and powerful weapon to use against our foes."

"The maidens may well have come from the Seelie Court," the Selkie king mused. "If you desire the Spear, you might seek it there."

"The Seelie Court?" repeated Jean, confused. "But isn't this it, Majesty?"

There were muffled laughs and titters from the court, and Morgana gave one of her cold smiles. "'Seelie' does not mean *seal*, but *holy*," she said. "Among the true fairies—those who have no mortal blood—there are two great courts or hosts. The Unseelie fairies are hideous and brutish, and hate all things that live. They are the ones who lean towards the Dark. But the Seelie fairies are closer to the Light: they are noble, and fair of face, and generous—when it pleases them." Her mouth twisted ironically.

"Well," Gwenlian said, "let us hope that we can find them, and persuade them to give us the Spear. They are very powerful, and we could never take it from them by force though we marched upon them with ten thousand men."

Fingal nodded. "You may have to be content with the knowledge that your foes cannot take it from them either. But now, as I promised, I will take up your cause against the Lochlannach."

Jean was beginning to regret having spoken. "I'm sure none of us wants you to fight for us, Majesty," she protested. "We wouldn't want any of your people to be hurt. The Lochlannach are great fighters, and they're very cruel." Her voice shook as she recalled the sacrificial grove.

Fingal smiled slightly. "We do not fight our foes with weapons, as you do on land. We have other ways of settling accounts with those who incur our displeasure."

"They carried iron, so I could not magic them. But I could use the Spell of Sedna," offered Morgana. "I learnt it from the Ice People in the far north—the children of the Blue Hag of Winter, the *Cailleach Bheur*. It is an incantation by which one may summon every sea creature that is hot-blooded and breathes above the waves."

"Very well, you may work your spell, though I doubt," the Selkie king said, looking stern, "that it will be needed."

The human travellers were dismissed from the royal audience chamber, but permitted to roam at will through the cold corridors of the undersea palace. They were given a change of dry clothing to wear, warm gowns and tabards in heavy fabrics and muted shades of bronze, maroon or dark green. But the damp chill of the place still reached their bones. The Selkie folk were plainly accustomed to it, as they had to be in a dwelling where no fires could be lit. Nor did the dim light trouble them: they used no lamps or torches to brighten their halls, at least by day. Perhaps their eyes were as keen as seals' even when they were in human form.

Owen and the king and queen found a small chamber—a solar, one might have called it, had there been any sun to shine in at its windows—and there they sat talking in low voices. Dubthach had remained in the throne room with Morgana: evidently he wished to be part of whatever action would be taken against the Lochlannach. Jean was beginning to wonder what she had started with her fortuitously worded plea, and hoped that none of their hosts would come to harm.

Wandering apart from the others, she found and climbed a narrow winding stair, thinking that more of their surroundings might be visible from a window in one of the towers. In fact, she found to her surprise that the upper room of this tower was all window: a little dome or cupola made entirely of glass. It must have been exceptionally strong glass, for there was no seepage where its panes joined together, and none had cracked from the vast pressure of fathoms upon fathoms of water pressing down on it. All around her were the green sea depths, and the reflecting surface lay far above her full of creases and dimples—how strange and amazing to see waves from *beneath*, instead of above! The sea below was quite clear: she could see for a considerable distance through the water. To one side a vast, shadowy shape loomed, sloping steadily up towards the surface. Saint Michael's Mount. The Selkies had explained to her that their sea castle stood on the side of the island's underwater base, and looking up at it she realized that Michael's Mount was, indeed, a mountain: a sea mountain whose peak vanished above the surface, just as the summit of a mountain on land may sometimes be lost in clouds. The causeway must lie atop a sort of knife-backed ridge, connecting it to Avalon. She suddenly recalled the dead tree trunks she had seen below the tidemark, remains of a vanished forest. Might this palace have stood once in the open air, on the side of a wooded mountain? Even as she thought this she had a mental picture of green forested slopes where the vague shadow now loomed, rising to a peak of stark rock—a high place, a holy place, long before the coming of the monks and their abbey.

As abruptly as it had come the vision faded, and there were only the green deeps as before. Glancing upwards, Jean noticed a long, dark shape up there by the top of the mountain—where what she thought of as the "island" began. It looked at first like a floating log, or some other piece of debris. Then she saw another appear, and another, and knew she was looking at the hulls of the longships, putting out to sea. The Lochlannach were leaving—again without their prize, she thought with fierce satisfaction. She watched as the hulls advanced across the ceiling of the sea. No oars dipped below the surface: they were under sail, then. She glared at them, hating their evil occupants, and at the same time wondering dismally what a few seals could possibly hope to do against such a strong and confident foe.

The Selkies were swimming up from the deeps now: streaming out of the submerged tunnel below the keep. In great waves the seal folk came, gliding over the walls and turrets of their castle, rising towards the surface of the sea. She thought she saw the silver-muzzled king, and the large pale seal that was Morgana, but she could not be sure. Several Selkies sped right past her tower, one coming so close that she saw his dark eyes turn down to look at her, and the tiny bubbles beading his pelt like pearls.

There were other creatures out there, too. The sea was alive with swimming shapes: in addition to the grey spotted Selkies there were other seals, harbour and harp seals. And there were little harbour porpoises, and pot-headed whales, and the sleek, grey, graceful dolphins that the fishermen called squidhounds. In the distance she saw a huge, dim shape—so huge that it could only be one of the great whales—rise up from the lower deeps like a dark cloud. She saw its enormous forked tail beating up and down as it passed between her and the surface. There were curious sounds, too, high-pitched whistles and trills carrying through the brine like the voices of birds. She fancied that the dolphins and the smaller whales were making them.

The light had begun to fade rapidly, though it could not be more than mid-afternoon. The sun no longer blazed down through the surface overhead; clouds must have scudded across its face. The formerly tranquil pattern of dimples and furrows had grown wild and chaotic. The seaweeds that clung like ivy to the castle walls waved their long tendrils, and bits of flotsam spun past the glass dome on invisible currents. A great storm was brewing, whipping up huge waves and stirring the upper deeps into turmoil. Jean doubted it had arisen by chance, and was suddenly afraid.

High overhead the longships tossed helplessly. Their oars had come out as the Northmen trimmed their sails against the rising wind. But the sea creatures swam up, grabbing and fouling the oars, striking the lapping oaken strakes of the hulls. Soon there were men in the sea, too: and the sea creatures seized hold of their flailing limbs, dragging them downwards to drown. The unmanned ships tossed, capsized, hung upside-down in the sea.

Jean had seen enough. She turned and fled for the stairs.

"It is done," Fingal said. The companions stood before him again in the great audience hall, this time unflanked by guards. "Your enemies are no more. We were granted the power in ancient times to cause a sea tempest to avenge the killing of any one of our kind. Today we have called on this power, naming the men of the monastery our kin; and the Lochlannach who slew them are all drowned. Our obligation is satisfied: I trust you are content?" He directed this question to Jean, who could only stare back at him, stricken. Gwenlian spoke for her.

"Our thanks, King Fingal," she said, bowing her golden head. "If you will now help us return to the mainland, we will go and trouble you no more."

He gestured to a pair of grey-clad guards standing at his side. "Give them sealskins, and guide them back to dry land. Farewell, Morgana. If ever you should desire to leave the dry realms and dwell here in the deeps, we would welcome you."

"I thank you for your offer," the sorceress replied, "but I was born upon the dry land, and my heart is still in Avalon. It is my home."

They made their farewells, and followed the two Selkies down to the sea cave. Jean trailed behind the others, her eyes downcast.

Chapter Thirteen

THEY SET OUT SOUTHWARD THAT SAME DAY, journeying across the barrens since there was no road, weaving their way around scattered boulders and clumps of low-growing tuckamore. They had retrieved the pony and cart, and Morgana had drawn out, from its hiding place between two great rocks on the beach, her feathered raven-mantle. Jean shuddered a little at the sight of it, wondering if the sorceress was going to transform herself again before their eyes; but she only tossed it around her shoulders, said "Come" in a curt tone and walked on ahead of them, leading the way. They travelled in silence, each occupied by his or her own brooding thoughts.

They had been walking for about an hour when they saw ahead of them a little cluster of man-made structures, lying along the shore to their left: long, low-roofed huts or sheds of some kind. Columns of grey smoke rose from their roofs, and a smell of roasting meat came to them on the sea wind. Goats and some cattle grazed the sparse grass of the meadow a short distance away. As the travellers drew nearer they saw that the structures were built from strips of sod, mounted on wooden frames; grass still grew thickly on the sods that roofed the huts, giving them the look of small, natural mounds. But for the livestock and the smoke curling up from the cooking fires within, the structures would not have been at all noticeable from a distance. There were no human figures to be seen, but the sound of voices carried on the wind along with the smells of cooking.

Owen stood still. "That is the Lochlannach tongue!"

They all halted in alarm except for Morgana, who continued to walk unconcernedly towards the sod huts. Jean's heart lurched.

"I would never have dreamed," said Diarmait in a harsh voice, "that they would dare to build settlements here—on *our* land."

"And those beasts are likely stolen," Owen added.

"Hadn't we better run for it?" asked Jean nervously. "If it is the Lochlannach we'll be in for a fight."

"I will gladly fight them," Owen said grimly, hand on sword. "Must the seal people have all the pleasure of punishing these barbarians? Let us teach them a lesson."

Jean recalled, unwillingly, the forms of the drowning men in the sea above her, and felt again the horror of their helplessness. The wind brushed her face, bringing with it more voices and the wail of an infant. "No!" she cried, appalled. "There are women there—babies—" Perhaps these were the wives and sisters of those same Lochlannach who had died by the Selkies' magic, and were even now waiting and wondering why their men did not return . . . She turned in appeal to Gwenlian and Diarmait, but their faces were hard. They had not seen what she saw from the sea tower, they remembered only the desecration and carnage of Saint Michael's Mount. Diarmait said nothing, but drew Fragarach from its scabbard.

As they drew closer to the tiny settlement, Jean trailing reluctantly behind, Sir Owen pointed to a moored boat rocking in the swell far below. It was smaller than the longships they had seen, wider and higher at the sides, with no ornamental carving at the bow. "A *knorr*," whispered Owen. "Not a ship of war, but the sort they use for carrying cargo, and livestock—and settlers."

"Then the animals *are* theirs," said Jean.

"I wonder how many of these *knorrin* have now come to our shores? They truly mean to take this land."

"Well, we shall not give them a welcome," said Gwenlian grimly.

At that instant a figure appeared at the doorway to one of the sod houses. It was a woman in a drab brown dress with her hair pulled back under a dirty white head scarf. When she saw the armed men she screamed and fled back into the hut. A babel of agitated voices rose within.

Morgana and the men strode forward, followed by Gwenlian and Jean. When they reached the door they found it blocked by another figure: a tall young woman, with big arms bared by her short-sleeved gown. Masses of red-brown hair, matted and tangled, fell about her firm-jawed face, and her callused hands held a naked sword. In the dim fire-lit interior behind her they glimpsed other figures, some women and children and an elderly man. A girl held a swaddled baby who uttered loud hiccuping cries.

The three men held back, and Jean sensed their change of

heart. None of them, not even the fearsome Fianna, was going to challenge this desperate young woman and her harmless household. Morgana, however, kept walking towards the hut, her features set and cold as though sculpted out of ice. The tall woman raised her sword, shouted a warning.

Then she shrieked, as if in pain, as the sorceress waved a hand at her. The sword dropped from her grip. At another gesture from Morgana the Lochlannach woman doubled over and fell to her knees. The stubborn courage in her face was replaced by terror as she stared up at the black-clad figure towering over her.

"Steel!" declared Morgana, looking down with disdain at the fallen sword. "Only fools take up alloyed iron against those who are of fairy blood." She kicked the weapon aside contemptuously.

"*Val* . . ." The Lochlannach woman's lips moved, made choking sounds. "*Valkyrie* . . ." she rasped. Behind her, the rest of the occupants of the hut dropped to their knees.

Morgana, who had been in the act of turning away, stopped dead. For a moment the anger drained from her pale face, leaving in its place an indecipherable expression. Then she swung around and strode away across the barrens, without a backward look.

The other travellers sheathed their weapons and followed her, subdued by the encounter. In the sod hut voices murmured, and the baby wailed on unheeded.

They turned inland after that, shunning the coast, and by late afternoon had come to a land of lakes, of flat barrens and scattered boulders: the bed of a vast glacier in ancient times. The lakes were not large or very deep—"ponds" New-foundlanders would call them; they were ringed about with reeds, and were home to small numbers of wildfowl, little speckled sandpipers and flotillas of quacking mallards. Owen wanted to shoot some of the latter with his bow. "No more suppers of cheese and bread," he said. "A man cannot march all day on such stuff."

"I would not shoot anything in this land, were I you," Morgana warned. "It belongs to the fairies, and for what you take they may demand a price."

Owen blanched. "You have led us into the lands of the Tylwyth Teg?" he exclaimed.

"I led you inland. It is better to avoid the sea with so many Lochlannach about. No harm will come to you while I am with you, so long as you heed my warnings."

Owen looked appalled, and even the king and queen seemed uneasy. But Jean's heart gave a little fluttering leap. The fairies! At last, they had come close to the beings she most longed to see. *They may help me go home again—help my world. I must see them!* She looked around her eagerly as they walked, but saw only the sombre barrens stretching in all directions under the overcast sky.

As they passed one long wind-rippled pond, Jean saw a glimmer of white among the tall rushes at its far end. A swan slowly glided out of the green stalks, closely followed by another: together they headed for the middle of the lake, apparently quite unafraid of the human intruders. A beam of stray sunlight escaped the lowering clouds to limn their long necks and their wings, furled with the soft feathers turned up like peony petals.

"Oh, how beautiful," breathed Gwenlian.

Diarmait grinned at her. "You do not fancy wild swan for supper?"

"Ah, you rogue!" retorted his wife, making a playful swing at him. "You would not dream of hurting those lovely creatures!"

"Swan is no good to eat in any case," said the practical Owen. "It is stringy and tough."

The swans ignored them, each sailing along just a few yards away with neck raised in an arrogant S, making the soft breathy huffs and hisses that were the only sounds they could utter. Jean noted the black knobs above their nares, the salmon pink colouring of their bills. She had seen birds like these before, drifting on the duck pond at Bowring Park. Her father had told her they were imported from Europe. "They're mute swans," she said. "They don't belong here."

"Don't belong?" repeated Diarmait.

She explained, and the travellers all stopped and stared at the elegant birds. "They might have flown across the sea," suggested Gwenlian, "like the little bird in the forest near Saint Michael's Abbey—do you remember it, Jean?"

"The chough. Yes, I suppose it's possible," Jean admitted.

"True," Owen said, "but this is the country of the Tylwyth Teg. The fairy people are skilled at changing their shapes, as we have seen. Any creature that seems out of the ordinary should be avoided." He turned away from the shore, and the others followed him, Dubthach with a little shrug of the shoulders. Morgana was already walking ahead. As they hurried to catch up with the priestess Jean glanced back at the lake, but the two swans were nowhere to be seen on its pewter-coloured surface.

Hidden by the reeds, no doubt.

That one brief ray of sun was the last they would see that day. Within hours an early dark was descending, deepened by the dense canopy of cloud above. They were close to a lake many times larger than any they had yet seen. In its centre was a small island, completely covered in trees.

"I do not like the look of that," said Owen.

"What do you mean, Sir Owen?" Gwenlian asked.

"That lake is too large, my queen: it looks as though it is very deep. There could be evil creatures dwelling in its depths—kelpies perhaps, or water dragons—"

"*Péisti*, you mean?" Diarmait said. "Do not worry, Owen. Even if it were so there would be no danger to us. A *péist* cannot leave the water. And I never heard of any kelpies dwelling in Gwynedd."

"The *Gwragedd Annwn* do," said Owen darkly.

"What are *they*?" Jean asked, looking uneasily at the stone grey surface of the lake. She did not much care for this talk of "water dragons." In this world they were more than likely to be real.

"They are spirits in the form of beautiful maidens. They dwell at the bottoms of lakes such as this, and can be seen at times rising from the waters to walk the dry land. It is ill luck to meet with the fairies of the land, and I am sure the water fairies are no different."

"Water fairies?" repeated Jean. "But they might be good and helpful, Sir Owen. Remember the story about the Lady of the Lake, and how she gave King Arthur his sword,

Excalibur. He was out walking by a lake, and a woman's arm came up out of the water and held the sword out to him." Her hopes began to revive at the thought. "Do you think this is a fairy place?" she asked Morgana.

"I feel a power here," the sorceress replied. "But it would be unwise for us to meddle with it, or to stay any longer in the area than is necessary."

Diarmait frowned. "Then let us not camp too near."

They walked on in the grey half-light for a few more minutes, then Diarmait called a halt. "Let us settle here for the night," he said. "We have no tent, and the cart will not shelter us all if it rains. That tree, there, may prove useful: there are no leaves on its boughs, but we can hang our cloaks on them to keep any rain off." They all looked at the tree. It was a huge overgrown shrub, at least a century old by the look of it: its thick, twisted trunk was all seamed and knotted with age, and its massive branches bent low over the ground. On their tips sprouted little white blossoms, shining like pale stars through the gloom.

"It is a may-tree," said Gwenlian.

Owen scowled. "I would not care to shelter under it. Any tree growing alone upon a plain is always full of the fairy magic, and may-trees have an ill name."

"Enough!" exclaimed Diarmait irritably. "Are we to be afraid of every bird and beast and stick and stone we see in this place? I say we sleep here."

They settled down, tethered the pony, and prepared their meagre bedding. Only Morgana did not lie down. "You may as well sleep now, while you can. I will stand guard."

Jean lay down, but the chill seeping from the earth below

and the worries filling her mind kept sleep beyond her reach. What if they did not, after all, meet any fairies? Or if the fairies refused to send her home? Would she be trapped in Annwn forever? And what of her family, who must surely think she was dead by now? She tossed to and fro in her damp cloak, moaning softly. She realized, with a stab of guilt, that she had not been thinking of her parents as much as might be expected, even when there were no immediate dangers to drive them from her thoughts. It was—she thought with a new stirring of terror—as though her memories of her own world and life were beginning to fade.

At length she managed to fall into a weary doze. But she woke again, cold and uncomfortable, to find it was still dark. A pale light, not at all like moonlight or starlight, was faintly illuminating her surroundings, the boggy ground and the figures of her sleeping companions. She sat up, puzzled, and looked around for its source. Then she gasped.

The may-tree was alight—not with fire, but with dozens of pale lights that clustered upon its boughs. They were each about the size of a candle flame, but rounded in shape, and gave off a dim, greenish-white glow that did not flicker. *I've seen this before*, she thought confusedly.

"What—what is it?" Jean whispered to Morgana, who was standing a little way off facing the tree. The others were still sleeping soundly.

"There is a power here, and our presence has disturbed it. No—do not wake the others. They will only be filled with fear, and try to flee. That could be—unwise." Morgana continued to gaze steadily at the tree with its adornment of unearthly lights.

And then the lights moved. Though there was no breath of wind to stir them, the pale green globes shifted in their places on the tree's black boughs. They moved of their own volition, as though they were alive. Jean thought of the luminous insects she had read about in books, which shone like little lanterns in the night—fireflies and glow-worms. There were none in Newfoundland, but she had always imagined that they would look something like this. The green lights were flowing all about the tree now, from its crown all down the twisted trunk to the roots, and as she watched several broke away to float out into the air. Soon all the lights were streaming through the darkness, bobbing and hovering as though held aloft by unseen hands. Some hung over the sleeping travellers, illuminating their faces with a cold green radiance. One came within inches of Jean's face, so that she clearly saw the core of pure white light within its green aureole. Then it darted away again. Morgana was surrounded by them, and seemed quite unalarmed. She raised her arms, and the lights settled on her hands and head so that she glowed too. She spoke softly, in one of the ancient tongues. All at once the living lights clumped together again, hanging in a dense swarm about a yard above the ground. Then the whole mass of them went whirling away through the darkness, trailing a few stragglers, heading for the black surface of the large lake, and the island at its centre.

Jean turned towards Morgana, speechless. The tall woman shook her head. "No—now is not the time for talk. Go back to sleep."

"I doubt I'll sleep now. I'm too nervous. What were those lights, and what does it all mean?"

"Knowing that will not help you to sleep," said Morgana cryptically.

And with that Jean had to be content. But she did not sleep. She lay down, gazing with wide eyes at the lake and the distant island, its mound of dark trees now shot through with glimmers of green.

When dawn touched the eastern sky Jean sat up, stiff and sore, and quickly abandoned any further attempts at resting. She sat and watched day break, as she had so often watched it from her window at home: watched as the whole sky turned a soft indescribable colour, neither gold nor grey but holding something of the warmth of one and the coolness of the other. The sun appeared, casting its yellow-white brilliance on the undersides of the clouds and outlining smaller cloud-tufts hanging suspended beneath them. The ponds on the barrens blazed beneath the sunrise, lakes of light almost too dazzling to look at directly. But it was chilly: Jean's breath steamed visibly on the morning air.

As the sun inched upwards she saw that the lakes, too, were breathing. From their sun-bright surfaces seethed and billowed tall columns of airy vapour, glowing in the golden light. She had seen such a thing before, on other lakes and rivers and on the ocean. Sea smoke, the sailors called this gauzy exhalation of the water: her father had told her that it occurred when the air was cooler than the water beneath it. The surface of the largest lake was smoking like a cauldron, and the island at its centre was nearly obscured: only the tops of its tallest trees could be seen. As Jean stood, stretching her arms and stamping her feet, her eyes caught a movement in the sky. Two shapes were flying towards her, out of the sun: she could not see them properly for the glare, but as they drew nearer and crossed the sky above she saw that they were birds. A pair of swans, their white plumage tinted with gold as they flew westward, out over the great lake, heading towards the half-hidden island. Could these be the same swans they had seen yesterday?

Jean glanced at the camp. The others slept on, as though enspelled. Morgana as usual had vanished: out flying in bird-form herself, the girl thought with a tiny shudder. She did not like to wake her friends, weary as they were, but neither did she want to lie down again on the dew-sodden ground. She helped herself to a little dry bread from one of the packs, and a drink from a water-skin; then for no particular reason she walked towards the large lake. Mist-shapes hung on the air before her as she stood on its shore. The longer she looked at these pale plumes and filaments, the more she began to see shapes in them: branching trees, fairy towers and arches, dancing figures. But they were thinning, fading . . . No, the whole *lake* was fading, wisping away before her eyes.

As the mist lifted, Jean saw stretching before her a long valley, its smooth grassy sides green-golden in the rising sun. Far down at the bottom there was a wide, shallow pond, and from its sparkling surface rose a great outcropping of pale grey-white rock that glittered like ice, or like a tremendous crystal. Near its top the gleaming rock gave way to soil, and from this grew dense groves of flowering fruit trees, maples and dark evergreens. The two swans drifted placidly on the shining pond, not far from the shore.

Jean blinked. The island: it was there still. But the lake itself had gone—vanished somehow, leaving only that pond like a modest remnant, and exposing the island's base. She swayed where she stood, afraid but also fascinated. Magic—this could only be magic. That much water could not evaporate in an instant, and it would not leave green grass behind, growing where only mud should be. Peering at the island, she could see a little arched bridge crossing the sunlit water to link it with the shore. *Someone* lived here.

Jean had already begun to descend the slope into the valley, without even realizing she had taken any steps. She halted, considering the situation. There was enchantment at work here: she recalled what Sir Owen had said about the *Gwragedd Annwn*. They were fairies, whether Seelie or Unseelie he had not said; but she thought again of King Arthur, and the arm reaching up from the water to give him Excalibur, and she felt a warm rush of hope.

"Jean!" cried Diarmait's voice in alarm. She turned. Her friends were awake, and standing there staring at her in disbelief. "Jean, what are you doing?" the king called.

"It's all right," she replied. "I don't believe there's any danger. They must be the Seelie ones, don't you think? If they wanted to hurt us they could have done it by now."

"Jehane?" Gwenlian queried. "What do you mean? Who are *they*?"

"The fairies, down there in the valley where the lake was. Don't you remember? Last night there was a huge lake here, and that island looked different—most of it was underwater."

They gasped at her as though she were mad. "Enspelled—the child is enspelled!" declared Owen, making the sign of the cross. "The *Gwragedd Annwn* have her in their power."

"Jehane," the queen said, "there is no valley. The lake is still there, where it always was. You are up to your waist in water. Can you not feel it? It must be cold as ice."

Now it was Jean's turn to stare at them. "Water? There's no water here." She waved her arms about. "See? It's all gone now."

Owen, who had been striding forward, stepped back hastily. "Ugh!" he exclaimed. "Do not splash about so! Must you wet us all as well?"

"I'm not wet." Jean walked back towards them. "Look, my clothes are dry! Feel them!"

They approached her hesitantly, touching her ragged cloak. "Jehane, your clothes are sodden," said Gwenlian. "I wonder you can stand it, with the morning air so cold. You are under a spell."

"Am I?" A thought had occurred to Jean. "Or are the rest of you? Remember, Lailoken said I have the second sight. He said I'm able to see things most other people can't—magic things. What if that lake was only an illusion?"

"*Glamourie?*" murmured Dubthach. "I have heard my mistress speak of such things. We had best wait for her return."

"She might be gone for days," Jean argued. "And the lake might come back and be real again, or something. I must go and see if anyone's down there." She felt an impatient longing to enter that valley—to confront, at last, the real powers of Avalon. Perhaps they *would* help her! Perhaps, like the

Selkies, they could also be persuaded to take action on her friends' behalf. This time she would make her request more specific: she would just ask for the Spear in Michael's name, nothing more.

She headed for the valley again. After a moment Diarmait joined her. "You see," Jean said to him, "the water isn't there, Your Majesty."

"It certainly feels like water to me," he answered, "and bitterly cold water at that." His face was pale and he was shivering. Suddenly his boot slipped and he went down, sprawling on the grass. Eyes wide, he gasped and flailed about with his arms, making choking sounds. Jean ran to him, but he did not seem to see her; she had to dodge his waving arms.

"Diarmait!" his wife screamed, running to the top of the slope. "Jehane, he has gone under! Find him—he will drown!"

It took a great effort, but Jean managed to seize hold of the panicking young man and drag him a few feet uphill. Grabbing his arm, she helped him to his feet. He coughed violently, crawling towards Gwenlian and the others. "No use," he said as soon as he could speak. "There is a curse on this lake: I sank to the bottom, and yet I could not swim. Had I not been in the shallows I would have drowned."

"Jehane, do not go back in there, I beg of you," implored Gwenlian, throwing her arms around her husband and helping him back to the camp. "It is you who have been spellbound, I am sure of it. If you go into that water again you will die."

Jean turned back, gazing at the view she alone could see: the white island in its gleaming pool, the shining bridge, the swans. "There's someone there," she said. "Please, I'm sure it's all right. And it may be our only chance."

Ignoring their protests, she headed back downhill with a quick determined stride.

But soon her heart was wrung by the frantic cries of her friends: she could not bear their anguish. Unfounded though it might be, it was very real to them. She turned back uphill. Their eyes widened, and she knew they could see her once more. "Look—I'm all right, do you see? I'm not drowning. There really isn't any water here. I'll be back very soon, I promise." But her heart was beating fast, and she was not nearly as confident as she sounded. Her knees were shaking by the time she reached the bottom of the green vale and approached the pond. She saw the two swans suddenly spread their wings and soar gracefully over the lake and circle the island's green roof. The white wings dipped, and they dived down into the trees.

The island: that was where the fairies must be. There was no other place in the valley where anyone could live, no caves or dwellings of any kind. She remembered how the living lights had flown over the lake to the island. It was the heart of the magic. She must go there.

She was struck by the beauty of the island as she drew nearer to it. Its trees were clad in the young green leaves of spring, and the white blossoms of wild apple trees rose among them like showers of sea spume. Distant places so often promised enchantment, she reflected: summer-hazed hills blue against the sky; rainbows rising from far-off fields; the "tiny fairy houses" of the Southside hills. But always the magic and allure vanished on approach: the hills were not blue when you came to them, the rainbow retreated, the houses on the Brow were not tiny after all. This island, though, would be different. It would hold its magic even when you came to it, surround you with wonder and splendour. The place where you were would at last be the place you wished to be.

She was at the shore of the pond now. There was a glint of scales a few feet away, and the finned tail of some large fish briefly splashed along the surface; but there was no other living thing to be seen in the whole valley now that the swans had gone. She crossed the bridge, and saw that it, like the lower part of the island, was made of some cloudy, quartz-like crystal. Shallow steps cut in the shining rock on the other side led her up to the edge of the woods. Turning back, she saw her companions still standing at the valley's edge, and waved her arms over her head until they caught sight of her. They waved back and she heard them shouting, but could not make out the words at this distance. She raised her hand to them one more time, then turned and entered the wood.

The trees here grew close together, blotting out the sky with their branches, and thick moss grew over their network of roots. It was a tranquil place, quiet as a church; she was reminded of the great forest near Brigid's abbey. She heard no sound, not even birdsong; the moss muffled her footsteps, and no wind stirred the green branches above her. Then slowly she became aware of a faint music, coming from somewhere deep in the woods. Had the place not been so silent she would scarcely have noticed it; as it was, she half-thought she was imagining it at first. She turned her head this way and that, listening intently: it was definitely the sound of someone playing on a stringed instrument of some sort, but she could get no clear impression of the direction from which the music came. One moment it seemed to be straight ahead of her, but when she walked forward that impression changed and she became convinced that it was coming from somewhere off to her right. Again she changed direction, and again she corrected herself. Finally she stopped, frustrated. She could still hear the music, but it seemed no closer than when she had first heard it.

She was standing under the sweet-smelling branches of a grove of apple trees: petals fell from them like snow, dappling the forest floor. Glancing down, she saw on the moss among the blossom petals another shape, also white but bigger. A feather, from quite a large bird. Was it a swan's?

As she stooped to pick it up there was a little sharp cry overhead, and she looked up to see a small dark-plumed bird with red beak and legs perching on a blossom-laden bough. There could be no doubt about it. The bird was a chough.

The chough? she wondered. Could there be more than one in Avalon, after all? But even as she thought this she doubted it, just as she doubted now that it was an ordinary bird.

"You're something—someone—special, aren't you?" she whispered. "You helped me, that time in the forest. Are you a fairy in disguise? Have you come to help me again?" The bird watched her, its sleek black head cocked to one side. Its eyes were dark and bright at once, like shiny black stones.

"Chaw," it said.

Then it flew off in a soft rustle of wings, into the green heart of the forest.

She followed it promptly, stepping quickly over roots and

ducking under hanging boughs, never taking her eyes off its small dark form. Now and then it would alight and wait for her on some low perch, flying away again only when she came close. And as she walked she found she could hear the music more clearly: the glittering strains of a harp under the hands of some skilled player, performing a lively tune. Nearer she drew to it, and nearer, and finally the harpist came into view.

He was sitting on a mossy rock on the brink of a small pool; a young man, no more than twenty-five years old or so, with hair falling in thick wheat-coloured waves around a pleasant, handsome face. He wore sandals strapped nearly to the knee and a short white robe, like a Roman toga; a great green cloak lay over his shoulders, held fast by a bronze brooch; in his hands was a small bard's harp with a plain wooden frame.

In the pool a single swan drifted, idly preening the snowy plumes of its back and wings.

The man glanced up casually as Jean approached, her footfalls soft and tentative on the moss. She stood in front of him, her hands folded, and swallowed hard before she spoke. "If you please, Sir . . . I want to find the fairies. To speak with them—if I may?"

"Speak then," the man said. His voice was unexpectedly rich and resonant—a golden voice, she thought, to go with the golden hair.

"You're—one of them?" she asked. It was hard to believe. He looked so real, so solid and alive, so *human*.

The man had returned to plucking at the harpstrings, his blond head bent over the instrument; but at her timid query he glanced up once more.

"I am their king," he said.

Chapter Fourteen

JEAN STARED AT HIM, speechless.

"You did not know that the fairy folk had a king?" the young man asked, setting down his harp. "I had thought my fame reached farther. King Finvarra I am to the Gaels, Gwyn the White to the Cymri. Some call me Gwyn ap Nudd—that is, Gwyn son of Nuada—for they believe, in their simplicity, that I must have a father like any common mortal!" He laughed. "Nuada Silverhand has been dead for many an age, and I am older than he."

Jean continued to gape wordlessly at the man, who returned her gaze calmly with his clear blue eyes. In the pool the swan circled, its plumage now dazzlingly white in a shaft of sun, now dimming almost to grey as it glided into a patch of shade. Presently it reared up, beating its wings and hissing softly. He glanced at it, a smile curving his lips.

"There was—another swan," Jean said slowly. She still clutched the soft white feather in her right hand; slowly she opened her fingers and stared down at it.

"We enjoy taking that shape, Queen Oonagh and I," the man said, glancing at the feather. "We do not need clumsy feather-mantles such as mortal mages wear, nor enchanted animal-skins like the Selkies. If we wish to take on another form"—he made a careless gesture with one hand—"why then, we take it."

She studied his face: the healthy colour of it, the shapes of muscles and bones beneath the skin, the hint of golden stubble on the chin and cheeks. It all looked so real, so natural, but . . . "This isn't *you* either, is it?" she said. "You're not a man, not really."

"I am a man," he said simply, "at this moment." He looked at the swan. "Come, Oonagh! Will you not join us? We so seldom have guests!" The great white bird paddled close to the mossy edge of the pool and heaved itself out of the water, shaking droplets from its wings. And then— it was not there. There was no slow transformation: it vanished, like an extinguished flame. In its place there stood a woman.

Her hair was gold with a touch of red in it, and fell in one long rippling cascade to her feet. On her head was a woven chaplet of apple blossoms. Her loose floating gown shimmered, green as a leaf in one light, silver as hoarfrost or dewed gossamer in another. She looked Jean up and down with eyes of pure emerald green, and her bearing was as regal and arrogant as the swan's. "A mortal," she observed to the golden-haired man in a low mellifluous voice. "So. Do you mean to keep her? She is not so fair of face as the other mortal maidens you have fancied."

Keep me! thought Jean with a start of horror. "I can't stay," she said hurriedly, dropping the swan feather and backing away.

"Why else would you have come, if not to stay?" the king asked. "You sought the fairies, and you have found us. It is given to few to see past our *glamourie* lake and come to Ynys Witrin."

"Ynys—?"

"The name of this island, the seat of our court."

"Is this—the Seelie Court?" she asked him, her hope swelling.

"So it is called by some. Your names for our kind are so many! The Seelie and Unseelie courts; the Neutral Ones; the Watchers; the fairies. The Gaels name us the Daoine Sidhe; the Cymri, the Tylwyth Teg. Some call us gods. Even our mortal offspring, the Tuatha de Danaan, are sometimes called gods by your race. Nuada and Lugh and the mighty Dagda: they have passed out of this world long since, but they still stand tall in the tales of men." He quoted softly. "'And it came to pass, when men began to multiply on the face of the earth, and daughters were born unto them, That the sons of God saw the daughters of men that they were fair; and they took them wives of all which they chose.' So it is written in your book of Genesis, the book of beginnings. Have you never read those words?"

She shook her head, wide-eyed.

"It continues: 'When the sons of God came in unto the daughters of men, and they bare children to them, the same became mighty men which were of old, men of renown.'"

"It's not—possible." Could he be lying? Was there such a passage? She could not believe it. The "sons of God" were the angels: how could they marry—have children? She tried to state, again, that it could not be; but though her mouth worked no sound came out.

He laughed at her appalled expression. "No? Flesh and spirit were not so far apart in those early times. And my people have never believed that there should be any division between the two. But few mortals mingle with us now, and we do not seek them out as once we did."

She gazed at him in wonderment. *An angel—he's an angel. It's all true then, what they said about the fairies. The neutral angels—*

Queen Oonagh abruptly turned and began to walk away. "This one is not for you, King of the Sidhe," she remarked, over her shoulder. "She is not like the others, and by that I do not mean her looks only. There is nothing about her that can put her in your power."

"You think not?" he returned easily. "She does not wear garments of green, perhaps, but what of her eyes? Fairy-green they are. Yes, you belong to us, young one," said King Gwyn, turning back to Jean.

"She is no child of this world," the queen added as she moved away through the trees. "She is one of the Shadow-born: there is iron in her bones."

"Yes, she has come a long way, indeed. But what of that?" He gazed at Jean with interest, perusing her as though she were some intriguing curiosity. "You do not play *fidchell*, perhaps?" he asked, presently.

"I—I don't know what that is."

"A game of strategy played on a board: here in Gwynedd they call it *gwyddbwyll*." She shook her head, feeling bemused, and he sighed. "A pity. It has been long since I challenged a mortal to a game of *gwyddbwyll*." He gestured to a mossy log lying nearby. "But you are weary, being human: you may sit if you wish."

Jean gratefully accepted the fairy king's offer. Her legs felt far from steady. "Your Majesty, I came to ask for your help," she said, clasping her hands together so they would not tremble. "It's true that I come from the Shadow-world. My name is Jean MacDougall. I'm travelling through Avalon with—some other people, and I don't dare stay long in this place. There are bad people about, the Lochlannach—do you know about them?" He nodded. "We're trying to get to Caer Wydyr for safety. And . . . and we're looking for the Spear of Lugh." She looked closely at him, but his face showed no reaction. "Some fairies took it from the monastery on Saint Michael's Mount. I don't suppose you'd know where it is now?"

"I know," answered Gwyn, "for I commanded that it be taken. It is folly to leave such weapons in the hands of children."

"I'm glad you did," said Jean earnestly. She had no wish to annoy him by questioning his actions. "The Lochlannach might have gotten hold of it otherwise, and used it against the Avalonians. But couldn't we please have it—my friends and I?"

"And what will you and your friends do with it?"

"Defend Avalon from the Lochlannach, and their allies. The Lochlannach say that Woden—the Gallows Lord—sent them to take this island. It isn't fair. The people of Avalon can't hope to fight these men *and* their war god." He said nothing, and she drew a deep breath. "So I ask for your help—in the name of Saint Michael."

She searched his face again, but still King Gwyn appeared unmoved. "You think to bind me with a name?" he said, raising his brows. "Mortal men gave that name to the Prince of Light, long ago: do you know what it means?" She shook her head, and he spoke the name slowly, drawing out each syllable. "*Mikha-El*: 'Who Is Like God.' But you cannot begin to understand what he truly is—he whose name you invoke so lightly. You have seen only those quaint images in churches, carved or painted by mortal men, that cast him in their image. He is far more than that. A great, burning glory he is: like the sun, only fiercer. The essence of the true Light, of which all light in this world is only a shadow. But we are not his servants, child. We are the Neutral Ones, the Watchers. We belong to the middle world, and we will do nothing to support the cause of the light or of the dark."

She sat in silence, dismayed by this unexpected setback. "But come with me now, and I will introduce you to my court," Gwyn offered, holding out his hand to help her up.

At least he did not seem to be angry. She might have another chance to persuade him, if she humoured him and stayed a little longer. She took his proffered hand shyly—it felt warm and real, like living flesh—and let him lead her through the trees.

"I didn't see anyone else, on the island or in the valley," Jean ventured timidly as they passed under the flowering boughs of the apple trees. "But of course, your people don't always take human shapes, do you, Your Majesty?"

"Very few of us do, now that we have chosen to dwell apart from mortals. Most prefer to be beasts or birds, or trees—"

"Trees!" She stared up at a knotted old apple tree as they walked under its boughs.

"We can take any form we choose. Some like best to be trees, and dream long, green dreams of earth and sunlight and water. Others prefer more lively forms. One of my fairy courtiers goes about in the shape of a white stag; another is a hare; another a golden eagle. There is one who dwells in the pond surrounding Ynys Witrin: he wears the shape of a great fish, a salmon."

"I think I saw him." She looked up at a sound of whirring wings. The chough was accompanying them, fluttering from branch to branch as they walked. "Is he a fairy too, Your Majesty?" asked Jean, pointing. "I thought he was just a bird at first, but I don't see how he can be. He—he *knows* things a bird couldn't know, and he helps me whenever I'm lost."

"I know him well. He is not one of my people, though he often comes to Ynys Witrin," said Gwyn. "Long ago his was a name of great renown in Annwn."

"But—who is he, really? *What* is he?"

"He is a bird," said Gwyn simply. "That is what he is now, and what he desires to be."

He led her back to the crystal steps. She could see Gwenlian and Diarmait and the others sitting high up on the grassy slope to the south, where they believed that the lake ended. There was no sign of Morgana. They stood and shouted as she descended the steps—into what must look to them like water. She waved back, anxious to show them that she was safe. "Can they see you, Your Majesty?" she asked Gwyn.

"No," he replied. "They see nothing I do not wish them to see. I can cast illusions, *glamouries*, over some things, and make others invisible. If they tried to enter this vale, it would seem to them that they were sinking into deep water. They would feel the cold and the wet, believe that they were drowning."

She remembered Diarmait's panic. "It's all in their heads, then?"

"Even so. They see only what is allowed—unlike you, Shadow-girl."

They crossed the glassy bridge. An old white caribou with branching antlers was standing at the water's edge, beside a dappled grey horse. From the fields beyond a snow white hare came springing, while a great bird made wide circles in the hazy sky above. A sound of music came from the shore on the opposite side of the island: Jean turned sharply, and saw Queen Oonagh there. The fairy woman was seated on a sort of throne made of tree branches, their twigs still in leaf. A second throne stood empty beside her. She was surrounded by attendants: handmaidens in long trailing gowns with flowers in their hair, beautiful young men in robes like Gwyn's. Some of these were carrying harps like Gwyn's, or medieval lutes. The other Sidhe, Jean noticed as she drew closer to them, did not look as human as Gwyn or Oonagh did. They were a little too perfect, their faces too smooth and blank—like statues, animated with an unnatural life. She could not look at them for long: there was something about them that disturbed her.

The king led her before the assembled fairies and introduced her. "This is Jean MacDougall. She has come to us from the world of the Shadow." They murmured together as the king took his seat at Oonagh's side, staring at Jean with their strange glassy eyes.

"And what does she desire of us, O King?" asked one of the smooth-faced maidens.

Jean stepped forward, nervously clasping and unclasping her hands. "Please, my world is at war. My people's enemies are very strong and cruel, they want to enslave us and rule over us."

"But what is that to us?" asked Queen Oonagh.

"I—I've come to ask you for your help," Jean stammered, "Your Majesty."

"You must know we do not intervene in wars, be the warriors mortal or immortal," said Oonagh. Her tone was one of complete indifference.

"Please, Your Majesty, I don't expect that at all," Jean explained. "I only came to ask if you could let my Avalonian friends have the Spear of Lugh."

"To use in battle?" the queen inquired, a faint hint of a frown beginning above her emerald eyes.

"In defence, Your Majesty," Jean said quickly. "To stop the Lochlannach from conquering this island."

"You know of its second virtue?" she asked.

"I beg your pardon?"

"Each of the Four Treasures," Gwyn told her, "has its own particular virtue, granted by the Tuatha de Danaan who made them. The Spear of Lugh can turn the tide of any battle; the Sword of Nuada cuts through anything that its blade may strike, be it flesh or steel or stone; the Lia Fail sings at the crowning of a true monarch; the Graal furnishes a magical feast from which no one goes away empty, though ten thousand should sit down to dine. But the Spear and the Graal were sent away into your Shadow-world long ago, by powers unknown; and when at last they were brought back, each had been given a new virtue. Both can now heal any wound. I cannot say how this happened, for the fairies cannot enter the Shadow or see past its dark veil. But somehow the Spear and Graal were changed."

"I *have* heard that the Spear was used to heal people—"

"But you ask for it only so that its destructive power may be used. As always, mortals think only of killing." There was no rancour in Oonagh's voice, merely dispassionate assessment. "But tell me, girl, why should you care about Avalon's war? This is not your home. You were born in the Shadow-realm: your place is there."

"But I can't fight there, not in that war," explained Jean. "Here, though, I might be able to make a difference. I know the three worlds are really one, part of one universe, and it might help my own world if this one is saved. I can see how the war in Annwn is like the one in mine. Our enemies, the Nazis, are like the Lochlannach: they want to take other people's lands for their own. And they're cruel and dishonourable—they kill even women and children." She remembered the words Abbess Brigid had spoken in the chapel. "A nun once told me there's really one great war that we're all fighting together. And a Druid named Lailoken said—"

"Ah, Lailoken!" King Gwyn smiled.

"You know him?" asked Jean in surprise.

"I know *of* him. He is one of the last of the half-breeds, the god-men. The Tuatha de Danaan are gone now: long ago they retreated to the island of Tir Tairngiri and took fairy mates there, and their descendants have hardly any human blood now. There will be no more like the Danaan tribe, or old Lailoken. His sire was a renegade sprite, one of the Unseelie Court. Our kind do not breed with mortals any more, nor will we interfere with their lives."

"Gael, Cymri, Lochlannach," said a deep voice. Jean jumped violently, for it was the white caribou that had spoken. "All mortals are the same to us. It matters not to the Watchers which race holds sway in Avalon."

"Mortals are interlopers." This voice came ringing down, clarion-clear, from the wheeling shape of the airborne eagle. "When we first entered Annwn all was peace and harmony here. No living thing moved in it, the hills were barren beneath the sky and the sea that lapped the silent shores was empty."

"Then life came into the worlds." One of the fairy maidens was speaking now. "Annwn and its Shadow were filled with creatures that grew and breathed and bred. They were so unlike us, they interested us greatly, and we never tired of watching them. It was then that we first began to assume material forms. When your people first appeared, human, we went to them in their own form and likeness, and spoke to them in their language. We showed them the herbs that heal, and passed our wisdom on to them."

"But they were brutal and violent," said the white caribou. "They took the ores from the earth's veins, and made them into weapons to hurt one another. And they went into the Shadow-realm, and brought out of it the cold metal, iron, that makes the worst weapons of all. There is none in Annwn, and the feel of it is hateful to us."

"We drove them back into the Shadow-world," said a fairy youth, his perfect face as empty of expression as his voice. "And closed up as many of the portals as we could. But always they found a way back into this world."

Oonagh looked coolly at Jean. "Do you understand, now, why we take no interest in your mortal conflicts?"

Jean gathered her wits desperately. What evil fate had caused everything to rest on *her*? An older and wiser person, like Lailoken or the kindly abbess, might have succeeded in swaying these haughty beings with well-chosen words and reasoned arguments. *What use am I?* she thought in despair as she cudgelled her brains for a reply.

"You cared about us once," was all she could find to say, "Won't you guide us again? If you hate wars, then help us to end this one. Help us find peace."

"And you will never go to war with one another again? Can we believe that?" returned Oonagh.

She looked at the queen wretchedly. How could she promise that humans would never go to war again? The faces before her were mask-like, implacable. Suddenly she realized that she was wasting her time: absolutely nothing she said would make any difference. These beings were old beyond reckoning, powerful beyond imagining, and quite impervious to her pleas. Had they truly possessed a spark of compassion, they would have intervened on their own by now. The deaths of innocent humans, of little children, were nothing to them. For a moment Jean seemed to wilt where she stood. And then, in the very midst of her hopelessness, anger came.

"You could stop all this," she cried, furious. "You have the power! If you don't like our battles and fighting, you could help us to end them. You just don't want to be bothered. We're nothing to you, and you don't care how we suffer!" Even as she spoke she knew she had gone too far; but she was exhausted, and she knew now she had nothing to lose.

They began to move towards her menacingly. "You dare to rebuke us, the Immortal Ones?" they shouted. "Go! Leave us, mortal! We will not have you in this place, disrupting its harmonies! Return to your Shadow-world!" The caribou levelled his antlers at her, the eagle dropped screaming from the sky. She backed away, hands feebly upraised to fend them off. *Now you've done it*, said a dry little voice at the back of her head. But she was too miserable to care.

There was a whir of wings, and a small blue-black shape darted over her head. It was the chough. But he was not attacking her: he flew over the heads of the fairy host, uttering his shrill little cries, as if remonstrating with them. They ignored him, and continued their advance.

"Enough!" King Gwyn alone had remained motionless, seated in his leafy throne: now he rose. "Most mortals may be cruel and prone to wickedness, but this one is not. I sense no evil in her, and I will not have her treated so." At his commanding voice they subsided, and he waved imperiously to the fairy musicians. "Play!"

They obeyed. He walked up to Jean, who looked at him unhappily. "I'm sorry," she said in a low voice. "Please, may I go now, Majesty?"

"Jean, Jean." He shook his golden head in wonder. "Never have I known a mortal who would dare to do as you just did."

"Most mortals are too smart to talk back to fairies, I suppose." She was able to give a tiny smile. "I don't know why I was allowed into Avalon, but I'm sure it was for a reason, Your Majesty. It might even have been fairies who opened the doors and let me in. I—I was hoping it was your people, and that you could tell me what it is I'm meant to do here."

"It was certainly no one of my court who let you in, my sharp-tongued Jean. Your answer does not lie here. There are other powers besides the fairies who can control the portals between worlds. Otherwise, we would have shut them all long ago." He continued to gaze steadily at her, his blue eyes bright and intent. "I am not sorry you came to us, though. I would be interested to hear about the world I cannot see. Will you not linger here awhile? You must not blame us for refusing the help you sought," he added as she remained doubtfully silent. "It would be a departure from our true path of neutrality. Darkness blinds, but so does light—as you must know if you have ever looked rashly into the sun. We decided aeons ago that we would not exist at either extreme. That is why we chose to dwell in Annwn, the middle-earth that lies between Shadow and Light."

Jean was puzzled. "Chose—? But weren't you thrown out of Heaven?"

"No, indeed. We made a choice, when the great War was waged, to take neither side. We hoped thereby to restore peace and balance to the universe and to reconcile our brethren. But still the war raged on between light and dark, defenders and rebels: and in the end the latter were consigned to the Shadow where no magic can thrive. The hosts of the Light would have driven us thence too, but Mikha-El would not allow it. Instead, he let us stay in Annwn. Here we have practised our philosophy of neutrality—the Middle Way—for longer than your race has existed. We have sought, many times, to teach it to mortals, but they would not hear. You are different though: I believe that you could learn it, in time. Stay with us, Jean MacDougall."

She shook her head. "No—I'm sorry, Your Majesty, but time is the one thing I haven't got. I really have to go—"

He laughed. "Foolish mortal. I can alter time!" Gwyn gave a negligent wave of his hand; and the world changed.

The clouds no longer drifted across the sky above, but rolled and raced like steam from a boiling kettle. Seasons turned as she watched, amazed: leaves turned colour and fell and sprouted again; drifts of snow swelled up like foaming surf and ebbed away again into the green grass of spring; moon and sun sped through the heavens like flying birds as night flickered into day and back again; stars danced in the dark like the windblown sparks of a great fire. The universe moved in a vast pulsating rhythm before her bewildered eyes.

"Oh, stop it—stop!" she gasped, feeling dizzy.

He waved his hand again and the whirling dance slowed. She looked wildly around her: nothing in the valley had changed, her friends were still where she had left them. It had only been an illusion, a *glamourie*.

"I could speed the march of days in truth, if I willed it—or slow it down. Time is not my master, but my servant," said Gwyn.

He moved closer to her, staring into her eyes; and suddenly she was caught up in a vision, more vivid and real than any she had ever had. She saw a land covered in ice and snow, with mighty glaciers stretching as far as she could see. An old woman, white-haired and wizened, sat upon a throne of sapphire-coloured ice: her robe was white as the snow at her feet, and she gloated as she gazed on the icy wastes. She could not be human, for the cold did not seem to touch her. Then the sun broke through the grey clouds: armies of luminous figures seemed to march upon the glaciers, and the ice began to thaw and retreat, leaving behind it smoothed boulders and long gouges that became lakes. The hag of winter fled wailing into the north. Centuries passed before Jean's eyes in a long and stately procession. She saw cities spring up on the plains, towers and domes and spires reaching up like flowers seeking the sun, and among them moved a people as tall and beautiful as gods. She saw priests leading white bulls into a temple for sacrifice, where a golden bowl gleamed upon an altar; she saw a man like Gwyn, fair-haired and broad-shouldered, draw out of a roaring forge a spearhead whose heated bronze glowed golden. She saw the Lia Fail, standing not on its earthen mound but in the paved central plaza of a great city; and she knew that it was old even in that far-off time, older by far than the gold-roofed buildings that surrounded it. She saw Fragarach, blazing with its blue fire, held aloft by a handsome warrior: his sword-hand was clad in a gleaming silver gauntlet—or was it that the hand itself was silver?

Then there were clouds running before the sun, and white walls of foaming water crashing down upon gold and silver roofs, and a mountain belching fire from its cloven side into a blackened sky. The cities were gone, and in their place were islands surrounded by the sea. A wild people lived in them, dark-haired, copper-skinned, hunting the seal and the caribou with flint-tipped spears. Then a ship came from across the sea, a leather-hulled curragh, and its straining sail brought it to haven on a stony shore. A tall woman in a white robe with flowing red-brown hair stepped out of the boat, followed by eight others: the nine women walked inland, their hands linked, singing as they went. Later there were other curraghs, carrying dark-robed men with long beards or tonsured monks or plainly dressed men and women clutching small children in their arms. Finally, to another shore, came a great wooden vessel at whose prow a man stood, a band of gold about his brows.

The image faded. Jean blinked, realized she was still standing in the fairy vale. "You have seen the ancient history of Avalon," King Gwyn told her.

"You saw what *I* saw?" cried Jean. "But I thought the vision was in my head—"

"It was I who gave you the vision. Those things I saw with my own eyes, going back to the dawn of the worlds."

There was a goldenness all around her, a richer quality in the light. "The sun's *setting*!" she exclaimed in disbelief. "How long have I been here?" Was it even the same day? She looked for her friends and saw with relief that they were still there, sitting together in the grass, though there was still no sign of Morgana.

"The chief part of one day has passed while we stood here," said Gwyn. "Do you see, now, why your great war does not mean to us what it does to you? It will pass in what for us are mere moments; then life and order will come again. Grass will grow on battlefields where the vanquished fell, fortresses will fall in ruin, memory turn to myth—and what is all that to us?"

"I must go to them," Jean said in a dull voice. Her last shred of hope was gone: she could no more reach Gwyn, for all his sympathetic manner, than the rest of his people. How could she plead with him for the lives of Gwenlian and the others, for Andy and Jim? They were insignificant to him, their lives brief as the lives of flowers, and of scarcely more concern.

"Do not go yet," said Gwyn. "You interest me, Shadow-girl. You possess the inner vision: you could learn our ways."

"But I'm also a mortal, just as you said. I can't be like you. I won't live forever, for one thing. And I *do* care what happens to people."

The fairy king made no reply. On the far side of the pond a voice like a young man's began to sing softly.

> Come with me, O come my beloved,
> Unto the hill and the forest free:
> There shall be mirth, and merry feasting.
> Come, maiden fair, and dance with me.

"That is an old song," Gwyn told her. "Many songs that your people sing are in truth fairy songs that mortals overheard and copied in ages past." Oonagh and her fairy women were dancing now, holding hands as they spun about in a circle. The fairy beasts gambolled in the fields, tossing their heads and rearing up like heraldic beasts on coats of arms. The music seemed to come not only from the Sidhe instruments, but from the island too, from its blossoming apple trees: sweet strains flowed from their silver branches like the songs of hidden birds, blown to her on the breeze with their fragrant scent.

> High leaps the hart, and the hind follows after;
> Heark to the dove, crooning on the green bough;
> Full is the forest with joy and with laughter.
> Come, do not tarry; O come with me now!
> Better the grove and the leaf-roof living
> Than the cold stone of the castle hall.
> Sweet is the berry, and cooling the dew-draught
> Drunk in the shade of the willow-tree tall.

Another wooden throne was brought by the fairies and set by the side of the pond. Gwyn seated himself, and motioned to Jean to take the new chair. Though she was anxious to leave now, she could not summon the nerve to disobey the fairy king.

A lovely woman came towards them, carrying a golden platter piled with twigs covered in white apple blossoms. She held the platter out to the king with a curtsey, and he waved his hand over it. At once the petals fell away, green leaves grew before Jean's eyes and little green apples swelled on the twigs, then turned plump and golden. "Eat," he invited her, plucking an apple and holding it out to her.

She stared at it and at the other fruits, beautiful and impossible on their platter. Her mouth watered. She had eaten nothing all day except for the bread and water she'd had for breakfast. But wasn't there some warning in the old stories about fairy food—didn't eating it put you in their power? She shook her head regretfully. "No, thank you."

Gwyn smiled. "Are you afraid our food will ensorcel you? Tell me, why *should* the thought of remaining in Ynys Witrin fill you with horror? You cannot really prefer to go back to your Shadow-world! Loved ones you have there, no doubt—perhaps a young man, a suitor?" She thought of Jim, but even his memory had begun to fade slightly: she could no longer picture his face as though he stood before her. The thought of him brought only pain. "Of what use is your love for them?" Gwyn continued. "Some will die before you, and fill you with grief; others, outliving you, will mourn you in their turn. Is this grief and loss what you truly desire? Stay here with me, my green-eyed Jean."

"Chaw!" cried a tiny voice overhead. The chough was circling above them, his shape black against the golden sky. Gwyn looked up at the bird with a frown.

"No, my friend," he said, as if the chough had spoken. "You are welcome here, but I'll not be chastised by you. You have known the peace of Ynys Witrin: why should she not know it as well? Go!" He made an impatient gesture, and a wind seemed to catch the little bird's body and blow him away from them. Gwyn turned back to Jean. "You need not stay forever. You can remain here in a dream of happiness for as long as you wish before you return—a dream you can look upon with delight all the rest of your life."

Jean suddenly thought of Peggy O'Brien, aged and shrunken in one day, and felt a surge of panic. *All withered and wizened she was, like an old old woman* . . . Was this what had happened to her? And would Jean really be able to leave, once she was under the timeless spell of Ynys Witrin? Or would she sink into a kind of trance, and wake to find herself wrinkled and aged, her whole life dreamed away? Worse still, might she find that she was unchanged, but that many years had gone by in her world and everyone she knew was dead?

She was in the hands of beings both uncaring and capricious: she could not escape, and she could not risk angering them again. "No," she said out loud, beginning to tremble.

Gwyn leaned close and spoke softly, this time in a tone almost of menace. "I could *make* you stay, you know."

She recoiled. "You said you never interfere with us mortals! Then how can you force me to do something I don't want to do?" she protested. Her heart began to pound, and she could not meet his eyes. Their blue irises were unfathomable: one might as well try to plumb the sea's deeps by gazing on its surface, or try to see the stars beyond the midday sky. Her own eyes dropped, focused on the bronze brooch at his shoulder. It was shaped like an incomplete circle, held in place by a large pin; tiny serpentine creatures wound their coils along its curved length.

"I could make you want it," he said, still in that soft dangerous voice. "I could fill your mind with bliss, place you in a fairy spell so that you would forget everything but the vale of Ynys Witrin."

"You won't do that," said Jean, through lips stiff with fear.

"And why not?" She could feel his penetrating stare, even though she was not looking directly at him. He rose and stood over her, taking hold of her chin in a steely grip, forcing her to look up at him. "Why not?" he repeated.

With an effort she met his eyes. "Because then I won't be—*interesting*—any more."

He suddenly laughed, releasing her, and returned to his own seat. "Ah, Jean, I am no match for you!" he declared, smiling. "It is a thousand pities you do not know the game of *gwyddbwyll*: what a player you would be!"

The fairy musician had begun to sing again:

> Come with me, O come my beloved,
> Unto the hill and the forest free:
> There shall be mirth, and merry feasting.
> Come, maiden fair, and dance with me.
>
> Never did lantern shine so brightly
> As the white moon in the evening sky;
> Nor marble fountain make such music
> As the stream's murmuring lullaby.
> When you are weary with fairy revels,
> Under the stars you may take your rest.
> Moss for your pillow, the wildwood your chamber,
> Slumbering safe on the green earth's breast.

Jean roused herself in alarm; her eyelids had begun to droop. To her horror she saw that the last light had gone, and it was now dusk: even more time had passed while she sat enspelled. Rising, she was relieved to see a little campfire burning bravely on the slope: her friends were still there, they had not abandoned her. But for how much longer would they remain? And how could she get back to them?

Through the blue twilight swarms of glowing, green-white globes came, circling about their heads, hanging in the air like living lamps. "The Sheerie," said King Gwyn. "They are lesser spirits, and manifest only in this form. Your kind say that they are evil beings, and lead travellers to their doom in the marshes. Fools! What fault is it of the Sheerie if some drunken mortal should take one of them for a lantern, and stumble into a pool? They are our friends, and shall provide the lamps for our feast."

Feast! She was feeling faint with hunger. She would never be able to resist food now . . . But she must, even if she starved.

He pointed to the few bright stars which were now piercing the eastern sky. "Behold the high houses of our brethren. Some of the Neutral Ones chose long ago to return to the heavens, and dwell now within the stars that are the gateways to the realm of the Light. Dana, Gwydion, Arianrhod and the rest: we call them the Shining Ones. Soon you will see them all assembled in their glory. But it is not their time yet; only the sky's brightest and greatest lords are assembled. Dawn and dusk are *our* times. When it is neither day nor night, light nor dark, that is when the fairies hold their revels."

The music played, the fairies danced; overhead the Sheerie wove ribbons of light across the sky where the stars shone—their greater, loftier kin, as it now seemed to her. Their glowing patterns were mesmerizing; she could not seem to draw her eyes away from them. Was it the Sheerie who spun above her, or the stars themselves? Dark and light whirled together, and she watched their dance from a distance, admiring but at the same time removed from them, a passive observer on the edge of a dream.

Then there was a raucous cry, and a black shape plunged towards her out of the spinning heavens.

It was a huge raven, flapping through the dusk, scattering the Sheerie as it came. Her senses cleared. She watched as the bird settled on one of the glacial rocks in the meadow, cocking its head at them. Its jet black eyes glittered on either side of its great spike of a beak, and its shaggy throat-feathers and the plumes atop its head bristled outwards like an anger-stiffened mane. It croaked again—and then its squat dark shape was replaced by the figure of Morgana, standing tall and regal on the boulder like a statue on a pedestal. Jean's heart leaped with relief.

"Give me the Shadow-girl," the sorceress commanded, without any preamble or show of reverence. Jean held her breath, suddenly glad of the sorceress's proud and haughty presence.

Gwyn and the other beings looked unimpressed. "Perhaps I am enjoying her company, and do not desire that she leave yet," the fairy king replied, meeting Morgana's challenge with calm insouciance.

She glared at him. "You of the Sidhe say that you take no sides in mortal conflicts," the sorceress said. "But if you do not free this girl, those stubborn fools yonder will not leave, and the company of Lochlannach who are marching across the barrens even now will capture them. You will have helped the foreign barbarians greatly by placing in their hands the King and Queen of Avalon, and the Sword of Nuada also."

"The Sword would be of no avail to the Avalonians in any case," Gwyn said indifferently. "The one called Woden has the protection of the ancient runes, and can turn any sword blade and quench any flame. Only the Spear of Lugh can strike him down, as he well knows."

"The Spear!" Morgana hissed. "Where does it lie? What have you done with it?"

"We will not give you a weapon to use against your kin or ours. Woden the One-eyed may lean towards the dark, but he is still our brother."

All this time Oonagh had been gazing intently at Morgana, without joining in the verbal exchange. Now, as the king ceased speaking, she suddenly addressed the sorceress. "Tell me of your father, mortal. Was he a Druid perhaps, by name Morfessa? Did he not dwell in a little hovel on the eastern barrens, among the old stone circles?"

Morgana stared; for the first time Jean saw the sorceress completely taken aback. "You knew my father?" she said at last, stepping down off the stone. "Then—is my mother also known to you? She was of the fairy folk. I have been seeking her for years upon years."

"Seek no more, then—for I am she. I, Oonagh, Queen of the Fairies."

There was a long silence. Both Morgana and Jean were speechless; Gwyn looked on in amusement, one eyebrow slightly raised.

"I was with the man Morfessa for a time, long years ago," said Oonagh. "It was a pleasing idyll for me, a change from seclusion at Ynys Witrin. And there was a child, which I left with him when I returned to my own place."

Morgana stood gazing at her mother: a woman seemingly the same age as herself, if not younger, smooth of face and golden-haired, lissome as a girl. Green eyes looked into green for the space of several heartbeats. It was hard to tell from the sorceress's face if she was disappointed, surprised, awed or angry. There was only a blankness there.

At last she spoke, and her tone was bitter. "There was a child—aye, there was indeed. So it was *you* who conceived and bore me, then left me behind!" Morgana snapped. She took a swift stride forward. "You struck off a spark of fairy fire, and you stifled it in flesh. I have the spirit of a Sidhe, but my powers are small and feeble next to yours. I cannot walk the wave, nor ride the wind, nor change my form, save with the aid of some talisman or spell. Only take them from me and I am no more than any mortal!"

Oonagh's face was cool, unmoved. "Do you say, then, that you would rather you had never lived? Perhaps you are right; for you will never feel at one with the common mortals, nor can you find a place here with us. Yes, I should not perhaps have had you—a half-human child, fit neither for one world nor the other."

Don't talk to her like that! Jean wanted to cry. *Can't you see how you are hurting her? Your own daughter . . .* But Oonagh neither knew nor cared that her words wounded, she only spoke her mind. She was cruel as a cat is cruel, without any thought of malice.

Morgana swung away, anger plain now on her face. Jean felt pity stir. A meeting between mother and daughter, long separated, should not look like this. Morgana should not have searched so long, so hard, to be met with a reception so cold and uncaring. But Jean dared not let her pity show. Nothing, she knew, would anger the sorceress more, and Morgana could easily vent on Jean the fury she could not loose upon the fairies.

"The girl may go," King Gwyn said suddenly. He took the bronze brooch from his cloak, flinging the garment aside, and pinned it to Jean's blouse. "Take this. It will allow you to come again to your own home in your Shadow-world, to the very place and time from which you left it, when the fates that govern your comings and goings are pleased to return you there. As to the spear that you seek, it is not here; and were I to tell you directly where it lies I would break my sworn oath of neutrality. But if those at Caer Wydyr have the wit to unravel a riddle, then tell them this: the Spear of Lugh lies both near to them, and far; it lies between the sky and the sea; in Avalon, and not in Avalon."

She could only stare at him in confusion.

"Come, child." Morgana turned her back on her mother and strode off, heading for the slope atop which Gwenlian and the others still waited by their fire. Jean turned and ran after her. "They will only toy with us further if we linger," snapped the sorceress. "It was ever their way. Never will I have aught to do with the Sidhe again! Lies and trickery are all that can be expected from them." Jean realized Morgana was not really speaking to her. The sorceress was merely venting her frustrations, talking to Jean as one might to a cat or dog, or to the air. She would never reveal so much of her private emotions to a person of any importance. As always, Jean was just *there*: a half-perceived presence.

The young king and queen of Avalon and the two warriors stood up, giving glad cries, as Jean and Morgana drew near and they were able to see them again. Jean ran to her friends and was eagerly embraced by both.

"We feared you were gone forever," said Gwenlian. "But, tell me, what took place there in the lake's depths? Did you see the *Gwragedd Annwn*?"

Wearily, Jean gave them a quick sketch of her story. They peered curiously at the bronze brooch, and pondered Gwyn's riddle, but could not understand it any more than she could. "So I haven't really helped you at all, I'm afraid," said Jean.

"That remains to be seen," Diarmait replied. "If the riddle has an answer, we may find it yet. We will tell it to our wisest councillors at Caer Wydyr, and send a messenger to Lailoken the Druid."

"Never mind! I care only that you are back safe, Jehane," said Gwenlian. "I have heard many tales of this Gwyn ap Nudd. He entices mortal maidens into his realm and keeps them there, enspelled and helpless. You have had a lucky escape."

"It was Morgana who saved me—" Jean began, but the sorceress interrupted.

"There is no time for this chatter. As I flew in the upper air I saw a great company of Lochlannach warriors, armed with iron, and marching this way across the barrens."

Owen and Dubthach swung round, and Gwenlian paled. "They are hunting us! Those people in the settlement have told their warriors about us, and now they are on our trail!"

"Come," said Diarmait. "To the south and east then, with

all possible speed! Our only hope is to get to Beaufort. Leave the cart and pony, they will only slow us down."

"It is so dark," panted Gwenlian as they began to run away from the valley. "How will we know the way?"

"I will go ahead of you in raven-form," answered Morgana. "Follow the path of my flight." She sprang into the air, her great black cloak billowing up about her; and then there was the black bird, just visible against the dusky sky, flying away from them.

"Follow her!" called Diarmait. "But keep your hands on your swords. I can see the light of torches, far behind us—"

As he spoke his voice became fainter, like a voice on the radio when the volume is lowered. Jean found she was straining to hear him. Then she gasped. The forms of her companions had turned blurry, fading from her sight. But it was not her vision that was at fault: for they too were crying out in alarm, calling her name as though they could no longer see her. "King Diarmait! Gwenlian!" she shrieked. It was no use: soon even the faint, blurred forms were gone. She was plunged into a deep seething darkness, and then blinded by a burst of brilliant light.

Jean flung up her hands protectively and closed her eyelids against the blaze. When she dared to open her eyes again, rubbing at them, she saw that her companions had all vanished. Gone too were the barrens, the flying raven, the dark night sky. She was standing on the road below the Battery, looking towards the harbour where the troop ship carrying Jim and Andy to war was still pulling away from the docks. And the moisture streaming from her watering eyes turned to tears.

Chapter Fifteen

THE MAIL WAS LATE.

Jean stood looking out through the glass panels beside the front door. Ever since her early childhood she had liked to gaze out through these panes of tinted glass, seeing the world outside bathed in their bright colours. The green panes gave LeMarchant Road a dim underwater look, like a street in a submerged city; the yellow ones suffused it with a warm golden light, and the blue wrapped it in a ghostly gloom. She peered through the red one—but the strange fiery glow it gave to sky and street reminded her too much of her nightmare about the warplanes and the winged women. She drew back from the door and resumed her restless pacing.

She had had another bad dream the night before, the darkest and most sinister one yet: at least she hoped it was no more than a dream, though it had come to her while she still lay at the edge of sleep. In it she had stood on a steep rocky mountainside, looking up at a vast fortress of black stone. It was dark, but she could make out shapes running to and fro on the grey scree-slopes: black four-legged shapes like huge dogs or wolves, loping to and fro or standing watch with red eyes burning through the dusk; shapes like tall veiled women; huge black birds that circled about the towers. Then the castle's dark gate opened, and out of it came a creature of nightmare, many-legged as a spider but shaped like a skeletal horse, grey and gaunt with spavined ribs and a long angular head that made her think of the Hobby Horse. On its back was a dark, mantled figure. Suddenly a great wind gusted over the mountain, and all the strange dark figures were swept up with it: spinning light as dead leaves within the whirling vortices, they all soared away towards the west where a bank of cloud glowed dull red. As so often happens with nightmares, there was a fear that went beyond the images, a feeling of dread and horror that had remained with her all day.

After her return from Annwn and the departure of the two boys on the troop ship, life had continued as though nothing at all had happened. The school term ended; her sixteenth birthday came and went; her father went to work each morning as he always did and came home at suppertime with the *Evening Telegram* tucked under his arm. Only now the war news meant more to her than ever before. Occasionally a letter arrived from Andy, saying that he was well and had come through his training with flying colours. His brooding discontent was gone—why had she not seen that it came from a desire to join in the war? He wrote with enthusiasm of all the new places he had seen, of the port of Halifax and of England, of the daily rigours of life on board a warship.

There had only been one letter from Jim, brief and sketchy, as though he had written it in a rush. With every post she yearningly expected another, but weeks had turned to months and there was no word.

Jean tried to keep busy. Without the welcome distraction of school she occupied herself with household tasks, or accompanied Fiona to the library, or helped out with fundraising activities. Mrs. Macrae and Mrs. Ross had suggested holding knitting sessions in one another's homes to make warm socks and scarves for the servicemen, as women in the outports were doing: Jean, who had always been a good knitter, threw herself gladly into the work. She dreaded being alone. She would think too much of Jim and her brother, of the dangers that they faced; or of Gwenlian and Diarmait and the others, of what might have happened to them that night on the barrens three months ago. Had they made it safely to Beaufort, or not . . . ?

The mellow chimes of the grandfather clock rang out behind her, and she looked out the door-panels again fretfully. There was still no sign of the postman. Wandering into the sitting room, she gazed out the bay window, hoping to catch sight of him coming down the street. The house was quiet: Fiona was out with a friend and Mrs. MacDougall was talking on the phone at the end of the hall. Jean began to hum, then to sing softly, fingering the bronze brooch in her pocket:

> Come with me, O come my beloved,
> Unto the hill and the forest free:
> There shall be mirth, and merry feasting.
> Come, maiden fair, and dance with me.

High leaps the hart, and the hind follows after;
Hark to the dove, crooning on the green bough;
Full is the forest with joy and with laughter.
Come, do not tarry; O come with me now—

"Jean?"

She jumped slightly, and turned. Her mother had come into the room, looking pale and drawn, older than her years. "I don't know that song, Jean," she commented, frowning. "Where did you learn it?"

"In Mary's Bay," said Jean quickly. It was the first lie she had ever told her mother; she was afraid it would show in her eyes.

"In the outport?" Her mother still stared at her, and Jean realized that she must know all the traditional outport songs, having been raised on the Southern Shore.

"Or maybe I heard it on the radio," Jean amended. "I don't recall exactly. What is it, Mum?" she asked, suddenly frightened by the look on her mother's face. "Who was that on the phone?"

"It's bad news, I'm afraid. Oh, not Andy, don't worry—they'd send a telegram if it were . . . that."

Who then? Not Jim! Don't say it's Jim! How could I live if . . .

"I know you've not seen much of him lately, except for that dance back in May. But you played together as children, and I know it'll be a blow to you." She paused, drew a breath. Jean was not breathing at all. "That was Mrs. Macrae on the phone. She and Laura won't be coming to knit with us today. They've heard from Laura's uncle, and . . . It's her cousin Dan. The ship he was on was sunk, out in the middle of the ocean. Dan is dead, Jean."

She stared at her mother uncomprehendingly. Fear, relief, shame followed one another and were replaced by blank disbelief. Dan—Dan Macrae *dead*? How could that be? She suddenly saw his smiling face, the shyly proffered rose corsage. He had given it to her right there in the front hall. Dan dead? No, it was impossible. She collapsed slowly into a chair.

"I . . . danced with him," she murmured.

"Ah, I know. When you're young it always comes as a terrible shock. There'll be no knitting today. You can take a little holiday." Her mother laid a hand on Jean's shoulder, briefly, then left the room again.

But Jean wanted desperately to work, to use her hands, to find a way not to think. She got up and followed her mother into the kitchen. "Can I help you with that, Annie?" she asked, watching the apple-cheeked young maid mix batter.

"No need, there's two of us," her mother replied, kneading dough. Jean sat down quietly on a chair in the corner, watching them. Mrs. MacDougall patted the loaves into shape and made the sign of the cross on them with her forefinger. Jean still felt removed from everything: she found she was looking at her mother as she might look at an unfamiliar woman in a shop or on the street.

"Why do you always do that?" Jean asked her.

Her mother looked up, startled, in the act of drawing her finger through the dough. "It's just an old outport custom. My mother always did it, and my grannie from Ireland. They marked the loaves with the cross before baking them."

"When we does it back home," added Annie, "we always says 'Blessed bread.'"

"But why?"

Annie shrugged. "You never takes bread for granted." The front door opened and closed, and there were footsteps in the hall. "There's your dad back early," she said.

"Was there any mail for me, Dad?" cried Jean as Mr. Mac-Dougall put his head in the kitchen door, a sheaf of envelopes in his hand. He shook his head, and she sank back into her chair.

"I'm off to Placentia tomorrow," he said, "to see Ned Donahue. I'll be wanting an early breakfast, Annie."

Placentia. Memories came to Jean of a quiet cove and wooded hills, of picnics by the sea. On an impulse she pleaded, "Could I go too, Dad?"

He looked surprised. "I'm just going on business, Jean. I won't be staying over."

"Please! I haven't been to Placentia for years. I'd love to go back, even for a day—"

"We should all go," said Mum, her eye still dwelling worriedly on Jean. "I know unnecessary trips aren't right in wartime, but as long as you're going there anyway we might come along for the ride. We've done nothing at all special this summer, Allister. And things have been so grim lately."

Jean nodded vigorously. She longed to escape from the house. And Placentia was far down on the western coast of the peninsula. Not all that far from Cape St. Mary's. *From Caer Wydyr.*

If she should be allowed into Annwn again, she would be more likely to learn there of her friends' fate.

"All right then," Mr. MacDougall acquiesced. "But go to bed at a reasonable hour, Jean, and tell Fiona to do the same. I'll want to make an early start."

It took four hours to drive to Placentia. From St. John's to Holyrood there was a paved road, but after Holyrood the pavement ended and there was only a long zigzagging dirt road, the Salmonier Line, leading to the west coast of the Avalon Peninsula. But it was an old familiar route, full of memories. Halfway between Holyrood and Placentia they stopped, as always, at a small wayside tavern to rest and buy refreshing drinks, before driving on to the coast.

They arrived late in the morning, and had an early lunch in the dining room of O'Brien's Hotel where they had always stayed in the old days, when they used to come down and spend the night. Jean recalled her childish excitement on first dining here years ago—her very first meal in a restaurant. It still had the same dark wood trim and tomato red paisley wallpaper, and outside the front window was the big apple tree she remembered climbing with Andy. When lunch was over her father went up the street to talk to the store manager he had come to see. Fiona wanted to go down to the shingle beach, and Jean and her mother went with her.

They strolled on over the clinking stones, wrapped in memories of picnics and boat rides, of fair days spent on the beach and the hills and foggy ones spent playing indoor games. But for Jean the thought of U-boats kept intruding, even though the cove was not deep enough for them. How many might be lurking in the bay beyond? No: she must *not* think of that. It brought the memory of Dan Macrae's smiling face before her, and the pink rose corsage . . .

Fiona ran on ahead and began to skip stones across the water, as her father had taught her to do. She was already beginning to outgrow her clothes, Jean noticed: her legs seemed suddenly very long and thin beneath her cotton print dress.

Her mother cleared her throat. "Jeanie, I have something to say to you."

Jean looked at her nervously. "Yes, Mum?"

"You seem so far away sometimes, these days." Mrs. Mac-Dougall hesitated. "I hope that you don't ever feel . . . that is . . . I know you haven't always gotten as much attention as Andrew and Fiona. The child that's in the middle sometimes feels overlooked. If you think I haven't noticed all the little things that you do, the help that you give me every day, well . . . you're wrong. I do notice, and I wouldn't ever want you to feel that you weren't appreciated and—and loved—as much as your brother and sister." Her hands twisted awkwardly together as she spoke.

"Oh." Once Jean would have been glad to hear these words, would have lapped them up hungrily. But now her head was too full of Annwn and its peril, and the war in her own world. What did those old feelings of hurt and inadequacy matter? They were insignificant, a sign of childish insecurity: she had grown beyond them, maturing as she moved between the worlds. "No, I don't feel that way, Mum," she assured her. "Really I don't." Why did her mother look so worried? It was as if she was afraid that Jean would run away, or something.

"Look! Six skips!" yelled Fiona. "I'm going to try and do it again. Mum, when will Dad be back? Could we ask Mr. Donahue to take us out in his boat?"

"Perhaps Jean would like to do something else?" suggested their mother, smiling tentatively at her elder daughter. "You always loved walking in the woods, didn't you, Jeanie?"

Jean looked up at Castle Hill, at the ruins of the old fort on its summit. "I'd like to go up there again. Just for old times' sake," she said.

"Yes, that would be nice," Mrs. MacDougall said. "We'll all go, as soon as your father gets back."

That afternoon they climbed the hill to the ruin of old Fort Royal. It dated back to olden days, to the seventeenth century when Placentia had been called Plaisance and was ruled by the French. Nothing was left now but traces of a foundation and some crumbling walls, no more than waist-high in places. Jean had come here with her brother and sister on sunny days like this, years ago. They had played around the broken walls, pretended they were knights and ladies in a castle, slain dragons and repelled invaders. Her heart ached now for those carefree days. Did she and Andy and Fiona still laugh and play here as unseen, ghostly children, while her present self stood where they had been? And had she been here then, invisible and unknown to those children as they played, a ghost of the future? Time seemed to her more than ever like an illusion. The fairy brooch had turned the clock back for her; King Gwyn manipulated time as he saw fit. She remembered the phantom soldiers of Mary's Bay, carrying the body of their fallen comrade. Might she catch a sudden glimpse of a French soldier pacing to and fro in front of these walls, bayonet in hand, going about his sentry duties? How many people from how many ages were crowded invisibly atop Castle Hill, held apart only by the thin partitions of time?

And what of people in other worlds?

She sat down on one low wall and looked at the view, which was magnificent: there was no fog today, and she could see all the houses of Placentia spread out below, the broad sweep of the shingle beach and the tranquil cove and Placentia Bay all blue and hazy beyond. It was no wonder that the French and the British had fought over Placentia, with its surrounding hills offering commanding views to sentries, its large harbour, the stony beach for drying cod. It must look nearly the same in Annwn, she thought. Someone must surely have founded a settlement in Placentia's otherworldly twin—used the beach for drying fish—built a fortress, most likely on the hill that mirrored this one. There were certainly people there, on the other side of that unseen boundary. If only she could see and talk to them, learn what had befallen their island and their rulers in the intervening months.

Farther down the hill Fiona and her parents were walking slowly up the slope, her sister talking excitedly about something. Jean stood up again and closed her eyes, feeling the sun and the wind, trying with that extra, mysterious sense to reach beyond the curtain that separated her from Annwn . . .

"*Attention! Les flèches!*"

The shout, loud and urgent, made her eyes fly wide open.

The wished-for transition had occurred, this time in a mere instant. Gone were the weathered remains of walls, the view of the hills, harbour and town. Instead, high walls of grey masonry loomed up all around her. The quiet too had gone: everywhere men ran and shouted, speaking in some foreign tongue. Their faces were contorted with stress and fear. She was standing in the outer ward of a castle, halfway between keep and curtain walls. And it was under siege. As she turned around and around in alarm, a hail of arrows came hurtling over the walls and clattered down into the paved ward. Jean flinched back. Someone yelled behind her.

"Arrêtez!"

She froze as a man in a plain brown tunic ran up to her, a sword in his hands. She struggled to remember some of her school French. "Uh—*je*—*je m'appelle* Jean MacDougall. *Et je veux—je veux*—uh . . ."

"Dieu! Jean MacDougall? Vous plaisantez? Vous vous moquez de moi?" He scowled at her.

She stared at him helplessly. *"Ne bougez pas!"* He turned and shouted at another man. "Here, this girl says she is Jean MacDougall!"

"Oh!" Jean didn't know whether to laugh or just be relieved. "You speak English, too!"

"I speak all tongues of Avalon," the man replied, as the other ran towards the inner keep.

"Then I am in Annwn." She had thought so, from the arrows and the men's attire, but the French had momentarily confused her.

"You are in the fortress of Beaufort, home to the Knights of Saint George." He glanced up. A man in full knight's garb was running out the main entrance of the keep. It was Sir Owen!

"Jean MacDougall!" he exclaimed, running up and embracing her. "I cannot believe it! It is good to see you again!"

She was crushed against his heavy chain mail hauberk, but she did not mind: she was filled with joy at the sight of a familiar face. "Oh, you weren't killed, you weren't killed after all! Where are King Diarmait and Queen Gwenlian? Are they here too?"

"No, they left for Caer Wydyr months ago, with a host of knights—as many as the Grand Master could spare. Come, I will take you to him."

"But what's happening here?" she asked. "It's the Lochlannach, of course—but how many of them are there? Are we in danger?"

He hesitated. "I will show you." He led her back to the outer walls, to the entrance of one of the square watch-towers. Up the stone stair they went, all the way to the trap door at the very top of the tower. Two archers were crouching there behind the battlements.

"Look now," said Owen, "but keep low, and do not show any more of yourself than is necessary." He snatched up a shield that was lying on the stone roof. "I will hold this over you."

She hunched down and crept over to the crenellated edge of the parapet, and peered out through the narrow crenel between two big square merlons. Below her she saw dozens of Lochlannach fighters clad in furs and mail, some carrying swords and others axes. Archers with huge yew bows stood farther back, and some men were mounted on stolen horses. One of the riders was white-haired, but hale and strong with broad shoulders and well-muscled arms. There were about twenty warriors carrying a huge pine tree which they had cut down and were about to use for a ram, gripping the half-stripped boughs like handles. Behind them a man carried a banner with a black eagle on it. So familiar was its dark, spread-winged shape that Jean's eyes automatically swept down, looking for the swastika beneath its claws.

The Beaufort archers sent down a flight of flaming arrows, and the pine needles flared up and the men recoiled. Some fell screaming, with arrows in their chests or sides. Jean could hardly bear to look.

There were other figures there. Shapes like the living shadows of women stood among the warriors. As she watched they drifted soundlessly forward, stooped over the bodies of the fallen men.

Owen lowered the shield and led her away. "You saw the old warrior with the braided white hair and the scarred face?" asked Owen. She nodded. "That is their king, Einar—he is a brutal man, but brave."

Jean swallowed. "I saw—other things too."

"I feared you might. The Lochlannach messengers claim that they are accompanied by Valkyries—beautiful goddesses in battle armour who serve the god Woden. I did not want to believe them, but after some of the things that we have seen, I wondered."

"They're there. But they aren't beautiful." She trembled. She had recognized in them the veiled figures from her nightmare.

"Come, Jean. I will take you to the main keep."

He led her back down the stairs, and they ran across the pavements to the keep, which was like a smaller version of King Ciaran's. She followed him through a large austere hall with walls of unadorned stone, then through another door that led to a courtyard. In its centre stood an equestrian statue, the horse rearing on its hind legs while the rider leaned from his saddle to drive a lance into the coils of a writhing dragon. She recognized Saint George, patron of the knights. The sun-hero's warriors, pitted against Woden's wolves; King George's people battling Adolf Hitler's sea wolves; the angels of light warring with the demons of darkness in the chapel fresco. It was as Abbess Brigid had said: the ancient conflict raged in all times, in all worlds. And was it coming to a head now, in her time?

There was a steep stone stairway without a rail leading up the side of one wall, and she followed Owen up it to the battlements of the keep. Below lay a small town, occupying the same position as Placentia. There were several ships in its harbour, medieval-looking wooden vessels with tall castles fore and aft and fighting tops on their masts.

"The knights' naval base. There is more than one battle being fought this day," Owen told her.

He pointed westward, to where the cove and the hills opened out into the broad blue expanse of the bay, and there Jean saw more ships, sails and hulls moving swiftly before the wind. There were longships like those she had seen on Mount's Bay, only larger, some perhaps a hundred feet in length; and they had carved dragons' heads at their prows, snarling with open jaws. Other ships were there too, long galleys whose white sails bore the red cross of Saint George.

"The Lochlannach's main strength comes by sea," Owen said. "We have held them off thus far. But the Baie d'Espoir seems ill-named this day."

"What did you call it?"

"Many of the place-names in this area are in the old French tongue. That great bay that lies between Avalon and Tir Tairngiri is called *la Baie d'Espoir*, the Bay of Hope. I do not know why: it is an ancient name, and I have never heard the reason for it. But we should not be lingering here. We should all have gone to Caer Wydyr months ago, to add to its defensive forces."

"Oh. Why didn't you?"

"The Grand Master is a proud man. He will not leave Beaufort to be taken by the enemy."

A tall, lean man with shoulder-length black hair and a spade-shaped black beard was standing at the far end of the battlements, looking out to sea and talking to a group of armed knights. "That is Gilles Lamont, the Grand Master of our order—Gilles Le Vainqueur, as we call him." Owen led Jean up to him. "Here she is, Master: Jean Mac-Dougall."

The Grand Master ignored her and went on talking to his men. "Curse these devil's spawn, but they are cunning! See, they drive their longships, which lie low on the water, underneath a galley's bank of oars so that the rowers cannot move them. Then the *berserkers* swarm up the galley's side while it is immobilized, and attack the crew!"

Owen coughed and, securing the Grand Master's attention,

again indicated Jean. This time the man reacted, looking her up and down with a cold eye.

"And how came this slip of a girl to penetrate the defences of our fortress?" he demanded.

Owen smiled. "High walls and locked doors are naught to Jean MacDougall, Master. She is of the Shadow-realm, and comes and goes by unseen portals in the air."

"Then she is a witch." Le Vainqueur frowned.

Jean stepped forward. "Please, Grand Master, sir: Avalon is in danger. I had a dream about it, a sort of vision."

"It is true, Master," Owen said. "This Shadow-girl is a seeress as well."

"What would you have me do?" the bearded man replied. "Many knights I sent with the king and queen three months ago, to help them guard their keep. I can spare no more. We are besieged, as you can plainly see, and must protect our home."

"Our knights could cut through that rabble easily enough," Sir Owen urged. "If we all rode together we could force our way through, and ride on to the southern cape." Jean sensed that the two men had been having this argument for some time before her arrival.

"And leave Beaufort behind? This citadel has never fallen nor been occupied by any foe. Never. I will not give it to these barbarians to use for their base. How will we ever retake it?" Le Vainqueur started walking back along the battlements, towards the stairway. "No Templar fortress was given up lightly to a foe. Our knights fight always to the last breath."

"You're Templar knights!" Jean exclaimed.

"So our predecessors were called, when they dwelt in your

benighted world." He strode down the stone stair, his knights following. Jean and Owen trailed after them. "They fought for the faith against the Saracens in the Holy Land," he went on, not bothering to look back at her, "and their reward was to be arrested, tortured, burned as witches by the king of France. But some of our order escaped. From the naval base at La Rochelle the last Templars fled, in ships laden with priceless treasure. They sailed westward in search of sanctuary. And they found it—but not in the world they knew." He stood at the base of the statue, his hand on the sword at his hip. "We continue their order, under a new name in a new land. And we will not leave Beaufort."

Jean looked at him, trying hard to think of an argument that might convince him. But nothing came to mind; she had shot every bolt.

At that moment one of the men gave a shout. A bird, a small falcon, had flown right down into the courtyard. As they watched, it alighted on the stone head of the saint.

"An omen!" cried one man.

Le Vainqueur looked unperturbed. "Say you so? To me it looks more like a pigeon hawk."

With a cry the bird flew down onto the pavement. And then before their eyes its shape expanded and changed; in its place there stood a tall, white-bearded figure, clad in a grey feathered mantle.

"Lailoken!" cried Jean, and ran to him.

Chapter Sixteen

"I TOLD YOU THAT WE WOULD MEET AGAIN," he said.

So glad was Jean to see him that she clung to him like a child, gripping his arm through the feathered cloak, leaning her cheek against the woolly softness of his beard. He squeezed her shoulder reassuringly. "But I did not expect it to be here, I will admit. You are full of surprises, Jean Mac-Dougall! We must have a long talk, later." He patted her arm before withdrawing his own, then directed his next words to the Grand Master.

"Master Lamont, Caer Wydyr needs your aid," said Lailoken. "Why do you not answer the requests of your king and queen?"

The Grand Master stared back at him, unperturbed. "Am I right in thinking that you are the Druid Lailoken?" he asked in a tone of light irony.

Lailoken bowed courteously. "At your service, Master Lamont."

"Then I should warn you that I do not set much store by

conjuror's shows. Portents and magic and auguries are naught to me," said Le Vainqueur coldly. "I put my trust in God."

"But the prophets of the Bible worked many wonders, did they not, and foretold future events?" the Druid said.

Le Vainqueur raised a black brow. "Do you say that you— and this girl—are prophets sent by God?"

"I say that we serve the same cause as you do: the triumph of light and justice over all that is dark and evil. Alone and isolated we must fail: united in one force, we may stop this foe." He stepped closer to the Grand Master. "In bird-form I have flown far across the sea, to a nameless mountain that rises in the cold north of the world. There I saw a great fortress: Valhalla, the stronghold of Woden. The Lochlannach warriors believe that they go there when they die, to feast at Woden's table and be waited upon by the Valkyries, whom they picture as beautiful maidens. They are sadly deceived. The Valhalla I beheld was a dark place, of sheer ramparts and shadowy, haunted halls. There I saw the Valkyries: they were hideous creatures, wraith-women clad in tattered black rags. I saw them fly forth in raven-form from Valhalla's towers to all the ends of the earth, to inspire men in distant lands with thoughts of battle and conquest. Their war cries have penetrated even into the Shadow, as this maiden will tell you."

"It's true. And I've seen them right here outside your castle, sir," Jean warned the Grand Master. "There were some dark shapes standing among the Lochlannach—like horrible women. You've got to leave this place while you can!"

"The Valkyries can do no real harm as yet," Lailoken said. "They are not come to their full power. Their strength at this time lies mainly in their evil influence, their ability to inspire the Lochlannach to brutal acts. They are not Slayers, but only Choosers of the Slain. When their Master comes, that will be a different matter.

"I lingered as long as I dared near Valhalla, but at last the winged watchers saw me, and they pursued me back across sea and sky, even to the shores of Avalon. I could sense their fell minds reaching out to enslave mine: without my magical arts I could never have escaped. Grand Master, this war is larger than you can imagine. It encompasses many lands, and more than one world. It is larger than the Lochlannach, who are only the most minor of Woden's minions. When they march on Caer Wydyr, they will not march alone. Will you not come to the aid of your king and queen? What is Beaufort that you prize it above all Avalon?"

"*I* serve their royal majesties," declared Owen. "If the Master gives me leave, I will go." His tone made it plain that the Grand Master was keeping him from his real duty. There was a murmur of agreement among the other men, and Le Vainqueur scowled.

"You think to frighten me with these Druid's tales? I have said that I can spare no more men."

"But the main attack will be against Caer Wydyr, not Beaufort. Something draws our foes to that place: their dark master is sending his greatest force there. For that reason I have left King Ciaran's *dún* for Caer Wydyr, and advised him to send as many of his men as he can to Gwynedd where the need is greater. You see how few Lochlannach have gathered at your gate: thousands more are marching to the south. You need not fear for your knights and vassals. I can use my magic to assist you when you meet the enemy at the gates, and I can fill the sails of your warships with a strong wind that will carry them to safety. Is your love for a pile of old stone so great? Will you not go to Caer Wydyr in her hour of need?"

There was a restless motion among the assembled knights, like the sea rising before a strong wind. The Grand Master's lips tightened. If these men had to serve him or their sovereign rulers, it was plain where their sympathies lay. Rebellion was a real possibility. His pride must choose between remaining here in his castle alone, or riding out at the head of his men to answer the call of Caer Wydyr. Either way, Beaufort would still fall to the Lochlannach.

In the end, to Jean's relief, reason won out. "So be it," Le Vainqueur said, his tone bitter. "We ride out this day." And with that terse pronouncement he walked away from them with a swift angry stride, vanishing into the keep. There was a pause, then the other knights followed their leader.

When they were all gone from the courtyard Lailoken turned to Jean. "Well met indeed! But you must tell me all that has happened since you left our world, Jean. Their Majesties have told me the rest: how you advised them to disguise themselves, and went with them to seek the Spear at Michael's Mount, and persuaded the Selkies to fight the Lochlannach. And how you struggled with the fairy king, and wrested a riddle from him."

So as the knights prepared to abandon their fortress, running to and fro with weapons and supplies and belongings, filling the keep and courtyard with noise and urgency, she sat with the Druid on a stone bench in a quiet corner, and told him of the war in her world and how it went. She reached into her pocket and drew out the bronze brooch to show him, wrapped in its concealing handkerchief. As she shook it free, something else that had become caught in the handkerchief's folds fell out onto the pavement at her feet. It was a little morsel of bread.

"Now where did that come from?" she wondered aloud, looking at it blankly.

Lailoken stooped and picked it up, examining it closely. "Someone cares very deeply about you, Jean MacDougall."

"I don't understand."

"It is the custom for people hereabouts to put bread in their pockets to ward off the fairies. The bread is always blessed before it is baked, and so it is a potent charm against all forms of dark magic."

"But no one here has come near my pocket . . ." Jean fell suddenly silent. She remembered her mother and Annie blessing the bread dough at home; remembered her mother offering to press her skirt for her that morning, before they set out for Placentia. The skirt had had no creases that Jean could see, and there had been an odd furtive look on her mother's face when she brought it back. "Is it true?" she asked. "Would a little bit of bread really protect me from danger?"

"Not from physical harm, I fear: but your mind will be safe from the effects of fairy *glamour* and sorcery. No one can place you under any sort of spell so long as the blessed bread is on your person." She thought of King Gwyn, and the mesmerizing fairy dance that had almost claimed her will.

Lailoken now turned his attention to the brooch, which he pronounced to be very old, dating to the ancient kingdom of the Tuatha de Danaan when the four Treasures had been created. "A very powerful talisman, this," he said, handing it back to her. "It is not like the fairy folk to give such rich gifts. Guard it well, for it will be your link to both the worlds."

A few hours later they all rode up to the main gate, the knights leading, the common soldiers riding behind. The knights looked magnificent in full armour: not all wore the old-fashioned chain mail; some were clad in plate-armour of polished steel under their white tabards, and their helmets were crested with tall white plumes or with the figures of heraldic beasts. Jean rode behind Sir Owen on his big horse, near the front but still in the safe centre of the group where the servants and other non-combatants were. There were no women there apart from herself, nor any children: the knights were a celibate order like the Templars of old. At first she could not see Lailoken anywhere. Then she glanced up and saw the little falcon making sweeping circles against the sky. He gave a shrill cry as the gates were opened, like a call to battle, and dived towards the enemy in a long swift stoop.

The Lochlannach were taken aback only for an instant by the unexpected appearance of the besieged at their fortress gate; there was no time to work themselves into a *berserk* fury, but they quickly gathered themselves to charge. At the same instant, however, the falcon that was the Druid swooped low over their ranks. Jean saw long trails of vapour form wherever the bird flew, hanging heavy as smoke on the air. Lailoken was blinding the enemy, wrapping them in a thick veil of mist.

"Now!" commanded Gilles Le Vainqueur.

The knights all lowered their lances and charged. Right through the ranks of the bewildered enemy they raced, and the soldiers wielding swords and maces poured after them. Jean didn't want to look, but she was too afraid of falling to shut her eyes. She saw the shadowy wraiths, standing apart from the melee: one raised its hand, and at once, as if in obedience to a command, the white-haired King Einar rode up raging on his stolen mount. But his sword was struck from his grip, and he took the point of Le Vainqueur's lance in his throat and collapsed backwards off his horse, blood flying from his mouth as he fell. The rest of the Northmen were speedily overwhelmed. Few had horses, and they could not hope to meet the charge of these bold and disciplined cavaliers. They fell beneath the pounding hooves, were knocked aside by lances and whirling maces. The knights did not pause to wreak further carnage than was necessary, but went galloping on down the hill, helped by their own furious momentum: they could no more be halted than an avalanche. On they rode, to the foot of the hill and beyond, leaving behind the castle with open gate and the harbour from which all the ships had fled.

All the rest of that day they rode, with only the briefest of pauses so that the horses might rest. They galloped at first along a road that followed the sea, now running along the tops of high cliffs, now sweeping down beside long stony beaches. Then it changed direction, swerving inland across pastures where sheep grazed in placid flocks and lonely farmhouses stood small against the sky. Beyond the fields were barrens, rocky and wild, stretching for as far as their eyes could see. And above them flew the pigeon hawk, high against the clouds, leading the way.

Late in the evening the Grand Master called for a rest, and as it was a dark night with gathering clouds they decided to ride no farther, but to sleep and then start out again as soon as it was light. As they prepared to bivouac on the barrens one man gave a shout, and they saw flying towards them another bird, a solitary raven.

"Could it be—" said Jean.

"It is Morgana," declared Lailoken, who had come back to earth when they halted and resumed his human form.

As they watched, two black dots appeared in the dark sky: two more ravens, seemingly in pursuit of the first. They reached Morgana and overtook her, flanking her and matching her wingbeat for wingbeat. She flew down and alighted near the knights' camp, her wings mantled and her black beak gaping in anger. She croaked at her pursuers, a harsh and defiant sound. The other two made no reply, but hovered above her in tight circles. Then Lailoken approached, and they swung away to the east, flying at great speed. Morgana assumed her true form.

"You were well disguised, priestess of Dana!" The Grand Master spoke in his dry voice. "You deceived those birds into thinking you were one of their flock."

She threw him a contemptuous look, then spoke to Lailoken. "They were not birds, but servants of Woden. As I flew they spoke to my mind, sending me images of myself riding into battle with the Valkyries, and throned at Woden's side."

"They will tell him where we are!" said Owen in alarm.

"We are of little concern to him, I think," said Lailoken. "The Gallows Lord has other things in mind. But how did you know where to find us?"

"I wished to see what had become of Beaufort, and why no help has come from the knights of Saint George. I flew over the fortress and saw it full of Lochlannach, and thought all within must have perished; but since there were no bodies to be seen save those of Northmen, and no gallows set up to honour Woden, I concluded that the knights had escaped."

"We have given up our keep in order to give all our strength to Caer Wydyr," Owen told her.

"And well that you should. Already you may be too late: the forces of Woden also are on the march, and may come to the castle before you."

"I think not. We are all mounted, and they only have such steeds as they can steal."

"All the same, you would be wise to take your rest now, and not sleep for long."

It was decided that the Druid and the priestess should stand watch, as neither had need of sleep, and all the men of Beaufort settled down to rest. Later in the night, as she was trying hard to sleep, Jean overheard the Druid and the sorceress talking in low voices at the edge of the camp.

"We should use our magic to call upon the spirits of the earth," Morgana said, "on Medb and the Morrigan, on Cromm Cruach, on Cernunnos the Horn-Crowned King, and on the old hag, the *Bean Nighe*, who washes the battle garments at the ford and summons the souls of the dead. All these would come at our bidding, Lailoken, and aid us in our struggle."

"Only if we performed some great sacrifice for them. Cromm Cruach demands an offering of human lives, have you forgotten? The others are cruel and capricious, and may not destroy only our enemies once they are loose in the land. We cannot know what would happen in a war of gods. The Northmen say that if ever Woden and the earth-gods join in battle, the whole world will perish in *Ragnarök*—a fiery cataclysm."

"Well, what would you then? The Seelie Court will not help us, aside from taunting us with answerless riddles. There are no other great powers in Annwn—unless you consider Jean MacDougall to be our salvation!" Jean could hear the sneer in her voice.

"Her name means '*divine gift*,'" said Lailoken softly.

"A fine gift she is! Will she overthrow the forces of the Lochlannach? Will she duel the Gallows Lord for us? Our cause is hopeless, Druid. Those ignorant fools do not know it yet, thinking this merely another battle to be won with sword and lance! Woden has other servants than the Lochlannach, more terrible than they can imagine."

The unwilling eavesdropper rolled herself up in her cloak, and did her best not to hear.

They rode on before the dawn came, Lailoken and Morgana flying in bird-form before them; and early in the evening of the second day they came to Caer Wydyr.

Jean, who was expecting another grim and spartan fortress like Beaufort or Ciaran's *dún*, was filled with awe by her first sight of the Cymri citadel. They all saw it long before they ever came near it, as a great point of light burning on the barrens—as though a star had fallen to rest on the earth. Then as they drew closer, galloping along with the flat fields on their left side and tall sea-cliffs on the other, it grew ever larger and brighter, and Jean saw that the light was the sun's, reflecting off high walls that shone like sheets of glass or crystal. The beauty of those curtain walls stole her breath from her. No human hands could have raised their gleaming ramparts, or the translucent towers that joined them at the fortress's four corners. Above and within the square barrier that they formed, white towers soared, airy and graceful as floating clouds against the sky. From their cone-shaped tops long banners were hung, white with the red dragon of Gwenlian's house; and the banners streamed in the wild sea wind, so it seemed as though the dragons were flying.

"Caer Wydyr, the Fortress of Glass," Owen told her. "The Tylwyth Teg raised the outer walls long ago, by some great magic no one understands; but the White Keep within was built by Prince Madoc."

They rode in under the glassy gate, whose oaken doors were flung wide for them; and there before them rose the white-walled castle, built atop a green smooth-sided hill. On the grassy fields around it were many men, being trained for war: practising with pike and mace, or trading blows with wooden swords. In one corner archers aimed at targets that were already bristling with shafts. Jean saw Diarmait demonstrating sword-swings to the men with the wooden weapons. Gwenlian was there too. In a plain brown dress with a shortened skirt, her golden hair braided and twisted tightly at the nape of her neck, she was standing with the archers, bow in hand. The queen caught sight of Jean and Lailoken first, and ran towards them with a cry of delight.

"Jehane! Oh, Jehane, you have come back to us. Lailoken, you have found her again!"

"Not I," the Druid smiled. "When I went to Beaufort I found her already there." In spite of her fear and worry, Jean was overjoyed to be with her friends again. Diarmait saw her too, and came running.

"A sign—a sign!" he shouted. "Jean always comes to lend us her aid when times are darkest!"

They hugged, laughing and jumping about in their delight at seeing one another once more.

"All together again!" exclaimed the queen. "And safe within these walls—for the moment, at least."

"I cannot stay with you," Lailoken told them. "I must go and try to stop the Lochlannach fleets that are even now approaching Avalon. I will drive the wind from their sails, and wrap them about in impenetrable fogs so they cannot find the shore. But the sea is against me. The Fomori of Lochlan and Domnu, their dark goddess, tame the waves for the Northmen, to help them come safe ashore."

Jean was afraid. Of course she understood why the Druid must go and use his powers on the enemy. But he looked so weary, his face deeply lined and haggard. She wondered what it cost him to be always on the alert, lending his powers whenever and wherever they were needed, flying from one end of the island to the other to keep its borders safe. And what would the rest of them do here, without him to help protect the keep? There was Morgana—but could she really be trusted? Jean recalled her story of the raven spirit's offer. What if she were to change her mind and go over to the winning side?

Lailoken turned and laid a hand on her shoulder. "Jean, do not look so worried. Trust in yourself. Somehow I am sure you have a great role to play in this affair, or you would not have been sent."

She nodded, and with the other two she watched him walk through the gate and pass out of sight as it closed behind him. Moments later a falcon flew skyward beyond the battlements, its small form dark against the dwindling light.

That evening Diarmait and Gwenlian called a meeting of their chief councillors, which Jean was too tired to attend. Diarmait had promised he would tell her all that was discussed, and she went gratefully with Gwenlian's chief handmaiden, Morwenna, to be shown her guest chamber. She had come to know Morwenna quite well on the first half of the journey across the barrens, and liked her: she was a pretty, fair-haired girl, kind-hearted and dependable. It was she who had donned the queen's attire and pretended to be her on the road back to Temair. As the two girls passed the throne room Jean could not resist peering in, and Morwenna good-naturedly stopped and let her go in to look around. Jean was dazzled by the room's beauty. The walls were all faced with white marble, and hung with jewel-bright tapestries many yards across, showing battles and coronations and other scenes from Avalon's long and colourful history. The two magnificent thrones on the dais at the end were covered in gold leaf and flanked by the crouching marble shapes of two Welsh dragons. She moved closer to the dais; and then she saw the door in the back wall, behind the thrones. It was low and set deep into the wall, and was made of some dark metal, and something about it seemed sinister to her. She asked Morwenna where it led.

"That is the Iron Door," the handmaiden replied with reluctance.

"Iron Door?" Jean felt a tiny prickling at the nape of her neck.

"To keep the fairies out. It is no natural hill that this keep sits on, but an old fairy mound. Those who raised the walls of glass in ancient times dwelt within that mound, in secret chambers far from the sun and air. Once mortals began to settle in Avalon, you see, the Tylwyth Teg retreated beneath the earth. Prince Madoc and his people did not know this when they came: they saw only the walls and the fair green hill within, and thought this a perfect place in which to raise up a castle. No mortal would knowingly build on top of a fairy dwelling: it is an affront to the Tylwyth Teg and can only bring bad luck."

"Are the fairies still there?"

"Lailoken has been down there, and he tells us they are long gone; but the people still fear what lies within the mound. A foolish king once built this doorway, with a stair that leads down into the underground chambers. He and his courtiers used to go down there, and hold feasts and make merry. But in the end ill fortune came upon them all. There were strange apparitions seen coming and going through the door; and the sound of music in the night; and finally the young king lost his wits, and died before his time. Now a door of cold iron bars the way to the stair and the mound."

Morwenna shuddered. "No one but the Druid has dared to open that door for more than a hundred years, and even he has not ventured all the way into the mound's depths."

She headed quickly for the grand entrance again, and Jean made haste to follow her. Upstairs in the guest room Gwenlian's ladies had filled a wooden tub with hot perfumed water, and as Jean was soaking in it new clothes were laid out for her, a choice of several gowns. She decided on a soft dove grey cotte, with the trailing sleeves she loved, and when she was dressed they gave her jewels, a necklace of real pearls and a little gold fillet that rested lightly on her head. After a moment's thought she took the brooch and the little morsel of bread from her skirt pocket, and placed them in a pocket of her gown. Her hand shook a little when she held the bread. *Mum*, she thought, a lump coming into her throat. *Oh, Mum, it's all right; I'll come back. The brooch will bring me back to you and Dad and Fiona, on Castle Hill: you'll never even know that I was gone.* But she felt a twinge of misgiving. The fates that returned her to her own world had twice snatched her away when she was in danger, but they had also allowed her to come very close to death on other occasions. *Or did they—whoever they are—know that I'd escape each time?* she wondered. How could she be certain that she would survive *this* time? And if she were to die in Annwn, would she simply disappear from her own world?

It's no use worrying, she told herself. *Here I am and here I'll have to stay—and trust whoever it is to look after me. It's Diarmait and the others who are in the real danger.*

She decided to go back downstairs and listen in on the end of the council. Morwenna offered to show her the way, but Jean told her not to trouble. "The council's in the throne room, isn't it? I'm sure I can find my way back there."

The castle corridors were very quiet and almost deserted now that night had fallen. As Jean was walking through one darkened hallway, lit only by the occasional torch in a wall bracket, she saw a lone figure approaching her. It was a stocky, broad-shouldered man, walking with a powerful stride. He did not respond to her timid greeting, but came on in silence as though wrapped in thought. He looked vaguely familiar, though she could not quite recall where she had seen him before: his shoulder-length hair and thick beard were white, his face deeply seamed with scars, and animal hides were wrapped about his shoulders. In the next instant she realized where she had seen him before, and stopped short with a gasp.

King Einar!

Impossible. He was dead. She had seen him die a day ago, toppling from his horse with the Grand Master's lance-point buried in his throat. No man could survive such a blow. How could he be here, now, in Caer Wydyr?

The Lochlannach king scowled at her. Then as he walked into the circle of light cast by a wall torch, he vanished.

She gathered up her skirts and ran as fast as she could to the throne room. The council had just ended, and the king and queen were standing together near the dais. She sprinted up to them and told them what she had seen.

"It was a ghost, I know it was," she panted. "It wasn't just one of my time phantoms. He looked at me—he *saw* me." She was still shaking. "This isn't where he died. What is his ghost doing here?"

"Einherjar," said Morgana, overhearing. "The spirits of dead warriors who ride with Woden in the Wild Hunt. Ah, I see it now! He is building up an army—not of live men, but of dead ones."

"What do you mean?" demanded Gilles Le Vainqueur.

Her face was drawn and solemn. "I have been troubled by dreams and visions for many months, but I did not understand them until now. I saw all the earth in flames, and the sun and moon devoured by giant wolves, and the stars of Heaven quenched."

"Are you saying there is no hope?" asked an elderly councillor, blanching.

"Whether it is hopeless or not, we must fight to the end," Gwenlian told him. "Jehane has told me of the king and queen of England—her world's Logres—and how, after the sky warriors rained down fire upon their realm and left all in ruin, these brave rulers would walk about the burnt rubble of the buildings and comfort the people who had lost their homes. If they can summon such compassion and courage in the face of such fear and desolation, can we do any less?"

Diarmait turned and addressed the council. "They have also a wise councillor, a man named Church-hill, who speaks to the people and gives them hope. Jean memorized a speech of his, and taught it to me. The words are better than any I could devise, and so I repeat them now: We shall defend our island, whatever the cost may be, we shall fight on the beaches, we shall fight on the landing-grounds, we shall fight in the fields and in the streets, we shall fight in the hills; we shall never surrender!"

The young king's eyes flashed as he spoke, and the councillors applauded and cheered at his words. But Morgana rose in a swirl of black gown and feathered mantle.

"It is said that the bravest men of all are fools, for they do not know enough to be afraid," she said harshly. "This earthly war means naught to Woden. It is only a means to an end."

"And what end is that?" inquired Le Vainqueur, raising one eyebrow.

"He means to make war upon the other gods of Annwn. He will ride against them, with the Spear and his Einherjar. He will fight the earth-gods to win the lordship of the land; he cares not if he destroys it and us in the process. Then he will ride with his Wild Hunt into the sky to challenge the high gods, the Shining Ones: lords of the sun and moon and stars. Every Lochlannach we slay only adds to the ranks of the Gallows Lord!"

"Then we are doomed!" quavered the elderly councillor. "We cannot fight without killing, and we cannot fight a god!"

"Our only hope is in the Spear of Lugh: it can turn the tide of any conflict, even one as great as this. You can fight your useless fight if you wish, but I will have none of it. I go to the vale of Ynys Witrin, to seek once more after the hiding place of the Spear; and if I succeed, I do not promise that I will protect you."

"And what might you mean by that?" demanded Gwenlian.

Morgana's lip curled. "You call yourself a queen, and deny me *my* true title! Queen of Avalon am I, by right; and with the Spear in my hand I could rule this island as my ancestress Morgan did before me. All here would bend to my will!"

Gwenlian's cheeks flushed angrily. "Then we would fight you too!"

At that, the sorceress turned and stalked from the chamber without another word.

That very night she flew away from the fortress in raven-form, heading due north. "She may not have meant what she said. She is feeling angry and hopeless perhaps," said Diarmait the next day. "She may be going to look for the Druid, or fighting the enemy with her own magical powers. I am sure she will come back."

But many days passed, and Morgana did not return. Her absence began to worry them greatly. "She has gone to Woden, to accept his offer and reign by his side," declared Sir Owen.

"Nay, Owen." Gwenlian shook her head. "I cannot believe that of her. Morgana is proud: I saw her face when she claimed this island was hers. She could never share power with another. Certainly not this dark god, who seeks to rule over all things. He would end by ruling her as well, and she knows it."

Jean agreed. But she still felt troubled. Morgana had no one in Avalon who was like her. Lailoken and Queen Oonagh had both rejected her. She could no longer hope to join her mother's people. Who was left? The image of three ravens flying through a dark sky kept rising before her eyes.

Birds of a feather flock together, said a voice at the back of her mind.

"Morgana was right. If only we could find that wretched Spear!" sighed Jean a few evenings later.

She was standing on the crystal battlement with Dubthach, looking out across the sea. The sun was setting, shedding a fire red light on the waves. The Bay of Hope, she thought sadly. What hope *was* there for those trapped within these shining walls?

"The Spear was the god Lugh's: perhaps he will give us a sign. Lughnasa is but a few days away," said Dubthach.

"What is—*Lu*-na-sa?"

"It is our name for the first day of the month that you call August; to us it is the high festival of Lugh the Fair. In places where the Old Ways are followed worshippers of Lugh will gather at sacred places, hills and wells and holy groves; there will be prayers for the harvest, and much merriment. The Fianna hold horse races at Lughnasa in the warrior god's honour. I have competed in them myself, many a time."

There was a note of yearning in his voice. It must be hard for Dubthach to be so far from home, surrounded by people whose ways and customs were strange—and now he had been abandoned by his priestess-queen. He must feel terribly alone. Jean talked to him for a while, telling him of her own home, sharing with him her fears and hopes.

"You should not mourn your brother and your Jim, even if they fall in battle," he told her. "For they will have a special place in Tir nan Og."

"In—where?"

"You do not know of Tir nan Og?" He pointed towards the setting sun. "Far to the west it lies, an island paradise at the earth's end: it is there that the spirits of the departed go, to rest from their lives' labours. But the places of highest honour there are for those who go to war to protect their homes and families. Whether they die in battle or live to return home, their places are assured from the moment they take up arms and bid their loved ones farewell. So when your life's journey is ended, Jean Mac Dhughaill, and you are come to Tir nan Og's shore, seek for your brother and your beloved in the Hall of the Heroes. It is there that you will find them, feasting in the company of the mighty."

Jean was deeply touched by his words of comfort, and murmured her thanks. But he lapsed into brooding silence again, and she quietly left him to his thoughts. She saw the king and queen walking along the far end of the crystalline battlement, and went to join them in gazing out to sea. The air was full of flying birds, and ringing with their plangent cries. Directly below was the cliff's edge, one part jutting out like a barbican, and the sea further down; about twenty feet away reared the Craig yr Aderyn, the Bird Rock.

It was a huge sea stack, a sheer-sided granite column thrusting up through the surf, its top level with the three-hundred-foot cliff that faced it. Its upper third was capped with a thick whiteness, like snow on the slopes of a high mountain, save that it stirred and moved as one watched, revealing itself to be one solid living mass of nesting gannets. They were large birds, the size of geese, white with fawn-coloured heads and black-edged wings. Their downy grey young huddled close to them on the rock. Other gannets flew overhead, in flocks thick as whirling chaff, while on the surrounding crags and the sea rocks below roosted birds of many other kinds: gulls, kittiwakes, cormorants, murres. Jean had heard stories of the great bird colony at Cape St. Mary's, but had never seen it. She knew this at once for its otherworldly counterpart.

Presently she noticed a little black shape, fluttering about among the grey and white bodies atop the Craig. It was not large enough for a raven, and the gannets paid it no mind, but let it move freely through their crowded nursery. She pointed. "Look! Down there. Is that—"

Gwenlian smiled. "Yes, it is your friend, the chough. At least I suppose it is the same one; Lailoken believes that it is. It flies far, for such a little bird!"

"I wonder why he would come here?"

"I do not know, but he has been on the Craig for nearly a month now. There is a little hole, there, in the top of the rock—do you see it? Like a tiny cave no bigger than your hand. I think that he has made it his home, for I have often seen him fly into and out of it. Lailoken tells me that choughs like to make their nests on sea cliffs."

"He isn't just an ordinary chough, Gwenlian. He's a fairy, or something. He's helped me twice before, when I was lost and alone."

"You think that his coming is a sign of some sort?" asked the king.

"Didn't Lailoken think so?" Jean asked.

"He said very little, beyond what Gwenlian has told you. I think he knows more about that bird than he cares to tell."

"King Gwyn was mysterious about him too. He told me that he wasn't always a bird, but that was all he would say."

They all fell silent for a time, gazing down at the Craig yr Aderyn and its restive occupants.

"So close they are," mused Gwenlian presently, "and yet no one can ever hunt them. The gap between cliff and rock is too wide to jump, and if you killed a bird with an arrow you could not claim your prize. The Craig is too steep to be climbed, and any boat that came near it would risk being dashed to pieces against its rocky base. And so the gannets are perfectly safe on their own little island, and have been for countless centuries—within bowshot of Caer Wydyr, yet forever beyond reach."

Jean went rigid. "Beyond reach," she whispered. "Their *own* island . . ."

"What is it, Jehane?" Diarmait asked.

"Near, and yet far; between the sky and the sea; in Avalon, but not *in* Avalon. That's what King Gwyn was hinting at! Don't you see?" Jean jumped up and down and yelled in excitement. "It's *there*! The Spear of Lugh—it's somewhere on the Bird Rock!"

Chapter Seventeen

"HUSH!" cried Gwenlian, laying hold of Jean's arm. "Not so loud, Jehane!"

"What's the matter?" asked Jean, taken aback.

"It would be a terrible thing if Morgana were to learn of this," said Gwenlian, looking alarmed. "What if you are right? The sorceress is the only one of us who has the power of flight, and can go to the Craig. And once she had the power of the Spear in her hand, I am sure she would take Avalon for her own."

Jean had to admit that was a strong possibility. "Still . . . she's abandoned us, hasn't she? I don't think she's coming back here."

"We cannot know that for a certainty. She may yet return. Did her man hear?" She gestured in Dubthach's direction.

"I think not," said Diarmait. "He is standing far away, and the noise of the birds is loud."

"Oh, why doesn't Lailoken come back?" groaned Jean. "He can fly, too. He could go over to the Rock and look for us."

"Say nothing of this until he returns, I beg of you!" urged Gwenlian.

Jean reluctantly gave her word.

Two more days passed with no sign of the foe approaching, and no news of either Lailoken or Morgana. Jean went out the main gate now and then with the sentries, to add her second sight to their unaided vision as they patrolled the plain. The fortress that had once seemed so large and strong and comforting to her now looked like some great beast held at bay with its back to the cliff, preparing to fight for its life.

As time passed the very atmosphere seemed to grow more oppressive, as if at the approach of a summer storm. Soon no one at all was allowed out of the main gate any more, and it was opened only for the occasional messenger to come and go. The scouts had all returned, with news of a Lochlannach army marching on the barrens, and of fleets of dragon ships coming ashore to the east and west of Caer Wydyr, where the cliffs dipped down into flat stony beaches and welcoming coves. But the exact number of the enemy was unknown to them.

There was still no sign of Lailoken. Surely, surely, nothing could have happened to him! But Jean felt her unease swell into real anxiety as time passed and the Druid did not reappear. If the longships were coming ashore, then he had failed in his attempts to ensorcel them. She did not like to think what that might mean.

When night fell, people huddled together in the common rooms of the White Keep: the story of Jean's ghostly encounter had spread, and soon many swore that they too had seen phantom figures drifting through the halls and courtyards of the castle. Jean herself was afraid to be alone. But it was the sight of the stars in the night sky, great glittering stars strewn thick as salt across the heavens, that filled her with foreboding. She recalled what King Gwyn had said of the Shining Ones, how they stood watch over the stars of this world's sky—the gates of the Light, he had called them—and also what Morgana had said of Woden's plan. Could it be true? Was it possible for Woden and his dark hosts to ride up into the skies and beyond—into the black, cold, upper reaches of space where the sun and stars burned, and there challenge the guardian spirits that tended those celestial fires?

Horror filled her at the thought. She pondered, also, Lailoken's explanation of the solstice rituals and evergreen wreaths, the fear of ancient people that the sun might not return to warm the earth and grow the crops again. That was only superstition, but . . . *could* the sun of this world, its moon and stars and planets, be destroyed? And if so, what of the other realms—the Light that lay above Annwn and the Shadow that lay below? Annwn was the middle realm that joined and linked the two. If it were to disappear, would her own world wink out too, like a shadow when the object that casts it is removed? Or perhaps Light and Shadow would still remain, but with nothing to bridge them—nothing to keep them in contact with one another and connect the benighted mortals of the lower realm to the Light. Without a trace, a hint of that higher plane of being, what would life in her own world be like? How often had she admired some beautiful vista or piece of scenery, never guessing that it shadowed forth an even more beautiful part of Annwn—which in turn expressed the beauty of the World of the Light? *All the good would go out of things, all the inner beauty. We'd be lost in the darkness forever, lost* . . . Lailoken was right: the fates of the three worlds hung together. The loss of one could only harm the others irrevocably.

Her thoughts turned to her family back on Castle Hill, enjoying their day's outing and respite from the war, little knowing what greater danger hung over them. This was not like her previous adventure, when the faces of her loved ones had seemed to fade, obscured by the barrier between worlds. With Gwyn's brooch to link her to the Shadow, she could see the faces of Fiona and her parents as clearly as though she had just left them. Once more she wondered what would happen if she were to die here. Would she simply vanish before her family's eyes, never to be seen again? Had it already happened? Days had gone by, for both worlds: if the brooch did not again work its magic and turn back time, they would think by now that she was missing, dead.

And this time will they be right?

There was still a chance to do something, to prevent Woden's plan from coming to fruition. He had not ridden to war yet, at least. Perhaps he wanted to add more souls to his Einherjar, to make up some necessary number only he knew. And the Spear—*Gungnir*—he needed that as well . . .

Could it really be on the Craig yr Aderyn?

Oh, Lailoken, where are you? she cried silently. *Come back to us now!*

The day came when all but the fighting men were confined to the keep. The enemy had been sighted from the watch-towers on the curtain walls, and looking out through the narrow windows those within the keep could see the crystal battlements being manned by rows of archers, while mounted knights and pike men and foot soldiers gathered in the outer ward. The curtain walls, Jean knew, were like glass, too smooth for the enemy to scale, but also hard and unbreakable, like diamond. But the mighty doors were man-made, built of wood; they could be rammed, shattered, burned down.

She asked to join Diarmait when he went out to the curtain walls and stood with him on the battlements, gazing north across the barrens. They saw, far out on the plain, the enemy massing like hordes of insects, tents and fires dotting the landscape. "So many," she murmured.

"Not enough to threaten Caer Wydyr," he opined.

"They look like more than enough to me—" Jean began; then she stiffened as she suddenly realized what she was see-ing. More than half of those milling figures were grey and translucent, moving like drifting smoke on the air: the young king and his men could not see them. The Einherjar were present too.

When she told the king this, Dubthach, who was also standing nearby, said bleakly: "Today is Lughnasa. I had hoped for some help from the god of the Spear. But no help comes."

Jean longed to tell him her idea about the Craig yr Aderyn, but a warning look from the king silenced her. She stared unhappily across the plain. Presently they all saw a horseman come galloping from the enemy's ranks towards the castle. Another horseman followed, at a more leisurely pace; two great broad-shouldered warriors of the Lochlannach walked with him, one to either side.

After a few minutes one of the knights came running along the battlement towards them. "My liege," the knight said with a bow, "a messenger has come from the enemy. The king of the Lochlannach seeks to parley."

"The king of the Lochlannach is dead," said Diarmait, "or so I am told. The Lady Jean here says she saw him die. She even saw his ghost."

"You speak of Einar, Majesty," the knight replied. "It is true that he was slain. But these barbarians have crowned themselves a new king, Ulf by name."

"Jarl Ulf?" exclaimed Jean.

"And by what authority does Jarl Ulf declare himself a king?" asked Diarmait coldly.

"I do not know, Sire. But he awaits you upon the plain below."

They looked down at the horseman with the two guards, now standing motionless a short distance from the castle gate. "He is very bold," observed Diarmait. "I would have thought he would be afraid to come so near, lest we capture him and demand a ransom from his men."

Jean felt a little flare of anger. "He knows you won't," she said indignantly. "He knows *you* always behave honourably, even if his people don't." Though Ulf was too far away for her to make out his features, she almost imagined she could see the contemptuous sneer on his face.

"Well, let us go down and see him," said Diarmait.

"Shall I inform the queen, Sire?" the knight asked.

"Nay," he replied reluctantly. "I will go alone, with a few guards. If it is a snare of some kind they shall not have us both."

Jean, who had been quietly wrestling with herself during this exchange, now gained the upper hand on her fears and blurted: "I'll go with you, Majesty."

"There is no need, Jean."

"Yes, there is," persisted Jean, desperate to get the words out before she lost her courage again. "If there's any evil magic down there, I'll be able to see it and warn you."

They rode out the main gate together with a small company of knights, Diarmait on a tall warhorse and Jean sitting uncomfortably on a small grey pony. Jarl Ulf—King Ulf— watched them come with no sign of alarm, even though he and his guards were outnumbered.

"Do you see aught amiss, Jean?" Diarmait asked her when they were only a few yards away from the foe.

She shook her head. "There's nothing—no Valkyries, or anything like that—but something about this still feels wrong." Why did Ulf sit there so fearless and confident? What did he know to make him so unafraid? He looked haughty and proud, as he had looked even when he stood in chains before the kings and queens of Avalon—but now there was an ugly gloating look on his sharp-featured face, the look of a man who knows that he has already won.

"Well," Diarmait called out when they were close enough to see one another's faces, "I am here. What would you say to me, Wolf?"

"I desire to discuss terms of surrender," the Lochlannach replied curtly.

The Avalonian king was taken aback. "Your surrender?"

"No. Yours."

There was a brief, incredulous silence from the Avalonians.

"I do not know what traditions your people observe, Wolf," said Diarmait at length, "but in Avalon it is customary for surrender to follow upon defeat. We are, as you may plainly see, undefeated. Do you hope to frighten us into giving you a victory you dare not take by force? You still have not the numbers you need to take Caer Wydyr."

"Allies we have whom you cannot see," Ulf answered.

"They do no fighting either, it appears," Diarmait retorted.

"They have not yet gained their full strength, *boy*," sneered Ulf. "When they do, they will be well able to fight—but there will be no need for it. You will fall on your faces before them in terror."

"I do not fear your ghosts. The spirits of the dead cannot harm the living."

"I speak not of the Einherjar, but of the Choosers of the Slain. They will soon be joined by their Master, and any mortal will be able to see them then. It will do you no good to cower behind your gates on that day, boy-king. I give you a chance: surrender now, and I will suffer you and your people to leave unharmed. It is only the fortress I want, not you."

Liar, thought Jean in disgust as she watched his face. *Does he really think we'd believe that? He would never let the king and queen live!* She glanced out across the barrens, towards the dark army of living and dead. Then she gave a little gasp, too soft to be heard by any save herself. But Sir Owen, who sat his warhorse a few feet away from Jean, saw her face. "What is it?" he asked, leaning over in his saddle.

Ulf leered. "Yes, little witch. Tell them what it is you see."

"I see . . ." It was as though she dreamed again, only now she could not wake. With an effort she said, "There are—things out there. Like—like horrible animals and birds—and women. Valkyries." Something black and long-legged loped across the plain, and a flight of black winged shapes rose up to hover overhead.

"Those are ravens," said Owen, seeing her glance up at them. "Only ravens, waiting for battle. Carrion birds can always tell when war is at hand—"

"They're waiting, yes—but they're not ravens." As she watched, the birds changed, expanded in size; became black-clad figures with wide-spread wings gliding and wheeling on the grey air. "It's not carrion they've come for, it's something else." More Einherjar. The Valkyries, the Choosers of the Slain, were biding their time. Their own battle was yet to come, and would lie on another field than this.

Owen looked up quickly, but from his face she could tell that he still saw only circling birds. The horses knew otherwise, however. Her little grey pony snorted and shifted his feet, and all the great warhorses—steeds trained to withstand the shocks and terrors of battle—were rolling their eyes and tossing their heads. Ulf's mount took a jittery sideways step, and he checked it with a sharp tug of the reins.

Jean spoke to him directly. "You don't understand, King Ulf. You don't realize what you're doing. You think you'll get

Avalon for yourself, but you're wrong. Your god doesn't want to conquer the world. He wants to destroy it. When that happens you'll be destroyed too—along with everyone and everything in Annwn. It's the *Ragnarök* that is coming."

For the first time, for the merest instant, there was a flicker of fear in the grey eyes. Then they were cold and gleamed like steel once more. "Fool of a girl," he said flatly. "You wish to frighten me with old hearth tales. The world will not end for an age and an age—not until the All-father finds *Gungnir*. He has not found it in all this time; it is hidden, and will most likely remain so for many years to come. What care I what becomes of the world, after I am gone?"

"You'll be killed, you and your men," argued Jean urgently. "That's what he wants. You'll be turned into Einherjar to fight his war."

"No. It is you and your friends who will die." With that Ulf turned his horse's head, jerking savagely at the bridle so that its neck was forced painfully around, and galloped off across the barrens with his men running after him.

"It begins." Diarmait's voice was heavy as they rode back to Caer Wydyr. "The war that no one can win."

At dusk the enemy made their first move.

Jean and Gwenlian and her handmaidens were sitting in one of the solars when they heard the commotion in the outer ward, and looking out they saw men rushing to defend the gate, heard the hollow booms of a giant battering ram echo around the crystal walls. Through them a red glow could be seen, like fire shining through ice.

"They have come!" cried one handmaiden, throwing

down the embroidery at which she had been nervously working. "The Lochlannach will kill us all—"

Gwenlian stood, her face calm. "Nay, we must not give in to panic. Our enemies are rash: they have not enough men to take the White Keep, and if they break through the gate it will cost them dear. Once they are all within the curtain walls our fighters will be upon them, and they will be caught in a trap."

Jean, looking up, saw ravens hovering right above the outer ward. They were not alone. Perched atop one crystal watchtower was an immense shape, too large for a raven or for any mortal bird, a still black shape that sat with folded wings and watched the scene below. The men in the outer ward had not seen it, so absorbed were they in the defence of the castle, but those stationed on the walls were waving and pointing and she could hear their thin, distant shouts of fear. The smaller birds circled the great shape in a black eddying cloud, as hornets swarm about their queen. A sudden horror filled her, and she ran from the room and down the passage, to the stairway of one of the castle's towers. She took its steeply climbing steps three at a time in her haste. Once in the chamber at the top, she leaned panting against the wall and peered fearfully through the narrow glassless window at the shape on the tower. The ravens still spun about it in a whirling dance, uttering their guttural cries. The thing looked to her for a moment like another raven, grown to gigantic size; but then as the fires below flared up they lit the perching shape, and she saw the beak with its cruel curve like a meathook, and the equally cruel talons that grasped the battlement. It was an eagle, a huge black eagle like the one on the enemy's banners. Horribly, its eye socket was only an empty hollow, so that it looked more dead than alive. Then its head swivelled, facing the keep, and she saw in the other socket an eye of living flame.

Terrified, she ran back down the stairs even faster than she had mounted them, and searching out the king and queen she told them what she had seen.

"It cannot be—*he*," said Diarmait, paling.

"He has only one eye, Lailoken said—and all immortals can change their shapes. And the ravens, the Valkyries, were flying around him. As if they were—*worshipping* him." Jean's teeth chattered uncontrollably.

Gwenlian went and looked out the nearest window. "I see something on the tower," she reported, her voice shaking a little. "But it looks to me more like a serpent. A great black serpent with an eye of fire." Jean joined her at the window, and saw that it was true: the shape of the thing on the tower had changed. Now huge night black coils were wound around the upper portion of the tower, as if it would crush the crystal to shards. But from the dark, weaving head above the coils one red eye still burned.

"The men are fleeing the walls," Gwenlian added. "There is no one left to defend them."

"The Gallows Lord—*here*?" said Diarmait. "But why?"

"Maybe he knows the Spear's nearby, and he won't trust his servants to get it for him: so he's come here himself, to take it." Jean was surprised at how normal she was able to sound. If only she could stop her teeth from chattering . . .

Gwenlian said, "Jehane, find every page you can and tell them to get everyone down to the lower levels of the keep.

They are not safe here now." There was a roar of noise from the outer ward. "They have broken through the gate! The castle is our only defence now, and it too may be breached. Diarmait, there is no choice: the Iron Door must be unbarred. There is nowhere else for the women and children to take refuge."

"They will not go into the fairy mound. They fear it too much."

"They will go," said Gwenlian, "when they see what is on the tower. Go, Jehane, and tell them. They must choose now between the mound and the enemy."

The pages ran to and fro in the halls, shouting urgently, and the people of the castle began to stream out of their chambers and down the wide stone staircases to the throne hall. At the dais they halted, looking in terror at the unbolted Iron Door; but the noises of battle coming from without were loud and near, and in the end one terror overcame the other as Gwenlian had predicted. Down the dark stair behind the forbidden door they stumbled and ran: women and children, the old and the injured, and as many men as could be spared to protect them—for their fear of what lay within those dark subterranean halls was still nearly as great as their fear of the enemies outside. By the light of torches and candles they gazed with awe on the works of fairy hands: on vaulted ceilings, on halls lined with columns carved like branching trees. Only Dubthach, who had joined them, showed no fear of the mound's dark chambers. Perhaps, Jean thought, serving a woman who was half-fairy herself had inured him to the usual dread people had for the Neutral Ones.

For hour after hour they waited, dreading to hear the noise of the Iron Door being beaten down; but there were only muffled sounds from above, shouts and distant thuds that might have been caused by anything. They all moved as far from the stone stair as possible. Time dragged on, and some tried to sleep, but they complained that they were haunted by the sounds of voices and music, or had strange dreams. Jean did not even try. She lay wide awake, huddled at the base of a tree column, and when something brushed her face, light as a moth, she cried out. Then she saw what had touched her, and exclaimed in astonishment: "It's the chough!"

The little dark-plumed bird stood before her on the stone floor, head cocked to one side. "Chaw, chaw," it said.

"How did you get down here?" she asked him. "Can you understand what I'm saying? Is there another opening somewhere?"

"Can you understand the speech of birds and beasts?" asked Morwenna in awe, watching her.

"No: I was hoping he'd be able to communicate with me somehow. He's not just an ordinary bird, you know. There's something magical about him."

"He's not a—not one of *them*?" asked Morwenna, shrinking back. "The Good People?"

"I don't know. But I'm sure he's friendly, Morwenna. He's helped me twice before." She squatted a few feet from where the bird stood and it hopped away on its scarlet legs, but did not open its wings. "If he didn't come in by the door, there must be another entrance to the mound. Maybe we can use it to escape, if the enemies break down the door!"

"Or they might get in by it," said Morwenna fearfully.

"Well. We'd better go and look for it, hadn't we?"

"Look for it!" the other girl exclaimed in horror. "You don't mean—wander about down *here*, in the *dark*? With the place full of fairy spells and enchantments?"

Jean put her hand in her pocket. The bronze brooch and the piece of bread were still where she had placed them when she changed her gown.

Morwenna relaxed slightly when she was shown the bread. "Ah—that is a strong charm, I know." She quoted softly:

> Who carries Blessed Bread
> Cannot be fairy-led.

"You see, I have protection against spells. Don't worry, Morwenna—you don't have to come with me. In fact, you probably shouldn't. But I'll be safe, I promise. I just have to go and see what I can find." It was better than waiting about, she thought, for the door of iron to be broken down and the enemy to come rushing in . . .

"I will accompany you," offered Dubthach. But at that some of the people around them began to wail and plead with him to stay. There were so few fighting men with them: the rest were all defending the castle. If the Lochlannach came—

"It's all right, Dubthach—I'll be safe enough on my own, with this guide." Jean hoped she sounded more confident than she really felt. She started to walk towards the chough, and at once he fluttered away a few feet, then glanced back at her. "There, you see?" Jean said excitedly. "He's leading me somewhere!"

As no one else was willing or able to follow, Jean collected some candle stubs and rolled them up in a bundle. Then she took up a lit candle and set off after the bird.

It darted ahead, pausing to light on the paved floor, then on a branched candelabra protruding from a sconce in one of the walls. As soon as Jean drew near, it flew on, but never strayed far out of the pool of light her candle cast.

It seemed to her that she walked for hours. On and on the bird led her, and down and down: she descended great stone stairs into gloomy halls, and walked along endless corridors. One room was all lined with mirrors, so that as she walked she saw her own candlelit figure repeated endlessly. Half-pillars were set against the mirrored walls, their reflections making them whole; and they too were endlessly repeated, colonnade upon colonnade, so that Jean and her numberless reflected selves seemed to walk through a palace of infinite size. She grew confused by the images at last, and would likely have lost her way but for the chough, who kept fluttering just a few yards ahead, and waited patiently for her when her pace slowed.

Her candle burned down, and she lit another, and another. The farther down she went, the larger the chambers became, and the more wonderful were they to behold. Jean felt light-headed with fear, fatigue and hunger, and her surroundings began to seem unreal. Room after room opened before her, hall after hall, all dark and strange as fever dreams. In one vast, shadowy chamber she was certain she heard music, a faint piping tune coming from a long way off. Through the darkness between rows of mighty pillars the music wove, thin as a spider's thread, and eventually faded away again. Another time she found herself in a grove of trees: not carved columns this time, but trees of metal so beautifully wrought that they looked almost real. Their bark and leaves were of beaten gold, of bronze and silver. Presently she saw ahead of her a lithe form, gleaming in the candlelight: a statue of a deer on a golden base, a golden hind with one delicate foreleg crooked, and wide ears angled warily forward. Its eyes were red jewels, their glinting depths almost alive. Walking on, Jean saw there was a hart for the hind, standing with golden antlers proudly raised. There was a golden fox, too, and a silver hare, arrested in eternal motionless flight across the floor; and farther on she came across an artificial pool, with sculpted water lilies and a bronze heron standing at its centre, long curved neck raised and beak half-open.

She paused by the pool, trying to imagine this place as it must have looked when the fairies dwelt here. Lamps would have shone down from the unseen ceiling, high above, banishing the darkness that loomed beyond her candle's glow. Had the fairies danced here in their artificial forest, feasted and made merry, trailed their hands in the pool . . . ?

The chough flew down and perched on the head of the heron, and chirruped at her. Jean set aside her wonder, and followed him obediently as he led her on. In the room beyond long glittering strands of crystal beads hung from the ceiling in rows, like rain; and the leaves of the trees were spattered with crystals, and dripped sparkling prisms. In another chamber it was winter. The trees were silver and diamond, the animal statues were white—marble or ivory, she was not sure which; there was a great, white, blank-eyed bear prowling across the marble floor, and a caribou with gleaming antlers and open mouth silently lowing. And in the midst of the winter scene there was a large throne, carved out of blue-white crystal that shimmered in her candle's light as though it were made of ice.

After that there was another stair, spiralling down a steep shaft, on and on until she felt she was descending into the earth's bowels. Her little store of candles was running low, and she began to worry. Still he led her on, along a flat-floored tunnel with dark rough walls and a strong smell of the sea: then up another spiral stair, up and up until her legs ached and her lungs burned, and she thought that if she stopped now she would never get up again.

An hour, a day, an eternity later—she could not say which of these it was—she emerged at last from the stair into a room with rough-hewn walls and a rocky, uneven floor. In fact it was hardly a room at all, but a cave that must have formed naturally. Yet to one side she saw a sort of backless couch, or bier, made of wood covered in gold leaf. On it lay a silver helmet topped with a golden crown.

And beside the bier, lying on the rock floor, was a long, gold-pointed spear.

Chapter Eighteen

JEAN WALKED FORWARD into the rock-walled chamber, towards the spear. *The* Spear—it could be no other, she knew. She had seen Lugh draw that golden spearhead from the forge, in the vision given her by King Gwyn. The shaft was longer than she was tall, and the head of the Spear glowed, as though the fires of its forging had never cooled.

"You knew," she said softly to the chough. It was perching on the scrolled end of the couch, gazing quietly at her. "Somehow, you knew this was what I was looking for. You brought me here on purpose."

"Chaw," the bird said softly.

A dim, pale light fell on the scene from one of the rocky walls. Looking in that direction, she saw a jagged hole in the granite at a level with her eyes. She stepped up to it, realized that a current of fresh air also came through it, bringing the smell of the sea and a curious musky odour. Guttural, croaking cries came from outside the aperture: the ceaseless calls of nesting gannets. She peered out. There were big white bodies and sharp-billed heads all around her, and straight ahead was the moonlit face of a cliff, dotted with more nesting birds and surmounted by Caer Wydyr's gleaming crystal wall. And her tired mind understood at last. "I'm inside the Craig yr Aderyn!" she said aloud. "Right inside it. So I was right, after all. And you knew. This is it, isn't it: the little hole that you kept flying in and out of." She turned back towards the couch, and then caught her breath.

There was a man lying on it.

She could see him dimly, in the faint moonlight: a bearded man, not young, dressed in fine raiment like a king's or great lord's. Going closer, she saw that his form was diaphanous, like mist: she could see through him, and his transparent shape lay only where the moonbeams fell. The perching bird, too, looked strangely transparent, as though the moon were shining through him.

What are you? Jean wondered as she gazed at the chough. *And who is that man on the couch? A ghost? Some great fairy lord? A vision?*

"May I take it?" she asked, gesturing to the Spear. "Is it all right? If it belongs to him, he won't mind, will he?"

The bird flew down and stood next to the glowing head of the Spear, looking up at her expectantly. Its meaning could not be plainer. She knelt down, closed her hands around the shaft.

"Thank you," she whispered to the bird. "Whoever you are. We need this badly—the Avalonians, my own people in the Shadow. We'll be safe now, and it's all because of you." She felt dizzy with exultation. Safe—they would be safe. The Spear would soon be in the hands of Gwenlian and

Diarmait, and Woden would be thwarted. Neither he nor any other enemy, mortal or immortal, could oppose the wielder of the Spear of Lugh. She stood, clasping the heavy shaft in her hands, and knew a moment of sheer joy.

"Stop!"

She jumped violently at the voice, which came from behind her even as she turned towards the entrance to the cave. The moon's light was eclipsed, and the spectral form on the couch immediately vanished away. A face filled the little hole in the rock. In the dim light she did not recognize it, but she knew the voice only too well. It was Morgana.

"I knew it!" the sorceress declared angrily. "When I felt that sudden surge of power here, I knew it was the Spear! So you knew all along, little sly one, and did not see fit to tell me."

"That's not true," said Jean, wondering even as she spoke if she would be believed. "I only guessed after you left. And I wouldn't have known to come to this place; it was the chough who led me here."

Morgana's face drew back a little, and a long white arm reached through the hole. "Pass it through to me."

Looking at the grasping hand, Jean was filled with doubt and fear. "What will you do with it?" she asked.

"Do not question me, you impudent chit! Gwyn ap Nudd may find your insolence amusing, but I do not. Do as I say!"

Jean remembered the angry words Morgana had spoken before she quit the throne room. Had they been spoken in the heat of passion, or had she truly meant them? Would she seize control of Avalon once she had the Spear, and use it to frighten all the people into compliance?

"Well? Why do you hesitate? If you are hoping that Lailo-ken will come to your aid, that hope is vain. The Valkyries have driven him from Avalon, away across the sea. And they did so at *my* command."

"You—you're helping Woden?" *So Owen was right—*

"I *pretend* to do so, fool. The Gallows Lord does not guess that I will never serve him. I will wield the Spear against him once it is in my hand. Then the Lochlannach and the Valkyries will have to serve *me*, for I shall be the bearer of *Gungnir*. I shall have them both in my power."

Jean saw, in her mind's eye, the red-haired Lochlannach girl kneeling in reverence before Morgana. *Of course—the Northmen will worship her. To them she's like a Valkyrie; and as for the Valkyries, they'll likely accept her as one of their own, too: a raven-woman, with supernatural powers . . . Birds of a feather . . .* "And after Woden's gone? What will you do then? Take Avalon for your own, with the Valkyries to help you? Hand it over to the Lochlannach, so they can drive the Ava-lonians out? You'd prefer them to the Avalonians, wouldn't you? Because they'll be your subjects, and serve you, and the Avalonians never will." The witch-queen's plans were laid bare before Jean, as clearly as if she had seen right into Morgana's mind. The icy glare the woman gave her told Jean that she had guessed right.

"I owe you no explanation for my doings," Morgana snarled. "Give me the Spear!"

Jean took a step backwards. "I'm sorry," she said, swallowing hard, "but I can't do that."

"You speak as though you had a choice, Shadow-child. Do you not know that I can enslave your will?"

The long white hand gestured sharply, but Jean stood firm. Holding the Spear in one hand, she took out her mother's fairy bread, and held it up in the moonlight so the sorceress could see.

Morgana hissed through her teeth. "So: you have some protection."

Jean replaced the bread; then grabbing the Spear in both hands, she dragged it as fast as she could towards the stone stair. But at a wave of Morgana's hand the way was blocked by an invisible barrier: Jean reeled back, as if from a wall. "You cannot escape! Your mind may be safe from my magic, child, but I can still make walls out of air and bar your way. You cannot reach your king and queen now. There is but one choice, and a little morsel of bread cannot change it. You must pass me the Spear, before Woden comes to claim it. *Now*."

Jean turned back to face Morgana. Her glorious hope, so newly born, was dead; but a part of her still could not give in. "No," she said quietly. "You'll have to take it from me. I can't stop you once you've got it. You can have your way, take over Avalon and drive out Gwenlian and Diarmait's people and kill anyone you want to." She took a step forward, her hands tightening on the spear shaft. "But it will all be because you *took* the Spear from me. Not because I gave it to you."

Morgana wasted no more words. She immediately became a raven, and proceeded to squeeze her black feathered body through the hole. But Jean made a frantic thrust with the Spear, and the raven recoiled with a harsh cry from the blazing golden point. In the same instant the chough flew out through the hole at the bigger bird, crying its defiance. There was a wild flurrying sound outside, and Jean ran to the hole with the Spear in hand, and looked out.

Morgana had returned to human form, standing tall on the Craig's top with her feet planted on the rugged rock: protesting gannets were all about her, but she paid them no heed. With one hand she waved at the chough, which was circling her head furiously; its wings folded to its body, and it tumbled into the abyss below.

Jean cried out in grief and fury, but there was nothing she could do. Morgana turned to face her, and motioned with her hand as though she were throwing something at the hole.

Then there was a great noise and a flash of blinding light, and Jean leaped back as the stone wall cracked and exploded inward, showering her face with granite fragments. She lay for a moment, dazed and bleeding from cuts on her cheeks and forehead and arms, and half-stunned with the force of the blast. The gannets screamed, and there were white-and-black wings beating the air above her, and a shower of broken stone and feathers and guano and the downy bodies of flightless nestlings tumbling to the stone floor. The sea wind blew Jean's hair about her eyes as she sat up, blinking. The rock wall now gaped before her, the little hole widened into a huge opening several feet across. In it, framed against the night sky, stood Morgana with her hand outheld.

Other things Jean saw too, behind that menacing figure. She could see men fighting on the high crystal wall of Caer Wydyr, sword blades glinting in the moon. One warrior stood aloof as the others fought; even at this distance she recognized the white triangular face and heavy dark beard.

King Ulf took no part in this final battle, he merely waited calmly for his *berserkers* to finish off the last of the castle's defenders. And then she recognized two more figures, standing together by one watchtower: one dark-haired and wielding a fiery sword, one slight and fair. Diarmait and Gwenlian. The White Keep had fallen to the Lochlannach and they had been driven, with their men, to the southernmost curtain wall; but they fought on to the end, as they had promised.

She reached for the Spear of Lugh. At the same instant, Morgana sprang down, and seized hold of it; but Jean still could not surrender it. She clung to the oaken shaft as it was lifted up by Morgana, knowing the effort was futile, feeling the other woman's vast unnatural strength. And then Jean cringed in terror, for there was a great clamour from the sky, a baying and shrieking, and the roar of thousands of voices raised in war rage. Behind the battlements a black cloud boiled up, swift as steam, high as a thunderhead, reaching out to devour the moon; and with it there came a howling wind.

It was too late for either of them: they had quarrelled, desperately, like two dogs in dispute over a bone; and now, even as one claimed victory, the wolf came with his pack in full cry behind him, to seize the prize from both.

Out of the burgeoning cloud he came, riding the edge of the storm that he commanded, and before him the Valkyries flew in savage fury and exultation, some in raven-form, some as raven-winged women, still others as night black wolves leaping the chasm of air. With them came all the legions of the Einherjar, white-faced and ghastly, with tattered garments streaming in the wind. But Jean could not look at any but the lord of the Wild Hunt. He rode his many-legged steed, and under his dark mantle he was armoured for war: his mail glinted dully in the failing moonlight, and he wore a steel helmet beneath which blazed his one red eye. His flowing beard was grey as the thready mane of his mount, but his shoulders and chest were broad and strong, greater than any living man's. Swifter than an eagle's plunging stoop on its prey was the war god's flight from cloud to Craig: his steed shrilled loudly as its hooves came clattering down onto the rock, scattering the crying nestlings and their frantic parents. On six splayed and spindly legs it stood, straddling the summit, while two more limbs flailed the air before its hideous head.

Morgana fled with a shriek of fury and defeat; taking her raven form once more, she circled the pinnacle along with the Valkyries. Jean fell back into the rock chamber, and her numbed hands lost their grip on the Spear.

She scrabbled for it wildly among the shattered rock and screaming nestlings, but even as her fingers found it again the dim light was blotted out. Down through the broken gap in the wall there reached a massive arm, larger than any man's, the arm of a giant: and its huge hand closed like a talon of steel about the shaft of the Spear, and lifted it up into the open air.

"*Gungnir*," said a deep booming voice, like the tolling of a great bell.

Even at the end she could not release the Spear. And so she was lifted up with it, clinging with ice-cold hands that seemed to have frozen around the shaft—even though she knew it was no use, that the war was already lost. A brief glimpse she had of the mighty head and shoulders, black against the sky, and of the single red eye blazing down on her like a living ember; and then she ducked her head in horror. She need not have feared his gaze, however. To him she was of no more account than the birds that squawked helplessly at his feet. The eye of fire looked only on the Spear. But as he hefted it in triumph, he gave it a little impatient shake, as a man might brush a fly away; and at last Jean's grip gave way, and she fell helpless to the rock. Over and over she rolled, dislodging still more flapping birds and their young; and then with a terrified shriek she tumbled over the edge of the Craig.

Wildly she clawed for a hold as she dropped down the sheer northern face of the stack, and her grasping hands found a small, protruding ledge and caught at it. And there she clung, with her whole weight hanging from her already cramped and aching fingers; unable to climb either up or down, hundreds of feet above the roiling sea.

Above her, the Gallows Lord hoisted the Spear, then with one mighty motion he loosed it at the wall of Caer Wydyr. It crossed the grey gulf in a golden streak, swift as a meteor trailing its fires across the sky, and struck Diarmait's back as he stood hacking the swordblades of his foes; and it pierced him through. His head snapped back as the spearhead thrust out of his chest beneath the left shoulder; but if he gave a cry as he fell upon the battlement at the Lochlannach's feet, Jean could not hear it.

Yet she thought she could hear, blown down to her on the buffeting wind, the despairing wail of Gwenlian.

Then the Valkyries, at a gesture from their master, were

flying to the crystal battlement to retrieve the Spear of Lugh for him. "No!" Jean screamed aloud. And then, more softly, "No—no . . ." until the word was only a sob.

The air was full of cries now, seeming to echo her grief. From the stony shelves where they waited and watched, the white drifts of roosting birds came suddenly to life, great squalls of them billowing outwards. In the steel grey murk beneath the Craig a thousand gulls and gannets whirled and scudded, their bodies gleaming palely as they drove upwards between rock and cliff. They flew among the Valkyrie-ravens, breaking up the black flights, and for a moment they swirled together like soot and snow.

Jean could no longer see the figures in the curtain wall, nor did she want to look any more. She wept and clung to her precarious handhold. There was nothing left to do, nothing more to feel beyond fear and sorrow. She had only to let go her grip and her own anguish would end in the chill and foaming water far below. But she continued to hold on, though only with a stubborn animal's will to survive.

There was a rasping cry in her ear, and a flurry of black followed by a stabbing pain in her right hand. The flesh was grazed as if by a knife cut, and peering up she saw a raven flying away from her. One of the Valkyries—or Morgana? She guessed the latter. The sorceress must be filled with hate at the loss of her chance for power, and she would certainly blame Jean for refusing to hand over the Spear. Jean watched dully as the bird came winging back, her blood on its beak. It was, she realized, going to peck at her hands until she fell.

Her vision was blurred by her tears, so she did not at first realize that the whirling shapes of white and black above her no longer had the forms of birds. It was their cries that alerted her, the voices no longer screaming wordlessly but calling out challenges and commands in ringing tones. Winged figures were engaged in aerial battle overhead— some were black-winged Valkyries, others flew on wings of white and were clad in shining robes. The raven Morgana saw them too: she broke off her attack and sought to flee, swinging out from the Craig, but a white-robed being with flowing golden hair lunged down, and rose with the torn feather-mantle in its hands. The sorceress fell screaming to the whitened sea far below: frothing waves closed over her head and outstretched arms, and Jean saw her no more.

Woden's steed leaped skyward, towards the spinning melee of white and black wings. But at that instant one shining figure rose triumphant, holding aloft the Spear. Swiftly he cast it at the lunging foe. Too late the war god reined in his steed, making it rear up in the air so that its gaunt form made a shield between him and his doom. Had he not loosed the fateful weapon first at that small and helpless human target, he and his spirit hordes might have gone on at once to bring down greater foes. But his malice would have its way, and its satisfaction was dearly bought. Down came the Spear of Lugh, tearing the air asunder, trailing long bolts of lightning from its golden tip: it smote through steed and rider both, and passed through them to the sea below, still burning; and they fell from the sky in flames. All the spirits in his train felt that blow, united as they were in his thralldom: from every spectre and Valkyrie the same blue fire sprang and spread, and with their master they too plunged burning to the sea like a shower of falling stars, and were engulfed and quenched by the waves.

The white-winged victor flew to the rock of the birds, and hovered over Jean as she looked up in wonder.

"Do not fear, Shadow-girl!" he called to her. She stared at the glorious golden-haired face, and to her amazement she recognized it.

"Gwyn," she croaked.

But how different he looked! His face was changed and radiant, and his white robe shone now in its own light. Bright bird-wings winnowed the air above him, yet she felt no wind from them.

"Jean, do not let go!" he said urgently. "I cannot touch you, nor catch you if you fall. I am of the Light now, and my hands would pass right through you. But you will not die, my good, brave Jean! You shall live, and be a mother and grandmother, and die an old woman in your bed! Only keep your grip a little while longer. Help is coming."

Two winged figures approached as he spoke, bearing the Spear of Lugh between them; and he took it from them, and held it out to Jean. "An object of power like this I can still touch, as can you. Lay hold of the Spear, my Jean, and I will lift you up."

She grabbed for the smooth shaft as he raised it before her face. Then she shut her eyes tight, clinging for her life as he carried her and the Spear across the chasm.

As they flew down out of the sky she saw Ulf stare up at her and the winged Gwyn, his face a white blur of fear; then he sprang back, and flinging up his arms he tumbled backwards over the crystal parapet. His howl of terror grew faint as he fell to the ground far below, and suddenly ceased. But Gwenlian did not look up. She was bent over her husband's motionless form, her head next to his, her empty quiver still strapped to her bent back. Jean wanted to call out to her, but she could not find her voice.

Then she was standing safely on the glassy parapet.

Jean let go the Spear and stood, swaying unsteadily. Before her Gwenlian was sobbing as she sought, uselessly, to staunch her husband's terrible wound with the hem of her gown. "Diarmait, Diarmait, do not die before me," she sobbed. "We swore we would die together, my love—do not leave me now!"

Jean wept quietly where she stood. But Gwyn stooped over the weeping queen, with his wings curved over her like a protecting shield, and said: "Little sister, do not mourn him. There is naught done this day that cannot be undone. You forget this is the Spear that Wounds and Heals."

And he held out the Spear with its tip to the king's breast, touching the deep wound that it had made. The head of the Spear began to glow again—not golden this time but red, as red as blood. It was a warm, living colour, and presently an answering colour came into Diarmait's pale cheeks, and his eyes opened to look up into Gwenlian's tearful face.

"Diarmait!" she cried. "Look, the wound has gone!" It was true: where the great gash had been there was now only the faintest scar. She looked up in wonder, and saw for the first time the radiant figure standing over her. And Diarmait saw too, and murmured in amazement.

"Is this the end of all things then?" he asked, looking up at Gwyn. "Am I dead, or has the world itself ended?"

"It is not the end, but the beginning," Gwyn answered, "for you, King of Avalon, and for your queen and people. The forces of Woden are vanquished. The spirits he held in thrall are gone, and his living warriors are left without their ruler."

"You struck him down," said Jean. "I saw. It's Gwyn, Diarmait—the king of the fairies."

"The Sidhe?" repeated Diarmait, sitting up in his wife's arms. "Then is he not—an angel?"

"I am as I once was, in the beginning of things," Gwyn replied. "But it is the girl Jean you have to thank, and not I. She it was who came to us, who rebuked us, who touched us as no mortal has ever dared to do; what we of the Seelie Court did today was all for her sake. When we saw her peril we could not allow her to die, nor anyone else that she held dear. We turned, in that one instant, from Watchers to Warriors. We follow the Middle Way no more."

And as he spoke the sun broke through the clouds beyond, all golden.

That morning Gwyn went to and fro among the wounded in the ward below, healing with the Spear all who had been injured in the fight, including the Lochlannach. He even healed the gash that Morgana had made on Jean's hand. Jean watched Sir Owen and Le Vainqueur revive from their own mortal wounds, and look up in awe at the winged Sidhe—no doubt imagining themselves dead and in Heaven. Some of the Lochlannach made obeisances to the white figures; others fled in terror.

Queen Oonagh was there also, but she stood aside, a sad cast to her radiant features: she held in her pale shining hands the feather-mantle that she had seized from Morgana. "It is useless now," she told Jean. "See, it is rent and ruined. It belonged to Morgan le Fay, long ago, and has passed from her to every high priestess of Dana. But the virtue is gone out of it forever."

"I'm sorry Morgana died," Jean said awkwardly. "I don't think she was really wicked, Your Majesty, only proud—and terribly lonely."

Oonagh inclined her golden head. "Do not think that I am altogether without feeling, mortal child. When I turned to the Light again I knew that I loved my daughter dearly. But I knew also that it was I who birthed her into this world, and for all the evil she has done I too must bear some blame. But do not mourn for her. When I let her fall into the sea, I knew that the Selkies were watching the battle from beneath the waves. They have taken Morgana with them to safety."

"Oh—she's alive then! I'm glad, I really am. But she won't stay down there in the sea with them, will she?"

"Alas, she will not. Her love for this isle of Avalon is too great, and her desire to rule it undiminished. She will return to her tower of sorcery in the northern barrens, like a wounded beast seeking its lair, and she will be filled with hate and anger. I shall place a binding spell on that tower, so that she may not leave its confines. But even a magic barrier cannot stand forever. We must pray that she will learn wisdom during the years of her imprisonment."

Dubthach came up to them, weary and battle-worn, and bowed to the queen of the Sidhe. "I beg leave to join her there, Majesty. For I know the other Fianna will continue to serve her, whatever her circumstances may be, and her priestesses also. She is our queen, and ever shall be."

"That leave is not for me to grant," said Oonagh, "but for the mortal king and queen."

"Leave is granted you," Gwenlian told him. "For you have been a good friend to us. I only wish you had a better mistress, Dubthach."

He bowed stiffly, and walked away out of the ward, through the burnt timbers of the broken gate and across the sunlit barrens beyond. They watched him go, feeling rather sad. But in the next instant they forgot their sadness, for there was a soft flurry of wings, and a falcon's call, and they turned to see Lailoken standing behind them, his face beaming.

"It was as I said!" he declared, as Jean ran to him with a glad cry. "The greatest role in this struggle was yours, Shadow-child."

"We all did what we could," she replied. "Some people here gave their lives, and some nearly died. But what happened with the Valkyries, Lailoken? How did you escape them, in the end?"

"I fled out to sea with them in pursuit, then after a day or so of flight I folded my wings and affected to fall from weariness. My pursuers thought I was drowned, and flew away. But I changed my shape again, once I was beneath the sea foam. I became a fish, and swam as fast as I could back to the land." He smiled. "And you, Gwyn ap Nudd—you are changed most of all, I think."

"I am—and the blame for that lies with this girl." Gwyn also smiled at Jean, then turned to gaze northward, and so did Lailoken. "There is a great fire to the north, Druid," said

Gwyn. "Do you see?" Jean looked, but saw nothing. "It is Valhalla: it burns, now that its lord is gone."

And then she saw, in her mind, the terrible towered fortress on the mountain peak, with blue-white flames roaring through its gate and high narrow windows. Slowly one tower bent, bowed and collapsed. Then the image vanished.

"It is done," said Lailoken. "The wolf age is ending; a new one begins, full of hope and promise."

There was a soft chirruping sound, and Jean suddenly saw a little black bird perching on a mounting-block nearby. She ran towards him. "Look, the chough! I thought he was dead!"

The Druid approached the bird too, and bowed his head and spoke to it. "My liege," he said, respectfully yet sternly, "it is time to wake."

And suddenly, standing next to the bird was the form of a man, a mere shade of a figure. It was the same ghostly form Jean had seen lying upon the bier in the cave. The shade answered the Druid in a low whispering voice. "I had a dream, Myrddin. Such a wonderful dream . . ."

"My liege," said the man they had called Lailoken, "you have *been* a dream. Morgan le Fay brought you hither to Avalon, to sleep and dream in peace until your wounds of mind and body were healed. And I too, confined in the forest of Broceliande for an age and an age, before I escaped: I too have had my long rest. But it is time to wake from the dream, Sire."

"Ah, but it was glorious," whispered the shade. "I dreamed I was a bird, Myrddin, flying freely through the air. You used to point out birds to me, do you remember? Hawks, larks, curlews—you knew them all by name. You could even become one, and for that I envied you. In the last days I came to envy even the real birds: the way they soared, free and unfettered, above the world of men."

"Arthur—" said the Druid, gently. "You must return to us."

Jean started. "*Arthur*," she whispered.

The ghostly king spoke again. "A nightingale sang in the woods on the eve of the last battle, knowing naught of the horrors to come, of the strife and sorrows of men; only pouring out its joy upon the air. I heard it as I lay in my tent, sleepless and grieving. And at dawn the larks rose up to Heaven singing. It seemed to me then that man was a vile thing, a blot on the face of creation with his wars and his hatred and cruelty . . . And I, who once claimed to strive for the good, was the vilest of all men. If I die this day, I said to myself, and my soul passes into a new body, let it not be the body of a man. Let me take a bird's form, as old Myrddin once did. Let me fly the skies and sing, and care naught for the world of men below!"

"Arthur—Merlin." Jean breathed the names. Behind her Gwenlian and Diarmait were sinking to their knees.

The Druid said, "Sire, hear me. You did not die, but only dreamed. That dream is ended now. It is time to take up arms again, and defend the weak and helpless. A hero is needed still."

As he spoke the ghostly figure grew more firm and real, while the shape of the bird faded and diminished. Gwyn held out the Spear to the king, but he stepped back in dismay. "Nay—not a spear! It was with a spear that I slew him—Mordred, my son—my poor, treacherous son. I will never go to war again, not though all the angels in Heaven asked it of me. Let me be! I prayed to be a man no more, and to have no more to do with men and their quarrels. And my prayer was answered. Leave me to my dream!"

The king's figure faded again, and colour and solidity went back into the body of the bird. It spread its green-glossed wings for flight.

"Arthur!" called Merlin urgently. "You say you will have no more to do with the human race; yet there was one, King, whom you helped even in the midst of your dream. Do you remember?"

The bird's wings furled to its sides again; the shade of the king spoke in a low, wondering voice. "There was a young maiden, alone in a wood, lost and fairy-led. Lost . . ." He fell silent for a moment: his eyes rested upon Jean. "I saw in her nothing that was vile, only innocence and youth and a brave spirit. She would not give up her attempts at escape, though the fairies in that wood led her astray time and again . . . I pitied her in her need, and I admired her courage."

"And you helped me. You showed me the path," said Jean. "And I'm grateful, Your Majesty. Without you I might still be wandering there." She moved towards him, eyes wide and adoring. "You—you're King Arthur! I know about you, Majesty, your life and your battles. You're famous even in my world—the perfect ruler, brave and noble . . . They said in the old stories that you would come back one day!"

"Do you hear, my liege?" Merlin said. "Will you deny her plea?"

Gwyn addressed Arthur then. "This maiden's world, and the lives of all those whom she loves, are still in peril. She comes from the Shadow, and it too is torn by war." His great swan white wings lifted and stretched to their full span as he spoke. "I and my host must now ascend to the heavens, to stand with those who guard the Light. With our help the balance has been tipped in the Light's favour, and the Dark Ones sent into retreat. But in your land of Logres the Northmen still fight in Woden's name, and no king reigns and the people live without hope. They dream of the return of Arthur, the Once and Future King. And in this maiden's Shadow-realm the twin of Logres, Britain, has a king, but he stands alone and comfortless. There is no ally who can deliver his realm from his foes. Yet if you take the throne of Logres, Britain may also be saved. Even through the wall of Shadow that divides their world from yours, its people may yet feel your coming, and hope may be reborn in their hearts. The three worlds are in truth one, King, and their fates all hang together."

His words seemed to ring on the air like a trumpet-blast even after he had ceased to speak. There was a little pause as his mortal listeners quietly reflected on what he had said. Then the fading form of the chough flew up into the air with a shrill cry, and vanished like a breath of steam into the clear air; and there was only the tall bearded man standing there before them, real and solid now, clad in the vestments of a king with a red dragon emblazoned on his tabard.

"It is time for us all to depart," said Gwyn. "You to your last earthly battle, Arthur, and I to the celestial one, to fight by Mikha-El's side. Merlin will convey you across the sea to Logres with the aid of his arts." He held out the Spear again.

Slowly Arthur reached out to take it from him. "I will do as you ask of me, emissary of Heaven. But when all is done,

I shall hide this spear where no mortal hand can find it and use its destructive power."

"There is still great danger," agreed Merlin. "For anything that happens in one world may be echoed in the other. In your world, Jean, both sides may seek after a deadly weapon too, a power as deadly to one side as to the other, one that can either bring life or destroy. But our winning of the Spear may at least keep that weapon from your foes until your war is won."

Jean turned to him anxiously. "Yes, the Shadow-world—what will happen there? Can it really be saved? There's still Hitler, and the Nazis—"

It was Gwyn who answered her. "I can see through the Shadow's veil, now that I belong to the Light . . . I see your dark warlord's fate sealed with the defeat of the war god; I see the flames of Valhalla spreading into your world. Yes—for him, also, it ends in fire: a burning pyre I see, in a conquered and broken city. His ashes will mingle with the ashes of his realm, and both shall be scattered to the winds."

"And your New Found Land can never fall to any enemy, now that Avalon is saved," added Merlin. "They shall not set foot upon its shores, save as prisoners of war."

Jean looked at the angelic Gwyn, and felt a sudden sorrow for the merry and carefree forest lord that he had been. As he reached out to her his hand passed right through hers. The blood in her fingers showed bright red, as though they were held to a strong light. "I have forsworn the Middle Way, and with it the middle realm of Annwn," he told her. "I belong here no longer."

"I'm sorry. I didn't know—I never meant this to happen to you."

"Do this one thing for me: cherish your mortal world. Love it always for my sake, to your last dying breath."

"I will," Jean promised. Then she turned back to her human friends. "But will we ever meet again?"

They came forward and hugged her warmly, king and queen and Druid.

"We *know* we shall all meet again, whatever befalls," said Gwenlian with confidence. "For we shall all be reunited in Paradise. Our souls go always on and upwards, Myrddin says, until we find the World of the Light. And in that place we shall never be parted again."

"Tir nan Og," said Jean softly, remembering Dubthach's words.

"Aye," Merlin said, smiling. "If you have not all won places in the Hall of Heroes, who then can hope to enter it?"

One last time they all embraced, holding one another close. Then Gwyn called Jean apart, and waved his insubstantial hand over her; and the bright walls and towers faded from Jean's eyes, and she felt herself falling away, out of the light into shadow. And then the shadow too was gone, and she found herself standing alone atop a windy hill, dressed in her plain blouse and skirt again, with the ruins of old Fort Royal all around her and the sun beaming down. Her parents and her sister were calling out to her as they came up the slope behind her, and her heart swelled with joy to hear their cheerful voices. She turned to run down and meet them. But her eyes lingered for a moment on the hazy blue expanse of Placentia Bay.

The Avalonians, she remembered, called it the Bay of Hope.

Chapter Nineteen

"THAT'S A LOVELY BIT OF WOOL, Margery," said Mrs. Macrae.

"Nothing's too good for our men," replied Mrs. Ross in proud patriotic tones.

They were all knitting together in the sitting room of the Ross house: Mrs. Ross and Penny, Laura and her mother, Jean and Fiona and Mrs. MacDougall. The older women conversed in solemn tones while Fiona—who was too young to knit very well and was really only there so that she would not feel left out—chattered to Penny and Laura. The latter was uncharacteristically subdued, as she had been for the past two weeks since the news of her cousin's death. Every now and then the conversation drifted into a lull, and the faint clicking of the needles was all that filled the silence. Outside, the summer evening was turning golden.

Jean worked quietly, her head bent over her own knitting project—a navy blue scarf for Jim—and thought of the letter she had received from him just this week. "The first time we had a U-boat alert a few days ago," he'd written, "I thought my heart would shoot out of my mouth. It turned out to be a drill, fortunately. As for the food and the sleeping arrangements, well, I see why the other fellows call this the 'HMS Hardship'! But whenever life on board seems unbearable, and I start to wonder why I ever let myself in for this, I think about you, Jeanie, at the dance in your pink dress, and then it all makes sense. I know that we're all here to protect everyone we love back home, and that alone is worth any kind of trouble. Jeanie, I can't wait to see you again!"

And I'm longing to see you, too, Jim—but when will it be? When oh when oh when . . . ?

It was mid-August already. Lughnasa was long past: in Annwn the Gallows Lord and his minions had fallen, and Avalon was free. King Arthur had returned to Logres with Merlin. Surely there should also be a change in the Shadow-world's fortunes by now? Jean set her knitting aside briefly to reach into her skirt pocket and touch the bronze brooch she had secreted there. Perhaps her world was *not* so closely linked to Annwn as Merlin had thought?

Fiona fidgeted in her chair, then got up and peered through the lace-curtained window for a while. Presently she gave a shout. "Look, it's Daddy. He's coming to the door!"

Jean looked up sharply, and her mother blanched and put a hand to her heart. "Allister? Why is he coming *here*?"

Jean threw down her knitting and ran to join her sister by the window. "It's all right, Mum, he's smiling!" she said quickly. "It can't be anything bad."

Mrs. Ross went to let him in, and he came into the room beaming, a copy of the *Evening Telegram* in his hand. "There!" he said, slapping it down on the coffee-table. "Look at that!"

They all crowded around the table, staring at the big banner headline. "CHURCHILL AND ROOSEVELT HAVE MET AT SEA."

"They've come together for an official meeting," Mr. Mac-Dougall explained, "on board a U.S. navy ship out in the ocean. The location's top secret, but there's a rumour going around that it was right here in Newfoundland waters—in Placentia Bay."

The Bay of Hope, Jean thought. She suddenly felt giddy.

Mrs. Ross bent down to read the article. "It says the British Prime Minister and the American President have drafted an eight-point declaration, supporting rights and freedoms for all nations."

"But what does it mean for *us*?" Mrs. MacDougall asked.

"It's an important statement," her husband replied. "By meeting with Churchill in this way, Roosevelt's making it clear to the whole world, as well as his people back home, whose side he's on. You see?"

Slowly, wonderingly, as though she did not dare believe it yet, Mrs. Ross said, "America's in the war."

A brief hush descended. Then Fiona gave a loud whoop, and she and Mrs. Macrae and Laura started jumping up and down, laughing and cheering, saying it over and over again: "America's in the war! America's in the war!"

"Not *yet*," said Penny.

"But they will be," said Jean. "They *will* join the fight, and help us to win it." It had happened, just as Merlin had promised. The tide had turned.

"And there'll be American soldiers on the bases here. I hope they're all good-looking—and rich!" Laura sounded like her old cheerful self again. She threw a mischievous glance at Penny, who gave an exasperated snort.

"Yes," Mr. MacDougall nodded in satisfaction as he folded up the paper. "This is the end of American neutrality."

As they all talked on excitedly, Jean slipped out of the house and ran lightly down the street, hope filling her heart for the first time in days. The war would end—not soon, perhaps, but it *would* end, and for the better.

She ran on and on, until she came to the place where she and Jim had stood after the dance, looking down through the trees towards the harbour.

"I will see him again," Jean said aloud. *But not in Tir nan Og, not yet.* "He will come back *here*—to me." She spoke firmly, forcefully: trying to make it sound true. It was not enough. *Give me a vision, a sign, something to tell me he will come back!* At that very moment a tune blared tinnily from a radio in one of the nearby houses, and as it wafted towards her on the clear evening air she recognized the voice of Vera Lynn.

A coincidence—or a sign? She took it for the latter, and began to sing softly along to the lyrics:

> We'll meet again
> Don't know where
> Don't know when
> But I know we'll meet again some sunny day . . .